# ALICE
# AND THE
# BILLIONAIRE BOSS

## by

## SERENITY WOODS

# CONTENTS

# Chapter One

## *Alice*

It's Tuesday the twentieth of December, and a gorgeous early summer afternoon in Wellington, the capital of New Zealand.

I don't visit the city much, so I'm glad my sister has chosen this café on the waterfront, not far from Te Papa, our national museum. We sit at a table outside, overlooking Lambton Harbour. The water is a sparkling blue, reflecting the clear skies. At the table next to us, a group of businessmen and women in smart suits chat over a working lunch. Families and couples on holiday stroll along the waterfront, while a teenager dressed in shorts and a hot-pink vest weaves between them on rollerblades.

"So," my sister says once the waiter has delivered our meals and lattes. "Are you ready to get laid?"

"Charlie!" Giving an embarrassed laugh, I dart a glance at the people next to us, relieved they didn't hear her. "For God's sake, keep your voice down."

She helps herself to the bowl of chunky chips in the middle of the table. "Relax, girl. Nobody's going to be shocked by someone having a one-night stand in the city."

"Maybe not, but I'd still rather not advertise my desperation."

"I thought that was the point of coming to the city. To advertise yourself?"

"Well, yeah, but not via a loudspeaker. At least on Tinder, nobody knows who I am."

"That's true." Grinning, she dips another chunky chip in the aioli sauce and eats it. Then as she looks at me, her amusement fades, and she reaches out to hold my hand. "I'm so sorry. I shouldn't tease you. I'm glad you came to me. I think it's great that you're doing this, I really do."

I study her purple nails, thinking about what different lives we lead. Charlie has just finished her third of four years at university. She's been working in the city for a few weeks to earn some extra money, and I'll be driving her home to Gisborne on the east coast in a couple of days. She's embraced the student way of life with all her heart and soul and is loving every minute of it. Only four years separate us, but sometimes I feel a lot older, almost as if we're a different generation. She uses Tinder all the time, and I'm sure she's had a few one-night stands.

When she first suggested I download the app, I was excited at the thought of finally putting myself out there. I joined the Tinder subreddit on Reddit and read a lot of posts by people who'd used it to get an idea of how it works. At first, I have to admit I was surprised at how quickly conversations turned to sex. I'd expected people to take a while to sound each other out before they shared themselves in such an intimate way, but I soon realized how naive that was. Sometimes it only took them a few minutes before one of them mentioned hooking up.

I thought I'd gained a good understanding of how it all worked, and I thought I was prepared. Now I'm here, though, I'm beginning to have second thoughts.

But I'm not going to tell Charlie that. Instead, I say, "Thanks for helping me."

"You've given up so much for me. I know I'll never be able to repay you. So, helping you get a date is the least I can do."

We smile at each other for a moment. We rarely talk about it, so it warms me to hear her say she appreciates the sacrifices I've made through the years.

"Come on," she says, releasing my hand and taking another chip. "Get your phone out, and we'll create your account."

My pulse immediately starts to race as I pull out my phone.

"Have you downloaded Tinder yet?" she asks.

"Yes, I did it at the airport. But I haven't created an account."

"All right. We'll start at the beginning. Hold on, I'll come and sit beside you." She gets up and moves around the table to take the chair next to mine, bringing her food and latte, and we huddle together, looking at the screen.

I open the app and tap 'Create Account', then connect it to my Facebook account.

Now I have to set up my profile. I input my name, my age, gender, and sexual orientation. "How much of this does the other person see?"

"Only your age and your first name. It uses the other information to match you with suitable people."

"Okay."

"Now, photos. You need to pick a great one for the main page of your profile, then maybe five or six others."

"I got Mum and June to take some new ones," I say, bringing them up. I flick through the recent collection they took of me in the garden wearing different outfits.

"Oh, that's a nice one." Charlie points to a shot of me from the chest up. I'm laughing at something June said, and my hair is up, although strands frame my face. "That jacket looks really classy, and you're wearing red."

"So?"

She winks at me. "It suggests you're up for some fun, shall we say?"

"Oh, seriously?"

"Yeah. I mean, you could put ONS or FWB on your profile…"

"Meaning?"

"One-night stand, and friends with benefits. But most guys are going to be open to that anyway."

"Right. Jeez. I feel so old. I should have a photo of me wearing a hairnet with my teeth in a glass."

Charlie giggles as she examines the photo. "Wow, your makeup looks nice. Yeah, let's go for that one."

I choose that as my main profile picture, and then we select five others.

"Okay," she says when we're done. "Now the bio. You only need a few sentences. I looked up some ideas for you." She pulls them up on her phone. "You can describe yourself using only emojis."

"Can I just put an eggplant?"

She laughs. "Two truths and a lie?"

"Mmm…"

"How you'd survive a zombie apocalypse?"

"My answer to that would be far too nerdy. I've read every post-apocalyptic book out there."

"List your unpopular opinions?"

"Too negative."

"Pros and cons? Or what about obscure skills?"

"Does it mean, like, juggling?"

"Well, what about listing the things that stand out about you? Not generic interests like 'enjoys travel and good food.' You want to put unusual, funny things that only those who have the same interests as you will recognize."

"Right, that makes sense."

I think hard and type a few sentences, tweaking them until I'm happy with them. Charlie reads it and laughs. "It's so you."

"That's the idea. I know I'm not looking for anything long term, but it would be nice if he liked the same things as me." I read it back, pleased it doesn't reveal too much about me. I'm not looking to open my soul to anyone here. It does show that I don't get out much, but there's no point in lying and saying I travel and go paragliding. I'm pretty much confined to the house, so it's natural that my hobbies all take place indoors.

Charlie slides her arm around me and gives me a hug. "Are you sure about this? You wouldn't rather wait until you get home so you can find a proper date, and get to know the guy first?"

I shake my head. "That's not what this is about."

"If it all works out, and you find a guy, and you go back to his place... You're not going to tell him, are you?"

"Tell him what?"

"That you're a virgin?" she says softly.

My eyes widen, and we study each other for a moment.

"How did you know?" I whisper.

She smiles. "Intelligent guess. I know you've never had the chance to date anyone. But I only have one more year and then I'll be home for good. Then you'll have more time on your hands to date someone properly. Wouldn't you rather wait until then, and have your first time with someone you love and trust?"

"Charlie, no guy is going to be interested in going with a virgin. It's not the commodity it used to be. Guys want girls who are experienced and fun in bed. When I meet the right man, I want to know what I'm doing."

"Hmm, yeah, I get that."

"I mean, you weren't going steady the first time you slept with someone, right?"

Her lips twist. "No. It was at a party. You're right, I just wanted to get it done."

"Exactly. The same for me."

Because I've looked after our mother full time since I was sixteen, I've been unable to go to university, to have a proper job, or to enter the dating game. I was determined that Charlie would get to have the opportunities I missed out on, which is why, when she finishes her degree, she's insisting on returning home to help share Mum's care. It means I might be able to enter the dating game eventually. But when I do, I don't want to go in blind.

"So you're not going to tell him today?" she confirms.

"Hell, no. He'll probably run a mile. I might say something like 'I haven't had many one-night stands,' to show why I'm nervous." I hesitate. "Can I ask you something personal?"

"Of course, always."

"Did you… um… bleed the first time?"

"No. Only half of all women do. You use tampons, and ride a bike, right? So I doubt you will either. If you do, and he notices, just tell him it's the last day of your period or something. Men don't have a clue about anything like that." We exchange a smile. "I know you're not looking for the love of your life," she says, "but I hope you find someone nice, that you click with. It'll make it easier."

"Well, shall we take a look? I've only got two nights here to get my leg over, so we might as well get going."

She laughs. "Yeah, come on, then. Now, remember, swipe left for no. Right for yes."

"How many times can I do that?"

"I think it's unlimited. When you've both swiped right on each other, you'll get a match. Then you'll be able to chat, if you want."

My stomach flutters with butterflies. "How long do you think it'll be before I get a match? Maybe I should have done this at home before I came here." I felt too guilty asking June to look after Mum for more than two nights as her free time is so limited.

"No, you'll be fine, you're gorgeous! You'll definitely get matches soon. Come on, let's see who's available."

I look at the first contender. He's wearing a baseball cap and posing in a gym.

"Left," Charlie says.

"Let me read his bio."

"He's flexing, for Christ's sake."

"I'm not averse to a few muscles."

"Alice, you have an IQ of 130. He lists his interests as beer and rugby."

"I like beer and rugby. I don't need him to write an essay."

"Yeah, but it would be nice to choose someone who didn't sign his name by holding a pen in his fist and making an X."

"Aw, don't be mean. He won't know if I swipe left, will he? I don't want to hurt his feelings."

She laughs. "No, he won't know. You're so sweet."

Guiltily, I swipe left. "This feels awfully shallow."

"It's the same as what we do face to face, just condensed into a few seconds. We all know with one look whether we're attracted to someone. No," she says, looking at the next guy, "left."

"What's wrong with him?"

"Sunglasses. It means his eyes are probably too close together."

"It could just be sunny."

"Look at his other photos."

We check them out.

"Told you," she says.

"I can't do this," I tell her helplessly. "He might be the loveliest guy in the world. If someone only checks out my photo, they're going to find all sorts of things wrong with me."

"They won't because you're perfect."

"I'm not—my mouth is too wide, and my front teeth are too big. I look like Bugs Bunny."

She starts laughing. "You really don't."

I blow out a breath. "I think I'll do this later. I want to take time to read their bios as well. It's not fair to choose just on looks."

"You do whatever makes you feel comfortable," she says. "As long as you tell me all about the dates in great detail."

"Dates? Plural?"

"Well, sometimes you have to kiss a few frogs…"

"Jeez. I don't want to think about the fact that I might have to go through this more than once. I just want to meet a nice guy, go back to his room, and… you know…"

"Have him shag you senseless?"

"Um, yeah. It's not much to ask."

"I don't think you're going to have any trouble finding someone who's willing to fill the role. Your only issue is whether you're going to feel comfortable enough taking your clothes off with them."

I blink at the thought of stripping off with a stranger. "Eek! I can't even think about that. I might wear a skirt and go commando and just ask him to get it over with."

She tries not to laugh, and fails. "Aw, Alice. Sex is such fun with the right person. You want someone gorgeous who's going to make your heart race, a guy who knows his way around the bedroom, and who's going to take his time to make it good for you."

"Eventually," I say, "that's definitely my goal. But this first time, even if he only knows to put tab A into slot B, I'll be happy."

"I dunno. Slot C is pretty good. And D can be a lot of fun providing you have plenty of lube."

"Oh my God." I blush, and she giggles.

"Well, good luck," she says, tucking into her chicken salad. "And don't forget, if you don't get a date this evening, you're welcome to come to the party at my place."

"Okay." It's lovely of her to offer, but we both know I'd never go. For a start, everyone there is going to be twenty or twenty-one. And I don't do parties. My idea of a great night is a new fantasy book, a gin and tonic, and a box of Jaffa Cakes.

God, I sound old.

We finish our lunches, exchange a hug, and then head off, Charlie to the house she shares with three other girls to get ready for her party, and me to the cheap hotel in Cuba Street with the room the size of a broom closet. I'm hoping that if I do connect with a guy, we'll be able to go back to his place. Although I guess that if we come here, we'd only be using the bed, so it doesn't matter that you can't turn around in the bathroom without banging your elbow on the door.

Once I'm in, I take off my jacket and shoes, flop back on the bed, retrieve my phone, and bring up the Tinder app. Okay. Time to do some serious swiping.

When I originally decided I wanted to do this, it took me a couple of months to pluck up the courage. I knew I didn't want my first hookup to be near where I lived. It has to be with a stranger that I had no chance of bumping into again, because I'm pretty sure I'm going to be terrible at it. But it means I've thought about it for a long time. It's not an idea I came out with yesterday. I really want to do this.

With that in mind, I'm determined to be honest with myself. Even though I joked that all I need is for the guy to know to put tab A into slot B, realistically there's no chance of me going through with this unless we have some kind of connection.

So now I'm on my own, I read each bio as I slowly work my way through the guys that Tinder is offering me. I know what I'm looking for. He has to have a sense of humor. He's got to be genuine, nice, for want of a better word. And I'd like him to either enjoy reading or be into sci-fi and fantasy, because it will give us something to talk about. I need someone like me, really, a bit nerdy, but hopefully with a twinkle in his eye that suggests he's going to enjoy showing me the ropes.

Looks wise, I try not to be too critical. I'm not demanding he be six-two and muscular, or a Henry Cavill lookalike (although that would be nice.) I suppose it's a bit like porn—you know it when you see it. I'm hoping he'll jump out at me.

Fifteen minutes later, I realize that's not going to happen. I suppose it's a bit like looking for a new house. You start off by thinking you want four bedrooms, a quiet location, a huge kitchen, and a pool, and by the end you realize you'll be lucky to get just one thing on your list. None of the guys I look at mention reading, sci-fi, or fantasy in their bios. I'm sure some of them must read, surely? I guess they think it's not going to attract girls.

I perk up when I find one guy who states that *Alien* is among his favorite movies. He's relatively good looking, with short, dark-blond hair and a cheeky smirk. He's twenty-six and a dentist. Well, I won't hold that against him. It also says that he likes playing Minecraft. So that's two things we sort of have in common. I'm not super-keen on Minecraft, but at least he likes gaming.

Taking a deep breath, I swipe right.

I continue on, and also swipe right on three other men. One mentions Slytherin—I decide not to tell Charlie, who told me to only date Hufflepuffs—one mentions he has a beagle, which is my favorite breed, and the third also has a photo of him with a dog and, in the background, a World of Warcraft poster. All three of them are smiling and are normal looking, maybe seven out of ten, which is what I consider myself to be, so hopefully they're not out of my league.

I've just closed the app and I'm about to give Mum a call when I get a notification.

*You've got a new match!*

Holy shit. So that means one of the guys I've swiped right on has also swiped right on me?

Heart racing, I open the app again. *It's a Match!* it declares, and it informs me that 'You and Mark have liked each other.' It's the guy with the dog who plays World of Warcraft. Ooh, well, that's good, right?

I look at his photo and bio again. It says he's five foot ten, twenty-four, so a year younger than me, but that's okay, and he's a dentist. Well, he's going to love my Bugs Bunny teeth. He's quite cute, with interesting light-blue eyes and a nice smile.

Cute enough to have sex with?

For the first time, it really sinks in what I've got myself into here. Charlie said that most guys on the app, even if they're open to a longer-term relationship, aren't going to turn down a hookup. If I start talking to this guy, it could end in us having sex.

I think I'm going to hyperventilate. I really need to get myself a brown paper bag if I'm going to do this for real.

# Chapter Two

### *Alice*

I'm not sure whether to message him first, or whether I should wait and see if he messages me. I don't want to look desperate, even though I am, so instead I decide to call my mother.

She answers after two rings. "Alice!"

"Hey, Mum." I smile as her picture pops up on FaceTime. She's in her mid-fifties, with still-blonde hair she keeps long so I can put it up neatly for her. Today, June has plaited it into a French braid and slotted one of her pretty flower clips into the side, and her face has a little color. "Ooh, you look nice," I tell her.

"June gave me a makeover." She bats her mascara-brushed lashes and laughs.

"Are you having a great time together?" June, her sister, only lives half an hour away, but she has four teenage children and works full time as a nurse, so she doesn't have much free time. When she does have a holiday, I assume she must want to spend it with her own family, so I try not to call on her, but occasionally she offers to look after Mum for a few nights so I can visit Charlie or have time to myself.

"We are," Mum says. "Last night we watched *Mamma Mia* and June made us both a margarita. The drink, not the pizza."

I laugh. "Naughty girls."

"I know I'm not supposed to drink alcohol…"

"Hey, everything in moderation including moderation, right?"

"Yeah." She smiles. "How are you doing?"

"I'm good. I've just met Charlie for lunch. She's trying to get me to go to a party tonight, but it's not my sort of thing."

"Aw, Alice. You should go! You might meet a nice young man." She winks at me.

I wrinkle my nose at her. Although we're very close, I haven't told her my reason for coming to Wellington this time. Not because I'm too embarrassed, although I don't particularly want to discuss my hopes for a one-night stand with my mother, but more that I don't want to make her feel bad. She's obviously aware that having to care for her is the main reason I've never dated, and she feels terrible about it. The last thing I want to do is increase her guilt.

"There'll be plenty of time for that when Charlie comes home," I reply. Charlie only agreed to go to university on the proviso that she returns to Gisborne when she graduates so she can split Mum's care with me. I've tried to convince her that I'm happy to continue to care for Mum, but Charlie just gets upset, so at the moment I'm going along with the idea.

"What are you going to do this afternoon?" Mum asks.

Apart from hopefully having sex? I clear my throat. "I thought I might go to the cinema and treat myself to a meal out."

"Oh, okay. Have a lovely time, sweetheart. Enjoy yourself. You deserve it."

I stare at the screen as a notification pops up. *Mark sent you a new message.* Oh, holy shit.

"Take care, and you know where I am," I tell her.

She waves. "Speak soon!" And she ends the call.

I tap the notification. It opens in the Tinder app, and there it is. A message from Mark.

Mark: *Hi*

Okay, so not a lot to go on. He couldn't even be bothered to use any punctuation. Kids today…

My heart in my mouth, I reply with: *Hello!*

Mark: *Sup*

Me: *Not much! I've been hanging out with my sister. She's at Vic. What are you up to?*

Mark: *Work*

Me: *I see you're a dentist!*

Mark: *Assistant yeah*

Me: *That must be interesting?*

Mark: *It's okay*

Me: *You play WoW, right?*

Mark: *Yeah*

Me: *What class do you play?*

Mark: *Troll warrior*

Me: *Ooh, Horde? The enemy, LOL. I play a human paladin healer.*

Mark: *Okay*

Jesus, this guy's hard work.

Me: *You have a dog in one of your photos. Is it yours?*

Mark: *No*

Fuck me. I decide to take the bull by somewhere even more aggressive than his horns.

Me: *Look, I'm new to Tinder. Do you normally chat for a while? Or would you prefer to meet up?*

I wait for him to reply.

Ten minutes goes by.

I know he's at work, so maybe he's in the middle of an appointment or something? While I wait, I ring room service and ask for a latte to be sent up with a piece of chocolate cheesecake. Then I watch half an hour of a ridiculous game show on the TV.

Finally, I come to the conclusion that he's not messaging back anytime soon. Ghosted on my first attempt. I sigh, toss the phone on the bed, grab my book, turn off the TV, and start reading.

Within five minutes, I've dozed off.

I wake about an hour later. It's warm in the room, and I have a slight headache, but I feel a whole lot better when I look at my phone and discover I have another match, and he's already sent me a message.

His name's Tim, and he's the first guy I swiped right on. He's twenty-six, a dentist, he plays Minecraft, and he likes *Alien*.

Oh well. Here goes.

Tim: *Hey! Looks like we matched :-)*

He used punctuation and a smiley emoji. Things are looking up!

Me: *Yeah. You are my lucky star!*

Tim: *LOL wot?*

Shit.

Me: *Sorry, it's a quote from Alien. Ripley sings the song at the end?*

Tim: *Oh yeah, sorry, I haven't watched it for ages. LOL cool. You into sci-fi?*

Me: *Yes, and fantasy. Books and movies. You?*

Tim: *Yeah, some, I like horror movies mainly.*

I'm not a big fan of horror, but at least he's talking to me.

Me: *What are your favorites, apart from Alien?*

Tim: *Oh, The Exorcist, The Shining, Saw, that kind of thing. You?*

Eesh.

Me: *I enjoyed The Thing.*
Tim: *Yeah that was okay.*
Me: *You gotta be fuckin' kidding me!*
Tim: *LOL why?*
Argh…
Me: *No, it's a quote from the movie.*
Tim: *Oh right, LOL.*
Me: *Sorry. I feel like an idiot now.*
Tim: *No, it's cool. You sound fun.*
Well, that's something.
Me: *I've only just started using Tinder. Do you normally chat for a while?*
Tim: *Sometimes. What are you looking for?*
Me: *What do you mean?*
Tim: *Are you on here for something long term? Or do you just want to hook up?*
I stare at the screen, my heart in my mouth. Oh my God. Am I really about to type this? I take a deep breath.
Me: *I'm just looking to hook up. You?*
Tim: *Yeah, sounds cool. And you're gorgeous! I'm totally up for that.*
It's clumsy, but at least it's a compliment.
Tim: *You wanna meet somewhere? Have a drink?*
I blow out the breath.
Me: *Sounds great. Can you suggest somewhere?*
Tim: *Murphy's Law in Courtenay Place? At six?*
Me: *Okay!*
Tim: *See you then.*
Me: *Yes, see you!*
I toss the phone onto the bed again and fall back, my hands covering my face. Holy shit. I'm actually going to do this.

It's only three p.m. so I have three hours yet. Too nervous to stay in, I gather up my jacket and purse and head out.

I walk down to the cinema and pick one of the movies that's about to start. It's some kind of historical drama, but two hours later, when I finally begin the walk back to the hotel, I can't recall anything about it.

It's not really surprising. Even though I tell myself that virginity is just a state of being, I'd be an idiot if I didn't accept that having sex for the first time is a big thing. Of course it is. Nearly every magazine article and book you read, and every movie you watch, tells you that sex is what makes the world go around. And the older you get, the more the thought of doing it is going to be nerve-wracking. But at least I'm trying to rectify the issue.

When I get back to the hotel, I take a shower, pluck out any stray hairs that remain after the wax I gave myself at home, slather myself in moisturizer, spray on a decent amount of perfume, and dress in what I hope is a sexy combination of lace bra and knickers beneath my dark jeans and a red top, because Charlie said guys think it's sexy. I nearly always wear my hair up in a scruffy bun, but tonight I leave it down in the hope that he might like to run his fingers through it. I apply a decent amount of makeup because it gives me confidence.

When I'm done, I stare at myself in the full-length mirror.

The clothes and makeup are good, but it doesn't look like me. I feel as if I'm on stage, wearing a costume. I suppose that is what I'm doing. I'm putting on an act tonight, behaving as if I do this all the time. I guess it makes it easier if I pretend to be someone else. Real Alice hasn't kissed a guy since she was sixteen, and that was only a playful peck. Sexy Alice is experienced and has one-night stands all the time. She'd totally be comfortable with going back to a guy's place and letting him strip off her clothes and have mad monkey sex with her.

Oh jeez. Deep breaths, girl.

I've already texted Charlie, and she messages me back, saying: *Good luck! Let me know how it goes! Just relax and try to enjoy it!*

I reply with: *Will do!* Then, at 5:45, I slip my phone into my back pocket, grab my jacket and purse, and head out again.

It takes me about ten minutes to walk down to the bar on Courtenay Place. By the time I arrive, my heart's racing and my mouth has gone dry. I'm so nervous, but I want to do this so much that I force myself to cross the busy road and head toward the Irish bar on the corner. I double check my phone as I walk, reminding myself what he looks like.

Although it's a Tuesday, it's close to Christmas, and the bar is busy, with people milling about outside, gathering with drinks to chat, or sitting at the tables, sharing food. I was hoping he'd wait for me outside, but I can't see him anywhere. After scanning the crowd, I go through the open doors into the dimly lit interior.

I pause on the threshold, waiting for my eyes to adjust. Then I hear someone say, "Alice?"

I turn and see a guy standing there, beer in hand. He's only an inch or so taller than me, and I'm only five foot seven. But that doesn't matter, right? He's not bad looking, although his hair is a lot longer than it was in his photo, and hangs around the collar of his jacket with a kind of surf-dude look.

"Tim?" I ask, breathless.

He nods. "Want a drink?"

"Um, okay, thanks." I follow him to the bar, feeling a little queasy.

"What do you want?" he asks.

"Gin and tonic, please."

He waves to the bartender and asks for a G&T. I swallow hard. Should I offer to pay?

"How are you doing?" he asks, raising his voice above the sound of the music and conversation.

"Good, thanks."

He nods and looks at his phone. I wonder whether he's double-checking my profile on Tinder, but when I glance down, he's checking his messages.

I stand there awkwardly, waiting for him to finish. When he's done, he pulls up Google, and I see the cricket score of the Black Caps match against Sri Lanka on the page.

"Two hundred and eight for two last time I looked," I tell him.

He glances up, surprised, then pockets his phone. "You're into cricket?"

"Yeah. I think they're going to cream Sri Lanka in this ODI."

He shrugs. "I don't know much about it."

Oh jeez. This is going well.

The bartender passes me my G&T. "I'll pay for mine," I say to Tim.

"Okay," he says.

I touch my credit card to the keypad. Then I wait for him to suggest sitting at a table, but he doesn't. He has a mouthful of beer and looks around the bar.

"So you're a dentist," I say, determined to have a conversation with this guy.

He looks back at me then. "Yeah. You've got good teeth."

I laugh, then sober as he just raises his eyebrows. Oh, he wasn't making a joke. "Thank you. I've always thought the front two were a bit big."

"They're large, but they're not buck teeth. I've seen much worse."

"Oh. Well, that's something."

"Yeah." He eye-dips me then as he takes another sip of beer. Wow. That's obvious. My face is up here, bro. Maybe I should check out the size of his knob and see what he thinks of that.

I have a large mouthful of G&T, glad of the burn of the alcohol down to my stomach.

"What do you do?" he asks.

"About what?"

"As a job."

"Oh. Didn't you read my bio?"

He laughs. "No."

"Right. I'm a book reviewer."

"Oh, cool. What kind of books?"

"Sci-fi and fantasy novels."

"Nice." He finishes off his beer and puts the glass on the bar.

Okay. I already know that Tim isn't going to be the love of my life, but that's not why I'm here. It doesn't matter that there's no real connection between us, right? I just want what's in his trousers. It's not going to be the best sex I'll ever have in my life. But it will be sex, and after this, at least I'll know how it all works. It's what people do all the time nowadays.

I have a couple of quick mouthfuls of my G&T, then say, "Do you live nearby?"

His eyes light up. "Yeah, a few streets down."

"Shall we go back to your place?"

"Okay, cool." He heads for the door, and I follow him out.

It's a beautiful early summer evening. We walk for five minutes, then turn left onto a quieter road. We pause at a pedestrian crossing and wait for the lights to change.

"Can I kiss you?" he asks.

I blink. "Here?"

He shrugs.

There's nobody else waiting to cross, so I take a deep breath and say, "Okay."

He moves closer to me, lifts a hand and slides it into my hair, then pulls me toward him for a kiss.

It's not my first ever kiss—that was reserved for Jimmy McCaffrey when I was twelve—but it's the first I've had as an adult, and I'm therefore surprised when he thrusts his tongue into my mouth straight off the bat. I stiffen, fighting the urge to move back. He tilts his head and deepens the kiss, and I close my eyes, trying desperately to stand still. Where his arm is raised to cup my head, I can smell his armpit. Oh God... this is awful. I knew it wouldn't be romantic, but holy shit, this is even worse than I imagined.

I don't know this guy. We have no connection at all. Am I really going back to his place? Can I see myself taking off my clothes, and letting him touch me in the most intimate way?

And what about safety issues? How do I know if he'll be gentle and kind, and not rough or even violent? Oh my God, this is so ridiculous. Why did I ever think this would work?

I move my head back, and he lowers his arm.

"Tim," I say gently, "I've changed my mind."

"Aw," he says.

"I'm very sorry to have wasted your time."

"What happened?" He doesn't look angry, just disappointed.

"I haven't done this much, and I'm a bit nervous. I thought I could do this, but actually I don't think I'm ready to sleep with someone straight after I've met them."

His eyebrows rise. "You've never had a one-night stand? Wow."

"No."

"Okay." He looks puzzled at that revelation, but just says, "So you want to go back to the bar?"

I smile. "Actually, I think I'll head off. It's not you, it's me. Again, sorry to waste your time."

"Ah," he says, "don't worry about it. Happens a lot."

Yeah, I think, I bet it does if you stick your tongue down a girl's throat straight away. But I don't say it. Instead, I say, "It was nice to meet you," and then I turn and stride back down the road, walking fast, all the way back to my hotel.

I go straight up to my room, lock the door, take off my jacket and shoes, then flop back on the bed with my hands over my face.

Tears prick my eyes. I can't believe I thought this was a good idea. How did I ever think I could meet a guy, go back to his room, and be intimate with him when I've only just met him? It was absolutely ridiculous. It was never going to work. Maybe it does for people who are sleeping around regularly, and therefore for them sex is just a small step further than kissing. I wanted it to work. I really, really did. But I should have known the reality was going to be nothing like the fantasy.

My phone buzzes, and I pick it up and see it's a text.

Charlie: *How's it going? You in bed yet? LOL*

Me: *Total disaster, I'm afraid.*

Charlie: *Oh no! What happened? Did you meet him?*

Me: *Yes. He was okay. Not horrible at all. But there was no chemistry. And it was all so cold and clinical. I froze and had to back out.*

Charlie: *Aw, honey, I'm so, so sorry.*

Me: *Yeah, well, I suppose I should have guessed that would happen. It was a nice fantasy.*

Charlie: *Oh don't give up! You have another night to go!*

Me: *I know, but I can't see it working. I'm just not the type of person who can sleep with someone they don't know. Not the first time, anyway!*

Charlie: *Well keep checking your messages. You never know. The next one might be the right one!*

Me: *Yeah.*

Charlie: *Look, why don't you come to the party? There are lots of guys here! They'd be all over the confident, sexy older woman.*

Me: *LOL thanks, but I'll pass. I'm going to take a bath then go to bed. Start again tomorrow!*

Charlie: *Okay, fair enough. You still on for the zoo in the morning?*

Me: *Absolutely! See you there at ten?*

Charlie: *Yeah, sleep well. Love you!*

Me: *Love you x*

I put the phone down and stare up at the ceiling.

*You never know. The next one might be the right one.*

It could be true. But I'm abandoning my idea of a one-night stand for now. I'll have to hope when the time comes—if it ever does—that whoever ends up being my first isn't turned off by the thought that I have no idea what I'm doing.

For now, though, I think I'll order myself another G&T on room service, take a bath, and watch a movie.

Looks like it's going to be a while before this girl loses her V-card.

Bummer.

# Chapter Three

## *Kip*

"I'm off."

I look up from the monthly financial report I'm halfway through checking, glance at my watch and see it's only six-thirty p.m., and give my twin brother a wry smile. "You're taking this relationship thing a bit seriously, aren't you?"

In the past, the two of us and our younger brother have worked until seven or eight p.m., or even later when it's busy, often sending for Uber Eats so we don't have to worry about getting dinner when we go home. Since his girlfriend moved in with him, though, Saxon has been keen to leave the office early to be with her.

He lifts one hand, palm up. "Reading financial reports." Then he lifts the other hand. "Spending time with a gorgeous redhead who's prepared to let me kiss every freckle she possesses." He pretends to weigh the options, then rolls his eyes.

"Go on then," I tell him good naturedly. "Fuck off. And give Catie a kiss from me."

He throws me a wry look. "Absolutely not."

We exchange a smile, and he leaves the room.

I sit back for a moment, my smile fading. Somehow, he managed to sidestep the dating arena by knocking a girl up on a one-night stand and then having her turn up on his doorstep four months later, pregnant with his twins. I'm genuinely thrilled he's found himself a girl he seems crazy about, but it's impossible not to feel a touch of envy.

It's been a few months since I had a woman in my bed, and I'd be lying if I said I didn't miss sex. I don't miss the emotional turbulence that always seems to accompany dating, though. I wish I could jump to the four-month stage and have done with the getting-to-know-you part.

Sighing, I return my attention to the financial report, and I'm a good three-quarters through before I'm interrupted again by the phone on my desk ringing.

I check the display and see it's an internal call—my younger brother, Damon.

I pick up the receiver and say, "Yo," my standard, somewhat unprofessional greeting to my siblings.

"My office," Damon states. "Now."

I tuck the receiver under my chin as I turn the page over, frowning at his curt demand. "I'm in the middle of checking the financial report."

"Dude," he says. "You're going to want to see this." He hangs up.

Still frowning, I get up, poke my head in the office next door and tell my PA, Marion, where I'm going, then walk along the corridor and into his office.

Our rooms reflect our personalities and interests. Saxon's is untidy, with his desk covered in sheets of paper and folders like the mad scientist he is. He's a big fan of Dr. Who, and he has a framed poster on the wall of his favorite: the tenth doctor, and a TARDIS mug on the desk. He's also into music, and he's always playing one of his vinyl albums on his record player.

My office is much neater. I like space, and furniture with clean lines. Lack of clutter helps me think, and I always make sure to leave a clean sheet of white paper on the large drawing desk by the window so if I get a new idea, I can start it straight away. I also have framed posters on my wall, but mine are of old sci-fi movies.

People who don't know Damon very well might expect him to have photos of fast cars or the All Blacks. He's young and flash, and it's true that he loves both of those things. But his offices bear beautiful oil paintings of Greek goddesses and angels in flowing white gowns with golden hair. Nobody ever guesses that he's the artist.

When I walk in, I discover him pacing up and down. One glance at his face tells me he's furious.

"What's going on?" I ask.

"Shut the door," he says.

I close it and come into the room. He gestures at his laptop and continues to pace. Puzzled, I go behind his desk, sit in his leather swivel chair, and look at what's on the screen.

It's an online article from a popular New Zealand news site, dated to just fifteen minutes ago. The headline is 'Wellington companies to close multi-million deal for revolutionary software.'

I read the article with growing disbelief.

"A senior member of staff at the computer software company, Kingpinz Robotics, revealed today that the company is on the verge of selling a revolutionary text-to-speech software called MOTHER to computer hardware company Sunrise Ltd. for the production an augmentative and alternative communication or AAC device, in a deal rumored to be over ten million dollars. Directors at Sunrise have been battling rumors of pay cuts and problematic working conditions for the past few months, and the acquisition of this software is a huge coup for them."

Slowly I lift my gaze to Damon. "What the fuck?"

He lifts his hands in bemusement, then puts them on his hips.

MOTHER is my baby, and I've been working on it for years, using our cousin Titus's AI program to completely revolutionize text-to-speech software for use in for an augmentative and alternative communication or AAC device for people who can't speak—either because they have a condition such as ALS, motor neurone disease, or cerebral palsy, or because they've had a stroke or a traumatic brain injury. I chose the name MOTHER because it refers to the phrase 'mother tongue,' and also because we're all fans of the movie *Alien*, in which the computer is called Mother.

Our senior leadership team or SLT at Kingpinz consists of five members, including me, Saxon, and Damon. I met the fourth member, Craig Worthington, at university. He's a talented computer engineer, and a good friend. When Saxon, Damon, and I decided we were going to set up our own company, we were quick to ask Craig to join us, and he's been with us ever since. The fifth member, Marama Taylor, joined the company four years ago, and we promoted her to the team in June. She's married to a member of the Māori All Blacks and they have two kids. She's also an excellent software engineer, and she's slotted into the team nicely.

At our monthly meeting in November, for the first time we discussed which company we were going to sell MOTHER to for production of the AAC device. Saxon and I favored a company called Genica Inc., mainly because we've worked with its CEO, Jack Evans, before, and we get on well. Craig then put forward Sunrise Ltd. as a possibility, speaking at great length about the CEO's commitment to producing advanced medical equipment. His enthusiasm rubbed off on Marama, who was leaning toward them as an option. Damon was on the fence.

I gave Sunrise some serious thought, but I was uncomfortable about the rumors of pay cuts and working conditions, and I also didn't mention to Craig that I don't like Sunrise's CEO, Renée Garnier. I met her recently at the hospital at a health professionals meeting. She was brash, forceful, and overconfident, and when one of the doctors mentioned the CEO of another one of Renée's competitors, she mimicked his speech impediment, which made me dislike her even more.

Last week, I spoke to Damon again, voicing my reservations about Sunrise, and in the end he voted for Genica Inc. That made us three to two, and just a couple of days ago I had a preliminary meeting with Jack Evans to talk about his vision for the AAC device. He's going to read this article, which is going to make me look like an unprofessional idiot. I'm so angry, I can barely speak.

"Looks as if someone wanted to force your hand," Damon says. "I wonder who that could be?"

I already know it wasn't Marama. She's a sweetheart, and she'd never do something like this. Craig is my best friend, but he can be ruthless and cutthroat in business. Shocked that he'd extend that work ethic to me, though, I walk out and along the corridor to the next office, and stand in the doorway.

Craig is the same age as me, a little shorter and stockier, with dark-blond hair. He's smart, witty, and hardworking. We used to go out socially with him a lot; less so since he got married and had a baby, but we're still good friends. Or I thought we were, anyway.

He looks up, sees me, and leans back in his chair. He doesn't smile.

"Why?" I say.

He turns his swivel chair from side to side. "I'm guessing you've seen the article?"

I walk into his office, with Damon following behind me. "Yeah. I've seen the article. Why did you do it?"

Marama also enters, drawn by our raised voices. I hear Damon murmuring to her, and her intake of breath as he tells her what's happened.

"I was talking to a friend of mine who's a reporter," Craig says. "I thought it was off the record."

"Bullshit," I snap. "You know I favored Genica. You wanted to force my hand."

"No," he says, but I know I'm right.

"Why Sunrise?" Damon asks, as he and Marama come to stand on either side of me. "Even the article mentioned the issues they've been having with their workforce."

"I'd never sell to Sunrise," I snap. "I don't like their CEO."

"What's wrong with her?" Craig asks.

"She's a bitch, and I'm not letting MOTHER within a mile of her."

He gets slowly to his feet. "She said she'll offer twice what Genica or any of the other development companies would pay."

"Even if that is the case," Marama states, "Kip's the project director, so the choice is up to him."

"This is nothing to do with you," Craig snaps. "Keep your fucking nose out."

"Whoa," Damon says.

"Craig," I say sharply as Marama reddens. "That's out of order. We're a team. We all get a say. And I don't care what that article says. I'm not going to let you force my hand. Nobody's going to think twice about me going back on a deal with Sunrise after all the hassles they've had recently. Money isn't everything. I've made the decision. I've already spoken to Jack Evans. I'm selling MOTHER to Genica."

He glares at me. "You arsehole," he says bitterly. "I should have known you'd shaft me. You said we'd discuss it before you made a decision."

"Marama's right—money's not always the most important thing," Damon says.

Craig glares at him. "Oh, fuck off. I might have known you'd take your brother's side. Do you even have a brain of your own?"

Damon's eyebrows rise into his hairline. "I think you should take that back," he says carefully.

"You can't do this," Craig snaps at me. Jesus, I actually think he's close to tears. "I'm a member of the team, and I get to have a say in what we do with our work. Why would you sell to a company that's offering half what Sunrise would give for it?"

"This is for everyone," I say, confused as to why he's so upset.

"Don't quote Tim Berners-Lee at me," Craig yells, getting to his feet. "I bet the people he thought were friends didn't screw him over like this."

I try to suppress my temper, recognizing there must be an undercurrent beneath all of this. He's never spoken to any of us like this before, and it's not like him. Is it the money he's worried about? Whilst, if we sold MOTHER for higher price, we'd funnel most of the money back into the company, it would inevitably lead to some of the cash filtering through to the staff.

"Craig," I say, "if you're having money problems, maybe you'd like to go down to my office and we can discuss this in private?"

He slams his laptop shut. "Go fuck yourself." He picks up his laptop.

Damon twitches as if he's going to move and block his path, but I put a hand on his arm, and he stays put. Craig strides past, out of the room.

We fall quiet and stare at each other.

"Holy shit," Damon says eventually. "That came out of nowhere."

I'm upset, but I don't want to explode in front of Marama. "I'm sorry that Craig was so rude to you," I say to her. "I'm not going to let that slide."

She nods. "Let me know if there's anything I can do."

We head out, Damon and I go back into his office, and we close the door.

"Jesus Christ," he says.

"I'm not going mad, am I?" I ask him. "I'm the project director. It was my decision to make, in the end?"

"Of course it was," Damon replies. "Plus we're directors, and he's just a member of SLT. We don't need his and Marama's consent on who we sell to. You discussed it as a courtesy. He's being an idiot." He studies me for a moment. "Do you want to backtrack? Sell it to Sunrise instead?"

Anger sears through me. "I'm not letting Craig bully me into doing that."

"Fair enough," he says. "Fuck him."

I give a short laugh, and his lips curve up.

"Are you going to talk to Saxon about this?" he asks. "He'd want to know."

I hesitate. He's had a huge amount on his plate lately, with Catie and the babies, plus he's in Auckland every other week running Titus's AI company while our cousin is in the UK. He doesn't need more to worry about. "No. Let's keep it to ourselves for now."

"He'll probably see the article."

"You know what he's like, he doesn't read the trade news. He relies on me to tell him what's going on."

"He won't be happy," he says, but he holds up a hand when I glare at him. "All right. What are we going to do about Craig, though? He had no right to discuss anything with a reporter."

"I know. I could fire him for it. I want to. I'm so angry with him. But there's something odd about all of this. We've been friends for a long time. Why would he do something like that?"

Damon perches on the edge of his desk. "He's always been your friend rather than mine. If I'm honest, I don't think he's quite the nice guy you think he is. He has a nasty streak. It stays well hidden, but sometimes it pokes through when he's well oiled."

I know he's right. "I'll talk to him," I say reluctantly. "Hopefully he was just frustrated, and he spoke without thinking. I'll try to talk him around."

"If you can't, we're going to have to think about how we handle this." He stops as the phone on his desk rings and picks it up. "Hey, Marion," he says. He listens for a moment, then closes his eyes briefly. "All right, hold on, I'll tell him." He glances at me. "Apparently Lesley is on the phone for you. She says she's in town and wonders if you'd like to catch up."

It's my ex. Damon gives me a look that says, 'For fuck's sake.'

"Want me to tell her you're busy?" he asks.

I sigh. "No, tell Marion I'll take it in my office."

"Bro," he says, "Seriously? She's not good for you. You can do better."

"I'm just going to talk to her," I tell him. "Catch you later."

I leave his office, walk through to mine, sit in my leather chair, and turn it so I'm looking out over the view of Alexandra Park. It's the summer solstice tomorrow, so the sun won't set until close to nine p.m. The sun is low on the horizon, its evening rays painting the park in shades of orange and gold.

I turn back to my phone and pick up the receiver. Line four is flashing, so I press it and lean back. "Hey, Les, sorry to keep you."

"No worries," she replies. "Hello, you. How are you doing?"

"I'm good, thanks." I prop my feet on the windowsill, stretching out my legs. "How are you?"

"Yeah, all good."

"You're back in New Zealand?"

"Just for a few weeks." So a visit then. She's still not moving back.

I watch a blackbird hop along the window ledge before it takes off and soars toward the park.

"I wanted to wish you happy birthday," Lesley says.

I lean an elbow on the arm of my chair and rest my head on my hand. "My birthday's tomorrow."

"Oh… It's the twenty-first, isn't it? Shit." She got the day wrong every year we were together.

"Yeah, but thanks anyway." I wait for her to suggest hooking up again. Be strong, Kip.

"I wanted to tell you before someone else did," she says. "I'm getting married."

I go still. Then, slowly, I sit up. "Oh. Okay."

"His name's Harrison Ford—and no, it's not the actor, they just share the name. He's an architect, and we're really happy together."

"Congratulations."

"Shit, I didn't mean to say it like that. You make me nervous."

"Why?"

"I don't know. You always make me feel as if you're going to tell me off."

I lift my glasses onto my hair and massage the bridge of my nose. "I appreciate you letting me know, and I wish you all the happiness in the world."

"Don't be sarcastic. You were very special to me, Kip. *Are* very special."

"So special you moved to another country."

"See, there you go again, telling me off. I wanted you to come with me. If you had, we'd still have been together."

It's pointless to argue with her. To remind her that she made the decision to take the job in Australia before discussing it with me. Our relationship was far from perfect, but I loved her—or I thought I did, anyway—and even if she didn't exactly break my heart, she fractured it enough that it still bears the scar.

What is it about people trying to force my hand? I'm sick of it.

She clears her throat. "You wanna meet up? I've missed you." I can hear the smile in her voice.

Jesus. She's marrying another guy, and she wants to hook up with me. It's the proverbial nail in the coffin. I feel a spike of dislike, and my fingers tighten on the phone.

"I've got to go," I tell her. "It was great to hear from you. Good luck with the wedding."

I slam the receiver onto the unit, then yell, "Fuck!" Leaning forward, I rest my head on the desk, then bang my forehead lightly.

There's a long pause, and then my door opens, and someone comes in. I flop back in my chair and watch Marion walk across to the desk and place a cup of coffee in front of me. In her fifties, with graying wavy hair, she's worked for me for five years. She's the same age as my mother, but even though she does boss me around the same way all good PAs do, we get on very well.

"You okay?" she asks.

"Not really."

"I'm supposed to tell you that you have an extremely important call coming from the UK," she says, "that it might come at any time, and you can't possibly leave the office until it happens."

"You can tell my brother I'm not going anywhere," I say wryly. "Despite the fact that Lesley wanted to hook up."

"You said no?"

"I did."

"Should I say well done?"

"It was an easy decision in the end. She's getting married."

Her eyebrows rise. "And she still asked to see you?"

"Yeah."

"Jesus."

"I know. I mean, why would she even suggest it?"

"A last hurrah, I guess."

"But how can you cheat on someone you're going to marry?"

"Aw," Marion says, "you're so sweet."

I scowl at her.

"Damon said to tell you to go on Tinder," she says, "and find yourself a date for your birthday."

"I don't want a date. I'm done with women."

"Oh, I think we both know that's not true." She pushes my phone toward me with a finger. "In this case, I think he's right."

"I'm twenty-nine tomorrow."

"I know."

"I'm an old man."

"Practically drawing your pension. You'd better find a girl before you get false teeth."

That makes me laugh, and she smiles. "I'm off now. See you tomorrow."

"Yeah, thanks Marion. Goodnight."

She goes out.

Sliding down in my chair, I pick up my phone and look at the red flame logo of the Tinder app.

Dating in person is surprisingly difficult when you're a rich guy. No, correction, not dating per se. My bespoke suits, Apple watch, expensive phone, and brand-new Mercedes C-Class Cabriolet ensure that I have little trouble getting a girl to go out with me, but it can be tough to see past the dollar signs that light up women's eyes.

It's one reason I like Tinder. On the app, I'm not Kip Chevalier, billionaire CEO of Kingpinz. I'm just a guy, looking for a date. Despite the fact that it's easy to lie online, I find the app a surprisingly honest way to find someone.

I haven't been on it for a few months, and I paused my account the last time I used it. I open it up and check my profile. Then I un-pause it, and start browsing.

If I see a girl I like, the first thing I do is check her bio. I'm not looking for anything in particular. Just something that prompts a connection. Even a one-night stand is better when you have something in common.

For a while, I swipe left repeatedly, not finding anyone who shares my interests. A lot of the women name bands I've never heard of, activities I'm not interested in, TV shows I've never seen, or contain jokes I don't find funny. I'm not usually this picky, but tonight I'm in a strange mood.

And then I see her. Alice. She's twenty-five. Her profile photo is taken from the chest up. She's blonde, and her hair's up in a scruffy bun, with lots of strands tumbling around her face. She's wearing tasteful makeup, and she's laughing at whoever is taking the photo, revealing that her front teeth are slightly bigger, which makes her look cute. She has dark-blue eyes and a mole on her left cheekbone, and she looks intelligent and classy. She's wearing a necklace with a pendant in the shape of a playing card bearing the Queen of Hearts.

I pull up the rest of her photos. There's a very nice shot of her in a sundress. One of her gardening. A more serious one that shows off her stormy blue eyes. A slightly older one with a beagle. And a photo of her in front of a computer with headphones around her neck. Is that a microphone behind her? Interesting. There's also a bookshelf that holds a dozen different sci-fi and fantasy books, including *The Lord of the Rings*, my favorite book of all time.

Interested now, I pull up her bio. It's relatively short.

*Sci-fi and fantasy fan (books and movies)*. Well, that's cool for a start.

*Ravenclaw*. A Harry Potter nerd. That's okay, so am I.

*Shield maiden of the Rohirrim*. Oh, she's a real fan of *The Lord of the Rings*.

*Alliance healer*. She plays World of Warcraft? Saxon and I have played since university. We don't get online as much as we used to now we're working, but we still play from time to time. I like that she's a gamer. It means she's into computers, which is a big plus.

*Joss Stone sound-alike*. I don't know the singer, so I pull her up on Spotify and play her most listened to song, *Right to be Wrong*. Oh, wow. She has an amazing, husky, soulful voice.

I signed up for Tinder Gold some time ago, which means I get five Super Likes a week. I tap the blue star icon on Alice's profile. That should pop up on her phone soon.

Nothing else I can do now. I've used the app enough to know it's no guarantee of a match. She might not like the look of me or could already have matched with someone else. She might even be on a date now.

My experience has been that for every ten or so right swipes, I might get one or two matches, and often they don't come to anything. I should swipe right on a few more profiles to increase my chances of finding a match.

But I've got work to do, and besides, I like the look of Alice, and I'm willing to wait to see what happens.

I open my laptop, pull up a report, and start reading.

I've only been working for a couple of minutes when my mobile lights up. I lift it and look at the message on the screen.

*Match! You and Alice have liked each other.*

I get the usual dopamine rush at the connection, and smile.

Leaning back in the chair, I study the screen. I'm never sure how long to wait, but as I'm the guy, I normally message first. Fuck it. What's the point in playing it cool?

Me: *Hey Alice! Looks like we matched :-) How are you doing?*

Alice: *Hello Kip! I'm good, thank you. That was quick!*

Me: *I was worried some other guy might snap you up, LOL.*

Alice: *Ha! Thank you so much for the Super Like. I'm very flattered.*

Me: *You're welcome. Do you have time to chat?*

Alice: *Absolutely. How has your day been?*

Me: *Yeah not bad. Busy, just winding down now. Have you been working?*

Alice: *No, I have a couple of days off. I've been with my sister today - she's studying at Vic. I went to the cinema, too. I saw that historical drama that's just come out. Not my kind of thing normally, but it was okay.*

Me: *I saw in your bio that you like sci-fi and fantasy? And you mentioned being a shield maiden of the Rohirrim, LOL. You're a big fan of The Lord of the Rings?*

Alice: *Oh nothing's as good as LOTR! Embarrassed to say I've watched those movies about eight times!*

Me: *Only eight? Lightweight. I must have seen them all twenty times! I watched them all in one day once.*

Alice: *Me too, LOL. Have yet to watch all the Hobbit and all LOTR in one day though.*

Me: *That would be fun. Maybe we should try it.*

I press send, my lips curving up.

Alice: *Ha! The man has stamina.*

Me: *That would be telling :-)*

Alice: *Oh, I see what I'm dealing with here :-)*

The smiling emoji suggests she's not upset with the innuendo, which lifts her in my estimation. I like a girl who can tease me. I turn to face the park and prop my feet up on the window ledge again. It's been a long time since I've had a conversation like this with a girl.

Me: *So here's a question. If you had to choose one between sci-fi and fantasy, which would you pick?*

Alice: *Ooh. Hmm. For books, I do love epic fantasy. For movies, probably sci-fi. I'm a big Alien fan.*

Me: *You are my lucky star :-)*

Alice: *Aw… you don't know how happy that's made me.*

Me: *LOL why?*

Alice: *I'm embarrassed to tell you.*

Me: *We're best friends now, right? Spill the beans.*

Alice: *Ah, I matched with a guy today. He said he liked Alien, so I said that quote, and he had no idea what I was saying, LOL.*

Me: *Aw...*

Alice: *I also said you've gotta be fucking kidding me, which also fell on deaf ears.*

Me: *The Thing, right? Brilliant movie.*

Alice: *Wow.*

Me: *Am I getting points for this?*

Alice: *You've been so great, I give you a gold star.*

Me: *I'm better than the previous candidate, then?*

Alice: *Oh, you have no idea. That was a total disaster.*

Me: *Aw that's a shame. Well, not for me.*

Alice: *Me either, I'm beginning to think.*

Me: *<3*

There's a pause, and then she also replies with a heart emoji.

Alice: *<3*

I chuckle.

Me: *Yeah Tinder can be cutthroat at times. I had one girl turn me down because she said I wasn't tall enough.*

Alice: *How tall are you?*

Me: *Six one LOL.*

Alice: *Wow. That's fussy.*

Me: *I thought so. I've also had a couple of girls say I shouldn't wear glasses in my photos as they're a turnoff. I guess it's sexier to walk into lampposts and fall down stairs.*

Alice: *If they've swiped left because of your glasses, it's definitely their loss, not yours.*

Me: *:-) So what's the beagle's name in the photo?*

Alice: *Frodo, LOL.*

Me: *I actually did laugh out loud at that!*

Alice: *Haha! Sadly he died last year, but he was a sweetie. Are you a dog fan?*

Me: *Oh definitely. I don't have one at the moment because I work long hours, but my family has always had them.*

Alice: *Your bio says you're a computer engineer?*

Me: *That's right. We started off designing prosthetics.*

Alice: *Like, replacement limbs?*

Me: *Yep. We design the software behind myoelectric prostheses. I'm also working on a new communication device.*

Alice: *Like in Star Trek?*

Me: *Ha! No, actually, it's the text-to-speech software for an augmentative and alternative communication or AAC device. Think Stephen Hawking.*

Alice: *Oh, the speech synthesizer?*

Me: *Exactly. For people who can't speak. It's my baby :-)*

Alice: *Wow, that's so cool. It must be very rewarding.*

Me: *Yeah, I think so.*

Alice: *I see you have a photo with a Rickenbacker.*

Me: *Oh, you're into guitars?*

Alice: *I know John Lennon had one. And George Harrison had a 12-string.*

Me: *That's right. Mine isn't a 12-string. I can never keep them in tune.*

Alice: *LOL. Do you play well?*

Me: *At the risk of sounding egotistical, not bad. Can you play?*

Alice: *A little.*

Me: *And you sing?*

Alice: *Well not professionally. In the shower!*

Me: *I'm now debating whether to ask if I can put that to the test… :-)*

She posts a blushing emoji, and I smile.

Me: *I hadn't heard of Joss Stone, but I played Right to be Wrong. Wow, what a voice. And yours is similar?*

Alice: *Yeah, fairly close.*

Me: *But you don't sing professionally?*

Alice: *No. Not had the opportunity.*

Me: *Shame. I'm sure you'd have done very well.*

Alice: *Thank you! So… am I right in guessing that you play World of Warcraft?*

Me: *Ha! You're the first girl to guess that from my bio. And you play an Alliance healer?*

Alice: *I have a top-level pally, a priest, and a druid. My fave's the pally.*

Me: *Do you raid?*

Alice: *I have done. Took down the Lich King with my guild! Haven't played as much since Wrath, other commitments, you know.*

Me: *Yeah. Life intervenes.*

I look at my watch. I'm tired and I need to get some work finished before I go home. But I really like this girl. I wonder whether she'd be interested in seeing me tomorrow?

Me: *So… this seems to be going well.*

Alice: *It does, doesn't it? You've cheered me up, anyway.*

Me: *I am sorry your previous date didn't work out, even though it means I got to talk to you. Did you actually meet up with him?*

Alice: *Yes. Um, this is actually my first time on Tinder. I arranged to meet him at a bar, and it didn't go well, suffice to say. But then we didn't have a connection like this.*

Almost immediately, she sends another message.

Alice: *I hope I'm not being too forward in saying that.*

Me: *Of course not. I haven't chatted to a girl like this in ages. Maybe ever!*

Alice: *Oh! I don't know why. You're lovely.*

I smile, flattered.

Me: *So would you like to meet up?*

Alice: *I think so.*

She sounds hesitant. I'm not surprised, if she's new to the app, and she's had a bad experience. It's tough anyway to go on a blind date, and it must be extra hard for girls, who have the safety factor to consider.

Me: *I have an idea. It's my birthday tomorrow.*

Alice: *Oh, congratulations!*

Me: *Yep. I'm 29. Nearly a pensioner.*

Alice: *LOL.*

Me: *My brother lives in town with his girlfriend. How about we all go to dinner?*

Alice: *Really?*

Me: *Yeah. It'd be fun. And then afterward, if all goes well, you and I could go for a drink?*

Alice: *That would be nice.*

Me: *No pressure. But I've enjoyed talking to you, and it would be great to meet you.*

Alice: *I'd like that very much.*

Me: *I'll contact him, then get back to you. Don't go anywhere!*

Alice: *Okay!*

I quickly text Saxon.

Me: *Hey bro, would you and Catie be up for dinner tomorrow? I've been chatting to a girl I really like who's a bit nervous and I think it would help if we went together?*

It takes him about fifteen minutes to come back.

Saxon: *Sorry, we were having a bath and then… other stuff.*

Me: *Jesus. Do you two ever stop?*

Saxon: *What can I say? I'm irresistible.*

Me: *And I'm jealous.*

I grin, though, pleased that he's found someone.

Me: *So, dinner tomorrow?*

Saxon: *Yeah, sure, if we can keep it relaxed? Catie's keen but still nervous about eating out. Maybe we could do Red's Rib Shack?*

Me: *Good idea. Shall I book? For seven?*

Saxon: *Sounds great. What's her name?*

Me: *Alice.*

Saxon: *All right, see you tomoz.*

I call the restaurant and book a table, requesting the best one in the house. Then I message Alice again.

Me: *Okay, all done! Seven p.m. at Red's Rib Shack. Do you know it?*

Alice: *Yes! Thank you so much. I wasn't sure if you'd actually do it, LOL.*

Me: *Of course! I'm excited to meet you. I'll wait for you out the front of the restaurant, okay?*

Alice: *Thank you so much.*

Me: *You're welcome. I look forward to it. See you then!*

Alice: *Bye, Kip. And thanks again.*

I smile as I turn back to my desk. Right, I have a fair amount of work I need to finish. Time to get stuck in.

I start reading the report on my laptop. But my mind keeps drifting to the girl in the red top.

It's been a long time since I've been excited for a date like this. I just hope she's as lovely in real life as she seems online.

# Chapter Four

## *Alice*

I put down my phone and blow out a long, shaky breath.

I've got a date! I cover my face with my hands. Tomorrow I'll be meeting him for real.

Oh my God, oh my God, oh my God, oh my God...

I still can't believe how it happened. I'd gotten out of the bath with the intention of deleting the app, convinced the whole thing was a terrible idea, but discovered a message waiting announcing that someone had sent me a Super Like. I was flattered, but told myself it didn't matter, I was still going to delete the app. Then I pulled up his profile... and my stomach did a strange little flip. He's gorgeous.

Picking up the phone, I look at his profile again. Kip, aged twenty-eight. Twenty-nine tomorrow, obviously. It's an unusual name. I forgot to ask him what it was short for. Kristopher, I'm guessing. His profile picture shows him from the chest up, dressed in an All Blacks shirt, looking at the camera and smiling. He has short dark-brown hair with a super sharp fade cut that's longer on top, a neat beard and mustache, brown eyes, and slightly arched eyebrows that give him a bit of a wicked look.

I bring up his other photos. One is a full-length shot of him in a dark-gray suit with a white shirt and gray tie, probably taken in his office at work. The second is of him on a beach in a pair of swim shorts—he has his hands on his hips and he's giving the person taking the photograph a look that suggests he didn't want his photo taken, but it does show off his nicely muscular body. The third shows him sitting in a chair playing the guitar. The fourth is of him standing next to a mirror, looking off at an angle, obviously photoshopped because he's wearing glasses but his reflection isn't, but it's an interesting shot.

I scroll down to his bio. The photo got me eighty percent of the way, but his bio sealed the deal. It's short but sweet and funny.

*If you're looking for a bad boy, look no further. I'm bad at everything.*

*Current relationship status: Made dinner for two. Ate both.*

*73% gentleman. 27% rogue.*

It made me laugh out loud and, despite the lack of detail, still told me a lot about him: that he has a great sense of humor, that he's single, that he can cook, and that he probably plays World of Warcraft. I thought he sounded fun. But he was so much more than that.

Have I found the right guy for my predicament? I love that he gave me quotes, and that he recognized mine from *The Thing*. He's a fan of *The Lord of the Rings* and he reads sci-fi and fantasy. He teased and flattered me. And now he wants to meet me.

I'm not marrying the guy, so we don't have to be soul mates, but I do need to like him, and for him to like me too. My meeting with Tim proved that to me.

I'm so excited, I have to tell someone. I bring up my messages and text Charlie.

Me: *Hey girl, how are you doing?*

Charlie: *Gooooood!*

Me: *LOL are you high?*

Charlie: *Only on life! It's a great party. You should have come!*

Me: *Didn't need to - got myself a date!*

Charlie: *WOT?!!!!*

Me: *LOL I'm meeting him tomorrow for dinner.*

Charlie: *Hold on.*

I wait for a moment, then jump as my phone buzzes. She's calling me. I laugh and answer it. "Hello?"

"Oh my God, tell me everything!"

"It's only a date, don't get over-excited."

"Yeah, but I would have sworn you were going to delete the app."

"I was! But he sent me a Super Like."

"Aw... that's so cute."

"He is. His name's Kip and he's twenty-eight. He's really funny, and he just got me, you know?"

"Oh, Alice. I'm so pleased for you! Can you send me a screenshot of his photo?"

"Okay, hold on." I take one and send it to her. "Should be coming through now."

"Yes, I got it. Ooh. He's got naughty eyebrows."

I laugh. "I know, I thought the same."

"Did he sound... you know, interested?"

"I told him I sing in the shower, and he said he was debating whether to ask if he could put that to the test."

"Oh, perfect! So when are you meeting him?"

"Tomorrow. I told him I hadn't used Tinder much and that I was nervous, and he said it was his birthday, and asked whether I'd like to go to dinner with him and his brother and his girl."

"That was a nice idea."

"I thought so. So I said yes. I'm meeting him at Red's Rib Shack at seven. He's going to wait outside for me." I can't explain how inexplicably happy that made me.

"I'm so glad. I hope he's fantastic."

The phone buzzes in my hand and I look at the screen. Oh, he's messaged me again!

I should tell her, but I have a sudden fear that he's going to cancel. I clear my throat. "Me too! Well, I'd better let you go." I can hear music and laughter in the background. "Have a great time, sweetie."

"All right. Still on for the zoo?"

"Of course. See you tomorrow."

"Bye."

I end the call, then bring up his message. Please don't let him say he's changed his mind...

Kip: *Question for you. I've just finished a book and want to start something new. Got any recommendations?*

My heart leaps. He's not canceling. He wants to chat again.

Me: *Hello! I thought you were supposed to be working?*

Kip: *I am. Sort of. Keep thinking about you.*

My face heats. Ooh! Play it cool, Alice!

Me: *Okay! What kind of book are you looking for?*

Kip: *I'm in the mood for some science fiction.*

Me: *Okay let me think...*

Kip: *Do you like it hard?*

I blink. Wow, that came out of the blue.

Me: *Sorry?*

There's a brief pause.

Kip: *OMG I meant the sci-fi. Do you like hard sci-fi?*

I giggle.

Me: *LOL okay.*

Kip: *Jesus, I'm so sorry, that was a genuine Freudian slip LOL.*

Me: *Haha don't worry about it. Yes, I read hard sci-fi! Have you read many of the classics?*

Kip: *Hold on, I'm busy saying every swear word I can think of.*

Me: *Kip, I'm not upset! It made me laugh.*

He doesn't reply for a moment. I picture him walking up and down, cursing at himself. I smile. He's quite sweet.

Me: *Have you read Neuromancer by William Gibson?*

Eventually he comes back.

Kip: *No, I haven't.*

Me: *You might like that. It's a cyberpunk novel.*

Kip: *Okay. Alice, I am really sorry for that comment. I would never say anything like that to a girl.*

Me: *Never?*

Kip: *Well, not before I knew her really well!!!!!*

Me: *I just assumed it was the 27% rogue coming out, LOL.*

Kip: *Thank you for not being insulted.*

Me: *Nah. I don't get offended easily. And now I'm just looking forward to getting to know you really well...*

Kip: *Don't be a minx. I'm still dying here.*

Me: *You're very sweet.*

Kip: *Gah. That's the second time today someone's called me that.*

Me: *Oh, who else said it?*

Kip: *My PA. And somewhere my brothers are laughing hysterically at that description of me.*

Me: *How many do you have?*

Kip: *Two. You?*

Me: *No brothers. One sister.*

Kip: *She's at Vic uni, right?*

Me: *Yep. Taking a business and communications degree. She's amazing, a lovely person. And I'm not going to tell you more about her in case you'd rather go to dinner with her tomorrow!*

Kip: *Aw, definitely not. You're my girl.*

I flush for the second time. I've never had any guy call me his girl before.

Me: *You'd better get on with your work. It's getting late.*

Kip: *Yeah, okay. I don't want to be too tired for our date tomorrow! Speak soon.*

Me: *Take care, and thanks again.*

Kip: *For what?*

Me: *For swiping right on me.*

Kip: *<3 :-)*

I put my phone down, smiling, flattered that he wanted to talk to me again.

Now I just have to wait until seven p.m. tomorrow. Argh! I'm excited and nervous in equal measure. But it'll be fun, and at least with his brother and his girl there it'll gives us time to get to know one another before things turn… intimate.

Oh my God. Now the nervousness is taking over the excitement. I'm never going to get to sleep tonight!

\*

### Seven p.m. the next day

I approach Red's Rib Shack from the other side of the road, pause in a doorway, and stare at Kip.

He's leaning against the wall not far from the door, looking at his phone in his left hand, his right in the pocket of his black trousers. He's wearing a white dress shirt, and I can see that the inside of the collar, the placket, and the cuffs where he's turned them back a couple of times are a silvery gray. The light breeze that's blowing across the harbor is ruffling the longer hair on the top of his head. He's wearing glasses, although he's looking over the top of them at his phone, so he must be short-sighted.

Oh my God, he didn't stand me up. I don't know why I was so convinced he would. He messaged me this morning, while I was at breakfast, to ask my opinion of a fantasy book he'd heard about, and we've messaged on and off all day in between his meetings and while I walked around the zoo with Charlie, who's been thrilled at the communication. It's mostly been inconsequential stuff, books, gaming, music, our favorite bands. But at around four he said he had a meeting and wouldn't be around for a while, and I haven't heard from him since. And three hours is a long time to maintain one's self-confidence.

But he's here, and my pulse is now racing at light speed. Gathering my courage, I check the traffic, then cross the road to stand in front of him. He's still looking at his phone, and I try to control my breathing as I wait for him to notice me.

He looks up then, straight at me, and we stare at each other for a moment. Then he slides his phone in his pocket and laughs. "I'm so sorry! I was just making sure you hadn't messaged to say you weren't coming."

"I'm nervous," I reply, "but I'm not crazy."

He smiles at that. His brown eyes are full of warmth and a kind of lazy interest that gives me goosebumps. "Hello," he says in a way that makes me tingle.

I blush. "Happy birthday."

"Thank you," he replies. "I'm glad you didn't stand me up. Best present ever."

I chuckle, and he smiles again and pushes off the wall. "My brother's inside. Are you ready?"

I nod, and he walks to the door and opens it to let me through.

Trying to stay calm, I go into the restaurant, and he leads me through to a table on a small dais by the window. Two people are already sitting there, looking as if they're trying not to laugh, so I get the feeling they were talking about us.

"Guys," Kip says, "this is Alice. Alice, this is Saxon and Catie."

My smile fades at the sight of the man sitting by the window. Although he's dressed in a navy shirt and jeans, and he's not wearing glasses, he's the spitting image of Kip.

The girl next to him, who's clearly pregnant, is wearing black trousers and a hot-pink top. In a soft Irish accent, she says, "They're twins, not clones. I know, they didn't tell me either." She holds out her hand, and I laugh and shake it.

"Your profile pic," I say to Kip, thinking about how his reflection hadn't been wearing glasses. "It wasn't a mirror!"

He grins, and Saxon gets to his feet. "It's always fun to see people's reactions to that photo. Pleased to meet you, Alice." We shake hands, smiling.

Kip takes the seat by the window, opposite Saxon, and I slide off my coat and hang it over the back of the chair next to Kip, opposite Catie. After yesterday's debacle, I decided I was going to wear something that made me feel comfortable and more myself, as I thought it might make me less nervous. I chose a cream sweater and dark jeans, and I've put my hair up in my usual scruffy bun. It hasn't worked. I'm still nervous. But at least I don't feel as if I'm acting tonight.

The waitress comes up with what looks like two Cokes and puts them in front of Saxon and Catie. She hands me a menu and asks if she can get us a drink.

"Catie's pregnant," Saxon says, "and it only seems polite for me not to drink when I'm with her, but please, you two have whatever you like."

"Would you like a glass of wine?" Kip asks me.

"That would be nice," I reply, thinking: *oh my God yes please give me alcohol.*

"Red, white, sparkling? Champagne?"

"Um, red please."

"Any preference?"

"No, I'm happy for you to choose."

He looks at the menu. "We'll have a bottle of the Kusuda, please."

I blink. It's the most expensive red on the list and costs more than I'd expect to pay for a three-course meal. Is it what he'd normally order, or is he trying to impress me?

"Show off," Saxon says.

Catie giggles, and I try not to laugh.

"Maybe this wasn't such a good idea," Kip says.

"Oh, I'm having great fun," Saxon replies. Kip glares at him, and Saxon gives him a look that says, 'I'm going to make your life a misery, and there's nothing you can do about it.'

"Ignore them," Catie says to me with a smile. "It's very nice to meet you."

"Likewise." I gesture at her bump. "When are you due?"

"End of March." Her top bears the words 'Make it a Double.'

"Twins?" I guess.

"Yeah. Two boys. Just like these guys."

"My commiserations," I tell her, and she chuckles, while the two of them smile wryly.

"Do you live nearby?" Saxon asks, leaning back and putting his arm around his girlfriend.

"Ah, yeah," I say. "Not far away." I haven't discussed that with Kip, and at the moment I don't intend to reveal that I'm only visiting Wellington.

"What do you do for a living?" Saxon continues, giving his brother a mischievous glance.

"I review books," I tell him.

"Nice," he says. "Kip likes to read. Mainly comics."

"Saxon," Catie scolds. "Stop it."

I laugh, recognizing that for some reason he's teasing his brother. "We've been talking a lot about books today, haven't we?" I smile at Kip.

"Yeah," he says. "I ordered that one you recommended... by William Gibson?"

"*Neuromancer?*"

"Yes. I liked the premise, and the reviews are great."

"Apparently Gibson was a third of the way through when *Blade Runner* came out, and he was convinced that everyone would assume he'd copied the film's look, so he rewrote that third a dozen times."

"That's interesting," he says. "It's a great movie."

"Yeah, it's one of my favorites. I love the music, too. I can't remember the musician..."

"Vangelis," he says. "He's Greek, although he recorded it in London, I think."

"Oh, that's right. I thought Sean Young was so striking as the replicant, Rachael." I continue talking about the movie, but I'm conscious of Saxon's expression softening as he observes his brother.

"*Blade Runner* is an adaptation of a Philip K. Dick novel, isn't it?" Saxon asks.

"Yes," I say, "*Do Androids Dream of Electric Sheep?*"

"That's right," Saxon says, adding to Kip, "we both read it when we were in our teens, didn't we?"

Kip nods, looking relieved that his brother has taken pity on him at last. "We went through a phase of reading some of the classics, although we missed *Neuromancer.*"

"I'm a little embarrassed to say I haven't read much at all," Catie says, and blushes. Saxon glances at her and rubs her back, which strikes me as sweet.

"We all lead such busy lives, and it can be hard to squeeze in time for reading," I say, wanting to put her at ease. "*Harry Potter and the Philosopher's Stone* had just come out when I was born, and Mum read it aloud to me while she was breastfeeding. She said it was the only time she had in the day where she was forced to sit still, so she made the most of it."

"That's a lovely idea," Catie says. "I'd thought about getting a rocking chair for the nursery. I could sit there while I'm feeding and read."

Saxon pulls her toward him and kisses her cheek, and she kisses him back. I glance at Kip. He's watching me, and my pulse speeds up again. He looks so gorgeous in the white dress shirt. He's not wearing a tie so it's open at the neck, revealing the hollow at the base of his throat, beneath his Adam's apple. His skin there is tanned, and I can see a touch of chest hair. Ooh.

His lips curve up a little. Embarrassed to be caught staring at him, I drop my gaze to where his arm is resting on the table, but that doesn't help. His arms are also tanned and scattered with light-brown hairs, and his hands are large with long fingers and nice manicured nails. How can I get turned on by his hand? Oh dear, I'm in big trouble.

Both guys are wearing Apple watches, and it occurs to me then that even though they're not in suits, they both look wealthy. It's obvious in their sharp haircuts, the cut of their clothes, their expensive cologne, and the way they carry themselves. Their self-confidence suggests they don't give a fuck what anyone thinks of them.

"We'd better decide what to order," Saxon says. "I was wondering whether a couple of platters would be a good idea?"

"Sounds great," I say, and so when the waitress comes up, the guys order the platters, which come with ribs, corn on the cob, onion rings, and fries that I call "curly pommes de terre," which earns me a puzzled smile from Kip. We chat while we wait for the food to appear, then exclaim when the platters arrive at the table piled high, with several dishes of barbecue sauce for dipping.

"I love ribs," I state. "I have a curious appetite." Kip glances at me, and I smirk at my private joke. "They're not exactly the perfect food for a date," I scold him.

"At least you don't have facial hair to deal with," he says, taking a bite and then wiping sauce off his mustache.

"No, I waxed my top lip this morning," I reply, and they all laugh.

We're gradually relaxing now, and I'm actually enjoying myself. The two guys have a great sense of humor and bounce off each other, and Catie, although quiet and, I think, a little nervous herself, teases Saxon in a way I think is adorable.

Kip and I join in with the conversation, but I feel as if our bodies are having a private conversation of their own. I'm acutely conscious of him sitting so close to me, our knees bumping occasionally under the table.

My gaze is constantly drawn to him as I familiarize myself with the way he moves and his gestures and expressions, and I see him looking at me the same way from time to time, too. When he licks his fingers after eating the ribs, I can't help but watch, my pulse speeding up as I wonder what's going to happen after the meal. He glances at me then, and something in his eyes tells me he's thinking the same thing.

His gaze drops to my mouth, and he grins. "Look away," I scold, wiping my lips free of the sauce I know must be at the corners.

"I meant to ask, what's your favorite type of sci-fi?" Saxon says.

I've had a couple of glasses of wine by this point, and although I'm still nervous, I'm a lot less anxious than I was. Unfortunately, alcohol encourages my naughty streak.

"Oh, I definitely like it hard," I announce.

Saxon's eyebrows rise, Catie's eyes widen, and Kip coughs into his wine. I giggle.

Kip wipes his mouth and gives the other two an amused look. "When we were messaging yesterday, I asked Alice if she liked it hard. I was referring to sci-fi. It was a genuine mistake."

They both burst out laughing.

"Yeah, yeah," I tease. "I'm still not sure I believe you."

"Jesus," he says, "have pity on me. It took me about half an hour to stop cursing myself after that."

I wink at him. "You poor old thing."

"You think that's bad," Catie says, "last weekend, Saxon and I were at his parents' house, and his Mum asked him what he was going to give me for Christmas, and he said a pearl necklace. I nearly spat my dinner across the table."

"I did say that," Saxon admits.

"Guys," Kip says with exasperation, "I'm on a first date. You can't just bring up things like that."

"Alice started it," Saxon points out.

"I'm a bit embarrassed to say I don't get the joke," I confess.

Saxon looks at his brother with amusement. "Be a nice guy and explain it for her."

"Jesus." Kip brushes a hand over his face.

Catie giggles and leans forward to speak to me conspiratorially. "It's when a guy... you know..." She makes a gesture as if she's throwing confetti over herself. I frown and shake my head. She leans closer so her mouth is near my ear. "When he comes across your throat," she whispers.

"Oh, shit." I laugh.

"I'm so sorry," Kip says.

"No, it's great," I reply. "I'm learning a lot."

Saxon grins. "Do you two want a dessert?"

I blow out a breath. "No thanks, I'm stuffed."

Catie giggles, and Kip throws her an amused glare. "Will you stop?" That makes me giggle too, and the guys both laugh.

"Shall we?" Saxon says, and we all get to our feet and start heading out.

"So," Catie says to me as we turn toward the door, "Will you send me some recommendations for books?"

"Of course. I'll have a good think." I follow her out, then stop as I realize the two guys have gone over to the till.

"I didn't offer to go halves," I say. "Shit. Do you think he'll mind?"

Catie laughs. "I very much doubt it." Her eyes dance, although she doesn't elaborate.

"Okay." I blow out a breath, looking through the window at him. He's talking to Saxon, and as I watch, he nods, glances at me, then looks back at Saxon and smiles. They're talking about me. Maybe discussing what's going to happen next. Oh jeez. Now my nerves have returned a hundredfold.

# Chapter Five

## *Kip*

"You really like her, don't you?" Saxon says as we stand at the till.

I touch my card to the reader. "Yeah."

"She's got that classy, cheeky thing going on. I knew you'd be head over heels as soon as I saw her."

I give him a wry look and pocket the card. "I'm not head over heels. We've only just met." I look outside, where the two girls are waiting. "But yeah. She's gorgeous. And funny." My gaze lingers on her as she glances at me. Then I smile at Saxon. "Thanks for coming tonight."

"You're welcome, and it was fun. We haven't done this much, have we? Double dated, I mean."

"One of us was always in between relationships."

"Yeah, I guess."

We turn from the till and walk slowly toward the exit. "Did you have any luck with Craig?" he asks.

This morning, we had a couple of reporters call to ask for details on the sale of MOTHER to Sunrise. Saxon burst into my office to ask what was going on, and so I had to tell him the stunt that Craig pulled yesterday. Craig called his PA to say he was staying home sick today, and we haven't been able to get hold of him. I'm kinda glad. I think Saxon would have ripped his head from his shoulders.

I shake my head. "His phone's still going to voicemail."

"Shit."

"I'll go to his house tomorrow."

Saxon nods. "So… where are you going now?"

"Thought I'd take her for a drink."

"To talk about sci-fi? See if she likes it hard?"

"Ah, Jesus, don't. I felt so bad when I sent that."

He slaps me on the back. "Happens to the best of us, and at least she found it funny. She's lovely, bro. Hope it works out for you. Happy birthday."

"Happy birthday. Can't believe we're twenty-nine."

"I know," he says. "Have you got any gray hairs?"

"Not on my head."

That makes him laugh, and we're both grinning when we finally open the door and go outside.

Saxon and Catie say goodbye and head off to his Aston. I see Alice's gaze linger on it before we turn and walk slowly down the street.

"I'm so sorry," she says, "I forgot to offer to pay my half of the bill. I really didn't mean to assume. Catie was talking to me, and I got distracted."

It's a sweet thing of her to say when she must have guessed that the two of us have money. "Not a problem at all. I'm old fashioned enough to want to pay on a first date." I smile at her. Saxon's right—I do find her classy look with her cream sweater, gray coat, and hair in a bun attractive. The mischief in her eyes is a bonus. A good sense of humor is always sexy, and promises fun in the bedroom. But I don't want to assume anything. I like this girl, and it's more important to me to secure a second date than it is to get her into bed tonight.

"Would you like to go for a drink?" I ask.

"That would be nice."

"Anywhere in particular? Murphy's Law isn't bad."

"No," she says hurriedly. Then she clears her throat. "Um... I mean... I'd rather not go there."

"Okay." I wonder if that's where she met the guy yesterday. "Let's try The Pour House."

We walk across Courtenay Place to the bar, but it's heaving with people, and not the kind of place where you can sit and have a conversation. I suggest York Tavern on Cuba Street, and we wander up there, but that's packed too.

"Christmas parties, I guess," I say, listening to the raucous crowd inside.

Alice glances up the street. "The bar in the hotel where I'm staying is really nice, and it's quiet."

"Which hotel?"

"The Elite."

I've never stayed there, but I know that despite its name, it's a three-star, cheap and cheerful. Still, our options are limited, so I say, "Sure."

We head along Cuba Mall, past the iconic kinetic sculpture called the Bucket Fountain that's happily splashing the tourists taking photos, toward the hotel at the end of the street.

"You don't live in the city, then?" I ask her as we walk.

She shakes her head. I wait for her to elaborate, but she doesn't. I guess she lives in one of the suburbs, although wouldn't she have caught an Uber home if that was the case?

She hasn't told me a lot about herself so far. I know she has a sister at university here, and that she likes fantasy and science fiction. She knows a bit about music and guitars. But that's about it. Still, I haven't volunteered much information either. But that's why we're going for a drink, right? To chat and find out more about each other.

We arrive at the hotel and go into the lobby. It's large and busy, but as we cross and walk through to the bar, we find it quiet, with only one other couple sitting at a table and a single businessman at the bar, drinking a beer while he studies his phone. Tinsel on the Christmas tree in the corner sparkles as the fairy lights flicker, and Dean Martin croons to *Silver Bells* in the background.

"What can I get you?" I ask her.

"Red wine, please," she says.

I ask the bartender to recommend a decent Merlot and order two glasses, and we take them to a table in the corner. Alice takes off her coat, then slides onto the cushioned bench seat, while I take the chair opposite her.

The lights are low, and a candle flame dances in a jar on the table. It's warmish in here, and Alice's pale skin bears a slight flush.

She puts her purse on the edge of the table. From the zip hangs a keyring with a few charms—a red heart, an open book, and a pink bird. I pick it up and turn it in my fingers with a smile.

"I like flamingos," she says. After delving her hand into her coat pocket, she brings out a tiny box and places it on the table. "Got you a birthday present."

My eyebrows rise. "Seriously?"

"It's only something small. It doesn't mean we're engaged or anything."

I point at her. "That's from *Aliens*."

She laughs and pushes the box over to me. "I love that you know that. Go on, open it."

I take the box. The lid closes like a flower, and I unfurl the petals. It contains a single chocolate truffle. I smile and take it out.

"Happy birthday," she says.

"Thank you." I bite it, dividing it in two, and offer her the other half.

She looks at it for a moment. "I bought it for you."

"And I'm choosing to share it." I gesture for her to take it, and she does, popping it in her mouth.

"Off down the rabbit hole," she says.

I don't quite get the reference, but I smile anyway, because she's quirky, and I like that. She also has an amazing voice. When we first met, I was sure I recognized it, but I can't think where from.

We eat the truffle, which is rich and dark, then have a sip of wine.

"Thank you," I say, genuinely touched that she bothered.

She wrinkles her nose. "Least I could do after you paid for dinner."

"Like I said, I'm old fashioned."

She smiles. "So come on then, tell me. *Alien* or *Aliens?*"

"Oh, good question. They're both superb. Different kinds of movies, right?"

We talk for a while about movies and TV series, while Dean Martin works through his Christmas repertoire. A couple more people come into the bar, but they sit further down, and it remains quiet where we are.

When we finish our wine, I ask her whether she'd like something a bit stronger, and she asks for a G&T. I order a whisky, and we sip those while we talk more about the kind of TV we like to watch, the books we enjoy reading, and the music we listen to.

I'm feeling nicely mellow by now, relaxed and comfortable, enjoying the company of this beautiful, intelligent girl who seems into me. Eventually, though, there's a lapse in the conversation, and I take the opportunity to smile at her. To my surprise, she drops her gaze, and I'm sure I see her blow out a shaky breath.

"Don't be nervous," I say.

"What makes you think I'm nervous?"

"The fact that your knee is bouncing under the table."

She stills her leg and gives an embarrassed laugh. "Sorry."

"What are you nervous about?" I ask, amused.

"I dunno. You're…" Her gaze slides down me. "Nice," she finishes lamely, bringing her eyes back to mine.

I grin. "And that makes you nervous?"

"I don't do this much," she admits.

Her knee is bouncing again. I don't think she's aware she's doing it.

This girl fascinates me. She's twenty-five, so she's not that young, and she seems oddly naïve at times, although her eyes hold heat when she looks at me. I think she finds me attractive. But there's something I'm not getting… My spidey senses are tingling.

"So you don't live in the city?" I ask.

She shakes her head.

"You live in one of the suburbs?"

She turns her glass in her fingers. "Not quite."

"You live further away? That's why you're in a hotel?"

"Mmm." A non-committal grunt.

We've mostly talked about non-personal things. Wanting to know more about her, I ask, "So you review books? Is that your main job?"

She hesitates, then nods, but doesn't elaborate. Can you make a living from reviewing books? I'm sure there's something she's not telling me. I frown, disappointed at her reticence.

She has a big swallow of her G&T, then leans on the table. I take off my glasses and slide them into my top pocket. Then I lean on the table too. She looks into my eyes for a long moment. Hers are dark-blue and beautiful, and the longing in them warms me all the way through.

"You don't have to talk to me," I say. "Or tell me anything personal. That's your prerogative. But I don't think what I'm feeling is all one way."

"No," she whispers, "it's definitely not."

I study her face, puzzled, trying to work out what she's thinking. I really like this girl, but I can sense that she's nervous and worried about something. I'd hoped that meeting Saxon and Catie would convince her I can be trusted, but maybe she's still concerned about being alone with an almost-stranger.

"The 27% rogue comment was just a joke," I tell her. "You can trust me."

Her face flushes, and she closes her eyes for a moment. "Dammit," she says, and huffs a big sigh.

I frown and watch as she opens her eyes. "Come on," I scold gently, "we're friends, aren't we? Tell me what you're thinking."

"I'm thinking you're a really nice guy, and I should have been more honest in my bio."

Oh… It dawns on me then. Girls often put 'No ONS or FWB' to make it clear they're not interested in hooking up, and her profile hadn't contained anything like that. She thinks I'm only after sex.

"Ah, honey," I say, my heart going out to her, "I'm so sorry, I should have made it clear much earlier. I'm not expecting anything tonight. I want to see you again. I'd love to get to know you better."

"Oh God." She covers her face with her hands.

I frown. "Is this about what happened yesterday? Did the guy try to force himself on you? Sweetheart, you don't have to do anything you don't want to do. You were right to put him in his place if that was the case."

"Please stop," she says.

I blink, bewildered.

"Shit," she says, her voice muffled against her fingers. "Shit, shit, shit."

"What's the matter?"

"I've fucked up big time," she says.

Now I'm baffled. "Come on, you haven't fucked up."

"You've got it the wrong way around," she whispers.

"The wrong way around?" I frown, trying to work out what she means. I told her I wanted to get to know her better. I tried to explain that I wasn't only after sex…

My eyebrows rise as it sinks in. "You mean… you're only looking for a one-night stand?"

She nods behind her hands.

Whoa. My head spins. I didn't expect that. Not because I haven't met girls who are only interested in sex, but because she hadn't struck me as being one of them.

She only wants to sleep with me? I feel a strange mixture of pleasure and disappointment. I want her; of course I want her—she's gorgeous. But I was hoping for more than that.

"Why are you embarrassed?" I ask. "There's nothing wrong with that. People have one-night stands all the time."

"I wasn't going to say anything, but you're such a nice guy, and I can't lie to you."

"Alice, I'm confused. Why weren't you going to say anything? And what do you mean, 'I can't lie to you'?"

"I thought you might not notice, but it's not fair not to say anything…"

I might not notice? I take her hands and pull them away from her face. "Alice…"

She drops her hands and huffs an exasperated sigh. "I'm a virgin."

\*

## *Alice*

Kip stares at me. "What?"

"I haven't had sex," I say grouchily. "Ever."

"What? You're gorgeous. How on earth have you got to twenty-five without sleeping with anyone?"

I give another long sigh, flattered by his compliment but too annoyed with myself to react to it. "I have family commitments that mean I don't have much free time. And now I'm twenty-five and inexperienced, and I mean *completely*. I haven't even kissed a guy since I was sixteen."

"Jesus." He's looking at me as if I've told him I'm a mermaid, with a kind of wondrous disbelief.

Then he tips his head to the side, his brows drawing together. "I still don't quite understand. It's nothing to be ashamed of. It's something to be celebrated, surely? When you meet the right guy, you can get to know one another slowly. Any man worth his salt will be patient and gentle your first time."

I scowl. "I'm not in a Jane Austen novel. I'm not able to date right now, and I don't want to wait for Mr. Right. I hate my virginity. It's like a millstone around my neck. I'm sick of listening to jokes about sex and reading about it and watching people having it in the movies, and not being in the secret club. And the more that time goes by, the more anxious I'm getting. I know it's no big thing. It's just sex. Tab A into slot B, right? Or C or D, as my sister kindly pointed out."

He gives a short laugh. "Technically, yeah."

"In that sense, who does it is irrelevant, right?"

He gives me a pained look. "Alice…"

"I just want to get it over with. So I thought I'd try to find someone on Tinder. And I met this guy yesterday for a drink, and we didn't have much of a connection, but I thought well, it doesn't matter, does it? I just need his... equipment."

He closes his eyes and strokes his thumb and forefinger over his eyebrows. "Alice..."

"So I suggested going back to his place, but on the way he kissed me, and he shoved his tongue in my mouth, and..." My voice trails off at the look on his face as he lowers his hand. "Let's just say I ended it there," I finish.

"Jesus."

"And then I met you, and we've gotten on so well, and the opposite has happened. You want to see me again, and I can't do that. And I like you so much... But I can't just take you back to my room and have sex with you without telling you. It's not fair on you. You're going to expect a girl to do all kinds of stuff, and I'm so clueless. I'm going to be terrible. And now that's it. I've ruined it. God I'm such an idiot." I put my face in my hands again.

He's silent for about thirty seconds. Finally, his chair scrapes, and he gets to his feet. I lower my hands and watch as he tucks his chair under the table. My heart sinks. He's going to leave. Nice one, Alice. Way to screw up a wonderful evening.

But he doesn't leave. He walks around the table, picks up my coat and hangs it over the back of his chair, then slides onto the bench seat beside me. Turning a little, he leans on the back and props his head on a hand. I'm now nestled against him, almost under his arm. I tingle all over at the sensation of being so close to him. Oh my God, he smells amazing. His neck and jaw are so close I could lean over and kiss them.

I look up into his warm brown eyes.

"Hello, crazy girl," he says, and smiles.

I know my face must still be scarlet because it's burning.

"Let's go back to the beginning," he says. "So you're a virgin. So what? It's no big thing. It's just a state of being. It's like saying you haven't bungee jumped or driven a car."

"It's a little bit more complicated than that."

"Not really. We've all got things we haven't done."

"Yeah, but when you get in a car with a twenty-five-year-old, you normally expect them to know where the handbrake is."

That makes him laugh. "I do get it," he says.

I feel a surge of frustration at his understanding, so immense it's as if I've swallowed a rock that's lodged in my throat. "If I'd not told you I was a virgin, and you'd realized it while we were having sex, would you have been angry?"

"Angry? Of course not. Sad that you couldn't have confided in me, and worried that I'd hurt you, maybe. But not angry."

"Aaahhh… dammit. I shouldn't have said anything. It feels like a chicken and egg situation, you know? I can't go with a guy because he's going to expect me to do stuff, and I can't learn stuff until I go with a guy."

"Well, I'm sure most men prefer to take charge anyway, and they probably wouldn't even notice you were inexperienced. Technically, you're right, if all you want is to get it done, any guy will do. Tab A into Slot B, as you so colorfully put it—it's pretty simple, on the surface. But that's taking a very basic, pessimistic view of sex."

"What do you mean?"

"It's not just about what goes where." He studies me for a moment, and then his lips curve up. "Don't sulk."

"I'm cross that you're having to educate me. I hate being naïve."

"Yeah, I understand. Bear with me. I'm trying to say that it would be a crying shame for your first time to be with a random dude from Tinder that you had no connection with. I'm so glad you didn't sleep with that guy yesterday."

"So am I."

He laughs. "Not everyone wants to go steady, and you shouldn't be ashamed about wanting a one-night stand. We live in a free country and in modern times. Providing everyone consents and uses protection, what the hell does it matter who does what with whom? Nobody cares. But it's not just about scratching an itch. It's about sharing yourself with someone you find attractive. Exploring each other, and giving each other pleasure."

My face warms. "You're obviously an expert," I say, a little tartly.

He shrugs. "I like sex. I'm not ashamed of that. And I'm sure you will too, once you've tried it."

My face heats, and his lips curve up.

"Look," he says softly, "you can go on Tinder, and any man you swipe right on is going to be as eager as hell to take you to bed, whether they know you're a virgin or not. But I'm the lucky guy you chose. And you're attracted to me, right?"

"Yeah…"

"And I'm attracted to you." He sighs. "I would've liked to have seen you again. But if you're only offering one night… Why don't you spend it with me?"

My eyes widen and I stare at him for about thirty seconds. He waits patiently, looking into my eyes, trying not to laugh.

"Are you serious?" I ask.

"Yeah."

"You want to go to bed with me?"

He rolls his eyes. "Of course I want to go to bed with you. You're gorgeous."

I'm genuinely surprised. "Even though I've admitted I've not done it before?"

His gaze drops to my mouth. "Despite the fact that this isn't a Jane Austen novel, some would say that's an attraction."

"What? Seriously?"

His lips curve up. "Guys like writing their name in the snow."

"Oh my God."

"You can't see why it's a turn on to be someone's first?"

"No." I can't believe this is happening. "Have you done it before?"

"Slept with a virgin? No. I'm intrigued."

"So your first time wasn't with another virgin?"

"No. She was four years older than me."

"Four years!"

"She was nineteen."

"You were only fifteen!"

He laughs. "Yeah. She thought I was eighteen."

"Jesus. Technically that makes her a pedophile."

He just chuckles. "Guys don't care about that when they're desperate to get laid."

"So you were desperate at fifteen? You understand, then, why I'm going crazy at twenty-five?"

"Oh, I get it, absolutely. Of course you want to have sex. And I understand that there are obviously complications in your life that make dating impossible. I get why you decided to go on Tinder. And like I said, when we went out tonight, my plan was to hopefully get a second date, because I really like you. But if I can't… I'll happily take you to bed."

My gaze falls to his mouth. "And show me what's what?"

"And show you what's what."

"If I ever do date someone for real, I don't want to look like a fool."

"So you're saying you want me to show you everything I know, to prepare you for meeting another man?"

"Ah…"

He rolls his eyes again. "Whatever. Can I kiss you?"

This is the litmus test. I think about Tim last night, and how kissing him couldn't have felt less sexy.

I glance around the room, concerned that someone's watching. But the lights are low, it's quiet, the bartender's busy at the other end of the bar, and the other people here are all concentrating on themselves.

"Don't look at them," he says. "Look at me."

I bring my gaze back to his. He's thinking about kissing me. About what I look like naked. About having sex with me.

I hold my breath as he tucks a strand of my hair behind my ear. Then he cups the side of my head, his thumb stroking my cheek. Behind him, the fairy lights on the tree flicker and change from red, to blue, to gold.

Finally, he lowers his lips to mine. They're warm and dry. His mustache brushes my Cupid's bow as he kisses me slowly, pressing his lips across mine. Small, light kisses like Christmas wishes. I close my eyes, concentrating on his mouth. Thinking about the fact that this gorgeous guy is kissing me. And that he wants to take me to bed.

He lifts his head, and I open my eyes to see him giving me an amused look. "Don't forget to breathe," he says.

I let out my breath in a rush. "You didn't use your tongue."

"I didn't want to send you running for the hills."

"But you do normally?"

His brows draw together. "That phrase makes me uncomfortable. I'm not Casanova. I don't 'normally' do anything. I've not done this before."

"Done what?"

"Tried to seduce a girl who's like a rabbit in the headlights."

"I'm sorry."

"Okay, rule number one, let's concentrate on me and you. Forget about everyone else. And rule number two, no apologizing. You're nervous. That's okay. We'll take it slow. Take our time." His eyes have acquired that lazy, sleepy look again.

"You're thinking about me naked, aren't you?" I ask.

"Well, yeah. That's sort of part of the process."

"I don't know if I can do this."

He tries not to laugh, and fails. "You want another G&T?"

"No."

"You want me to go?"

"Oh my God, no, absolutely not. Can I think about you naked?"

"Oh yes. You can undress me with your eyes, if you like." He smiles.

"My heart's racing," I admit.

"It's supposed to."

"Is yours?"

"Of course." He takes my hand and presses it to his chest. Sure enough, I can feel his heartbeat, maybe not as fast as mine, but still faster than it should be considering we're sitting down.

"You're sure about this?" I say hesitantly. "I'm not joking, I really am clueless. I mean, obviously, I've seen actors do it, and watched a bit of porn, but it's hard to know how real it is." I glare at him. "Don't laugh."

"Sorry. You're a very unusual girl."

"Why?"

He shakes his head. "Look, I'm not an expert."

"Oh, I'm pretty sure that's a lie."

"I'm really not. But I promise I'll do my best to educate you."

I narrow my eyes. "You're making fun of me."

"A little. Do you want me to ask reception if they have a whiteboard?"

"Kip…"

"Actually, I am serious. I really like you. I'll be gentle. I'll make sure you know exactly what to do by the end of the night. And I'll make you come at least twice. How does that sound?"

I flush scarlet. "Holy shit."

He smirks. "Come on. Let's go down the rabbit hole together, and see if we end up in Wonderland."

# Chapter Six

## *Kip*

Her eyes widen. "How did you know?"

"How did I know what?"

She stares at me for a second, then says, "Oh, nothing."

I have to stop torturing the poor girl. Her eyes are like saucers. But I'm having a lot of fun, and it's impossible not to tease her.

"You're enjoying my misery far too much," she says.

"Tell me you're not having a good time."

Her lips curve up then. "Maybe. I'm so glad you don't mind me asking questions."

"Ask away. Can't promise I'll know the answer, but I'll try."

"Did you mean what you said about showing me everything?"

"Well, let's start with the basics and see how we go."

"What do you mean by the basics?"

"Tab A into slot B."

"Oh, okay. I get it." She sucks her bottom lip. "Can I ask a question now?"

"Honey, you don't have to ask if you can ask a question every time you want to ask a question."

"Right, got it. What does slot C refer to?"

"Probably oral?"

"And D?"

"Anal, I'm guessing."

"Oh, right. Both of which you've done, of course."

"Do you remember rule number one?"

"Concentrate on me and you, and forget about everyone else."

"Right."

She studies my mouth, then lifts her gaze to mine. "I like that you're open about stuff. It's refreshing, and it's such a relief. I thought I'd just have to shut up and let the guy get on with it. I like being able to talk about it."

"I'm glad. Now, rule number three…"

"You have a lot of rules."

"I do."

"You're very bossy."

"You have no idea. Yet." I watch her eyes widen. "So, as I was saying, rule number three, I like being open too, so I'm going to say right now that I won't be asking you every five seconds for your permission to do something, because that's not romantic or sexy. But if at any point you want me to stop, you just say, and I'll stop. Okay?"

She nods, wide-eyed.

"It's not a problem," I tell her. "I won't get angry or annoyed."

"Okay. Can I ask another…" She stops herself. "I've got a query."

"That's just another word for a question."

"Yeah, I know. Um… you mentioned two orgasms."

"I should have said a minimum of two."

"Oh. Um… look, I know you're going to quote rule number one at me again, but how do you know?"

"How do I know what?"

"That I'll have two?"

"I have a sixth sense. I can predict the future."

"Kip…"

"I don't quite understand the query."

She purses her lips. "Well, it's not up to you, is it? Aren't my orgasms down to me?"

My lips curve up. "I can safely say you're the first girl who's ever assumed that."

"You've lost me."

"Do I have to talk about tabs and slots again?"

"Possibly."

I grin. This is such fun that I'm almost tempted to stay here all evening and just talk to her about it. Almost.

"Well, most women assume the guy is the one responsible for her pleasure."

"Weird," she says. "Why's it his responsibility?"

"Wow. I think I love you."

She laughs. "I don't understand. Guys don't assume their pleasure is the girl's responsibility?"

"No."

"So why the other way around?"

"I don't know," I admit with some surprise.

"And surely no two women are the same? How can you assume that what turns one girl on is the same as the next?"

"I guess it's a ballpark thing. They have the same buttons, and if you press them in the same order, something good normally happens. More or less."

"More or less of what?"

"Jesus. It'll just be easier to show you. Basically you're right; you're not all the same. Some girls like different buttons being pressed."

"Are you talking about slot D again?"

We both start laughing.

"You're a lot of fun," I tell her, smiling. "And that's even before we've gotten to the bedroom."

"I thought that—" She stops as my phone, which is sitting on the table, vibrates.

I glance at it. It's a text from Lesley. The first line of it is visible. Just wondering if you've… I exhale, then look back at Alice.

"I don't mind if you want to read it," she says.

"No, it's okay. It's not important."

"You're sure?" she asks. "You frowned."

I look back at the phone. "It's someone I don't particularly want to hear from."

"A girl?"

I turn my glass around in my fingers.

"Your girlfriend?" Alice asks.

"I wouldn't be here with you if I had a girlfriend."

"All right. Don't glare at me. Not every guy is as honorable as that. So… not your girlfriend. But someone who was special to you?"

I sigh. "She's my ex."

"Okay. How long ago did you break up?"

"Oh, a couple of years ago." I stretch out my legs. Alice's face is kind, encouraging me to talk about it. "She got a job in Australia, without telling me. We ended up breaking up over it. Then a year later she came back to New Zealand. I thought it was for good, and we dated for a couple of months. Then out of the blue she said she was going back. I felt like such a fool. I thought she'd come back to be with me." I scowl at the memory. "She called last night to say she's here again."

"And she asked to see you?"

"Not at first. She told me she's getting married."

"Oh."

"Then she said she wanted to meet up."

Her eyebrows rise. "Meet up? Or hook up?"

"Not sure."

"Even though she's marrying another guy?"

"Yeah."

"What did you say?"

"I ended the call."

"It hurt your feelings to hear she's getting married again?"

I frown. "No. Not the way you mean it. It depressed me to hear from her, actually. I thought she was out of my life."

"Is that why you went on Tinder?"

"A bit, yeah."

"Are you broken-hearted?"

"No," I reply, realizing it's true. "I'm annoyed, if anything, that she thinks she can say jump and I'll jump, no questions asked." Yeah, it's anger and resentment I'm feeling right now. Not hurt.

Alice's dark-blue eyes study me. Then she gestures at the phone. "So what does she want now?"

I pick up the phone, open the message, and read it out. "Just wondering if you've changed your mind and you'd like to come over. I'm at the Five Palms." I put the phone down and look back at her.

"Nice hotel," she says.

"Yeah."

"You want to go over there?"

"No."

"I'd understand."

"The answer's still no."

"I bet she knows where the handbrake is."

I give a short laugh. Then I pick up my phone. "I'm not interested in any woman who'd cheat on her partner."

"So you're seriously telling me you'd rather stay here with a twenty-five-year-old virgin who can't even work out which slot is which?"

"I'd rather stay with the gorgeous blonde who makes me smile."

Her brows draw together. "She didn't make you smile?"

"Not nearly enough." I hold down the off button on my phone, then slide the power button to the right, and the phone goes dark. I put it down, feeling a swell of relief. She can't contact me now. It's surprisingly liberating.

I look back at Alice. She meets my eyes and gives a beautiful, shy smile. "Are you going to kiss me again?"

"Oh, I think so, don't you?"

"Will you use your tongue this time?"

I just adore this girl. "Do you want me to?"

She thinks about it. "Mmm."

I check the bar; nobody's watching.

"Come here." I slide my hand to the back of her neck and pull her toward me.

Dean Martin has given way to a general Christmas playlist, and now George Michael is singing *Last Christmas*, telling his partner that they still catch his eye. I brush my thumb across the soft skin of Alice's neck, think about kissing her, my senses leaping into life. I can smell the cinnamon and orange from the pot of potpourri next to the candle, and the deep scent of her perfume, something with jasmine. The bar suddenly seems rich with color—the dark burgundy of the carpet, the green foliage of the wreath pinned above the bartender, the scarlet of the poinsettia sitting on the corner of the bar, the golden wall lights, the blue of Alice's eyes. Man, she's beautiful. She makes my heart race.

I kiss her slowly, starting with soft butterfly kisses. She sits stiffly at first, and then gradually, like a chocolate button placed on a radiator, softens and melts against me. Encouraged, I open my mouth and touch my tongue to her bottom lip. She inhales and her lips part. I do it again, giving gentle, subtle touches of my tongue to her lips. Each one makes her inhale with a little gasp. And then eventually, she brushes her tongue against mine.

Heat rushes through me, but I hold back, letting her explore, as if I'm encouraging a deer to come toward me in the forest. She rests her hand on my chest, then slowly slides it up until her fingers find the hollow at the base of my throat. She strokes it with her thumb, then continues to move her hand to my neck and jaw, her fingers brushing my beard, while she grows bolder and thrusts a little with her tongue.

I give a half-sigh, half-growl deep in my throat and slide my tongue into her mouth, and she inhales again, sharply this time. For a moment I think I've gone too far and she's going to move back, but instead she gives a sexy little moan and tilts her head to the side to change the angle—subconsciously, I think—a move that tells me she wants more.

So I slide my arms around her, and she lifts hers around my neck, and we indulge in a long, deep, luscious kiss that sends my heart banging on my ribs and makes other parts of me stir like a bear coming out of hibernation.

When I finally lift my head, I'm breathless and hungry for more. Alice stares at me, the Christmas lights filling her eyes with flickering red and gold stars.

"Oh my God," she whispers, "yesterday I was close to never wanting to kiss anyone ever again. Why was that so amazing?"

"Skill." I mean it to sound sexy, but my voice cracks and comes out as a squeak, and we both laugh. I clear my throat. "Finish your drink, and I think maybe we should go to your room."

She nibbles her bottom lip. "It's the smallest room in Christendom. I'm not kidding. It's miniscule."

"Does it have a bed?"

"Well, yes…"

"Then it sounds perfect."

She gives an impish smile. "Is this really happening?"

"Looks like it."

"You really want to go to bed with me?"

"I really want to go to bed with you."

"Oh my God, I'm so happy right now."

"Maybe you should wait until afterward and see if you still feel the same way."

"Kip, I already know it's going to be amazing. How can it not be when we're already having fun?"

I feel suddenly humble, flattered and touched that this adorable, naïve, innocent girl has chosen me to share herself with for the first time. She has no idea what I'm like in bed, or whether I'll be able to give her pleasure. But because we've taken the time to talk, and we seem to have a connection, she's excited purely at the thought of being intimate with me.

When you're a teenager, even though you're excited about having sex, you don't analyze things much. By twenty-five, I'd been having sex for ten years, and quite a lot of it. I can't imagine having got to that age and not having done it. But I can see how, as the years go by, she must have thought about it a lot, and fantasized about how her first time would go. What should be a simple act has understandably become a big deal in her head, and I get why she's nervous, as well as intrigued and excited.

I finish off my whisky, and she has the last mouthful of her G&T, and then we get to our feet. I pocket my phone and slide on my glasses, she collects her coat, and we head out through the bar, across the lobby to the elevators.

We wait with two other couples for the doors to open, then go into the car. Alice presses the button for floor twelve, and then moves in the corner next to where I'm leaning on the wall while the other couples come in.

The doors close, and we all stand quietly as the car rises. I put my arm around her, and she turns and slides her arms around my waist. I kiss her forehead, and the woman standing opposite us smiles. I smile back, then look down at Alice. She must be around five-six or seven, and she's wearing Converses, so she's about six inches shorter than me, and she fits nicely under my arm. I didn't bring a jacket with me this evening, and she fiddles with one of the buttons on my shirt.

"This is nice," she murmurs, touching the silver-gray placket of the shirt.

"Thank you." I look down at her flushed cheeks, the fine curves of her eyebrows, her long dark lashes. I want to kiss her again, but even though I was happy to do so in the bar, it doesn't seem appropriate here.

Then the car stops at floor five, and both couples go out. The doors slide closed again, and the car begins to rise.

I turn Alice so her back is against the wall of the carriage, and move up close to her. She looks up at me with wide eyes. "Can't wait," I say, and, taking her face in my hands, I lower my lips to hers.

We indulge in seven floors' worth of kissing, and we're just getting into it when the elevator stops and the doors slide open.

"Dammit," she says, and I grin as she takes my hand and marches out. She leads me along the corridor, turns right, then strides up to door number twenty-eight. After scanning her key card, she opens the door and goes in, flicking on the light switch.

I follow her, stopping as the door closes behind me. "Wow. You weren't kidding."

The room is barely big enough to hold the Queen-size bed. Two tiny bedside tables sit either side of it, and there's a single chair by the door to the bathroom, with a narrow in-built wardrobe to its left. That's it. There's no room for anything else.

I could go down to reception and see if they have a larger room available. I can easily afford any room in this hotel, and often the penthouse suites and other, bigger rooms aren't booked out. If I was on my own, I'd definitely do that. But I don't want to embarrass Alice. And anyway, the only thing we need is a bed, and this one is more than adequate. The wall lights are subtle, and it's pleasantly warm. It almost feels as if we're in a tent. I don't get claustrophobic, and I'm more than happy at the thought of getting up close and personal with this gorgeous girl.

She hunches her shoulders. "I did say." She looks around. "Have you changed your mind?"

I laugh. "No." I take off my glasses and leave them on the chair, go up to her, take her face in my hands again, and kiss her fiercely.

"Mmm…" Wriggling out of her coat, she hangs it over the back of the chair, then lifts her arms around me. Still kissing her, I toe off my shoes, and she does the same. Then I bend and pick her up, wrapping her legs around me. "Ooh!" Her eyes widen.

I turn and pull back the duvet, then climb onto the mattress. Turning, I lie on my back on the pillows, letting her stretch out on top of me.

Propping herself up on her elbows, she looks into my eyes. "Do you want me to take my clothes off?"

"No. We're going to make out for a while."

"Kiss, you mean?"

"Kissing will be involved. As well as other fun activities."

"I like the sound of that."

I laugh and kiss her nose. Then her cheeks. Finally, I slide a hand to the back of her head and bring her lips to mine.

She sighs, and we exchange a few long, sedate kisses that nevertheless still send my heart racing. I rest my hands on her shoulder blades, then draw them down her back, following the curve of her waist, all the way down to the swell of her bottom. Clutching the soft muscles there, I squeeze, and she gives a long, throaty sigh, rocking her hips slowly against mine.

Then she lifts her head and looks at me. Her eyes sparkle in the low light. "You've got an erection," she points out.

"Yep."

"Wow." She tilts her hips, pressing against it. "That's amazing."

"That's all you."

"Mmm." Her gaze drops to my lips, and then she lowers her lips to mine again.

This time, she opens her mouth, and I feel the tip of her tongue brush against my bottom lip. Smiling, I stroke my tongue against hers, and she gives a sexy little moan and slides her tongue against mine.

I let her kiss me for a long time, allowing her to move at her own pace. She gradually grows bolder, grazing her teeth on my lip, delving her tongue into my mouth. It's hard to stay still, and my hands wander down her back, over her bottom, then back up again, getting used to her curves, without turning intimate. Eventually, though, I can't stop my fingers sneaking beneath the hem of her sweater, and although I only skirt them around the waistband of her jeans, the feel of her skin, and her answering shudder, prompts me to step things up a notch.

Holding her around the waist, I twist so she's on her back, then stretch out beside her. Leaning on an elbow, I look down at her and kiss her again. This time I'm able to go at my own pace, and, growing hungry for her, I crush my lips to hers, kissing her fiercely, until I'm breathless with need, and I know she's feeling the same because of the way she's moving against me.

When I eventually lift my head, she blinks a few times and says, "Oh jeez."

"Do you like making out?"

"Oh my God I love it."

I laugh. "Want to do it naked?"

"Oh!" Her eyes widen, and she slides a hand down to my shirt. "Can I undo your buttons?"

"Of course."

Propped on an elbow, I watch as she slowly pops the buttons through the holes, then pushes the sides of the shirt apart. "Ooh, Kip. You work out." She brushes her fingers down over my pecs and abs, her eyes alight with admiration.

It's difficult not to feel flattered. "When I can."

"Do you do a lot of sport?"

"I used to. A lot of rugby in my university days. Some cricket, tennis, and football. Golf occasionally."

"Croquet?"

I laugh. "No. I haven't done as much sport over the last couple of years because I've been so busy. I still swim most days though." I have my own pool, although I don't tell her that.

She traces across my abs. I haven't quite got a six pack, but I'm not in bad shape.

I shiver at her touch. "Tickles."

She gives a beautiful, shy smile. "Take your shirt off."

I sit up, tug it off, and toss it over the side of the bed. Next, I take out my wallet and leave it on the bedside table with my phone before undoing my trousers, sliding them down over my hips, and taking them off with my socks.

Alice's face lights up as I lie on my back and stretch out beside her, arms above my head so she can drink her fill. I'm now wearing only my black boxer-briefs.

Her gaze skims slowly down me. I feel it as if she's brushing a feather over my skin, starting at my biceps, moving over my shoulders and down my chest, across my abdomen, lingering for a long while on the erection that strains against the fabric of my underwear, then finally continuing down my legs before returning to my face, by way of the erection, again.

"Fuck," she says.

"Is that a good fuck?"

"It's an oh-my-fucking-god-look-at-you fuck. You're amazing. I want to get out a magnifying glass and examine every inch of you."

"I'm hoping you won't need it to look at the family jewels."

She giggles. "I didn't mean that. The jewels are very notable without the need for magnification." She looks at my crotch, then gives me an impish glance.

"Go on," I say. "Ask whatever question is burning inside you."

"I've read that the average size of a man's erection is just over five inches."

"Sounds about right."

"Jesus, I'm the luckiest girl alive."

"I'm not that big. It must look bigger because I'm wearing black."

"God, you're so modest. It looks enormous. Now I'm thinking about the tiger I saw at the zoo this morning. I'm not sure if I dare let it out of its cage."

"It's probably more like a meerkat, actually."

We both laugh. She reaches out a hand then and runs a finger just under the waistband of my underwear. "Will you take it off?"

"Absolutely. But first you need to lose some clothing. It's only fair that I get to look as well."

# Chapter Seven

## *Alice*

Oh no, he wants me to undress. Suddenly nervous, I notice that my hands are shaking as I lift them to unbutton my jeans.

He puts out a hand to stop me, though, and lifts up so he's straddling me, his knees either side of my legs. "That's my job."

"You'll never get these off. They're very tight."

"Maybe, but it'll be fun to try." He pops open the button, slides the zipper, and begins peeling them down over my hips.

I lie back on the pillows and watch him. "I can't believe this is actually happening," I whisper.

I'd seen the way his shirt sleeves stretched over his biceps, so I knew he was muscular, and I was pretty sure he was going to be gorgeous beneath his clothes, but the reality has surpassed my meager imagination. He's better looking than any guy I've seen in any of the porn I've watched, more like a male model, all taut and tanned. How on earth did I manage to land a guy like this for my adventure?

I reach out a finger and draw it over a tattoo he has on his upper right arm. It's an elaborate cross, with an infinity sign beneath it. "Are you religious?" I ask.

"No." He tugs my jeans over my feet and tosses them on the floor, then removes my socks.

"I feel as if I've won the lottery," I tell him, "and I only have you for one night. If I had a man like you forever, I'd never let you out of my bed."

He moves back up the bed to lean over me and looks as if he's about to say something, but thinks better of it. Instead, he looks down at my breasts, still covered by my cream sweater. He gives me a mischievous look. Then he takes the bottom of the sweater in his hands. "Arms up." I raise them above my head, and he lifts the hem of the sweater up over my head and halfway up my arms.

Then he stops. The main part of the sweater is still covering my head, so I can't see him. I feel his fingers push the sweater up just enough to reveal my lips. Then he lowers on top of me, lying between my legs, and kisses me hungrily, plunging his tongue into my mouth.

"Mmph…" I draw my knees up, shuddering at the feel of his erection pressing against my mound, but unable to move because of his weight on top of me, and the fact that my arms are imprisoned in the sweater.

Ooh, he's deliciously heavy, and he smells amazing, of some kind of sexy cologne that makes my pheromones all perky and attentive. He rocks his hips, grinding the root of his erection, right against my clit, sending shocks as fast as a Japanese bullet train to my nipples and mouth, and making me clench deep inside.

His kisses are amazing, causing sparks to fly through my body, and I'd have been happy for him to go on forever. But eventually he lifts his head, and then I feel him press his lips down my neck.

I raise my arms, intending to remove the sweater, but he lifts a hand to press them back. "Lie still," he instructs.

My pulse is racing now. I do as he says and try not to squirm as he kisses down my neck. I'm wearing a lacy cream push-up bra, not because I need it as I'm a C cup, but because I like the cleavage it gives me. He pauses for a moment, and I think he's admiring my breasts. Oh jeez.

He shifts on the bed, and I feel his lips brush the curve of my left breast above the cup. He kisses across it, then dips his tongue into my cleavage before continuing across to the right breast.

I'm breathing fast now, my chest rising and falling. Part of me expects him to stop and tell me to calm down, but he doesn't. Instead, I feel him take the lace of the left cup, pull it down, and tuck it under my breast. His hot breath whispers across the sensitive skin of my nipple before he covers it with his mouth and sucks.

Holy shit… oh my God… I groan and arch my back as he does the same to the other breast, tucking the bra cup beneath it, then sucking on the nipple, gently at first, then more firmly. He does it a few times, then blows across them, and they tighten until it's almost painful.

Sliding a hand under my back, he finds the catch of my bra and squeezes the two sides together. Amazingly, it comes undone, and he pushes the entire garment up, then cups a breast in his hand and sucks the nipple again. He continues doing that for a while, going from one breast to the other, until I'm filled with a desperate ache, and throbbing between my legs.

He lifts his head, moves up and lies on me again, and kisses me. "Stop wriggling," he scolds.

"I can't help it." I tilt my hips up and groan as he matches the movement, stroking against me right *there*. "You're making me ache."

"Aw. Poor Alice." He nips my bottom lip with his teeth.

"You didn't tell me you were a sadist."

"Torturing you is fun, it's true."

"Kip..."

"Relax. I'm going to make you come with my mouth now."

"I thought the first time you'd... wait, what?"

"Just relax."

"After a revelation like that? God, you're so confident. I don't know whether that's sexy or arrogant."

"Let me put it like this. Do your best not to come." He removes the sweater, and I look up into his eyes, which are full of amusement.

"Challenge accepted," I tell him, and he grins.

He draws the straps of my bra down my arms and drops it over the side of the bed. Then he pauses. "Can you take your hair down?"

For some reason, despite everything he's doing, that's such a sexy thing to say that I feel my face flush. I lift my hands to the bun, pull out the couple of Bobby Pins holding the stray hairs, remove the elastics, and let my hair unfurl.

He slides his fingers into it. "It's so silky." He blows out a breath. "Fuck, that makes me so hard." Muttering something else, he moves down the bed until he's kneeling between my thighs.

He tucks his fingers in the elastic of my underwear, moves it down, and lifts my legs so he can remove it. Pushing my knees apart, he lowers onto the mattress. He glances up at me. "Remember, try not to come." Then he dips his head and brushes his tongue right the way up through my folds.

"Ohhh..." Immediately I know I'm in trouble. His mouth is warm, and he knows exactly what he's doing. He starts by teasing my clit with the tip of his tongue, alternating that with long licks up my core. Although he doesn't slide his fingers inside me, they do join in with the fun, stroking and sliding through my sensitive folds.

I start counting in my head, trying to distract myself, but all that means is that I'm aware it takes this gorgeous guy less than one minute to make me come.

He obviously feels the approach of my orgasm because he covers my clit with his mouth and sucks. I curl my toes and arch my back as the pulses hit, and cry out, gasping with each magnificent clench of my muscles, until I finally fall back with a groan.

Lifting his head, he blows lightly on my tender flesh. Then he lowers his head again and flicks his tongue, laughing as my body jerks.

Placing kisses as he goes, he moves up the bed to lie beside me, propping his head on a hand. "This is called the refractory period," he says. "The recovery phase between orgasms. It's shorter for women than for men."

I look into his eyes, still reeling from the pleasure he gave me so casually. "How long?"

"Usually minutes or even seconds for women."

"And for you?"

He shrugs. "Fifteen, twenty minutes? Maybe more now. I'm getting old." He smiles and trails a finger down between my breasts before teasing a nipple with a finger. "Don't want you to cool all the way down," he states with a smirk.

I study his face, filled with wonder. He's so handsome and charismatic. I can't believe his ex let him go. What a stupid, stupid woman.

"Penny for them," he says, sliding his hand down between my legs.

I push it away. "You promised you'd remove your underwear."

"I did." He rolls onto his back, lifts the elastic over his erection, and slides them off. Then he rolls back to face me and props his head on a hand.

He's naked. O. M. F. G.

Occasionally I've ventured onto a porn site because I've been so curious about sex, so I know what guys look like, and how sex works. But it's the first time I've seen a man naked in real life.

"Do you mind me looking?" I ask shyly.

"As long as you don't laugh."

I give him a wry look. Laughter is the furthest thing from my mind right now. "Can I touch you?"

"Help yourself." He shifts onto his back and tucks his arms under his head.

I feast my eyes on his magnificent body. He has an attractive scatter of hair across his chest. On his taut abdomen, it narrows to a thin trail that deliberately leads my gaze to the thicker patch on his groin, from which emerges his impressive erection.

I stare at it, then lower my hand and run a finger up from the base to the tip. His eyelids lower slowly, then lift again.

"You're not circumcised," I observe.

"No. Any porn you've watched is probably made in the States. Eighty percent of men are circumcised there. Only twenty percent here."

"I didn't know that." I'm not sure how to touch him. "Show me how it works."

He lowers a hand and strokes himself a few times, showing me how the foreskin slides back to reveal the head, then forward again to cover it. Then he returns his hands behind his head and his eyes meet mine. Keeping my gaze on his, I lift a hand and lick from the heel of my hand to my fingertips, the same way I've seen girls do online. His eyebrows lift a little. Then I lower my gaze to his erection and close my hand around it.

It's firmer than I thought it would be, and long, despite his protestation that he's only average. I can feel the veins beneath the soft skin, and I study the head as I stroke him, loving the way it swells. Intrigued by the tip, I lower my head and brush my tongue over it.

"Whoa, fuck," he says.

I lift my head. "Sorry, I couldn't resist it."

He blinks. "No, it's fine. I had my eyes closed. I wasn't expecting you to do it, that's all."

"Why not?"

"Because… not all women like doing it."

"Really?"

"Only about two-thirds do it, and only about a third enjoy it, apparently."

"Hmm. Well, it sounds as if you're breaking rule number one there."

His lips curve up. "Just me and you?"

"Just me and you." I stroke him again, fascinated by the way it reveals the head. Now I see why it needs lubrication. I add some, then close my mouth over the end, scooping my hair over one shoulder so he can see what I'm doing.

"Fuck." He falls back and covers his face with his hands.

Feeling powerful and in control, I wash my tongue over the end and then slide my lips down the shaft. Oh wow, this is hot. I lick and suck, thoroughly enjoying myself, thrilled when I feel his hand slide to the back of my head, his fingers tightening in my hair. He holds me there with gentle pressure, encouraging me to go further, and I take him deep into my mouth, as deep as I can, and suck.

"Alice…" He releases my head and puts his hands on my upper arms. I carry on, enjoying myself too much. "Alice," he says more urgently when I don't move.

I lift my head. "What?"

"You've got to stop."

I sit back on my heels and wipe my mouth. "Sorry. Was I doing it wrong?"

He gives a short laugh. "No. Quite the opposite. But I'm only human, and it'll defeat the whole point of this exercise."

"I don't understand."

He holds me and twists so I'm on my back, then looks down at me. "We're here to take away your virginity, and if you carry on like that, I'm going to come."

"You mean in my mouth?"

"Yeah."

"Ohhh… yes, do that. I want to know what it tastes like."

"Jesus." He rests his forehead on my shoulder.

I stroke his hair. "You okay?"

"Just counting to ten."

I kiss the top of his head. "I'm sorry. I'm like a kid in a sweet shop. There are so many wonderful things to choose from."

He lifts his head and studies me for a moment. "I want to make love to you this first time, okay?"

"We're 'making love' now?" I tease.

But he only smiles. "Yeah, I think so, don't you?"

Touched, I say, "Maybe." I look up into his beautiful brown eyes, cup his cheek with a hand, and brush my thumb across his beard. "Even this fascinates me," I murmur.

"My beard?"

"Facial hair. I love the way you're so different from me. Bigger, stronger, heavier. You smell so good."

"My cologne?"

"Yeah, but not just that. Your skin." I nuzzle the crook of his neck. "I like this." I touch his Adam's apple. He swallows, and I laugh as it rises and dips. "I like your haircut." He turns his head, and I brush my fingers from the longer strands on top to where it fades almost to nothing at the nape of his neck. I stroke him there, and he shivers. "It must be very strange for you," I say, "being with someone who's so naïve. Is it frustrating?"

"No." He doesn't elaborate, but his expression suggests he's actually enjoying himself. His gaze drops to my mouth. "I like this." He bends his head and kisses my Cupid's bow. Then he gives me a proper kiss, and our tongues tangle as he delves his into my mouth.

At the same time, he rests a hand on my knee and pulls it so my legs part, and then he moves his hand up to cup my mound. He slides his fingers down into my folds, and I sigh.

He lifts his head and looks at me again while he teases my clit. "Ready for me, Alice?"

I nod, suddenly breathless.

He strokes me for a while though, kissing me at the same time, until my heart is hammering on my ribs, and it's impossible to stop my hips moving to meet his fingers. Only then does he lean across, pick up his wallet, extract a foil packet, and toss the wallet back on the table.

Looking back at me, he thinks for a moment, then he rolls over and gets to his feet. I watch him go through to the bathroom, and then he comes back out with a towel.

"Lift up," he says, and when I do, he tucks the towel beneath me. "Just in case," he adds. "Saves you getting it on the sheets and being embarrassed to tell housekeeping."

Oh… he means if I bleed. Oh my. That was thoughtful. And now I'm nervous again.

Lying back beside me, he holds the packet up and nods at it. "Go on."

I take it, tear it open carefully, and take out the condom.

"Make sure it's the right way up," he says. Then he shows me how to put it on him, ensuring there's no air in the end, and rolling it slowly down. "Lock and load," he states.

When it's done, he moves between my legs. He pushes up my knees and shifts closer. Then, sitting back on his heels, he strokes the tip of his erection down through my folds. He does it a few times, and I realize he's lubricating himself with my moisture. Then, finally, he presses the head against my entrance and lifts up to lean over me, hands braced on either side.

Fixing his gaze on mine, he pushes his hips forward.

I inhale sharply as I feel a sharp sting, and my body gives an involuntary jerk. He moves back and withdraws, glancing down. His eyebrows rise, just a tiny bit, and I look down and see blood on the condom. It occurs to me then that he wasn't a hundred percent sure I was telling the truth about being a virgin.

"You okay?" he asks, leaning back over me. His eyes are filled with tenderness.

I nod, heart racing. "Do you want me to get a tissue?"

"Nah. It's not much. I hope you won't be too sore, but there's not a lot I can do about that, apart from stop."

"Oh God, don't do that."

He laughs and guides himself back inside me, and this time pushes firmly inside. I gasp at the amazing sensation of being stretched and filled so completely, right to the top. I close my eyes. He moves back and pushes forward again, and now his hips meet the back of my thighs, and he pauses and bends to kiss me.

"That's it," he murmurs. "All the way in."

"It feels amazing," I whisper, wrapping my arms around his neck.

"Not too sore?"

"Not enough to stop."

He lowers on top of me, and he starts to move, giving long, slow thrusts while he kisses me hungrily. "Fuck me, you're tight," he murmurs, his voice a deep growl.

"Sorry."

"It wasn't a complaint. You feel fantastic."

Pleased he's enjoying it too, I feel almost tearful at the thought that I've done it, I've taken that step, and I'm not a virgin anymore. No longer will I feel resentful and puzzled when I watch people making out in the movies. Relief flows over me, along with a fierce, brilliant joy.

I sink my hands into his hair and plunge my tongue into his mouth, and he groans, his hips speeding up. Oh wow, this is amazing. Oh, I like having sex. I'm definitely doing this again.

We carry on like that for a while, kissing while he moves inside me, and then he lifts up.

"Where are you going?" I ask.

He stops and looks down at me. "I was going to change position."

"Can we stay like this?"

He smiles. "I thought you wanted me to show you everything I know?"

"I did. But this is nice."

"You might prefer being on top?"

I shake my head. "You're heavy. I like that."

He lowers down again. "Okay. I'll do this, then." He shifts his hips up an inch. This time, when he thrusts, he grinds right against my clit.

"Ooh." I gasp.

"Lift your legs around my waist."

I do as he instructs, which changes the angle a little. Mmm, that feels good too.

"Good girl," he says.

Our eyes meet, and our lips curve up. "You like being in charge, don't you?" I tease.

In answer, he lifts up, takes my hands, and pins them above my head, holding me there. "Yeah," he confirms, giving long, slow thrusts again.

My eyelids drift closed as he arouses me, and I feel the first glimmers of an orgasm, twinkling in the distance like fairy lights. "Mmm…"

Holding my hands with one of his, he strokes the other down my arm and over my body, then back up to cup my breast. He teases the nipple while he moves, and I groan and clench around him, which makes him say, "Jesus," and his hips speed up again. Now he's thrusting with purpose, and he's breathing faster. Ooh… he's losing control. I like that.

In the porn I've watched, the girls are always vocal, which suggests to me that men like that. I wouldn't want to fake moans the way they sometimes seem to, but luckily I don't need to, because as things heat up between us, I can't help but groan each time he thrusts. He releases my hands, and I slide them around his back, enjoying the movement of his muscles beneath my fingers. It's grown hot in the room, and his skin is damp to the touch, which only seems to make this sexier.

Pleasure is building deep inside me, and I tighten my legs around his waist and lightly dig my nails into his back. "Oh God, that feels so good," I whisper, wanting to encourage him, "don't stop… I think I'm going to come…"

"Ah, yeah, come for me, baby, that's it…" He thrusts harder, pressing down with each movement of his hips, and that does it. Ooh, it's different with him inside me… the blissful feeling starts deep inside and spreads out like a wave… and I gasp… and then the pulses hit, damn, they're strong, five, six, seven, holy shit… and I'm crying out, almost in tears at how amazing it feels…

And then it's gone, and I flop back, but he doesn't stop; he pushes up my knees and he's thrusting hard and fast, oh my God… I hadn't realized there'd be so many sexy sounds—his hips meeting my thighs, the sound of him moving inside me, our harsh breathing—and his eyes are closed, oh holy shit he's so incredibly gorgeous, and then he shudders, oh wow… he's coming…

I watch him, drinking in the experience, observing his fierce frown, the way his body stiffens, the jerk of his hips, his guttural, sexy groan. Oh… now I understand why everyone talks about sex so much. It's amazing.

And even though we've only just finished, I want to do it all over again.

# Chapter Eight

## *Kip*

My heart's thundering. I take several shaky breaths, then open my eyes and stare right into Alice's dark-blue ones.

She's stunning, her hair mussed, her lips rosy, with the edges blurred from all the kissing, and a flush in her cheeks.

"Do I look just-fucked?" she asks, and laughs. Sliding her hands up my chest and neck, she cups my face and brushes her thumbs across my cheeks. "You're so gorgeous," she murmurs. "I can't believe I lost my virginity to the best-looking guy in Wellington."

There's no end to the way this girl chooses to flatter me. I kiss her, sighing as she brushes her hands down my back. When she gets to my butt, she gives the bit she can reach a slap.

Giving her a wry look, I carefully withdraw. She's bled a little; it was a good job I put the towel there. I dispose of the condom, then reach over to her bedside table, take a tissue out of the box, and hand it to her.

She touches it to herself and winces. "Ouch."

"I'm sorry."

"No, don't be. I'm glad. At least it proves I wasn't lying."

Bringing the duvet with me, I stretch out beside her, and when she finally lies back, I pull her into my arms and tug the duvet up to our chests. "I didn't think you were lying," I tell her.

"You looked surprised when you saw the blood."

"That was more because I thought at your age you probably wouldn't bleed."

"You forgot the word advanced. At my *advanced* age."

"I can't criticize. I'm thirty next year."

"I didn't spot any gray hairs."

"There are a few." I gesture at my crotch.

"I'll have a look later." She gives a mischievous smile.

Pulling a pillow beneath my head, I make myself comfortable, and she leans on my chest, resting her chin on a hand. Outside, the world continues to spin around us—a police siren sounds off in the distance, a car toots its horn, a door bangs further along the corridor—but in here it's warm and quiet. Just the two of us, basking in the afterglow of really good sex.

I reach out a hand and touch the pendant around her neck. It's the same as the one in her photo—the playing card with the Queen of Hearts. "I like this," I tell her.

"My mum gave it to me," she says.

I let it go, and it rests on her collarbone.

"Thank you so much," she says.

"You're welcome."

"I mean it. You answered all my questions, and you were patient and kind. I'm so lucky I met you."

I pull a strand of her hair through my fingers. "Me too. You were amazing."

"Aw, don't do that."

"Do what?"

"Give me false flattery. I know how clueless I was."

"Experience doesn't matter. You were enthusiastic and eager."

"Isn't everyone?"

"Have you never read the AskMen subreddit? Guys on there are always complaining about how many girls lie there like starfish."

"Seriously?"

I shrug, not wanting to go into details about my own experiences. Rule number one and all that. But a high percentage of the girls I've been with expect the guy to do all the work. I don't mind; it's not an onerous task. But it was pleasant to sleep with someone who seemed to enjoy turning me on, too. I think of the way she fixed her gaze on mine and licked her hand before she stroked me. Man, we could have some fun, if she stuck around.

"Hmm." She traces a finger in a circle on my chest. "I don't get why anyone wouldn't want to participate actively."

I play with another strand of her hair. It's so silky. And it smells nice.

"Poor Lesley," she says. "All alone in the Five Palms."

I give a short laugh.

"There must be something wrong with her brain," she adds. "Letting you go. She's crazy." Her eyes are wide and honest. She totally means it.

Slipping my hands beneath her arms, I lift her up a few inches so her face is level with mine, and then I kiss her, long and slow. When I eventually release her, she says, "Mmm. I can't believe I thought using your tongue was gross."

"You don't think so now?"

"Mmm. No." She licks her lips, then stretches out next to me, and we face each other, heads propped on our hands. "I'm sorry you got that text today," she says. "You looked very fed up at that point."

I sigh. "It came at the end of an odd couple of days."

"In what way?" She looks genuinely interested, and suddenly I want to talk about it.

"I told you that I work for a company that does research into robotics?"

"Yeah."

"Actually, I own the company with Saxon and my younger brother, Damon."

"Oh?" Her eyebrows rise.

"We have a senior leadership team of five. One of them is someone I went to university with. He's a smart guy. Normally hardworking and supportive. But yesterday he blew up, yelled at me in a meeting, then walked out."

"Oh, that's awkward."

"Yeah. I've tried to call him, but his phone is turned off. I'm debating whether to go and see him, but I don't even know if he's at the family home."

"Does he have a landline there you could call?"

"I think so."

"It might be slightly less awkward if his wife answers the phone than if you turned up at the house and he wasn't there."

"True." I hadn't thought of that.

I smile at her. She smiles back.

"I can't believe you wouldn't let me change position," I tell her. "Out of all the things I have up my sleeve, you chose missionary."

"I was enjoying it. Not to say I wouldn't enjoy trying your catalog. Shame we only have the one night." She sighs.

"We'll see."

She frowns then. "Kip… I told you, I'm not in a position to have a relationship."

"Okay."

"I just can't right now."

"Fair enough."

She glares at me. "You don't mean that."

"You're right, I don't."

"That's not fair," she says softly. "You should respect my wishes."

Used to getting my own way, I narrow my eyes. "Can you tell me why you can't have a relationship?"

She drops her gaze and plays with a fold of the bedsheet.

"We're friends now," I say gently. "And I'd like to see you again. If you're going to refuse, don't you think I deserve to know why?"

She lifts her gaze back to mine. "I guess." She sighs. "It's not a state secret or anything. My mum has M.S."

My eyebrows rise. "Multiple Sclerosis?"

"Yes. PPMS—primary progressive, the kind that isn't relapsing remitting. It means it just gradually gets worse."

"I'm so sorry."

She gives a sad smile. "Thank you. She was first diagnosed when she was thirty-nine, the year after my father died, when I was fourteen. Some doctors think a shock like that can bring it on. How much do you know about it?"

"I know the immune system attacks the protective sheath that covers nerve fibers."

"That's right. It causes communication problems between the brain and the rest of the body. She suffers from muscle weakness, especially on the right side, and she's confined to a wheelchair. She has problems controlling her bowels and bladder, and blurry vision and slurred speech sometimes. Extreme fatigue also means that even activities like brushing her hair can exhaust her. But we've established a routine now that gives her as much independence around the house as we can, and we manage the disease well. She occasionally suffers from low moods, but in general she stays positive, mainly for me and Charlie, I think."

"Shit, I'm so sorry."

"She's an amazing woman, and does everything she can to be as self-sufficient as possible. But the truth is that she needs twenty-four-hour care."

We fall quiet. She watches me as I process that information.

"So you've looked after her since you were young?" I ask.

She nods. "Full time, since I left school at sixteen. Obviously, I couldn't go to university. And I haven't been able to get a full-time job."

"You only have one sibling?"

"Yes. Charlie is twenty now, in her second year at uni. Mum and I saved up to make sure she could go. Charlie cried when we told her we were sending her to Vic. She said she'd go only on the proviso that she comes home when she finishes her degree to share the care with me. I agreed, because it was the only way to get her to go."

"And you don't have any other help?"

"My aunt, Mum's sister, June, comes over when she can. She's a nurse, and she has four kids, so she doesn't get much free time, and when she is off I try not to call on her as of course she wants to be with her family. But she's very sweet, and insists on giving me a day or two off a month."

A day or two a month… I've spoken to full-time carers at the hospital when I've been doing research there, and I know what pressure it puts on a person to have that kind of responsibility.

"You can't pay for someone to come in?" I ask.

"I get a Supported Living Payment, but I'd rather look after her myself and use it to buy things I need to care for her. Money's very tight. Coming here and staying in this luxury room was an extravagance I don't usually have." She looks around and laughs.

I find it difficult to echo her humor, though. The carers I've met have been much older, and often partners of the person who needs looking after. She's so young, and she's already missed out on so much.

"So," I ask, "Charlie's got, what, another year, or two years at uni?"

"One more. She's doing a law degree. She's hoping to do something part time when she graduates, so she can help share Mum's care. It means I might be able to get a part-time job. But if I can persuade Charlie to have a proper life, with a husband and kids, I will. I want her to have a normal life. I've come to terms with the fact that my life will never be normal in that way. My mum will always come first." She gives me a direct look. It's a warning. She's saying she would never abandon her mother and run away with me.

"I understand. But if a guy were to come around, because he liked you and wanted to be friends…"

"I don't live around the corner, Kip. I live in Gisborne. I'm driving home tomorrow."

I feel as if she's thrown a bucket of cold water over me. Gisborne is on the east coast of New Zealand, the first place in the world to see the sun each day. It's a good seven-hour drive, and probably more like nine hours because the more direct route along State Highway Two has road closures. She's going to have to drive all the way up to Lake Taupo before heading east. Jesus. Flying would take only an hour, but clearly that's out of the question money-wise.

I have money, and a plane, and could offer to fly her back and forth. But I already know she wouldn't accept it. And anyway, it wouldn't solve the issue of looking after her mum. She wouldn't want to hire a carer, even if she could afford it.

"I think you've just broken my heart," I tell her.

"Aw." She pushes me. "You'll forget all about me tomorrow. Soon you'll just remember me as the ditzy blonde who made you spend the night in a room the size of a postage stamp."

She snuggles up to me and sighs, and I wrap my arms around her. I wasn't joking. I feel genuinely gutted. There must be some way I can see her again. "You'll be bringing Charlie back here at the beginning of semester one, won't you? Can I see you then?"

"Don't make me promises like that, Kip. It'll hurt so much more when I get that message saying you've met someone else."

I don't reply, because she's convinced herself we could never have anything of substance, and she won't believe anything I say. It stings a little. I'd be prepared to travel, and to find a way for us to be together, but there's no point if she's going to say no to everything I suggest, and I know she will. I've already been with one girl who couldn't be bothered to fight for me. I don't think I can go through it again.

"Are you going to stay the night?" she asks. "I'll understand if you'd rather go." Her words seem emotionless, even cold. She doesn't care what I do.

I can't get angry at her, because she hasn't led me along at any point. Okay, she didn't tell me up front that she only wanted a one-night stand, but I don't blame her for that. I wasn't particularly looking for more, either. She's been very frank. I can't really get upset because she's treated me like a human vibrator. I should be thrilled. I had great fun, enjoyable sex, and no commitment. Every guy's dream, right? Don't be a pussy, Kip.

But for some reason, maybe because I heard from Lesley, because of the unpleasant exchange with Craig yesterday, or because the connection I've had with Alice has made me realize that I'm actually quite lonely, I feel a sweep of self-pity and resentment.

Then Alice moves, and I look down and see her rub her nose. I slide a hand beneath her chin and lift it so I can see her face. Her eyes shine with unshed tears.

I'm so selfish. She's not cold, and it's not that she doesn't care. She doesn't have a choice, for Christ's sake. She loves her mother with all her heart, and how can I criticize her for that? She should be applauded, in this day and age where young people are often condemned for being selfish. She's looked after her mum for eleven years, with barely a day off to do the things that young people do. She's so touch-starved that she reached out to a man she hadn't even met because she needed that human connection. I've made her feel loved and wanted. What we have here, tonight, is like a present under the Christmas tree. It's beautiful and sparkling and, in itself, it's a wonderful thing, no matter what's inside it on Christmas Day. I have to appreciate it for what it is.

Lifting up onto an elbow, I tip her onto her back and move up close. She sniffs and looks up at me with her huge blue eyes, and I'm not imagining it, they're filled with admiration and something a little deeper, not love, obviously, but dare I say adoration?

I kiss her, soft and gentle, my lips playing with hers, nipping, teasing, for a long time before I add my tongue to the mix. She sighs, opening her mouth, and our tongues touch, thrust, and dance with one another, our breaths mingling.

I once read a sci-fi novel where lovemaking with an alien species involved silver strands of energy wrapping around the other person like ribbons, and I imagine that happening now—snaking from us, intertwining, then pulling tighter until we're locked together, unable to separate until we reach the ultimate height of fulfillment.

Still kissing her, I stroke a hand down her neck to her breasts and cup them, teasing her nipple with my thumb. It's soft as velvet, like a light-pink rose petal, but as I tug it gently, the skin tightens and the nipple grows erect. I do the same with her other one, until they're both standing stiff and proud, and she's murmuring against my lips, wriggling a little.

Sliding my tongue deep into her mouth, which elicits a long, sexy moan from her, I brush my fingers down her body, across the slight swell of her stomach, and then over her mound. Pushing her legs apart, I slip my middle finger down into her folds.

She's still wet and swollen from her previous orgasms, and my finger slides easily through her slippery flesh. I know she's going to be sore, so I concentrate on her clit, teasing the tiny button with small circles and light pressure.

"Mmm... Kip..." she whispers.

I lift my head. "Does that feel good?"

"Yeah..." Her teeth tug her bottom lip, and her eyelids drift shut briefly.

"Tell me what it feels like." I slide my finger down an inch and gently collect some more of her moisture before returning to caress her clit.

She's breathing heavily now, and her hips are starting to move to match my hand. "Like swimming in a warm sea. Oh God... like being filled with melted chocolate..."

I kiss her. "Maybe I should lick it up?"

But she lowers her hand so it rests on mine and says, "No, don't stop..."

"Okay." I increase the pressure a little and kiss her again, deeply this time. Her long, sexy moan brings goosebumps out all over my skin, and my erection springs back to life. I press it against her hip, and she sighs. "See what you do to me," I murmur, stroking her firmly.

She closes her eyes and bites her bottom lip again. "Slow down or I'm going to come."

"I want you to. Tell me how it feels."

"Mmm... like a thread circling my stomach that's slowly being pulled tight... like the whole world, the entire universe, is in this room, buried deep inside me... like nothing else exists except... ohhh... you... and me..." And then she can't speak anymore, and she clamps her hand on mine and squeals as she comes. I watch her, feeling her muscles pulsing, and imagine the blissfulness flowing through her, the exquisite sensations of her climax. There's nothing like it, and there's nothing like being able to share yourself in such a vulnerable and open way with someone else. I'm so thankful I got to be the one she chose.

I lift my hand, and her eyes open. "Wow. That hit me like a freight train."

"Glad to be of service."

She laughs and wraps her arms around me, and we indulge in a long, sensual kiss.

Then I lift my fingers to my mouth and suck them.

"Whoa," she says. "Oh my God."

"What? It tastes nice." I slide my fingers down into her again, collect a little of her moisture, then bring them up to her mouth. "Try it."

"Kip!" She laughs and turns her head away.

Not to be foiled, I touch my fingers to my lips, then hold her face and kiss her, delving my tongue into her mouth. She struggles and complains, then sighs and goes still, letting me kiss her until I finally lift my head.

"Gross," she says, although her eyes are filled with that wondrous look again.

"There's not a single thing that's gross about your body. It's a work of art."

"Are you kinky? I'm beginning to think you're kinky."

"Kinky means unusual. I'm sure I'm not unusual in my tastes. You have a fascinating body. You don't have a single angle or hard bit— you're like a sexy marshmallow, all curvy and soft and silky. Why wouldn't I want to touch and lick every single part of you?"

"I've never been compared to a marshmallow before," she admits. Then her eyelids lower to half-mast. "Surely there are some parts you wouldn't want to stick your tongue?"

I kiss her. "Nope."

"Oh my." She blinks a few times, then looks down at my erection. "And now look what we've done. Are you going to do something with that?"

"No. I'm not going to make you sore. I'll cope."

"Seems a waste." She licks her lips, sits up, and gets to her knees.

"Ah…" I give a short laugh as she moves between my legs. "You don't have to do that. It goes down on its own eventually."

"I told you, I want to find out what it tastes like." She studies my erection, and just her hot, interested gaze is enough to make it swell even more. "It wants me to," she observes. "It looks very excited about it."

"Jesus." I look up at the ceiling. "Of course it's excited. It's only had my hand to play with for the past few months."

"Aw. Poor thing. Let's give it a party, then." She lowers down.

I lift my head and watch her apply plenty of lubrication, which is so sexy it makes my heart bang on my ribs. "You've been watching too much porn."

"Is that a complaint?"

"No, you go for it, girl."

She laughs, takes my erection in her hand, and then lowers her mouth over the head.

Ah… it's been a long while since a girl has done this for me. Lesley hated it, and I'm too much of a gentleman to demand a girl do it in return for going down on her. I understand. Women are gorgeous, but men's bodies are hard and hairy and unattractive, so I get why the majority aren't keen on it.

But Alice sweeps her hair over her shoulder and gives me a look that's so hot I nearly come on the spot, and then slides her lips down the shaft until I feel the tip touch the back of her throat.

I'm not going to last long like this, despite having come only twenty minutes ago. I watch her helplessly as she strokes me and licks and sucks. Ah Jesus… I slide my hand into her hair, unable to stop my hips thrusting up, and she gives a sexy little murmur of approval and takes me even deeper. Oh man…

Stroking me firmly, she lifts her head to watch and says, "You taste amazing," then takes me in her mouth again. At the same time, she slides her hand down, cupping my balls, then explores even lower with her lubricated fingers.

"Whoa! Alice…" Heat rushes through me, and I lose the ability to form words. I tug her hair, but she just sucks harder, and that unravels me like a ball of yarn. I come in her mouth, and I'm sure I black out for a moment when I feel her throat constrict as she swallows down everything I have to give.

When I'm finally able to talk again, I reel off a string of swear words, covering my face with my hands.

I feel her move up the bed, and then she leans over me. She moves my hands aside, and I open my eyes just as she kisses me.

I laugh and try to push her off, but she holds my face in her hands and plunges her tongue into my mouth. I groan, then just go limp and let her, and she gives me a long, deep kiss before she eventually lifts her head.

"Serves you right," she says smugly.

"Yeah, that's fair enough," I tell her guiltily. "I'm so sorry about that."

Her eyebrows rise. "About what?"

"Coming without warning you. I'm so sorry, that was very bad manners. I lost the power of speech. You and your naughty fingers took me by surprise."

"You did warn me," she says, amused. "You pulled my hair. I wanted to taste you. It was amazing. I could feel every jet." Her eyes flare.

I blink. "Oh. I thought that was why you kissed me—as punishment."

She laughs. "No. I did it because you did it to me, remember?"

"Oh…"

"Why would I want to punish you?" she asks, puzzled.

"I guess because it's impolite. It's called snow-blowing."

"Seriously?"

"Yeah. Except usually it involves returning the whole mouthful, I believe. A way to punish a guy when he doesn't warn that he's going to come."

"Well, I wouldn't do that. You lost control. That's super-hot." She stretches out beside me and licks her lips. "It's a bit salty," she adds. "Mmm. Nice."

I huff a sigh.

"I can tick Slot C off, anyway," she comments. "I like making you lose control. You swear a lot. I'm learning lots of words."

I give a short laugh. "What am I going to do with you?"

"You can spank me later. As I'm sure you're interested in doing, Mr. I'm-convinced-I'm-not-kinky-even-though-I-definitely-am." She yawns and snuggles up to me. "If I could have a man, I'd pick someone like you," she whispers.

And it's right then, at that moment, that I make the decision that I'm not going to let her go.

# Chapter Nine

## *Alice*

Kip gets me to turn away from him, then moves up close so his chest is to my back and wraps his arm around me. I sigh and close my eyes, assuming we'll cuddle for a while and then he'll announce he has to leave.

"Is this spooning?" I mumble as he pulls the duvet up to my shoulders.

"Sure is."

I pull his hand up to my mouth and kiss it. The light scent of his cologne rises from his skin, along with the essence of luscious, warm male. Having lost my father, I find the smell oddly comforting as well as attractive. "You smell terrific."

He kisses my hair. "So do you. Your hair smells of strawberries."

Smiling, I close my eyes.

Two seconds later, I fall asleep.

*

I rouse in the middle of the night, and it takes a few seconds for me to remember where I am. The window is on the other side to where it is at home. And not only that, but there's someone in bed with me.

I turn over, pleasure filling me as I realize he's still here, and that he didn't disappear in the night. He's lying on his back, looking away from me, sprawled out, sound asleep. It's dark now—he must have turned out the lights at some point—but the room is lit dimly by the moon outside, as the curtains are still open. The duvet rests over his chest, but his shoulders are free, and the moonlight highlights his muscles, and the scatter of hair below his throat.

He stayed. I curl up on my side and let my gaze wander over him as my eyelids droop again. I can see the short hair on the back of his head, his almost-shaved nape, and the curve of his ear.

I'm not foolish enough to assign any special meaning to what happened last night. People have one-night stands all the time, and I'm sure few of them think deeply about the act, viewing it as simple gratification. But despite all that, it was special for me. This man found me attractive enough to take me to bed, he took considerable time to give me pleasure—three times—and he was kind and gentle—well, until the end, anyway. As I remember how he lost control and thrust himself to a climax, I get goosebumps all over. I'll be pressing the rewind button on that memory a lot in the future.

I'm so glad I did this. It's only now that I realize how badly it could have gone. If I'd slept with Tim… let him kiss me and take off my clothes, let him slide inside me… I'd have been lying there, eyes squeezed shut, desperate for him to get it over with so I could leave. But Kip couldn't be further toward the other end of the spectrum.

His chest rises and falls with his even breaths. He's taking up more than his share of the bed, but I don't care. I lie there and look at him until I can't keep my eyes open any longer. And then I fall asleep, and dream of him for the rest of the night.

*

The next time I open my eyes, it's daylight. I blink, and then my eyes widen as I see Kip lying on his side, head propped on a hand, watching me.

"Morning," he says.

"Oh. Morning." I lift up, brush a hand over my face, making sure I haven't been drooling, then run my fingers through my hair. "Oh no. I bet I look as if I've stuck my fingers in an electric socket."

He smiles. "It is quite wild." He lifts a hand, picks up a strand, and runs it through his fingers. Then he slides his hand to the back of my head and pulls me toward him, rolling onto his back. Laughing, I fall onto his chest, and he gives me a long, luxurious kiss.

When he finally releases me, I glare at him and say, "I have morning breath."

"You taste *sweet as.*" He runs his hands down my back.

I kiss his nose. Reaching over him, I tap my phone where I left it on the bedside table. It's 07:19. Aw. I'd hoped to wake earlier, but I didn't think to set my alarm. "Ah. I need to get ready. Charlie's coming at eight. We wanted to get an early start."

"Yeah, I need to get to work. I'm normally in by seven thirty."

"Saxon will know you got lucky."

He chuckles. Then he slides his hands down and strokes over my butt. "How are you feeling today?"

I wince. "Tender."

"I'm sorry."

"So you should be. Ravaging me like that."

"Yeah, because you didn't enjoy it at all."

"Not one bit. Didn't you hear me complaining at great length?"

"No." He pulls my head down and gives me a long kiss. "It had to be done." He kisses my nose. "And I'm glad I was the one to do it."

"Me, too."

"I'd like to have made love to you again," he says reluctantly. "But I don't want to hurt you."

I am very sore, and as much as I want to have sex again, I think I'd wince all the way through it. "Kisses are almost as good," I admit.

So he smiles and kisses me again, and we smooch for a while, taking our time.

Eventually he moves back, and we study each other for a long moment.

"Are you going to tell me your surname?" he asks.

"I don't think so."

"Mine's Chevalier," he says.

I give him an exasperated look. "Kip…"

He shrugs and lifts an eyebrow as if to say, 'Too late now.'

"I'm still not going to tell you," I say, and he sighs.

I kiss him again, taking my time, trying to tell him without words that I'm sorry, and that I wish I could tell him everything about me, but there's no point, because this is hard enough, and I'm going to be upset anyway when we have to part.

"Come on," he says when I eventually move back. "Let's get ready."

We rise and dress. I showered yesterday before our date, and so I just have a quick wash and pin my hair up. Kip says he's going to go home and shower and change, so he pulls on his rather creased shirt and trousers he forgot to hang up last night. I get dressed in my jeans and a pink tee, then pack my small case. Finally, we have a long kiss and a hug before we go out and down to the elevator.

We don't speak as the car sinks to the ground floor. There are several other people in with us, and anyway, I can't think of anything to say. I want to blurt out my surname and where I live and tell him to call me, but what's the point? I need to sever this neatly, because I'm sure it'll make it easier than hanging onto hope that one day in a year or two's time, we'll somehow have a fairy tale ending.

The doors open, and we walk into the lobby. Halfway across, we stop and turn to one another.

"Thank you," I tell him. "I've had a fantastic time, and you were amazing. I really appreciate you being so patient and kind."

He tucks a strand of my hair behind my ear. "Thank you for letting me be your first." He brushes his thumb across my lips. "Can I give you a last kiss?"

I hesitate, because I know I should say no, but the word won't form. Taking that as affirmation, he slips a hand to the nape of my neck. He's wearing his glasses, but he lifts them onto his hair, then moves up close and lowers his lips to mine, and we exchange a long, slow kiss that sends tingles through me from the roots of my hair to the tips of my toes.

As he lifts his head and replaces his glasses, my gaze slides past him and falls on my sister, sitting near the front desk, watching us with shock and delight.

"Oh fuck," I mutter.

"What?"

"Charlie's here." I watch her get up and bring her suitcase over to us.

He turns and smiles as she walks up, and holds out a hand. "Hello, Charlie. I'm Kip."

"Hello, Kip." She shakes his hand, running her gaze down him, then glances at me with much amusement. "Have a good evening?"

He grins as I flush scarlet. "I hear you have a long journey ahead of you," he says and looks at me. "Will you text me when you get home so I know you got there safely?"

"Um…" Not expecting that, I flush even more.

He takes out his phone. "What's your number?"

I meet his eyes. He lifts his eyebrows, then looks at Charlie.

She reels off my number, and I glare at her as he programs it in. He types briefly, and then my phone buzzes in my back pocket. I take it out. He's sent me a message that says, *Sorry, but it had to be done.* That's becoming his catchphrase.

"You've got my number now, anyway," he states. He looks at Charlie. "Make sure she texts me when you arrive."

She nods, and he smiles. "All right. Have a good journey."

I stare at him, because it suddenly occurs to me that I won't see him again. A wave of sorrow sweeps over me, taking my breath away.

He's watching my face, and his brows draw together. He walks up, puts his arms around me, gives me a big hug, then a fierce kiss on the mouth, before he turns and walks away, striding across the lobby and out through the door without looking back.

I watch him go, then press my fingers to my mouth as I fight not to cry.

"Oh no," Charlie says, and she puts her arms around me. "Oh, Alice."

"I'm okay." But my voice is a squeak.

She squeezes me, then moves back and looks at me. "So it went well, then?"

I nod and rub my nose. "He was lovely."

"He was gorgeous. You lucky thing. So you... you know? Took him up to your room?"

Tears tip over my lashes. "Yeah. He was amazing." I dash the tears away. "I'm not going to regret it. It was the best thing that's ever happened to me."

"Of course you won't regret it. But you haven't agreed to see him again?"

"How, Charlie? I live nine hours away from him. How is that going to work, exactly?"

"Couldn't you see him when you come to Wellington?"

"What, the two times a year I make the trip? Yeah, he's totally going to wait for me."

"He might. He looked pretty keen."

I inhale until my lungs are full, exhale until they're empty, then smile. "No. It's over. But that's okay. We had a great time. I'm not going to make more of it than it was." I take the handle of my case. "Come on. I'll check out, and then we can get going. I vote we stop for breakfast soon, what do you think?"

*

As we set off on the state highway, I ask her about the party last night, and we chat for a while about other things until I finally pull over at a café for breakfast. We both order eggs and bacon and coffee, and take a seat near the window. It's a warm morning, and the sun streams through across our table. Mariah Carey is declaring that all she wants for Christmas is you, and the air is filled with the scent of coffee, cooked food, and warm croissants.

Charlie nurses her coffee when it comes, and then says, "Okay, so I can't keep quiet any longer. I need to talk about him."

I sigh and stare into my latte. "I thought it was too good to be true."

"Sweetie, you had sex. Amazing sex, by the sound of it." She looks at me for confirmation. Grudgingly, I roll my eyes and nod. "Come on," she says. "Tell me all about him."

"I don't know that much. He was twenty-nine yesterday. He's six foot one. He has a twin brother called Saxon, and a younger brother called Damon. They run a company that does some kind of research into robotics and prostheses. And he plays the guitar. That's about it."

"Have you Googled him?"

"No."

"Right." She pulls out her phone.

"Charlie…"

"Don't tell me you're not curious."

I hesitate. Then, after a few seconds, I give in and nod. I am curious. I'm so curious I would definitely kill a cat if there was one around. "His surname is Chevalier."

She grins and types it in, then waits for the results. After a few seconds, her eyes widen. Her gaze slowly rises to mine.

"What?" I say, heart racing.

"He's right at the top of the search results. Jesus, he has a Wikipedia page!"

"Really?"

"Yeah. I'll read it out. 'Kristopher Alan Chevalier, known as Kip, born 21 December 1993, is the joint CEO of Kingpinz Robotics, based in Wellington, New Zealand, along with his twin brother, Saxon Mark Chevalier, and his younger brother, Damon Stuart Chevalier.' There's a detailed section on the company. Oh shit, his cousin is Lawrence Oates. Did you read the article on him on Stuff the other day?"

"No."

"His nickname is Titus. He's a leading Kiwi expert on AI. It says here that Saxon is currently running the company here because Titus is in the UK. They've made a huge breakthrough in IVF by using AI to predict successful embryos."

"I met Saxon. I didn't know he did all that!"

"They sound like quite the family, don't they?"

"So what does Kip do at the company?" I'm intrigued now in spite of myself.

She continues to read. "'Kip is an innovative computer engineer with a Master's Degree in Software Development. He has an interest in maxillofacial prostheses. These can replace anatomy inside the mouth, which are called intra-oral, or a part of the face like the ear, nose, eye, or cheek, which are known as extra-oral prostheses. Some of them are worn daily like a pair of dentures, and others are permanently implanted into the body, like cranial plates. He is also currently working on an augmentative and alternative communication device or AAC that experts are saying will be revolutionary in the field." She looks up and gives me a look that says, *Oooh!*

"He told me about that," I say. "He said it was his baby."

"He must be pretty smart." She scrolls down. "Let's look at the personal section."

Suddenly, I don't want to know more in case I don't like what I hear, but she's already started reading. "'In 1999, Kip's father, Neal Chevalier, invented the Chev-X 490 Gaming Pro 3D—the world's first graphics processing unit—which offered a notably large leap in 3D PC gaming performance. This was followed five years later by the Chev-X 520 Elite, which again saw a significant rise in gaming performance and outshone all other GPUs at that time.'"

Her jaw drops. "'The Chevalier family's net worth is estimated at 7.2 billion dollars.'" She lifts her gaze to me.

I stare at her. "What?"

"Holy shit, Alice, he's a billionaire."

"What?"

"That's nine zeroes."

"What?"

Her giggle holds a touch of hysteria. "Oh my God. What was he doing on Tinder?"

My brain is refusing to compute. "I'm guessing he likes being anonymous. I would think billionaires have trouble with women being after their money, don't you?"

"Oh Alice. Did you have any idea?"

I think about Saxon's Aston Martin. The way Kip ordered the most expensive wine on the menu. His Apple watch and brand-new iPhone. His exquisite, tailored shirt. The inner confidence that radiated from him. "I guess there were signs he was wealthy. But that's different from being…"

"Fuck-off rich?"

"Well, yeah."

She looks back at her phone. "'When Kip was twelve years old, he witnessed the death of his cousin, Christian Chevalier, who drowned in a sea cave after a pile of rocks collapsed. Kip swam to get help while his brothers attempted to free his cousin, but Christian died before the paramedics arrived.'"

"Oh, shit. How awful."

"God, yeah."

We're both quiet for a moment, our hearts going out to the young lad who experienced such a traumatic event.

Charlie looks back at her phone. "It says 'Kip had a relationship with Lesley Nicholls for two years, but they parted in 2021." She clicks on Lesley's name. "She's a model."

"She texted him while we were together. He said they broke up when she accepted a job in Australia without telling him. Then she came back a year later, and they dated for a few months before she went back. She really hurt his feelings, I think."

"It says here that she's getting married now."

"She wanted to hook up with him last night."

Charlie's eyebrows rise. "But he obviously didn't."

"No." I smile. "He chose me."

"Over a model." Charlie puts on a stunned face, and we both laugh.

"Does it mention anyone else?" I ask her.

"No. It says 'Kip is currently single.'" Her lips twitch. "It doesn't mention you."

I give a short laugh at the thought of me being linked with a relatively famous billionaire. "What a shock."

"There's also a philanthropy and charity section here. 'Kip is the patron of a number of New Zealand charities, including the Kiwi

Cancer Society, and he has received several awards for the development of computer-aided technology in facial prosthetics, which are often required by cancer patients following the removal of facial anatomy. He is also the president of the Chevalier Trust, a family-run, multi-cause charitable enterprise that is active across a broad range of areas including young people and education. Kip himself takes a personal interest in the provision of computer technology in low-decile schools and is the patron of Computers in Homes, which aims to make computers and Internet services available to all New Zealand children.'"

She puts her phone down. "Is he a saint?"

"Most definitely not," I say, thinking about how he pulled my sweater over my head and told me off for wriggling.

"He sounds amazing though. Are you really not going to see him again?"

"Like I said, we live nine hours away."

"Only an hour by plane."

"I can hardly afford to fly all the time."

"He might be prepared to pay for you to fly, though."

I frown at her. "I don't think so."

"You never know."

"I can't let what we've found on the Internet change my decision. That's just tacky. The last thing he's going to want is for a girl to be after his money. That's obviously why he was on Tinder."

She sighs and rests her chin on a hand. "Would be nice though, wouldn't it? Having all that cash."

I'm not even going to think about it. I liked him before I knew he was rich. I'm not going to let his bank balance influence the fact that I've already told him I don't want a relationship.

"Come on, drink up. We've got a long drive, and we should get going."

She finishes her coffee, and the two of us head back out to the car. Soon, Wellington is in my rear-view mirror, and I set my mind to moving forward.

# Chapter Ten

## *Kip*

I go home, shower and change, pick up a breakfast wrap and a coffee on the way in to work, and arrive just before eight thirty, about an hour after I usually get there.

As I walk past Marion's desk, she says brightly, "Morning, Mr. Chevalier."

I give her a wry look. "Don't start."

"I only said good morning."

"You said it with a glimmer in your eye."

She grins. "Have a nice evening, did we?"

I pick up my post, then turn and rest my butt on the table. "I did, as it happens."

"The meal went well?" she asks. I told her yesterday that I was taking Alice to Red's Rib Shack with Saxon and Catie.

"Yeah. The ribs were amazing."

"Great, because I want to know all about the cuisine."

I sip my coffee. Then I smile. "She was lovely. Warm and funny. You'd have liked her."

"Will I get to meet her?"

I sigh. "She lives in Gisborne."

"Oh, shit."

"Yeah."

We study each other for a moment.

Then she says, "You're not going to let a little thing like four hundred kilometers come between you, are you?"

"Absolutely not. I'm working on it."

She laughs. "If there's anything I can do, let me know."

"Yeah, okay." I get to my feet. "Any news from Craig?"

"I'm afraid not. He called in sick again. Claire tried to ask what's going on, but he made some excuse and ended the call."

I sigh. I let it go yesterday, hoping he'd come in after he cooled down, but that didn't work, so I'm going to have to deal with it today.

"What's my schedule like?" I ask.

"Not too bad today. Nothing until the meeting with TalkTech at ten, and then you're over at the hospital at two."

"Okay, thanks." I pick up my coffee and go into my office.

I put the wrap and post on my desk, then go over and stand by the window. It's a beautiful day, a bit blustery, but then it often is in Wellington. It's nice and clear for Alice's drive back to Gisborne. Even so, she probably won't get there much before six p.m., especially if she stops a few times. I doubt I'll hear from her before then.

I sip my coffee, thinking about last night. About going down on Alice, and her surprised cries of pleasure when she came. About sliding inside her, and the stab of realization I felt when I saw she was bleeding. It wasn't that I thought she was lying about being a virgin, I was just so surprised that she could get to the age of twenty-five and not have had sex. She's so beautiful and sexy. It's an absolute crime.

But it's not as if it was her choice. Her commitment to her family has been amazing. I have nothing but admiration for the fact that she's looked after her mother and sent her sister to university. It's rare for a person to make such sacrifices in this day and age without expecting something in return.

Turning, I pull out my big leather chair, sit down, and roll up to my desk. I study my post for a moment. Then I open my laptop.

I don't even know her surname. She wanted to remain anonymous, and I should respect that.

Yeah, right. This was always going to happen.

I pull up Google and type "Alice Gisborne."

At the top of the search is a dentist called Alice Monroe who works in the city. I click on the profile—she's a brunette around forty, so I know it's not her. Second is an Alice Beecham who's a realtor. A click brings up a Gisborne real estate agency. A second click on staff reveals that Alice Beecham is in her fifties with gray curly hair.

The third search result is a Facebook entry for someone called Alice Liddell. I click on it, and it takes me to the Facebook page. It's set to private, so the rest of the information is hidden. But the profile picture is of a beagle lying on its back. Hmm.

I type in "Alice Liddell."

At the top of the search results is a series of black-and-white photographs of a young girl, maybe ten years old, clearly taken a long time ago. I click on the Wikipedia entry—yeah, it's not her. This woman was, in her childhood, the inspiration for Lewis Carroll's *Alice's Adventures in Wonderland* in the 1850s.

I type in "Alice Liddell Gisborne".

Once again, the Facebook profile pops up, but nothing else. The beagle picture still suggests it's her, though.

I decide to change tack. This time, I type "Alice Liddell science fiction fantasy reviews."

The first entry of the search results is of a website called Wonderland.

I stare at the screen. Oh shit. Surely not.

I click on the Wonderland link, which brings up the website of a podcast that reviews science fiction and fantasy novels, run by a woman called Alice. I click on the About section of the website. It says, "Alice Liddell has been a fan of Lewis Carroll's book *Alice's Adventures in Wonderland* since her mother named her after the character when she was born. Alice loves gaming, music, and chocolate truffles, and lives in Middle-Earth."

There's a photo of her. It's the one she used on Tinder where she's obviously sitting at her recording desk with her headphones around her neck, smiling at the camera.

I sit back with a short laugh. Holy shit.

I listen to the podcast every week, often while I'm working out at the gym. No wonder I recognized her husky voice. I just didn't put two and two together because it was out of context. She's huge in the New Zealand literary community. She publishes regular episodes on YouTube and Spotify and Apple in which she interviews famous sci-fi and fantasy authors from both New Zealand and across the world, as well as reviewing new books. On TikTok she does daily videos where she talks about her favorite novels. She's also active on Twitter, where she chats all the time to readers and writers. Jesus, I even follow her on there. In fact, I'm sure I've replied to a couple of her tweets over the last few years when she's been discussing books. She's appeared at several Kiwi fantasy conventions where she's done live podcasts interviewing movie stars and authors. She's really well known.

The reason I didn't make the connection is that I hadn't seen a photo of her. I've never looked at the About page of the website. The avatar she uses on the Wonderland social media sites isn't a photo of herself or her beagle but a cartoon of a rabbit with a pocket watch and waistcoat, an adaptation of one of the original wood-engraved illustrations done for the book. Otherwise, online she doesn't tend to show her face. Her podcasts are audio only. And her photos on Facebook and Instagram only include pictures of books.

Suddenly everything falls into place. The pendant she wears of a playing card with the Queen of Hearts. The keyring with a red heart and book, and her statement, "I like flamingos." They use flamingos as mallets in the story, don't they? I pull up the Wikipedia page of the book and read through it. Jesus! How many references did she make when we were together? I know she mentioned her 'curious appetite'. She called her fries 'pommes de terre'—I knew it was French for potatoes, but I didn't realize it was part of a language pun used in the book, 'digging for apples'. She jokingly asked me if I played croquet. And when I gave her half of the truffle, as she ate it, she said, "Off down the rabbit hole." Christ. She gave me all those clues, and I didn't get one of them! Now I know why she said, "How did you know?" when I said, "Come on. Let's go down the rabbit hole together, and see if we end up in Wonderland."

I sit back, thinking about her podcast. Dammit, I knew I recognized her. I listen to her because I love her husky voice and her quirky sense of humor. She never fails to make the people she's interviewing laugh. She's also really smart at analyzing books and movies, and I enjoy her critical mind. I think about some of the episodes I've enjoyed, and I'm filled with a sense of wonder. I already thought she was amazing, but now I've filled in the gaps, it's only amplified my admiration for her.

She told me that she cares for her mother twenty-four-seven, which must mean she's been confined to her home since she was sixteen. Reading must have been a comfort to her, something she could fit around looking after her mum. Maybe she started by doing a blog reviewing books and movies, and the podcast grew out of that. She's done extremely well for herself, though, to develop it as well as she has.

How does she make a living out of it, though? She must monetize her podcasts. I remember something then and google Wonderland and Patreon. Yeah, I was right—you can support her on Patreon and get extra interviews, reviews, discussions, and even merchandise. She's also running a Kickstarter campaign to fund a proper studio that's already passed its target amount. Wow. She's quite the entrepreneur. Now I'm really impressed.

Why didn't she tell me any of this? I'd have been fascinated and would have loved to chat to her about it. But even as I form the question, I know the answer. It's the same reason I didn't mention my company on my profile. Being anonymous is part of the attraction. She didn't want to share herself in that way. She knew that if she managed to hook up with a guy, she wouldn't be able to develop a relationship with him. All she wanted was the physical connection.

I turn back to the view and prop my feet up again. I'm so stunned. I just keep smiling. It all makes so much sense now. She came across as confident because she's used to interviewing strangers all the time, but she was also shy because she hardly ever leaves her house. Professionally, she's smart, innovative, and enterprising, but personally she's innocent and naïve. What a wonderful combination.

Jesus. I'm absolutely fascinated.

"You're not wearing the same shirt from last night," Saxon says from behind me. I turn to see him come into the office. "Do I interpret that as a bad sign?"

"I went home and changed." I smile.

His eyebrows rise, and he grins. "You spent the night?"

"I don't kiss and tell, bro."

"Excellent," he says, as if I haven't spoken. "I knew you two would hit it off. Are you seeing her again?"

"Not sure. She lives in Gisborne."

"Oh." He blows out a breath. "That's a bummer."

"Yeah." I look at my laptop. "I've got her mobile number. Do you think it could be called stalking if I look up her address?"

"I guess it depends what you're going to do with the information."

"I thought I might send her some flowers. But I don't want to invade her privacy." So far, I've only looked up what anyone could discover on the internet. Finding her address will take a little more delving, and I don't want to make her uncomfortable.

He purses his lips. "Only you know how well it went last night, and whether she's the sort of person to react in a negative way to that. Girls don't normally complain when you send them flowers. As long as you don't follow it up by appearing on her doorstep, I would think it would be all right."

"Yeah. Okay."

He hesitates. "No sign of Craig today, I hear."

"He called in sick again."

"Yeah. What are you going to do?"

"Try ringing his landline," I reply, thinking about what Alice said last night. "If that doesn't work, I'll have to go to his house."

"Want me to come?"

"Nah. He'll probably respond better if I'm on my own."

"All right," he says. "Give me a call if you need me."

"Will do."

He goes out.

I look back at my laptop. Take a few bites of the breakfast wrap, and have a sip of coffee.

I shouldn't.

Oh, what the fuck. I don't think I'm imagining the connection we had last night. She wanted to keep her distance because she's convinced we can't have a relationship and she doesn't want to get hurt. If she didn't get mad at me coming in her mouth without telling her, I don't think she'll mind me sending her flowers.

Whoa. Don't start thinking about that, Kip.

Mentally crossing my fingers, I start searching. It only takes me five minutes to track down her address.

I search for a florist, then give them a call rather than ordering online. Turning on the charm, I sweet talk the woman on the other end of the line into agreeing to the last delivery slot on their books today, and read out a message for the card.

"She's a lucky girl," the woman says as she types in my credit card number.

"I'm a lucky guy."

"Aw. You're a sweetie."

I roll my eyes—that's the third time I've been called that in the past few days. I thank her and end the call, then go over to my computer workstation, determined to lose myself in code for the next hour and stop daydreaming about Alice and her big blue eyes.

*

It works, partly. The morning is busy, and after my meeting with TalkTech at ten, I spend a couple more hours working on MOTHER, ready for the meeting with Genica in the New Year when we finally hand over the program.

At two o'clock, I force myself to accept that I'm putting off contacting Craig, and finally get around to dialing his home landline.

It rings five times, then goes to voicemail.

"Hi there," I say, "it's Kip Chevalier here. Craig, can you call me please? I'd like to chat about our meeting the other day." I leave my mobile number and hang up, already knowing he won't call back.

I work until five p.m., then go out and tell Marion I'm off for the day.

"I'm going to call in and see Craig at home," I tell her.

"Good luck," she replies.

"I hope I won't need it, but thanks. See you tomorrow."

I walk through the office and out to the car park, get in my Mercedes, and head toward the suburb where Craig lives. It's only a ten-minute drive, and when I arrive, I pull up outside his house and turn off the engine.

He lives in a beautiful five-bedroomed home in an area popular with young families. The house is surrounded by a decent-sized lawn and bush to the back, and must be worth a few million.

I get out, walk up the path to the front door, and ring the bell.

Inside, I can hear his baby crying. After about thirty seconds, the door opens. It's Craig's wife, Chloe, and she's holding her baby boy in her arms. He must be around four months old now. Chloe is about the same age as me, five foot four, curvy, dark-haired, and pretty, although she looks tired. We've always gotten on well, so I'm surprised now when she greets me with a hostile gaze.

"What do you want?" she snaps.

My eyebrows rise. "Hey, Chloe. I was looking for Craig."

She frowns. "He's not here."

"Okay. I've tried calling him but it just goes to voicemail. Do you know what time he'll be home?"

She meets my eyes and gives a short, humorless laugh. "He won't be home, Kip. He's left me."

My jaw drops. "What?"

Some of her animosity fades as she obviously realizes from my reaction that I'm telling the truth. She sighs and moves back. "Come in."

I walk past her into the house, toe off my shoes, and leave them by the door. My heart is banging. Craig's left her? Jesus. They've been together for years. I thought we were best mates. Why didn't he tell me?

"Go in the living room," she says, and I walk in there. It's untidy; kids' toys litter the floor, and an open suitcase sits on the dining table, half-packed.

Chloe comes in behind me. "Do you want a coffee?"

"No thank you, I'm fine."

She gestures at the sofa, and I take a seat.

"What's going on?" I ask softly.

"He left me," she repeats.

"When?"

"Two weeks ago."

"Ah, shit. I'm so sorry. I didn't know. He didn't tell us at work."

She leans back, cradling the baby, and sighs. "What made you come around here, then?"

"We had a… argument, I guess you'd call it, at work a couple of days ago. He's called in sick the last two days. He won't reply to my calls, so I thought I'd better see him in person."

"You argued?" She frowns. "What about?"

"The sale of the software we've been working on. I wanted to sell to one company, and he wanted another."

Her brow clears. She gives a short, humorless laugh. "I'm guessing Craig wanted Sunrise Ltd?"

I frown. "Yes. How did you know?"

"That's why he's angry, Kip. He left me for Renée Garnier."

Oh Jesus. I feel a little faint as I remember how I called her a bitch to his face.

"He probably promised her he'd be able to persuade you into selling to her," she says. "He always thinks he can talk anyone into anything."

"He was pushing for Sunrise," I say softly, remembering that he mentioned them at the meeting where he blew up. "Marama agreed with him. Damon was on the fence. But Saxon and I were convinced Genica was the right company, and in the end Damon agreed, so it was three against one."

"Well there's your problem. Craig was always very conscious of the fact that it was him against the three of you." She smiles as I frown at her. "I know you would never have shut him out consciously. He was jealous, Kip."

"Of my family?"

"Of the fact that you and Saxon would always have a connection that he could never have, no matter how long you were friends. As close as you and Craig were, you would never choose him over your twin brother."

"That's not true. I've sided with Craig many times in the boardroom against Saxon."

"I'm not talking about the boardroom. He loves you, Kip. He's always put you on a pedestal ever since you first met. But he knows he'll never mean as much to you as Saxon or even Damon, and I think that stings. The three of you are very tight. And that relationship you have with Saxon is very special, closer still. It can be tough for people around you. It was one reason Lesley left."

My eyes widen. "What?"

"She told me once that she knew she'd never mean as much to you as Saxon."

I give a short, incredulous laugh. "You're kidding me."

She shrugs.

I sit back, stunned. Lesley never mentioned anything about it to me. Is it possible that she could have felt that way?

It's true that I'd talk to Saxon about the company, obviously. But about personal things? We're close, but we're still guys. There's a lot we don't say to each other. And there has always been a level of competitiveness between us that has meant we often deal with problems ourselves rather than admit we're struggling.

"I spoke to her yesterday," I admit. "She told me I make her nervous—that I make her feel as if I'm going to tell her off."

"Well, yeah, you can be quite stern."

"Seriously?"

"Yeah. I've always thought it must be sexy under the right circumstances." She smiles with a flash of her old teasing nature, then her smile fades and she looks away.

"I'm so sorry about Craig," I murmur.

She straightens the baby's top. "I know some of it's my fault. I've put on weight, and I'm tired all the time. I haven't paid him as much attention as I should have."

"Jesus Christ, Chloe, you've had a baby. And that's bullshit anyway. You're still as gorgeous as you were the day I met you."

She presses her fingers to her lips and starts crying.

"Ah, come on…" I go over to the sofa and put my arm around her. I'm bitterly disappointed in my friend. "I can't imagine what women have to go through giving birth, physically and emotionally. You've been through huge changes. Guys need to be patient and supportive after their partners have had a baby."

"Oh Kip, shut up."

I close my mouth, not quite sure what I've done wrong, and just rub her arm.

She sniffles and snuffles for a while. Eventually she blows her nose, then gives me a shaky smile. "Don't mind me. I figured out a while ago that I married the wrong guy, that's all." She meets my eyes and gives a short laugh.

I know it's not a come on. We've never felt that way about each other. She's referring to the fact that she fell for Craig, even though he has an abrasive side to him that neither Saxon nor I possess. He's a little less respectful, and, it seems, a lot less honorable.

"You've always been the kind one," she says. "Damon's frank and naughty. Saxon's impulsive and hot-tempered. You're the kind, generous, sweet one."

"Jesus, please don't call me sweet."

"But you are, and I don't mean that in a patronizing way. I don't think you have a nasty bone in your body, Kip. And sometimes I think all two hundred and six bones in Craig's body are nasty."

I don't argue with her because she's hurting, and she doesn't need me to defend the guy who's hurt her so badly.

"What are you going to do?" I ask, gesturing at the suitcase. "Are you going away?"

"We were both supposed to be going to visit my parents in Australia for Christmas." She moves away a little, and I remove my arm. "It's going to be hard work traveling on my own with a baby, but people do it all the time. I'll manage. I need to see Mum and Dad, and have some time to think."

"Maybe he'll realize how much he misses you while you're away."

"Maybe. Honestly, though? I don't want him back. He didn't just have a one-night stand with someone else. He started seeing her over a year ago."

That shocks me. The baby was born in August, which means he was having an affair when they were trying to get pregnant.

"When he told me he was leaving, he didn't apologize or say he regretted it. He..." She stops and clears her throat. "He'd been drinking, and he was very cruel. Alcohol makes a person honest, so I know he'd obviously been thinking those thoughts all along. And why would I want to be with a person who felt like that about me?"

Anger sears through me, making my stomach churn. "I'm so sorry."

She shakes her head. "Don't."

My throat is tight with emotion. "Is there anything I can do?"

She gets to her feet, holding the baby. "No, but thank you."

I stand as well, shoving my hands in my pockets. "If you think of anything, just call me. I mean it. What he's done... I'm disgusted with him."

Her lips curve up. "I'm going to say it."

"Please don't."

"You're so sweet."

"Argh. I'm going." I smile and head out to the front door, where I put my shoes on. There I stop and turn to face her. "I hope your trip goes well."

"Thanks. We'll be fine." She hesitates and looks up at me. "I wish you were the one I'd fallen for all those years ago. I went for the bad boy, and it was a mistake. You're a good guy. I envy the woman you end up with."

Embarrassed, I study the carpet. "Thanks."

"Is there anyone at the moment?"

I chew my bottom lip. "Maybe."

"I'm glad. She's a lucky girl."

I sigh and open the door. "Take care of yourself."

"Thanks, Kip."

I walk down the path, and she closes the door behind me.

I head back to the car, get in, then sit there for a moment. I'm going to have to go and see Craig, wherever he is, but I don't think I can stomach that tonight. I check my watch. It's getting close to six. I think I'll go home, make some dinner, pour myself a whisky, and wait for

Alice to message me. I could do with a little trip to Wonderland tonight.

# Chapter Eleven

## *Alice*

The journey home to Gisborne is a long one. Luckily it's a nice day, and the roads are relatively clear. We chat for most of it, and also sing to music, but the couple of stops we take and a few bouts of roadworks mean it's nearly seven by the time I pull onto the drive and turn off the engine, and we're both knackered.

"Thank fuck," Charlie says. Then she turns to me and gives me a big hug. "Thank you so much for coming to get me."

"Oh, you're welcome. Anytime." I hug her back. "Come on, let's go and see Mum."

We get our bags out of the car and head down the path to the front door.

This is our family home—a moderately sized, four-bedroomed house in a quiet cul-de-sac. Luckily, the insurance money we received after Dad died paid off the mortgage. I don't know how we'd have coped if we'd had to find that money each month.

The surrounding lawns are neat—my uncle must have mown them while we were away—and the roses I planted around the front porch are blooming and smell gorgeous as we pass. I hung a homemade Christmas wreath on the door before I left, and the tinsel glitters in the evening sunshine.

We go inside, and I call, "We're home," as we walk in.

"In here," Mum calls, and we go into the living room. I smile to see Mum sitting in her chair, hair braided, makeup on, brimming with excitement to see the two of us home at last.

"Girls!" she squeals, and she holds up her arms, and we run over to her and give her a huge hug.

"Aw," June says, "you soppy bunch."

I laugh and break free to give her a hug, too. Like Mum, me, and Charlie, June has blonde, slightly fluffy hair, although she wears hers in a practical, tight bun at the nape of her neck. We also all have the same dark-blue eyes.

"It's wonderful to have you home," Mum says tearfully to Charlie. "I've missed you so much."

The two of us sit on the sofa, while June perches on the arm of Mum's chair. Before I left, I put up the tree, and Mum and I dressed it with tinsel and all the decorations we've collected over the years. It's always an emotional time for us because Dad loved Christmas, but I'm glad I did it now for Charlie's sake.

"Yeah," I say with mock-sarcasm, "because Charlie never calls." My sister rings her on FaceTime nearly every day.

"It's not the same," Mum protests.

Charlie smiles, flopping back with a sigh. "It's great to be home for a few weeks now."

"How about you?" June asks me. "Did you have a nice few nights away?"

"I did, thank you."

"Something you want to tell us?" Mum asks mischievously.

I glance from her to June, who's grinning, then look at Charlie. She raises her eyebrows and says, "I haven't said anything."

Mum looks away, toward the dining room table, and I follow her gaze. Sitting on the surface is a bouquet of flowers.

Slowly, I get to my feet and go over to the table. The bouquet is wrapped in cellophane and tied with a big red bow. I count the flowers inside—it contains two dozen crimson roses.

Charlie appears beside me, and says, "Ohhh…"

I remove the envelope that's stapled to the cellophane, open it, and retrieve the card inside. It says, "Thanks for a great evening. You left me smiling like the Cheshire Cat. Kip x." It ends with a red heart.

"Cheshire Cat?" Charlie says. "Oh shit. He knows who you are."

"What does it say?" Mum asks.

Charlie reads out the card, while I stare at the flowers and cover my mouth with a hand.

Did he know all along? Or did he just Google me when I left, the same way I did him?

"Who is he?" June asks.

I lift the bouquet, open the cellophane at the top, and sniff inside. Oh, they smell amazing. I turn to face them, still holding the bouquet. "His name's Kip Chevalier. I met him online, and it was his birthday yesterday. We went for dinner with his brother and his girlfriend."

"How old is he?" Mum asks.

"Twenty-nine. He's a computer engineer." I glance at Charlie. I don't want her to tell them that his family's rich. She just gives a small smile.

"What's he like?" June wants to know.

I hesitate and glance at Charlie. She grins. "He's absolutely gorgeous, and really into Alice."

"Charlie!"

"He is! You should have seen the way he kissed her goodbye this morning."

"This morning?" Mum asks. Her eyes widen. "Did you spend the night together?"

"Oh God…"

Mum and June both squeak, and Charlie giggles.

"Oh Alice," Mum says, "tell me everything!"

"Absolutely not," I reply, and they all laugh.

"I live vicariously through you two," Mum scolds. "So I need all the deets."

"I'll tell you," Charlie says with a wink. "Alice has to go and message him, don't you, Alice?"

I glare at them all. She's right though. I promised I'd message him, and I definitely need to now he's sent me flowers. "All right," I say. I throw Charlie a warning glare as I get up. "Don't give away all my secrets."

"Absolutely, I will," she says. "All the gory details."

I poke my tongue out at her and, gesturing at June with my head, go outside to the garden, carrying the flowers.

June follows. I put the flowers on the table outside, and we stand on the deck. The sun is going down, and it's warm and sultry. Bees are meandering through the flowerbeds, and at the bottom of the lawn, a couple of rabbits are having an evening silflay.

"Thanks for looking after her the past few days," I say. "I really appreciate it."

"Of course, no problem at all."

"How is she?"

She tips her head from side to side. "She's had problems with her left eye."

"She mentioned that before I left. Has it gotten worse?"

"A little, I think. But she's been in good spirits."

"That might be something to do with the margarita."

"She did enjoy it though."

I smile. "Then it was worth it."

"I'm glad you appear to have had a good time." Her eyes twinkle.

I glance at the house. "I wasn't going to tell Mum. I don't want her to think she's holding me back."

"She thinks that anyway, sweetie."

"Yeah, but it's going to be worse if she thinks I've met someone."

"Have you? Met someone?"

I hesitate. "No. It was just a… fling, I guess."

"But you're about to text him?"

"He asked me to let him know I got home safely, that's all."

"Right."

I give her a wry look. "He's a nice guy. But I live nine hours away."

Her smile fades. "Yeah, I know. I'm so sorry. I should do more…"

"Oh God, June, no, don't say that. Christ, you have a full-time job, and a husband and four teenagers at home. You already do more than enough. This is why I didn't want to say anything. I'm not looking for things to change. I'm happy with the way things are. I just wanted…" My brain fills in the blanks. A gorgeous guy to go down on me. Who'd take my virginity in a manly fashion while also being kind and gentle. Who'd then fuck the living daylights out of me. "A bit of fun," I choose lamely.

"You deserve so much more," she says, holding my upper arms and looking into my eyes. "You've looked after Penny since you were a teenager and never asked anything in return."

"She's my mum," I whisper, suddenly emotional at her outburst. "I lost my dad. I don't want to lose her as well."

She rubs my arms. "Yeah, I know." She clears her throat. "Well, go on, you message your young man. I'm going to go and quiz Charlie all about him."

I roll my eyes, and she laughs and goes inside.

I turn one of the outdoor chairs to face the setting sun and sit. I open my call record, add Kip's number to my contacts, then message him.

Me: *Hey, it's me. You asked me to let you know when I got home. Well, I'm here! A long day, but finally done.*

He comes back immediately.

Kip: *Oh, I'm so glad. I've been wondering how you were doing. I'm guessing there are closures on State Highway 2?*

Me: *Yeah, we had to go the long way around.*

Kip: *Well, it's good that you made it. How's your mum?*

Me: *She's good, thank you. Charlie's currently revealing all my secrets to her.*

Kip: *I thought my ears were burning.*

Me: *I doubt she's talking about your ears, LOL.*

Kip: *LMAO!*

Me: *She always enjoys spending time with her sister. The two of them are quite naughty. She's not supposed to drink, and they made margaritas.*

Kip: *She sounds as spirited as her daughter :-)*

Me: *Maybe! Kip, I just wanted to say thank you so much for a wonderful evening. And thank you so much for the flowers.*

Kip: *Oh… I wasn't sure whether you'd be mad at me.*

Me: *For sending me such gorgeous flowers? Hardly!*

Kip: *Well, more for tracking down your home address. I don't want you to think I'm stalking you.*

Me: *I'm guessing by the Cheshire Cat reference that you've worked out who I am, too.*

Kip: *I'm afraid so. I knew I recognized your voice. I listen to your podcast every week!*

Me: *Oh! Really?*

Kip: *I wish you'd told me while we were together. I'd love to have asked you about it. I've never had sex with a famous person before.*

That makes me laugh.

Me: *I'm not famous! Well not much!*

Kip: *Seriously though, I'm so impressed. You're amazing.*

Me: *Well, right back atcha, boy. I Googled you, too.*

Kip: *Ah.*

Me: *Yeah, Mr. Innovative-Computer-Engineer-with-a-Master's-Degree-in-Software Development. That's a pretty impressive bio. Not as impressive as your Tinder one, obviously…*

Kip: *It doesn't mention the 27% rogue, anyway.*

Me: *No, LOL. Hey, I wanted to say, I'm so sorry to hear about the death of your cousin.*

Kip: *Thank you.*

Me: *I'm so sorry, I feel as if I'm intruding, but Charlie Googled you on the way home, and she read it out, and I just felt so awful for you.*

Kip: *You're not intruding, and I'm touched you mentioned it. That's who my tattoo is for.*

Me: *Oh, really?*

It makes sense now. The cross—for Christian, and the infinity sign, a symbol of togetherness and eternity.

Kip: *I miss him a lot. He was a good lad.*

I don't know if I'm imagining it, but he seems kind of sad today, and not just because he's talking about his cousin.

Me: *Are you okay? I'm probably completely wrong, but you seem a bit melancholic.*

Kip: *Sorry. I miss you. And I've had a shit afternoon.*

I try to ignore the first bit and concentrate on the 'shit afternoon'.

Me: *Why so?*

Kip: *I went to see that colleague I told you about.*

Me: *You went to his house?*

Kip: *Yeah. He wasn't there. Turns out he's walked out on his wife. She has a four-month old baby. Fucking bastard.*

The curse surprises me. He swore during sex a few times, but this sounds positively vitriolic. He's upset.

I study my phone, fighting with myself. I promised I'd cut myself off from him when I came home. It was tough to leave Wellington knowing I'd never see him again, and I was convinced that keeping in touch with him would only draw out the disappointment of losing him.

But he sent me flowers. He asked how my mum was. He's upset. And I miss him.

Me: *Would you like to talk? Properly, I mean? It's okay if you'd rather not.*

I wait a few seconds for him to message. Then my phone starts ringing. Smiling, I answer it. "Hello?"

"Hey, Alice."

A shiver runs all the way down my back at the sound of his voice. "Hey, you. How are you doing?"

"Ah, I'm okay." He sounds tired.

"Where are you, at work?"

"No, at home. I'm on my second whisky, rather a large one, I have to say. It tends to loosen my tongue, so I apologize in advance if I say anything untoward. I wasn't expecting to talk to you."

I smile. "I'm glad you're at home. Where do you live?"

"Out in Brooklyn."

"Is it a mansion?"

He chuckles. "Not quite."

I toy with the ribbon on the flowers. "Kip, I want you to know that I'm not talking to you now because I know you have money."

"Well, if my fortune can't talk you into seeing me again, there's no hope for me."

I frown. "I'm serious. My situation hasn't changed. But…" I hesitate. I don't know how to tell him that I'm sad I can't see him again without giving him mixed messages.

"I miss you," he says.

I look at the flowers on the table, my lips curving up. "I miss you, too. So what happened today?"

"I've been trying to call Craig but it just goes to voicemail, so I went around his house. His wife, Chloe, was there, with their four-month-old baby. She told me he left her two weeks ago for another woman."

I close my eyes for a moment. I can only imagine how that must have shocked him. "Ah, jeez. That sucks."

"I didn't know what to say to her. He's my best mate. I've known him since university. He's a member of our senior leadership team at the company. He's a smart guy, the smartest I know, after Saxon and Damon. I've always admired him, looked up to him. And he treats his wife like this. They've been together since his last year at uni, so I've known her just as long. I'm just… speechless."

"I'm so sorry. Was she terribly upset?"

"She cried."

"Aw."

"She said he'd been seeing this other woman since Christmas. The same time they were trying to get pregnant."

"Oh, Kip." His voice holds indignance and disbelief. He's shocked that his friend would treat his wife like this. Actually, I think he's shocked that any guy would treat any girl like this. Oh my God, that just melts my heart.

He huffs a sigh. "I'm sorry, I'm mad, and I don't get mad often."

"Does she know the woman he's left her for?"

"Yeah. That's part of the problem. I told you I was working on a communication device?"

"Yes, like the one Stephen Hawking used?"

"Yeah. I know this sounds arrogant, but the software is miles better than anything on the market at the moment. It's called MOTHER."

"Like in Alien?"

"Yeah," he says softly, and I think he's smiling. "I've been working with my cousin, who runs an AI company."

"Titus, right? Charlie had read about him."

"Yeah, that's right. The predictive text component is especially advanced, and it's going to make a real difference for people with speech difficulties. In November, we discussed which company we wanted to employ to make the speech synthesizer. Saxon and I wanted one company, and Craig was super-enthusiastic about another. In the end, I went with the company I liked. Then we discovered that he'd talked to a reporter and told them we'd sold to the company he recommended, Sunrise."

"Shit, really?"

"I confronted him. He said Sunrise had offered double what Genica, the company I wanted, had offered. When I said it didn't matter, that I wasn't going to let him bully me into it, he hit the roof. And then his wife told me the woman he's has been having an affair with is Sunrise's CEO."

"Oh wow, so he's mad because you didn't sell to his girlfriend? How unprofessional is that?"

"My thoughts exactly."

"Have you spoken to him about it?"

"No. I was too tired tonight. I'll go tomorrow. I'm sorry, this must be very dull for you."

"Kip, come on. We're friends now, right? I'm glad you're talking to me about it. I can tell how upset you are."

He sighs. "Yeah."

"Are you more upset about the professional or personal side of it?"

He's quiet for a moment. "The personal. I just felt so sorry for Chloe. She's a lovely girl. She said it was partly her fault because she's not been attentive enough to him. That made me see red."

"Why?"

"She's just had a baby! What kind of man has an affair when his wife is struggling to recover physically and emotionally from the birth of their first child? Actually, what kind of man has an affair? I don't get it. Relationships end. People break up. I get that. But there's no excuse for cheating." He gives a frustrated sigh.

Smiling, I pull one of the roses out of the cellophane and sniff it, loving its sweet scent. This guy… I'm glad he's had a few whiskies. It's like he's opened up his heart and I'm peering inside.

"Chloe said something odd," he says.

"Oh?"

"She said Craig was jealous of my relationship with my brothers, Saxon especially, and that he always felt it was us three against him. I can kind of understand that, although I've always tried to include him in all decisions. But Chloe also said that it was one reason my ex left."

My eyebrows rise. "Seriously?"

"Yeah. That shocked me, actually. Apparently she told Chloe she thought she'd never mean as much to me as Saxon."

"You're twins," I say, amused. "You're going to have a special connection. Anyone who doesn't accept that is going to have a problem."

"You think?"

"Of course. There do seem to be some women nowadays who expect to be the priority in every area of their partner's life, but I don't personally believe one person can be everything to another. I think friends and family all bring something different into our lives. After saying that, obviously, I would imagine it's best if you don't confide in someone else to the extent that you keep secrets from your partner, but I can't imagine you doing that. Anyway, what do I know? I'm hardly an expert with all my zero years of relationship experience."

"You may have zero experience, but you make more sense than most other people."

"Well, thank you for that."

"Do you think I'm stern?"

I smile. "Stern? No. Why?"

"I told Chloe that my ex said I make her nervous, as if I'm going to tell her off. And Chloe said 'yeah, you can be quite stern.'"

"I wouldn't say that. Bossy, maybe. When Charlie read out your Wikipedia page, she asked if you were a saint. I thought about how you told me off for wriggling and said definitely not."

That makes him laugh. "So I don't make you nervous?"

"Only in a tummy-rumble kind of way."

We're quiet for a moment. I think he's smiling, the same way I am.

"I'm glad you said we're friends," he says.

I turn the rose in my fingers. "I didn't say no to seeing you again because I don't want to."

"I know. I understand."

"The distance is such a big obstacle, Kip. I don't want to string you along with promises I can't possibly fulfill. And if you're eventually going to meet someone else, I'd rather it didn't be after I've fallen for you, you know?"

He's silent for a moment. Then he says, "I wouldn't say obstacle."

"What?"

"The distance. It's more of a hurdle."

"A hurdle is an obstacle."

"Meh. Obstacles are huge and insurmountable, like walls and buildings. You can jump over hurdles. And I don't think my Wikipedia page mentions that I broke the record at high school for the four-hundred-meter hurdles."

My lips curve up. "You did not."

"Absolutely I did. Ask Saxon."

"I might just do that."

"He might deny it, actually, because I was always better than him at athletics. Ask Damon instead. He'll tell the truth."

"You're tipsy, aren't you?"

"I'm mellow."

"Has the whisky made you feel better?"

"You've made me feel better, Alice. Thank you for talking to me."

"Least I can do after the three orgasms you gave me."

He laughs. "I'm guessing you're on your own."

"Yeah, I'm out in the garden. With your flowers. They're so beautiful. You didn't have to do that."

"Least I could do after the orgasms you gave me."

I smile and blush. I did make him come. Several times. It gives me a warm feeling in my tummy.

I don't know what he meant about the distance between us being a hurdle rather than an obstacle. It's not just the distance. I look after my mum, and that's not going to change anytime soon. Maybe he's thinking of suggesting getting someone in to care for her, but she wouldn't want that. She's a very private person, and I know she'd feel terribly embarrassed about having a stranger do some of the intimate things I have to do for her.

I don't want to lead him on. But I like him so much.

On the other end of the line, I hear footsteps on tiles, the scrape of metal, then the squeak of furniture.

"What are you doing?" I ask.

"I opened the sliding doors so I could smell the jasmine," he says. "It reminds me of your perfume."

"Aw."

"Now I'm lying on the sofa. What's it like in your garden?"

"It's a lovely evening here. I'm sitting in front of the spare room that I use as my studio."

"I saw you're running a Kickstarter campaign."

"Yes," I reply, flattered that he's tried to find out about me. "It met the total I set last week. I'm so thrilled. I'm going to have the studio redecorated and get some new equipment."

"Who are you interviewing next?"

"Tomorrow I'm talking to Abby Richardson—she wrote *Life on Mars?*"

"That's sci-fi, right?"

"Yeah."

"What kind?"

My lips curve up. "You're a bad boy."

"I'm just asking."

"It's *haaaard*," I say in a breathy voice, and he laughs.

"I'm hoping *Neuromancer* will turn up before Christmas so I can get stuck in," he adds. "I'm thinking maybe we should come up with a list that I can work through. What would be on your list of top twenty sci-fi novels?"

I stretch out my legs in the warm evening sun, and smile as I begin the discussion of our favorite books.

# Chapter Twelve

## *Kip*

It's Friday the twenty-third of December, and the last day we're officially open at Kingpinz for several weeks. The girls in the office have put up a Christmas tree a few weeks ago, and they've decorated their desks with tinsel and other festive ornaments. The guys haven't bothered, as usual, and mostly complain about all the fuss while secretly enjoying the atmosphere. All morning the secretaries have been organizing our Christmas party. There's going to be a Secret Santa, and the caterers we've hired are just finishing setting up the food and drink in the boardroom.

I'm at my desk, signing some letters that Marion's left me, when there's a knock at my door, and Saxon walks in. My eyebrows rise. He's wearing a pair of antlers and a big round nose that's flashing red.

"Guess which reindeer I am," he says.

I lean back and lift my glasses onto my hair. "Wanker?"

He laughs, takes off the nose, and sits in front of my desk. "Just trying to get in the mood."

"What's up?"

"I wondered if you'd caught up with Craig?"

"Not yet. I'll pop out later." I saw Saxon and Damon earlier and revealed what Chloe had told me.

"I still can't believe he's having an affair with Renée Garnier," Saxon says.

"Yeah. It's incredibly unprofessional when you think we were considering Sunrise Ltd. for production."

"I meant more that she's only, like, two foot tall. And she does that weird thing with her hair. And her eyes are too close together. Chloe's a cracker. Why would you go out for a burger when you've got steak at home? I guess she must do great things to his dick."

"That's exactly what I said to Alice last night. Well, I didn't mention burgers and steak, or dicks, but, yeah, it had the same sentiment."

He grins. "You spoke to Alice? You didn't mention that."

"We talked for over an hour."

"Aw. Are you seeing her again?"

I shrug. Then I meet his eyes and smile. He smiles back. "Didn't think you'd let a little thing like that put you off," he says.

"That's what Marion said, funnily enough."

Looking at the red nose in his hand, he turns it over a few times. I wait, sensing he's about to say something. Eventually, he looks up.

"I'm going to ask Catie to marry me."

My eyebrows shoot up. I grin, and his lips curve up.

"Took your time," I say, thrilled for him.

"I've been thinking about where to do it. I know it's supposed to be romantic to, you know, take the girl to Paris and propose by the Eiffel Tower or something, but Catie would faint if I took her anywhere near a long-haul flight. She won't want a fanfare. But I thought it might be nice to do it on Christmas Eve, in front of Mum and Dad. Make her feel like part of the family, you know?"

I nod. Catie's parents are both dead, and she was brought up by her stepmother, who was apparently a right piece of work and made her life a complete misery. Our parents have already taken to her, and they're keen to look after her and include her.

"It's a great idea," I tell him.

He smiles. "Okay."

"Do you think she'll say yes?"

"Jesus, don't say that. I hadn't even thought about the fact that she might say no."

I give a short laugh. "She's not going to say no. She's crazy about you." I lean forward on the table and straighten some papers on my desk. "There's something I didn't tell you in front of Damon."

"Oh?"

"Chloe said that Craig felt it was him against the three of us, and that he was jealous, especially of our relationship." I gesture to the two of us.

He stares at me for a moment. Then he rubs the first two fingers of his left hand against his thumb. "That's me playing the world's smallest violin. Fucking jealous… Boo-fucking-hoo. We're twins. We're close. What did he expect?"

"Chloe said it was also one reason Lesley left."

That makes him pause. "Seriously?"

I shrug.

He studies me, thinking about it. "Are you saying you want to break up with me?"

That makes me laugh. "I dunno. It shocked me, I guess. She never mentioned it to me. But it made me think. Maybe we make others feel excluded at times. Perhaps it's something we ought to think about."

A frown flickers on his brow.

At that moment, there's a knock at the door, and then Damon appears. He's wearing a headband with a piece of wire that supports a golden halo. It sits at an angle, as if it's slipped.

"Wondered where you both were," he says, coming in. "I'm supposed to tell you they're going to do Secret Santa soon."

I gesture at his halo. "Really?"

"I'm a fallen angel." He sits beside Saxon. The three of us are alike in many ways, different in others. We look very similar. Damon's a younger, beefier version of Saxon and me—not so many lines at the corner of his eyes, a bit more energy, an inch taller, a tad heavier. But whereas Saxon and I are fairly similar in character, Damon is more irreverent, some would say cocky, impatient, easily bored, and yet brilliant for all that, both in his work and his painting. When he settles down, he's going to be truly exceptional.

"Why are angels difficult to understand?" I ask. When Damon shrugs, I say, "Because they're obtuse."

He frowns. "I don't get it."

"He means angles," Saxon explains.

"Oh yeah," I say, "sorry."

Damon snorts. "Fucking double act."

I chuckle, then sit back and study him. "Can I ask you a question?"

"Fire away."

"Do we ever make you feel excluded?"

"What?" He looks from me to Saxon, who just lifts his eyebrows. Damon looks back at me. "What's this about?"

"Chloe told him that Craig feels it's us three against him," Saxon says, "and that he's jealous of our relationship." He gestures from himself to me.

"She said it's one reason why Lesley left," I add.

Damon's smile fades. "Seriously?"

I shrug. "Do we? Make you feel excluded?"

He gives a short laugh. "No."

"Really?"

"No. I mean, you're close, but then you're twins. You've never made me feel like you were shutting me out, even when we were kids. You've always made me feel included. Always been there for me. You're great brothers."

Saxon looks from him to me and smiles.

"Most women misunderstand the way men think," Damon continues. "They assume we're the same as them, constantly analyzing the relationship. They don't get that when we're quiet, we're not thinking deep, meaningful stuff—we're usually thinking about sport or sex."

"Or food," Saxon adds.

"Or food," Damon agrees. "Lesley probably mistook your reticence for secrecy and thought you were hiding things from her, and assumed you shared those secrets with someone else. And Craig said he's jealous? What a cunt."

Saxon and I both laugh.

"Are we done?" Damon asks. "Are we going to braid each other's hair now?

"Go on," I say good-naturedly, "fuck off."

He gets to his feet and walks out. We hear him say, "Marion, I'm standing under the mistletoe, and I want to kiss someone."

"Damon Chevalier, I'm old enough to be your mother," she scolds. "Find someone your own age."

"You know you're my only girl. Come here."

She squeals, then laughs, so I know he's managed to sneak a kiss from her.

"I'm glad she knows him," Saxon says. "He's a walking lawsuit." We both grin. "Feel better?" he asks.

"Yeah."

"All right. Message your girl. Tell her you miss her." He gets to his feet. "And let me know what happens with Craig."

"Will do. Hey, hold on a sec. Put your nose on."

He reapplies the flashing nose. "Is this for Alice?"

"Yeah." He poses, and I take the shot. "Thanks."

"Anytime." He heads out, and I hear Marion exclaim, "Oh goodness! You're as bad as your brother," so I know he's snuck a kiss beneath the mistletoe with her as well.

Smiling, I pull up Snapchat—we friended each other on the app last night—and send the photo to Alice with the message, *Just an ordinary day at the office.*

She comes back: *That's Saxon, right?*

Me: *Yeah, how did you know?*

Alice: *You're better looking.*

I laugh.

Me: *We're identical.*

Alice: *Nah. You have naughtier eyebrows.*

I smile. She never fails to warm me all the way through.

A photo of her appears, and my heart gives a noticeable bump. She's taken a selfie at her recording desk. Her hair is up, rather scruffy, with strands tumbling around her face. She looks fresh-faced and beautiful.

Me: *Aw. You're so gorgeous.*

Alice: *You're crazy. I'm not wearing any makeup and my hair's a mess.*

Me: *You still look amazing. What time's your interview?*

Alice: *At midday. I'm just running through everything, making sure I've got my questions ready etc.*

Me: *I hope it goes well. I look forward to listening to it.*

Alice: *I'll include a message for you.*

Me: *LOL, okay. What'll it be?*

Alice: *You'll know it when you hear it :-) It should be up by the end of the day.*

Me: *All right. I'm off to do Secret Santa.*

Alice: *Have fun! Are you going to see Craig today?*

Me: *Yeah after work probably.*

Alice: *Good luck. Let me know how it goes.*

Me: *Will do. Catch you later.*

She sends me another photo of her blowing me a kiss.

Smiling, I slide my phone into my pocket and, hearing music start up in the main office, head off to the party.

\*

A few hours later, I slip out of the building and walk to my car.

The party will continue for a few hours yet, but I'm not in the mood for festivities. Saxon has already left anyway, keen to return to his girl. We've left Damon there being the life and soul of the party. Hopefully he'll stay sober enough to steer clear of the young secretaries who are all fluttering their eyelashes at him.

I haven't drunk any alcohol, so I get in my Merc and head out to Oriental Bay, where Renée Garnier apparently lives, and where I'm assuming Craig is now staying. I'm not sure what I'm going to say to him yet. I just know that I need to talk to him.

It takes me about fifteen minutes to get there. While I drive, I play one of Alice's podcasts. She's interviewing a Kiwi author of a series of fantasy novels, an older guy, and it's a great interview, with him chuckling constantly as she teases him and makes him laugh. I listen to her husky voice and imagine her singing that Joss Stone song to me in bed, whispering in my ear, pressed up against me. I want to see her again. I want to touch her, to make love to her, and listen to her sighs as she comes.

I refuse to accept it's over. My parents brought me up to respect women, and I know they'd say I should come to terms with the fact that Alice doesn't want to see me again, but I don't truly believe that's what she wants. She just can't see an answer to her problem, and I'm great at problem solving.

I have more pressing things to think about than my love life right now, though, and I try to focus on Craig as I follow the GPS instructions to Renée's house in a quieter part of the suburb, perched high on the side of one of the hills surrounding the city. It's a big place, bigger than Craig's. She doesn't have children, and she's a CEO, so she obviously has money.

I park outside, get out of the car, walk up the long flight of stairs to the front door, and ring the bell. About ten seconds later, the door opens.

It's Renée, and her eyebrows rise as she sees me. I try not to think about Saxon's description of her, but he was right—she is very short, she does have odd hair, and her eyes are too close together.

She looks at my glasses and says, "Kip?"

I nod. "Hi, Renée. I'm sorry to bother you at home, but I was wondering whether Craig was here."

She hesitates, then gives a slow nod. "He is. But I'm not sure he'll see you."

Impatience flares inside me. "What is he, twelve? Not answering my phone calls. Calling in sick. Tell him to grow up and come and talk to me, please."

Her eyes flash—she doesn't like being challenged. "Wait here," she snaps, and, leaving the door open, she walks down the hallway and disappears.

I listen and hear voices, slowly rising before dropping sharply as if one of them has warned the other to be quiet. I slide my hands into my pockets, wishing I was anywhere else but here. The sooner this is over, the better.

After about thirty seconds, she returns to the door. "Come in," she says grudgingly. "And take off your shoes."

I'm tempted to walk in with them on just to piss her off, but my mother would say you should always respect the rules in other people's houses, so I toe off my shoes, leave them by the door, and follow her along the hallway and into the living room.

Clearly, Renée's into minimalism. I thought I was too, but not like this. There's hardly any furniture, and it resembles a show home, spotless and far from cozy, with modern art on the walls, lots of mirrors and chrome, and a black leather suite that looks hard and uncomfortable. It's a stark contrast to Craig's own house, which has a comfy suite you can sink into, books and magazines on the tables, baby toys everywhere, and in a few years will have finger paintings on the fridge and a carpet scattered with LEGO.

Craig is standing in front of the fireplace, hands in his pockets, stiff and unsmiling. I walk in and stop a few feet in front of him.

"Can you give us a minute, please?" I ask Renée.

"This is my house," she states, sinking into an armchair.

I look back at Craig. "Can we talk alone?"

He glances at her, then back at me. "Anything you want to say, you can say in front of Renée."

"Fine." I only said it as a courtesy to him. I don't care whether she's there or not.

"How did you find me?" he asks.

"I contacted the FBI. They've had helicopters scouting the whole of Wellington the past few days."

He glares at me. "No need to be sarcastic."

"Chloe told me you'd moved in with Renée."

"You've spoken to her?"

"I went to your house."

He studies the carpet for a moment. "Is she okay?"

I feel sick to my stomach. "No, she's not okay, you fucking idiot. She's having to travel to the other side of the world with a four-month-old baby on her own."

"She doesn't have to go," Renée says.

I look at him, not her. "Maybe she felt the need to see her parents, to have some support after her husband walked out on her, you know?"

He lifts his gaze back to me. "It's easy to pass judgment when you don't know the whole story."

"No, I don't, because you haven't told me. I thought we were friends. I thought you'd talk to me if you were considering something as serious as walking out of your marriage."

"And have you lecture him about duty and responsibility?" Renée snorts. "Mr. Self-Righteous."

"Renée," he snaps.

"Oh, grow a pair," she tells him. "Stand up for yourself."

He meets my eyes and then drops his gaze again. And it's then that I understand.

"This is your doing," I say softly, looking at Renée. "What did you do, tell him you wouldn't see him unless he delivered MOTHER to you?"

I can see from the look on her face that I've guessed right.

"And now you've failed," I tell Craig. "And you've walked out on your wife. I don't think she's going to take you back. You've burned your bridges there."

"He doesn't want to go back," Renée says. "Why would he want to live with that fat, grumpy old bitch?"

I look at him in surprise, waiting for him to tell her to mind her mouth, but he stays looking at the floor, sullen and unresponsive.

"Oh, I see," I say softly. "Saxon was right. This is about her doing great things to your dick. Don't tell me you enjoy being humiliated. You didn't need to leave the office for that."

"Don't mock him," she says, getting up and coming to stand in front of me.

I look down at her. "And don't talk to me like I'm one of your subs. What you do in the privacy of your own home is your business, and so is his marriage. But you bring it into the office, it makes it my business.

Did you target him on purpose? Because you wanted the software for yourself?"

She shrugs. "I was willing to pay a small fortune for the software. Still am."

Disgusted, I look back at Craig.

She grabs my arm. "Don't you turn away from me."

I look at her hand where she's holding my arm. Then I lift my gaze to hers. She glares at me, refusing to back down, eyes blazing. I wait. Eventually, after about twenty seconds, she slowly lowers her hand and drops her eyes.

Lips curving up a little, I turn away from her, back to Craig.

Now that I understand what's going on here, I think I have an insight into his problems with Chloe. Craig obviously enjoys being dominated, and Chloe is too quiet and gentle to take on that role, which was probably why he was so cruel to her when he left.

"I don't care what you do in your private life," I tell him. "It takes two to tango, and I'm sure there are reasons why your marriage with Chloe hasn't worked out. But cheating on her when she's pregnant, and when she's just had a baby, is deplorable. I don't think you need me to tell you that, though. I think you know that already. You're obviously under the sway of this woman, and… whatever. I don't give a fuck. But promising her that we'd sell MOTHER to her… I can't overlook that. I want your resignation in my inbox tonight. No lawyer is going to find in your favor once all this comes out."

He inhales, looking genuinely shocked.

"If you resign, I'll give you a decent reference," I tell him. "But if you don't, I'll fire you, and I'll tell everyone I know just what a piece of weak shit you are."

"You won't," Renée screams, "you can't do this, he's done nothing wrong, how dare you—"

"Renée," he snaps. "Enough."

"Topping from the bottom?" I tell him. "She'll punish you for that tonight. But maybe you'll enjoy that." He flushes. I meet his eyes. "I wish it hadn't come to this. We've known each other a long time."

"Yeah," he says. "And back when we met, we were equals. But you put yourself on a fucking pedestal and then wonder why we try and knock you off it." His chest heaves.

I turn. Without looking at Renée again, I walk out, put my shoes on, and leave, closing the door behind me.

\*

A few hours later, I'm at home, in a tee and track pants, on FaceTime with Saxon and Damon, a glass of whisky in my hand.

"Jesus," Saxon says. "She's a dominatrix?"

"Well, I couldn't see any whips or paddles, but yeah, I'm pretty sure that's what's going on there."

"I didn't think he'd be into S&M," Damon says.

"I've always thought their cotton-rich socks are the best on the market," Saxon replies.

"That's M&S, idiot," Damon tells him.

I give a short, tired laugh. They're trying to cheer me up. It works, partly.

"I'm sorry," Saxon says. He's in his living room, and he looks over his shoulder as Catie walks up behind him and passes him a mug, probably of coffee. "Thanks, hun," he says.

She bends and waves at the camera. "Hey guys."

"Hey," I say, smiling. She's such a lovely girl, fragile and damaged, but positively glowing now she's with Saxon. She makes me think of Kintsugi—the ancient Japanese art of repairing broken ceramics with gold to make them stronger and more beautiful. He's healing her, helping her accept her past, and she's becoming more beautiful and precious than before she was broken.

She wanders off, and he watches her go, then looks back at the screen. "Sorry. Where were we?"

"Don't worry about it," I say softly. "Go and be with your girl."

"Are you okay?" he asks.

"Yeah. I'm going to listen to Alice's podcast in a minute." I told both of them about her secret occupation not long after I found out.

"All right. You know where I am if you need anything." He waves, then signs off.

Damon's also at home, sitting out on his deck, by the look of it. "Do you think he'll resign?"

"I don't know. She might talk him out of it."

"I don't get why guys like to be dominated," he says. "I mean, each to their own in the bedroom, sure. But I don't understand it."

"Nah, me neither. She didn't like me standing up to her, that's for sure."

"You're lucky she didn't pounce on you and tie you up with a ball gag."

"Jesus. That's an image that's going to stay with me." I shudder at the thought. I did not find Renée attractive in the slightest.

He laughs. "Who's Alice interviewing tonight?"

"An author called Abby Richardson."

"She wrote *Life on Mars*, right? I've read that."

"Yeah. Should be good."

"You going to call her afterward?"

"Maybe."

He nods. "I'm sorry about Craig."

I sigh. "Yeah. Me too."

"It sucks, especially right before Christmas."

"I know. Do you think I did the right thing?"

"Asking for his resignation? Fuck yeah. He couldn't continue to work here after that. But I am sorry. I know you've known him for a long time." He pauses. "Make sure you call Alice after the podcast."

I smile. "Yeah, all right. Have a great weekend. I'll see you tomorrow at Mum and Dad's, right?"

"Yep. See you." He ends the call.

I sit there for a while, sipping my whisky. The sliding doors are open, and I can hear birdsong from the trees beside the house. The sun hasn't set yet, but it's growing dark in the house. I should get up and put the lights on, but I can't be arsed.

I slide down on the sofa, resting the glass on my chest, and think about the night Alice took me up to her room, and about her soft, warm body pressed up against mine. I want to see her again. I want to hear her husky voice and have her mouth on mine.

But all I have is her podcast, so I sigh and pull it up on my phone, then start it playing while I inhale the jasmine and pretend it's her perfume I can smell.

# Chapter Thirteen

## *Alice*

Kip finally messages me just after eight p.m. *Just finished the podcast,* he says.

I'm in the living room, watching a movie with Mum and Charlie, curled up in one of the armchairs. Smiling, I text him back. *What did you think?*

Kip: *Loved it. Thought you really brought her out of herself. She seemed very shy.*

Me: *She was. Nobody remains shy with me for long though!*

Kip: *You're a very easy person to be with.*

Me: *Sorry did you just call me easy?*

Kip: *LOL no!*

Me: *I did sleep with you the first day I met you.*

Kip: *You were also a virgin. I'd hardly call that easy.*

Me: *Good point.*

"Are you texting Kip?" Charlie asks.

I put my phone down, blushing. "No."

"You are," Mum says. "You're smiling."

"I smile all the time."

"It's your bashful smile," Charlie says. "That's how you looked at him that morning after he kissed you."

Mum smiles. I know Charlie told her that Kip and I spent the night together. Mum hasn't mentioned it to me yet. I think she's aware I don't want that conversation—not because I'm embarrassed, but because I know she's going to tell me it's time I lived my own life, and I don't want to argue with her.

"He's just listened to the podcast," I reply, "that's all. I'm paying attention to the movie."

"It wasn't a complaint," Charlie says. "I think it's lovely. He seems really keen on you."

I study my phone. He's waiting for a reply. What am I doing? Every time I message him, I'm stringing him along. And every second that goes by, I'm falling for him more.

Then I think: Alice, it's just a text. I have to chill out more. He's a big boy, able to make his own decisions. I've made it quite clear that I can't have a relationship. All we're doing is staying friends. There's no harm in that, surely?

Kip messages that he caught the reference I made to him in the podcast. In Abby's book, her main character has to deal with a pair of young twin boys who manage to sabotage the generator on her Martian world when they pretend to swap places. I commented that it must be a nightmare having twins when you can't tell one from the other, and that I knew a pair of twins who I was sure still pulled stunts like that.

When I ask him if that's true, he replies: *That would be telling…*

Me: *Do people still get you mixed up?*

Kip: *All the time. It's why I wear glasses.*

Me: *Really? You don't need them?*

Kip: *Yeah, we're both short-sighted, but Saxon wears contacts.*

Me: *Oh I see! Well at least it showed you I was thinking of you.*

Kip: *:-)*

Me: *How did your day go? Did you manage to track Craig down?*

Kip: *Yeah. Kinda wish I hadn't.*

I glance over at Mum, who's watching me with a small smile. "Do you mind if I go and call him?" I ask.

"Of course not," she says softly.

Giving a grinning Charlie a wry look, I take my phone and, as the sun is going down and there will be moths fluttering around the solar lamps in the garden, I head through to my studio.

Once I've shut the door, I sit in my chair, prop my feet up on my table, and dial his number.

"Hey," he says after a few rings. "Didn't expect you to call."

"Are you at home? You're not busy?"

"Yes, I'm at home. No, I'm not busy. And yes, I'd love to talk."

I smile. "I just wanted to check you're okay."

He sighs. "Yeah. It's done anyway."

"Do you want to talk about it?"

"I don't want to bore you."

"Oh, hardly. So you went to the house of the woman he's having an affair with?"

"Yes, and he was there. It was a very strange turn of events."

"In what way?"

"I told you that she—Renée, her name is—is the CEO of one of the companies we considered?"

"Yes."

"It turns out she'd attempted to engineer the deal. She's been pushing Craig to make us sell to her. I think she told him she'd stop seeing him if he didn't make the deal."

"Shit, really?"

"Yeah. It turns out their relationship is… ah… I'm not quite sure how to put it."

"Now I'm interested," I say, amused. "Spit it out."

"I think there's a Dom/Sub thing going on there."

"I'm guessing you're not referring to a Subway sandwich?"

He chuckles. "No."

"I was going to ask if she preferred a six inch or a foot long."

That makes him laugh out loud. "I adore you," he says.

I smile. "I don't know much about this stuff. So you're saying she's his submissive?"

"No. The other way around." He sounds amused.

"Oh…" That startles me. I know it happens, of course, but I'm still surprised. "How could you tell? Was she dressed in leather and holding a whip?"

"Not quite. It was the way he acted with her, very subservient. It's odd, but with his wife he's always been the dominant one, telling her what to do, that kind of thing. I guess he wanted her to stand up to him, and when she didn't, he went elsewhere."

"Wow. I'm so naïve. I don't know about any of this stuff."

"Me neither."

"I bet you know more than I do."

"Well, that might be true, but it's not something I'm interested in."

"You don't want me to tie you up and walk up and down your back in high heels?"

"If there's any tying up to be done, it's gonna be me doing it, you can bet on that."

I blink at the vision of him tying me to the bed, and my whole body heats. "Ooh. I think I've just had a hot flush."

That makes him laugh. "You like that idea?"

"Um… honestly, I'm not sure. I don't quite get the whole power-play thing."

"I guess it's about giving up control for a while. And about trust. Putting your pleasure in someone else's hands."

We both fall silent for a moment. Suddenly, I'm filled with yearning. I wish I was there with him, so I could slip my hands beneath the hem of his tee and slide them over his warm skin and up his back while he kisses me. Oh God. I want that so bad.

He's quiet too. Is he thinking the same thing?

I clear my throat. "How did you end it?"

"I told him I wanted his resignation in my inbox by the end of the day or I'd fire him."

"Has it turned up yet?"

"Not yet. I'm hoping it will. If I have to fire him, I'm pretty sure lawyers are going to get involved. I don't care—I'll win. But I don't really want the hassle."

He speaks with authority and determination. It gives me goosebumps.

"You're definitely not a submissive, are you?" I say softly.

"Nope. Does that bother you?"

My heart is banging on my ribs. "No."

"Good. So, it's Christmas Eve tomorrow. What are you up to?"

"I actually have an Ask Me Anything on the IamA subreddit at ten a.m."

"Oh, really? Have you done that before?"

"No, my first time."

"That should bring you in some new listeners, right?"

"That's the plan. I'm a bit nervous, but excited too. What about you? What are you up to?"

"I'm off to my parents in the afternoon. I'll stay for a couple of nights."

"They have a nice place?"

"It's okay," he says. He's smiling. "Saxon told me today he's going to propose to Catie in the evening."

"Oh, how wonderful!"

"I'm just hoping she says yes," he says, and laughs.

"Why wouldn't she?" I'm genuinely puzzled. The two of them looked very much in love when I met them.

"She's had a tough upbringing. Her parents died, and she was brought up by an abusive stepmother. She actually ran away a few times, and lived on the streets for a while."

"Wow, really?"

"Yeah, she's a real-life Cinderella."

I'm touched he's confiding in me. "Where did she meet Saxon?"

"They had a one-night stand in Auckland. She left his hotel room in the middle of the night. He didn't know where she was or even her real name. He moped for weeks. And then one day she just appeared at our offices. She didn't know he worked there—she was there for a temporary job."

"Jesus. What happened when she saw him?"

"She saw me first and couldn't work out why I didn't recognize her. She didn't know he was a twin. I was really bemused as to why this pregnant girl was staring at me as if she knew me."

"I bet you thought Jesus, I must have been really drunk that night."

He laughs. "Well I hadn't been with anyone for about six months, so I knew I wasn't the dad."

"Seriously? You haven't dated for six months?"

"Nope. It takes a special girl to lure me away from work."

I smile and scratch at a mark on my desk. "You shouldn't say things like that."

"I shouldn't give you compliments?"

"You know what I mean."

"I'm not going to stop saying nice things to you, Alice. You'll have to get used to it."

I don't reply, not sure how I feel about that.

"You want kids?" he asks.

"We've been on one date, Kip."

"I meant generally."

"Oh. I... don't know. I try not to think about the future too much. I don't know whether it's even a possibility for me yet. The life expectancy of people with M.S. is five to ten years lower than average, but Mum's only fifty, and..." I trail off, feeling guilty for even thinking about it.

"I understand," he says softly. "I'm sorry, I shouldn't have asked."

"It's okay. It's just... I know what it must sound like, as if I'm some kind of martyr. I don't mean to be like that. And when Charlie's qualified, and she's home sharing the care, maybe I'll be able to get out and about a bit. I'm just conscious that Mum isn't going to get any better. She's only going to need more looking after. And so I can't make plans."

"I know."

"It's not that I don't want to…"

"I know, Alice. It's okay. I'm just glad we can be friends. I like you, and I enjoy talking to you. You make me smile, and that's not a small thing in this world."

"No, that's true."

"So what are you going to talk about tomorrow on your AMA?"

There's a soft knock at the door, and I say, "Come in." The door opens, and Charlie enters.

"It's just Charlie," I say.

"Tell her hey," he replies.

"Kip says stop smirking," I tell her.

She laughs and deposits a glass of wine on my desk, then bends closer and says, "Hey, Kip."

"Hey, Charlie," he calls, and she smiles as she hears him.

"She's brought me a glass of wine," I tell him.

She blows me a kiss and goes out again. I smile and have a sip, and then tell Kip about the AMA, while outside the sky slowly darkens, a lone star sparkling like a Christmas wish.

\*

The next morning, I help Mum get dressed and do her hair for her, and then Charlie offers to take her for a walk to the shops while I get to work. The two of them head out, and I make myself a coffee, then take it into the studio.

At least today I'm typing, not speaking, but I'm still nervous. My success with Wonderland so far has surprised me, and it seems to be getting bigger. I didn't expect it at all. I've always loved reading, but it was only when I was confined to the house when Mum fell ill that I started to write reviews and share them online. I was totally surprised when I started to get feedback, and even more surprised when I emailed a well-known Kiwi author that I loved to ask whether I could interview her, and she said yes. That was the start of Wonderland, and I've enjoyed every minute of it ever since.

I bring up Reddit, and the IamA subreddit, get myself ready and comfortable, introduce myself with the bio I've prepared as it strikes ten, then wait for any questions.

I imagine this is a bit like a book signing, when an author is terrified that nobody is going to show up. I sit nervously as questions begin to trickle through and start answering.

Half an hour later, my fingers can't keep up with the flood of questions, and my heart is racing as my fingers fly over the keyboard. People are asking about the interviews I've done, the books I've reviewed, and recommending ones they've read themselves. Several threads evolve into long discussions about various books, with readers arguing amongst themselves about which stories are the best. And all the time, readers throw compliments at me, about how much they enjoy Wonderland, and giving me ideas for future podcasts.

Then I spot it. The question says: Hey Alice! Love your podcast. I'm starting *Neuromancer* today. Thanks for the recommendation :-)

The username is KnightsInWhiteSatin. Isn't the French for knight Chevalier?

Smiling, I reply: *I hope you enjoy it! You can tell me what you think later!*

*Will do,* he replies. *Lots of people on here. You're very popular!*

Me: *Want my autograph?*

After that, about twenty people answer *Yes!* making me laugh.

I spend another twenty minutes answering questions. In one thread, someone asks where I got the Queen of Hearts playing card pendant that I'm wearing in my photo, and I tell them my mum got it for my twenty-first birthday. *When is your birthday?* another reader asks, and someone else says: *January 20, she mentioned it on the podcast about epic fantasy last year.*

*Don't tell everyone,* I scold, wondering whether Kip's read it. Probably not. I'm sure he's got more important things to do than trawl through hundreds of questions on Reddit.

As eleven o'clock nears, I promise everyone I'll check back regularly to catch up on any questions, then get up and stretch my legs. Phew! That was more intense than I expected. It's exciting though. I had so many new people saying they were going to check out the podcast.

My phone buzzes with a new message. It's from Kip. *So… your birthday's on the twentieth of Jan?*

My lips curve up. *I didn't think you'd seen that.*

Kip: *Oh, I saw it. Do you have anything planned?*

Me: *Not as such. We usually treat ourselves to a takeaway and watch a movie together.*

Kip: *Will Charlie still be there?*

Me: *Yes, she leaves the week after. She's going to the South Island with some friends for a few weeks before uni starts.*

Kip: *In that case… I'd like to invite you to join me for a few days.*

My heart leaps.

Me: *Oh, Kip… we shouldn't.*

Kip: *Why?*

Me: *Because it's just going to make it harder when we have to part.*

Kip: *Why don't we worry about that at some other time?*

Me: *Sigh.*

Kip: *You can have a few days away, right? Charlie can look after your mum?*

Me: *Yes…*

Kip: *You work very hard. Don't you deserve to treat yourself?*

I do deserve a treat, don't I? Other people have flings, and are able to concentrate on the physical rather than the emotional side. I know there's a lot he could teach me. It would be a lot of fun having him further my education.

Me: *Will there be sex involved?*

Kip: *Actually I was thinking probably not. We should slow down and concentrate on getting to know one another first.*

I feel a pang of disappointment. I was teasing him; I didn't expect him to say no.

Me: *Oh. Okay. I guess that makes sense.*

Kip: *Alice, I'm kidding. Do you seriously think I could be within twenty feet of you and not think about you naked?*

Me: *Oh LOL I was worried there for a bit!*

Kip: *I'm already thinking about positions and other enjoyable activities we can get up to.*

Me: *Oh God, don't say things like that! Now I won't be able to stop thinking about it!*

Kip: *I want you to think about it. Long and hard.*

Me: *And now I'm thinking about the foot-long sub again!*

Kip: *LOL. I thought you'd enjoy furthering your education.*

Me: *Will there be an exam at the end?*

Kip: *A sexam?*

Me: *LOL.*

Kip: *I think we'll concentrate on the coursework.*

Me: *Especially the practicals?*

Kip: *You did say you wanted to be well schooled for when you meet Mr. Right.*

That makes me blink. I did say something similar to that, because that was the idea when I first went on Tinder. It makes my stomach flip to hear him say it now, even though I'm very aware this is only a fling.

Kip: *Alice, I'm teasing you. This is purely a selfish endeavor. I'm expecting to be the only guy who benefits from your growing expertise.*

My lips curve up.

Me: *I'd be happy with missionary.*

Kip: *Me too, but hey, why not broaden your horizons?*

Me: *Are you talking about slot D?*

Kip: *Jesus, are you trying to give me a coronary? Let's start with you on top and see where we go from there.*

Me: *LOL are you sure about this?*

Kip: *Absolutely. I can have fun planning it over Christmas.*

Me: *So you'll have to let me know when you want me to drive down.*

Kip: *You won't need to drive. I'll send the family plane.*

Me: *Sorry, what?*

Kip: *The flight attendant is called Immi. She'll look after you. Then I'll pick you up from Wellington.*

Me: *Wow. Are you sure?*

Kip: *Just to warn you, I'll be taking you out somewhere nice to dinner.*

Me: *So I shouldn't wear shorts and a vest?*

Kip: *You're welcome to wear whatever you like. I'll be wearing a suit, though.*

Me: *Ooh.*

Kip: *You like that idea?*

Me: *I do. What kind?*

Kip: *Italian, navy-blue, single breasted, three-piece.*

Me: *A waistcoat? *fans self**

Kip: *Yep. And you get to take it off if you like.*

I feel a sudden swell of emotion. Is this for real? A gorgeous guy, who just happens to be incredibly rich, who owns his own private jet, and is so desperate to see me that he's willing to wait for weeks? This must be an elaborate joke.

Me: *Am I dreaming?*

Kip: *Saxon would say you're having more of a nightmare if you're dating me LOL.*

Me: *Dating?*

Kip: *For want of a better word. It's what they call it when you get the feels about someone.*

Me: *You have the feels for me?*

Kip: *I do. All the feels. And I've made my up mind that I want you, so you might as well get used to me.*

A shiver runs down my back at his statement. I'm not sure whether to feel flattered or alarmed. He speaks with such determination, even though I've told him I'm not in the zone to have a relationship right now.

Getting up, I wander over to the window and look out at the view for a moment. The garden is burgeoning with summer blooms. Mum likes to sit on the deck and watch the bees buzzing around the flower beds, so I try to make sure there's plenty of color.

There's no way this could work. Even if he told me he'd fly me to Wellington whenever I wanted, I'd only be able to go when Charlie's home, or on the rare occasion that June was able to look after Mum. I don't truly believe any guy would remain faithful in a relationship with a girl he could see only four or five times a year. Kip could have any woman he wanted. Why on earth would he pick me?

My phone buzzes.

Kip: *Have you fainted?*

Me: *LOL no I'm still here. I do feel a bit breathless though. You make me feel as if I'm standing in the middle of a tornado.*

Kip: *Good.*

I frown. *Is it intentional?*

Kip: *Absolutely not.*

I give a wry smile. It is. He's trying to dazzle me with sex and money. Well, I suppose there are worse things to have to deal with.

Kip: *How long do you think you could come down for?*

Me: *I don't know, I'd have to think about it. How long would you want me for?*

Kip: *Two or three months?*

I laugh. *Be serious.*

Kip: *Okay. Two or three years?*

Me: *Kip!*

Kip: *:-) As long as you can give me.*

Me: *I'll talk to Charlie.*

Kip: *Okay. I gotta go. We've got a meeting about Craig.*

Me: *Did he email you his resignation in the end?*

Kip: *No, hence the meeting. I'll let you know how it goes. Have a good day.*
Me: *You too, babe.*
Kip: *LOL.*
Me: *Sorry too soon?*
Kip: *Not at all. Gives me the warm fuzzies.*
I smile.
Me: *Never given a guy fuzzies before.*
Kip: *<3*

# Chapter Fourteen

## *Kip*

I pick up my iPad and take it and my phone through to the board room. Technically, the office is closed for Christmas, but Helen, our head of HR, has called a meeting to discuss the situation with Craig. She's in her forties, with short dark hair, and she exhibits a calmness even in heated situations that I've always appreciated.

Damon and Marama are also present.

"'Bout time," Damon says as I walk in.

I give him the finger.

"Both mature and professional," he states, and the two women snicker.

"Where's Saxon?" Helen asks as I take the seat next to her.

"I didn't mention this to him," I advise. "I'm trying to keep as much of this off his desk as I can."

"Okay," she says, and smiles.

"Still no sign of Craig's resignation?" Damon asks.

I shake my head regretfully. "I guess it's time to fire him."

Helen leans on the table and clears her throat. "Technically, Kip, he's done nothing wrong."

I go still. "What?"

"Legally, I mean. Morally, he's been a wanker—talking to the reporter was unethical, and offering MOTHER to Sunrise without your consent was out of order. But was it illegal? As far as I know, he hasn't signed any documentation, because all three directors' signatures have to be on the paperwork, and Renée would know that. The agreement was verbal, an attempt to force your hand out of embarrassment. I think a lawyer could easily argue that Renée offered double what Genica was offering, and Craig would have automatically assumed that would swing things in Sunrise's favor. I've checked the financial records, and although he paid for several lunches on his business account, there are no suspicious transactions, no sign of money having passed hands. It doesn't sound as if he's taken any bribes from Renée."

I look at Damon. His lips twist in a rueful smile.

She's right, of course. I hadn't thought it through. I've been so caught up in shock and disbelief that I didn't consider the fact that I might not have any grounds to fire him. I've never had to fire anyone before.

"It's unpleasant," Helen adds. "Situations like this aren't easy to handle. We have to be careful this doesn't turn toxic. In New Zealand there are several grounds for firing an employee. Serious misconduct, such as theft. Repeated misconduct, including poor timekeeping. Performance. Redundancy. Incompatibility. And incapacity, usually relating to health issues. The closest is probably incompatibility. A personality clash that's causing a substantial issue to the business would fall in this category. You can also fire an employee for being disrespectful, although he would be within his rights to sue the company."

"The problem is, it's a one-off," Damon says. His words suggest that Helen has already approached him to discuss the situation. Interesting. She wanted someone to back her up when she spoke to me. "It's not a repeated pattern of behavior," he continues. "There are hurt feelings on both sides, and we have a duty to try to address those before we turn to legal action."

I lean back in my chair. "Are you saying you're happy to just brush off what happened? With how he spoke to Marama?"

Damon frowns. "Of course not. He was out of order. But we need to do this by the book or we're going to open ourselves up to a whole can of worms."

"I'm a big girl," Marama states wryly, "you don't need to go into battle on my account."

"That's not the point," I reply. "I'd have issues with any employee of mine talking to another in that way."

"Fair enough," she says softly.

"You've given him a verbal warning," Helen says. "I suggest we invite him into the office after Christmas for a meeting. He would be able to bring in a support person, and maybe just you and I should be there, Kip, so he didn't feel as if we were ganging up on him. We also need to keep a record of every interaction we have with him until this is settled."

"And if he won't come?" I ask. "Or he comes and refuses to back down?"

"We follow it up with a written warning. If he were to continue to be difficult, we would suspend him, and then finally terminate his employment on the grounds of incompatibility. He's smart, though, and he's within his rights to sue us for wrongful dismissal. I don't think he'd win, but…" She shrugs.

Damon clears his throat. "Okay, we'll leave it there. Thanks, Helen. We'll get back to you."

She nods, picks up her laptop, and she and Marama head out, closing the door behind them.

I stretch out my legs, look up at the ceiling, and blow out a breath. "Fuck."

"I'm sorry."

I stare at the light for a moment, then lower my head. "I just want him gone. I'm so angry with him."

"I know."

"He's made a fortune out of us over the years," I say bitterly. "And I feel as if he's stabbed me in the back."

"I know, I feel the same. I'm disappointed in his behavior. He's let us down, and for what? A woman?" His disgust is palpable. I try not to smile. "But there are a couple of reasons we need to be careful," he says. "One of them is legal."

"And the other?"

He tips his head to the side. "He's your friend, and I know you. If you fire him now, you're going to be eaten up with guilt at the thought of what's going to happen to Chloe and the kid. You're going to feel the need to control this, but maybe everyone just needs a few days or weeks to calm down."

"You really think he can return to work here after what he said?"

Damon taps his pen on the table. "I know he's hurt your feelings. Professionally, though, he's an excellent engineer, and an asset to the company. Maybe we should consider trying to work through this?"

I get up and shove my chair under the table with a bang. "Over my dead body."

"Kip—"

"I don't want him to set foot in this building again."

"If you don't want to meet with him and Helen, I'll do it. But it's got to be done. We have to go through the steps. Helen will run the meeting. Hopefully Craig will shoot himself in the foot without us having to do anything. Then she can give him the written warning."

I grit my teeth. It's the last thing I want to do, but I know he's right.

"You want me to organize it?" he asks.

"No, I'll do it."

"All right." He gets to his feet. "I know this is tough, and he's hurt your feelings. And you're not going to want to appear as if you're backing down. But give him a few days to stew. Maybe he'll come to his senses over Christmas, when he realizes he might lose his wife and kid. Give him the chance to make amends."

I want to say 'Fuck him.' And it annoys me that Damon, who's usually the hot-headed one, is having to say it to me. But he's right.

I give a short nod, and he walks out. Gritting my teeth, I pick up my stuff and head out to Marion's office to get her to book a meeting.

*

### Later that day

"Bro," I say. "For God's sake, come on."

I'm at my parents' house in Brooklyn. Saxon and Catie are here, and so are Damon, my cousin, Kennedy, her husband, Jackson, with their baby, Eddie, and Brandon and Jenny, Kennedy's parents. Brandon is my father's twin brother. Pongo the Dalmatian, currently stretched out in front of the fire, completes the picture.

I've been waiting all evening for Saxon to pop the question. It's now nearly ten o'clock, and Catie's yawning. If he leaves it any longer, she's going to say she's off to bed, and then he'll have missed his opportunity.

Everyone looks at me, puzzled, then at him. He purses his lips, stretches out on the beanbag he's currently sitting in, rubs his hands over his face, then sinks them into his hair.

"I'm going to regret this," he mumbles.

I chuckle and settle back to watch the scene play out.

Saxon gets to his feet and holds his hand out to Catie, and she lets him pull her to her feet. She told me earlier that she's twenty-three weeks pregnant, and now she's put on a little weight, so she looks healthy and beautiful.

"Don't freak out, okay?" he says to her. "I mean, yeah, I could see why you might, but just remember the babies."

She looks confused and glances at me. I just smile. Saxon has had a few girlfriends over the years, some that lasted longer than others, but he's never fallen head over heels like this for a girl before. It's strange to see him so captivated.

He takes a small, black velvet box out of his track pants and opens it.

"Catie," he says, sinking down onto one knee. "Will you make me the happiest guy in the world and marry me?"

Most of us have been drinking, but that's enough to sober everyone up. Beside me, Damon says, "Wow," clearly shocked.

"What?" Catie says.

"Breathe," Saxon replies. "Hyperventilation isn't good for the boys."

Damon gets up and takes a look at the ring. "Wow. Bro. How many carats?"

Jackson also peers at it. "Must be at least three."

"Jesus," Kennedy says. "How much did that set you back? You're talking over a hundred K, right?"

Catie's face is a picture. For a girl who used to spend less than thirty dollars a week on food, she's clearly struggling with the thought of spending such a fortune on a single item.

"Guys, you're not helping," Saxon says. He glances at me, and I can see he's nervous that she's going to panic and say no.

"Well?" he asks her.

"Are you serious?" she says.

"Yeah."

"You're really asking me to marry you?"

"Yeah."

"For the babies? So they'll have your name?"

"Our name. You'll be Mrs. Catie Chevalier. My wife."

"Mrs. Chevalier?"

"Yeah. Unless you particularly want to keep your name. I'll be your husband. You can boss me around and tell me to pick up my socks."

I can tell he's suddenly conscious that we're all watching him. He rises, glancing around.

"All right," he says. "Sorry guys, show's over." Taking her hand, he leads her out of the room, onto the terrace. I watch him put a throw around her shoulders, then start speaking to her, head bent close to hers.

"Fucking hell," Damon says, "I didn't expect that."

"Damon," Mum scolds, then looks at me. "You knew he was going to propose?"

"Yeah, he did mention it. I thought he was going to chicken out."

"Aw." She looks out at them, her expression softening. I follow her gaze. Catie's looking up at him as if he's a movie star. It makes me think of Alice. She looked at me like that.

I glance back at Mum. She's smiling at me.

"How's Alice?" she asks.

I blink, then look at Damon. He pulls an 'eek' face. Giving him a wry smile, I say, "She's good, thank you."

"Alice?" Kennedy asks. "Who's Alice?"

"Kip's girlfriend," Damon says.

"She's not my girlfriend," I correct. "She's just a friend."

"With benefits?" Kennedy suggests.

I tip my head from side to side, and everyone laughs.

"Is that who you've been texting all evening?" she asks.

"Might be."

She grins.

"What's she like?" Mum asks.

"Yeah, spill the deets," Kennedy adds.

I hesitate, having the uncomfortable feeling that if I talk about her, it'll somehow jinx things. Usually, I'd have made a joke and changed the subject, but for some reason I think about what Damon said, that Lesley mistook my reticence for secrecy and thought I was hiding things from her. It's never been my intention to be secretive or to shut others out. Maybe it's because I'm the oldest—even though it's only by fifteen minutes—but I've always felt that a man should deal with things on his own. Chloe's statement that Lesley felt excluded has made me rethink that reticence, although it doesn't come easily to me to share.

"She's twenty-six in a few weeks," I tell them, and my mother's face brightens with delight that I'm opening up. "She's a podcaster. She reviews books and interviews science fiction and fantasy authors."

My father's eyebrows rise. "The podcast isn't called Wonderland?" When I nod, he says, "You're talking about Alice Liddell?"

"Yep."

He grins. "I listen to that every week. She's terrific. Got a lovely husky voice."

"I know."

Mum's busy googling on her phone. She pulls up the website and finds Alice's picture, then shows the others. "She's pretty," she states.

"She is. And funny."

"Where did you meet her?"

"On Tinder. We went for dinner with Saxon and Catie."

"Oh, how wonderful. When are you seeing her again?"

"That's kind of the problem. She lives in Gisborne, and she looks after her mother, who has M.S."

They all look startled.

"Oh," Mum says. "That makes it tough."

"Does she have any help?" Dad asks.

"She has a younger sister who helps out when she can. But she's at Vic, so she's obviously not around in term time. Alice's aunt also shares some of the care, but again, she works full time, so…"

"Does she get paid help in?"

"She prefers not to do that. It's delicate. I'm working on it."

"Well if there's anything we can do," Dad says.

I nod, then look over as the sliding doors open and Saxon and Catie come back in. I note that he's holding her hand.

"She said yes," he states with obvious relief, and she holds up her hand, showing us the ring on her finger.

We erupt into cheers, and everyone gets up to exchange hugs and kisses. I give Saxon a bearhug and murmur, "Well done, bro."

"Thought I'd blown it for a minute," he admits, "but I managed to wrestle victory from the jaws of defeat."

I grin and release him so I can give Catie a kiss on the cheek. "I'm so pleased for you," I tell her.

"Thank you, Kip." She gives me a hug. "I'm so happy."

"Aw." I put my arms around her and hug her back. "You're far too good for him."

"Ah, that's a nice thing to say, but I know I'm getting the better deal by far."

"Honey, I've never seen him so happy. You complete him."

She presses her fingers to her mouth and her eyes shine. "Aw, Kip…"

"Are you making my fiancée cry?" Saxon says, putting his arm around her as I release her.

"Fiancée," she squeaks, and we all laugh.

They turn to talk to my parents, and I watch Saxon lift Catie's hand and kiss the ring he's just placed on her finger. I feel a strange tightness in my chest. We're heading toward thirty, so we're hardly kids, but both of us have steered clear of commitment until now, hanging onto the last vestiges of boyhood. For some reason, it feels as if this is the final step into adulthood. Soon he'll be married with two kids. Catie is his confidante now, and I know there'll be things he talks to her about that he doesn't discuss with me.

Pulling my phone out of my back pocket, I bring up my text conversation with Alice and message her.

Me: *Saxon proposed, and Catie said yes :-)*

She comes back almost immediately. *I wondered how it was going! Oh, I'm so glad!*

Me: *He's pretty happy.*

Alice: *I bet. How are you doing?*

I study the phone, surprised at her astuteness.

Me: *Why'd you ask that?*

Alice: *Sixth sense. Are you sad?*

Me: *I'm thrilled for him.*

Alice: *Yeah, I know. Wanna chat?*

I hesitate. Then, opening the sliding doors and going outside, I dial her number and put the phone to my ear.

She takes a few seconds to answer. "Hello, you!"

"Hey. I'm not interrupting anything?"

"No, no. We were watching that new sci-fi movie that just came out. I'll do a review in a few days. They said they'd take a bathroom break, but I suspect it'll involve pouring another glass of champagne, you naughty boy."

I smile. This morning, I organized a hamper to be delivered to the house in Gisborne. It included a variety of fancy chocolates and biscuits, and two bottles of champagne.

"Oh, it turned up?" I say.

"It did. Mum and Charlie were very impressed. It was a lovely gift, thank you. I feel bad because I didn't get you anything."

"Ah, you can pay me back on your birthday."

She laughs. "So, Saxon finally asked Catie to marry him?"

"He took his time. I thought he was going to chicken out, but he got there in the end."

"So, are you a little sad?"

"I don't know. I feel odd. As if we've finally grown up." I give an embarrassed laugh.

But she just says, "It makes sense. It's been the two of you against the world for a long time, hasn't it? And now you sort of have to hand him over to her."

I don't say anything, but she's right, that is how it feels.

"Do you feel jealous of her?" she asks.

My eyebrows rise. "Jealous?"

"I wondered if that's what's bothering you."

"How do you know something's bothering me?"

"Like I said, sixth sense."

I slide my other hand into my trouser pocket and study the patio tiles. "No, I'm not jealous. Envious, I guess."

"Okay…"

"They're different things. Jealousy implies I'm jealous of her. I'm not. I'm a little envious of him, if I'm honest."

"Because he's settling down? Is that something you're looking for?"

"You're a very unusual girl. I'm not used to talking about my feelings like this."

"You are rather like an oyster. I feel as if I have to pry you open."

I chuckle. "I don't know, is the answer to your question. I've not thought about it before."

"You asked me if I wanted children. Do you?"

"Again, I haven't thought about it before. I suppose knowing Saxon's having twins has made me think about it. I've never pictured myself as a father."

"You'd make a great dad."

My lips curve up. "Well, thank you. I'm not sure you're right, though."

"Oh Kip," she scoffs. "You're honorable, smart, kind…"

"Please don't say sweet."

"I thought you were sweet before you took me to bed. I've changed my opinion, though."

"Have you now?"

"You're a very naughty boy."

"Is that a complaint?"

"Definitely not. I get quite breathless when I think about going to bed with you again."

I look up at the clear night sky. "I wish you were with me now."

She just sighs.

"Have you talked to Charlie about how long you can come down for?" I ask.

"I did."

"And what did you settle on?"

"I… um… wasn't sure how long you'd want me there. I thought… um… maybe three nights? I'm happy just to make it one or two if you like."

"Three nights sounds great. Five would be better. Imagine how much sex we could have."

She laughs. "I'd be lying if I said it hadn't crossed my mind. I don't want to leave Mum for too long, though."

"Fair enough."

It's a beautiful evening. The white Japanese wisteria that Mum grows against the wall glows in the semi-darkness, and its sweet scent reminds me that the hot days of January and February are just around the corner. Christmas Eve never fails to make me feel like a boy again—those memorable days when Saxon and I were seven or eight and Damon was only six, and we all still believed in Santa. I can remember one Christmas in particular, when the three of us decided we were going to stay up late and try to catch Santa delivering our presents to the end of our beds. We didn't of course. Damon fell asleep by about ten. Saxon and I made it until one in the morning before we crashed out.

It strikes me that a good portion of my memories involve Saxon. The two of us were inseparable when we were young. Even though my parents are wealthy, and we could have had separate bedrooms, we shared until we were fourteen, and even after that, we often stayed up late together watching movies. As adults we're used to spending time apart, but I finally accept that it is odd to have lost him to someone else.

"Are you outside?" Alice asks.

"Yeah. You?"

"I'm in the garden. It's warm tonight."

"It's a bit breezy here."

"Wellington blows, but Auckland sucks, right?"

I grin.

"Look up at the moon," she says.

"Okay."

"How much astronomy do you know?"

"Not much," I admit.

"Look to the south. Can you see that really bright planet? It won't be sparkling, just shining."

"Yeah."

"That's Jupiter. There's a theory that the star the Magi followed was actually the conjunction of Jupiter, Saturn, the moon, and the Sun in the constellation of Aries."

My eyebrows rise. "Oh, seriously?"

"It happened on April 17, in 6 BC, in the early morning hours, and the Bible describes the Star of Bethlehem as a rising morning star."

"It's a nice theory."

"I think so. I love Christmas Eve."

"Me too."

"It does make me a bit sad. My dad used to love this time of year. He was the one who used to help Charlie and me put the mince pie and milk out for Santa and the carrot for Rudolph."

We're quiet for a moment. I look at Jupiter, thinking how lucky I've been to have both my parents right into adulthood.

"Do you think your father's death had anything to do with your mum developing M.S.?" If it were anyone else, I'd hesitate to mention something personal like that, but Alice makes me feel as if I could ask her anything.

"I'm convinced of it," she says. "She was absolutely devastated, and she couldn't get out of bed for days. Her symptoms began shortly afterward."

"That's very sad."

"It is, although she always says she feels honored to have had him for sixteen happy years. Can you imagine being with someone for that length of time? Being that comfortable and content?"

Her husky voice sends goosebumps rising all over my body. "Kinda," I say.

We don't speak for a moment. Then, out of the blue, a shooting star falls, just to the east of Jupiter.

"Whoa," she says. "Did you see that?"

"Yeah."

"Make a wish," she says, "quickly!"

I look up at Jupiter and smile.

"What did you wish for?" she asks.

"I can't tell or it won't come true."

"Aw," she says. "Spoilsport." She sighs again. "It's funny to think we're both looking up at the same sky. It makes me feel closer to you."

"I miss you," I tell her. "Is that dumb considering we've only spent one night together?"

"Maybe. I miss you too, though."

"Can I call you tomorrow?"

"Sure," she says, and I can tell she's smiling.

# Chapter Fifteen

## *Alice*

On Christmas morning, we open our presents, and then we prepare dinner together, Mum sitting at the table peeling potatoes and carrots, while Charlie and I get the turkey with the trimmings ready. When it's done, we eat outside on the deck, reminiscing about old times, and then afterward while Mum has a snooze, I finally call Kip. We talk for over an hour, and then later, while I'm watching a movie, we text each other almost continuously.

The next few weeks pass in much the same way. I spend my days either working in the studio or spending time with Mum and Charlie, either just sitting chatting, watching TV, or occasionally going out for a drive. Mum doesn't like to be away from home for too long, but she enjoys brief trips to the beach, and she loves going to the park, where she can see the children on the swings and watch the dogs running around.

Kip messages and calls me every day. It's a strange relationship; we're not exactly boyfriend and girlfriend, because we've only slept together once, but I feel that we're closer than friends because we've shared that intimacy, and we flirt a lot of the time. After saying that, even though he talks all the time about my upcoming trip on my birthday, I'm beginning to feel nervous that I haven't seen him for a while. Maybe I imagined the chemistry that was between us? I can't help but think he might be starting to regret suggesting I come to the city. After all, I'm hardly a catch. But he insists he's looking forward to it, so I gather my courage with both hands and tell myself I'm going through with it, if only because there's the chance of some really hot sex.

I also think it'll be good for him to take some proper time off work. I know he's been in the office most days apart from Christmas Day.

He tried to organize a meeting to see Craig, but Craig emailed to say he was going away for Christmas and that he'd call when he got back, so unfortunately Kip has to wait. I know it's weighing heavily on his mind, so maybe I'll be able to distract him a bit.

For a while it feels as if my birthday is never going to come. But eventually it arrives, and I wake in the morning with bubbling excitement deep in my belly.

I open my presents that Mum and Charlie have bought me, and spend the morning setting up auto posts in my social media so Wonderland can continue to function while I'm away.

Kip messages me mid-morning to wish me happy birthday, then informs me he's heading off to a meeting for a few hours, and he'll see me at the airport when the plane lands at five.

With growing nerves, I spend a couple of hours getting ready. I've waxed myself within an inch of my life, so all that's left to do is to put on my makeup, do my hair, and then get dressed.

I'm not sure if I'll have time to change before we go out to dinner, so I put on my best dress for the restaurant he told me he's taking me to. I'm not really a dress kinda girl, preferring to hang out in jeans or black trousers, but today's a special occasion, so I'm happy to make an exception. The dress is calf-length and white, sleeveless with a V-neck, and the trim around the neckline and the band above the waist is a panel of broderie anglaise that reveals a tantalizing glimpse of skin through the lacy pattern. I team it with a pair of pretty silver sandals, and I leave my hair down with its natural curl but pin a white flower clip in the side, which gives me a Greek-style look.

Mum presses her fingers to her lips when I go out. "You look so beautiful," she whispers.

"You look hot," Charlie corrects. "You're going to do his head in."

"That's the plan." I give a slightly hysterical laugh.

"The taxi's here," Charlie says, looking out of the window. "Are you ready?"

"I hope you have an amazing time," Mum says when I bend to kiss her.

"I'm sure I will."

She holds my hand as I go to turn away. "Opportunities like this don't come around very often, sweetheart."

"I know." I look into her blue eyes, so like mine and Charlie's. She hesitates, then opens her mouth to speak. "Don't," I say hastily, knowing she's going to say something about the future. "Please, just… don't. This is hard enough."

She bites her bottom lip, then forces a smile. "Okay, I won't."

I give Charlie a hug. "Call me if you need me at all."

"I won't," she states. "We'll be fine, and I can always ring June. Go on. Don't think about us at all."

I pick up my case and open the front door. My stomach flutters with butterflies, and I pause on the doorstep. Is this a good idea? Either I've overestimated my relationship with Kip, and it's going to feel a bit awkward staying with him, or it's going to be amazing, and I'm not going to want to leave. Either way, I'm not sure it's the best idea.

But it's too late now. I've said I'm going, and it would be a shame to squash the seed of excitement blooming in my belly.

I wave goodbye, then head out to the taxi.

It takes me to the airport, and I head to the information desk and inform them I have a private flight. The assistant directs me to a quiet gate in the corner, and when I get there, I discover a tall, slender woman in her thirties waiting for me. She's dressed in a smart gray suit, and she introduces herself as Immi.

"Let me take that," she says, relieving me of my case. "Come with me. We're all ready for you."

Trying to look as if I've done this a million times, I follow her across the tarmac to the waiting plane. It's called The Knight Sky, and when I climb the steps I discover it seats eight, although I'm the only passenger today. In front of me, two light-gray leather chairs face another pair across a polished wooden table, with another group of four further down.

I slide into one of the chairs, smiling as I see the vase of six red roses fixed to the side of the table.

"I understand it's your birthday," Immi says as I buckle myself in. "Congratulations!"

"Thank you."

She proceeds to give me a quick safety talk, and then she takes her seat for takeoff. The pilot introduces himself as Sam and also wishes me happy birthday, and then we're speeding down the runway, and within seconds we're in the air.

"Would you like a glass of champagne?" Immi asks me when she comes over.

"Ooh, yes please." I decide it's pointless to try to hide my delight at the experience. I'm having the time of my life—why should I pretend I'm not? I accept the champagne and sip it with pleasure, and I also say yes when Immi brings over a small plate bearing a tiny, beautiful chocolate cake and a couple of chocolate mints.

Feeling as if I've stepped through the looking glass, I nibble the snacks and drink my champagne as the plane speeds above the clouds, thinking how different my life would be if I could travel like this to Wellington every time I needed to go. It would of course make it easier to visit Kip. Ultimately, though, it wouldn't change the fact that it's not a permanent solution. Mum needs me, she loves the home she made with my father, and the last thing she'd want is for me to leave her with a stranger so I could go and get my leg over regularly. I love her, and I couldn't do that to her, no matter how much she protests she wouldn't mind, because I know how she really feels.

It would be easy to persuade myself that seeing Kip is pointless because there's no hope of developing a relationship with him. But I'm not going to focus on that. The fact is that right now, I have this wonderful chance to spend some time with a gorgeous guy. It doesn't have to be about forever, right? People have short-term relationships for all kinds of reasons. There really is no reason we can't enjoy each other's company for as long as this whatever-it-is lasts.

Sam announces we're going to begin our descent. Immi clears the plate and glass away, I buckle myself in again, and soon we're dipping through the clouds, and the hills and buildings of Wellington appear beneath us, with the harbor gleaming in the summer sun.

The plane lands with a gentle bump and taxies up to the terminal. I thank Immi and Sam, then head across the tarmac with my case, and exit the gate.

I see him immediately, standing waiting, hands in the pockets of his trousers, and my heart leaps. He smiles, and I leave my case and run up to him, throwing my arms around his neck.

"Whoa!" he says, stiffening. "Alice!"

I step back, only then noticing his long brown coat, his white Converses, and the fact that he's not wearing glasses.

"Shit," I say, stepping back, "Saxon?"

He laughs. "Kip's stuck in a meeting, so I said I'd come and pick you up. I'm so sorry. I should have messaged you."

"It's okay. I suppose I should have made the connection. But Kip didn't actually wear glasses for very long when we were together." I realize what I'm implying, and my face heats.

Saxon smirks, then pulls me toward him and gives me a hug. "It's good to see you again. Happy birthday!"

I hug him back, touched. "Thank you. I hear you're a married man!"

"Yeah, we got hitched up in the Bay of Islands while we were on holiday." He releases me and collects my suitcase, and I walk with him across the lounge.

"I bet Catie was excited," I say, glancing up at the huge model of Gandalf astride the eagle from *The Lord of the Rings* that's suspended from the ceiling.

"Yeah, she didn't expect it."

"How is she feeling?"

"She's good. Blooming."

"As are you," I say as we exit the airport.

He laughs. "Yeah maybe."

"Being married suits you."

"Oh, I think I'd agree with that. There's something about putting a ring on your girl's finger so that every other guy knows to steer clear." He gives me a mischievous smile before checking the traffic and crossing the road to the car park.

I follow him, liking his somewhat possessive description of being married. It's strange, though. He and Kip are identical. Same eyes, same nose, pretty much the same short beard and hair. I don't get the tingle with Saxon, though. Why is that? Is it possible I won't get it with Kip now either? Was it all in my head? This isn't helping my nerves.

I clear my throat. "So how's Kip? Is he okay?"

"Yeah, he's really sorry he couldn't be here to meet you."

"He's meeting with Jack Evans, right? Genica's CEO."

Saxon looks surprised. "He did this morning, yeah."

"About MOTHER?"

"That's right." He stops and opens the passenger door of his car.

"Wow, I forgot you drove an Aston."

"Yeah. Boyhood dream. I wanted to be James Bond."

I give him a wry look and slide into the seat, and he grins and closes the door. I buckle myself in, my heart hammering. These guys aren't just wealthy, they're mega rich. What the hell am I doing here?

Saxon gets in, buckles his seat belt, starts the car, reverses out, and sets off.

I try to act casual, as if I'm used to traveling in 007's car every day. "So Kip met with Jack to nail down the production of the hardware?"

"Yeah. They hammered out the final details, to continue the metaphor."

"You said he met with Jack this morning? So he's not still in the meeting?"

"No…" He sighs. "He's meeting with another member of our team."

"You don't mean Craig?"

"He told you about him?"

"Yeah. I thought Craig was away?"

"He called yesterday to say he wanted to meet this afternoon. Kip tried to move it, but Craig was insistent."

I wonder why he didn't tell me. I guess he was worried that I might think he'd be too distracted during our time together. I don't care if he's distracted, but it would be a shame if Craig spoils it.

"I know he's very upset about what's going on," I say.

"He's taking it personally, which is fair enough after the things Craig said about us."

I watch him signal at the roundabout and head toward the city. "About you two being close?"

"Yeah."

"He does realize you're twins?"

Saxon smiles. "I can see why he likes you."

I'm not quite sure what to say to that. "Apparently Craig's wife also said it's one reason his ex left."

He snorts. "Lesley left because she was a selfish bitch who expected the world to revolve around her."

"She wasn't your favorite person, then?"

"She fucked him over, and not in a good way. Anytime you see him being cynical or wary, it's her fault."

"He loved her?"

He glances at me. "You don't have to worry about her. She's old news."

"I'm not worried." It's true; I'm not. My relationship with Kip is a shooting star. He's lit me up briefly, but I know he'll be moving on soon. In a way it gives our relationship freedom. We don't have to worry about baggage—not that I have any, where men are concerned—or laying down foundations for the future. There's only here, today, now.

"You should have told us at dinner you were Alice from Wonderland," Saxon says, heading toward the hospital. "I've listened to your podcast. I'd love to know more about it. I thought maybe the two of you would like to come to dinner over the weekend and you can tell us all about it."

"That would be nice. Have you mentioned it to Kip?"

"Not yet."

"I'll check with him. I don't know what he's got planned. I'm only here for three nights."

"Have you told him that?" he asks, amused.

"What do you mean?"

"I think he's hoping you'll stay a bit longer than that."

"I told him three nights."

"He's likely to ignore that."

"He's likely to ignore my needs and wishes?"

Saxon thinks about it. "Let me rephrase it. He likes to get his own way."

"Is that supposed to be a better way of putting it?"

"Maybe not. Can I take the fifth?"

"Your poor mother, having to cope with bringing you two up together."

"We were no trouble at all. Damon was the miscreant."

"Really?"

"Absolutely. He was constantly in trouble. We were positively angelic compared to him."

"Oddly, I don't find that reassuring."

He laughs, slows the car, and pulls into a parking space in front of a building that bears the sign out the front that says, 'Kingpinz Robotics.'

"Pretty cool having your own company," I tell him as I unbuckle myself.

"I think so. I'll drop your case off at his house, by the way. He wants to Uber into town so he can have a drink."

"Okay, thank you."

We get out, he gestures with his head for me to follow him, and together we walk up the path and into the building.

The foyer is large and cool. A young woman sits behind a long reception desk and smiles at us as we enter. To the right, a waiting area includes a group of armchairs, a water cooler, and a rubber plant that brings a splash of green to the otherwise white and light-gray decor. There's also an intriguing painting on the wall made up of rectangles and squares that I assume is abstract, but when I get closer, I can see it's actually a zoomed-in picture of a motherboard.

"I like this," I say, pausing in front of it.

"We've got a friend in Auckland who knows the Māori artist," Saxon explains. "I saw one of the paintings in his office and asked for the artist's name."

"You're talking about Mack Hart?" I ask. "The one who invented the supercomputer?"

Saxon smiles. "Is there anything Kip hasn't told you?"

"We talk a lot."

"I'm beginning to get that." He pushes open one of the swing doors, and we walk into the offices.

We're in a long corridor, with individual offices to our left and a large workroom to our right. The place is busy, filled with people at computers, or walking across the floor carrying files, coffee cups, on the phone, or talking in groups.

I follow Saxon along the corridor, feeling a little out of place. I've never worked in an office, and I'm unused to the dynamics, the atmosphere, and all the people. I love my job, but it must be fun sometimes to be around others during the day.

"That's my office," he says, gesturing to the left, but continues along the corridor. "Kip's is down here." He turns left, and I follow him into a large room with a desk behind which sits a woman who looks to be in her fifties. She's wearing a smart, light-gray suit, and her wavy salt-and-pepper hair is neatly clipped back.

"Hey Marion," he says, "I found her." He smiles at me. "This is Marion, Kip's PA."

"You must be Alice," she says, standing and holding out her hand. "How lovely to meet you at last."

I walk over and shake her hand. "So you're the one who keeps him in check?"

"She's the only one who can," Saxon states.

"Hardly," she says wryly. "The Chevalier boys are a wild bunch."

"Boys," he repeats. "We're nearly thirty."

"You'll always be boys to me." She smiles. "Their meeting's over. They won't be long."

I wander to the doorway of Kip's office and glance inside. It's large and spacious, the minimal furniture all chrome and glass. On the wall are framed posters of old sci-fi movies, like *Invaders from Mars*, and *The Creature Walks Among Us*.

"He likes space," Marion says from behind me.

"It's very neat," I reply. "Your doing?"

"Nope, that's all Kip," she says. "I think Saxon is so untidy that Kip goes the other way."

Saxon just laughs.

I turn as behind us someone says, "You found her, then?"

It's obviously the twins' brother. He's younger. Taller. Heavier. Cockier. Good looking, and he obviously knows it. His eyes are a shade lighter than the twins', and he has designer stubble rather than a beard.

"I did," Saxon says. "Damon, this is Alice. Alice, our younger brother, Damon."

We shake hands, my face warming as his gaze skims over me. "I've heard a lot about you," he says.

"Likewise," I tell him. "The word miscreant was used."

He grins and glances at Saxon. "I like her already."

Saxon grins. Then he says, casually enough that I know it's not casual, "How's it going in there?"

"He walked out," Damon says.

Who did? Craig? Or Kip?

Saxon glances at me, then gestures at Kip's office, and the two of them go inside and start murmuring.

I look at Marion, who smiles. "Lovely weather, isn't it?" she asks.

"Beautiful. Wellington's putting on a good show for me. Usually I'm blown to bits when I come here."

She laughs. "Can I get you a coffee?"

"No thanks, too nervous." I say it before I think better of it, wondering if she'll make fun of me.

But she just says, "Aw, don't be. He's a pussycat."

"It's been a while since I've seen him, that's all. I'm... ah... not quite sure what to expect. Out of sight, out of... you know."

"You've not been out of his mind," she states. "I can tell you that much."

"Oh. Well." I clear my throat. "How long have you worked for him?"

"Around five years. He works very hard. Twelve-to-fourteen-hour days, six or even seven days a week, most weeks. Usually I have to pry him out of his office with a shoehorn. This is the first week he's taken off in years.

"Oh, he's taking time off?" I hadn't expected that. I thought he'd go in to work during the day and I'd see him in the evening.

"He was quite adamant about it," she says. Then she leans forward conspiratorially. "I think he's a little nervous, too, actually. He's even wearing his best suit."

I smile. "He's taking me out to dinner."

"I know. To Le Soleil, of all places."

"Le Soleil?"

"You're in for a treat," she says. "It's the best restaurant in Wellington."

My mouth opens, but no words come out as, down the corridor, I hear voices, and I turn and watch as two people walk into the office. One is a woman with short dark hair, dressed in a smart dark-gray suit—he's mentioned his head of HR, Helen, and I wonder if it's her. The other is a guy in a three-piece navy-blue suit, a crisp white shirt, a light-blue-and-silver-striped tie, and glasses. Oh my God, he's gorgeous.

I needn't have worried that the chemistry between us had disappeared. As soon as my gaze falls on him, I inhale sharply, and my heart immediately bangs on my ribs.

He's looking at his phone, but as he enters the room he glances up. For a few seconds he stares at me as if he can't quite believe I'm there. To my left, out of the corner of my eye, I see Saxon and Damon emerge to watch the scene with amusement, but I can't tear my gaze from the guy whose brown eyes are fixed on mine.

I don't know what to expect—whether he'll come over and shake my hand, smile and politely say hello, or even just nod and turn to finish his conversation with the woman. But he doesn't do any of those.

Instead, he thrusts his phone and briefcase at Helen, who fumbles and almost drops them, and then he strides across the room, bends and puts his arms around me, picks me up, and spins me around in a circle with a triumphant whoop.

"Aw," Saxon says. "You old softie."

# Chapter Sixteen

## *Kip*

"I missed you," I tell Alice as I lower her down.

"I missed you, too." She smiles, looking up at me with that expression on her face that makes my heart race, as if I'm a movie star, and she's been waiting in line for my autograph for hours. She looks amazing, in a white dress that emphasizes her English-rose complexion, her wavy hair curling around her shoulders looking as soft as candy floss. Her makeup is subtle but sultry, her lips a dusky pink, and her blue eyes are sparkling. Jesus, I could eat her up in one bite.

"You okay?" Damon asks.

With some reluctance, I realize I should go over the details of the meeting. To my surprise, though, Helen says, "Don't worry. I'll fill them in if you want to head off."

I glance over and find Saxon smiling at me. "Go on," he says. "You two get going."

"Thanks for picking her up," I tell him, and he winks at me.

I look at Marion, who says, "There's nothing here that won't wait."

"All right." I collect my phone and briefcase from Helen, then hold my hand out to Alice. She slides her hand into it shyly, and I say, "See you guys later."

"Nice to meet you," they call to her, and we head out of the office.

We walk along the corridor, our fingers interlinking. "I'm sorry I wasn't there to meet you," I tell her.

"It's okay. I embarrassed myself by thinking Saxon was you."

"You're not the first and you won't be the last. Catie was completely confused when she first saw me and I didn't recognize her. She actually fainted when Saxon came in."

"Really?"

"Yeah. She was four months pregnant and she hadn't eaten any breakfast, which didn't help." He pushes the door open, and we go out into the foyer.

"Bye, Mr. Chevalier," the receptionist calls.

"'Bye Sasha." He leads me through the open front door and out into the sunny day.

"'Bye Mr. Chevalier," Alice echoes in a teasing voice.

"My staff is very respectful."

"Should I call you Mr. Chevalier?"

"Actually I was going to ask you to."

"Really?"

I just laugh, and she rolls her eyes and says, "I'm so gullible."

"It's one of the many things I like about you."

"I don't know why I thought he was you," Alice says. "You're nothing alike really."

"We're identical," I say, amused.

"Maybe. But he doesn't make my heart race the same way you do."

It's such a nice thing to say, and it makes me glow. I put my briefcase down, call for an Uber, then catch her hand, and she turns to face me. Slowly, I move toward her, fixing my gaze on hers. Her eyes widen, and she takes a couple of steps backward, stopping when she reaches the wall with a bump.

Closing the distance between us, I hold her hands down by our sides, linking her fingers with mine. She's wearing sandals, and she's a few inches shorter than me, so I have to dip my head to bring my mouth close to hers, where I pause.

"Oh," she says helplessly, her breath whispering across my lips.

I wait, savoring the moment. I've been thinking about kissing her all day, struggling to concentrate in my meeting, wondering how I was going to feel when I first set eyes on her again. I'd convinced myself she couldn't possibly be as beautiful as I remembered, and that I must have imagined the electricity that passed between us every time we touched. But she is beautiful. And I didn't imagine our attraction.

"Are you going to kiss me?" she asks.

I move closer so I'm pressing her up against the wall. "I'm enjoying the anticipation," I murmur, kissing up her jaw to her ear, and nuzzling behind it.

She shivers. "Normally I'd agree, but I'm dying here."

I inhale, breathing in her sweet scent, and kiss the delicate skin behind her ear. "You smell amazing."

"Kip, for Christ's sake…"

I laugh and brush my lips along her jaw to her mouth. She sighs and her lips part, and I slide my tongue inside and intertwine it with hers in a luxurious kiss that seems appropriate for the beautiful summer's day.

Then I lift my head and wrap my arms around her. She slides hers around my waist, and we stand there and hug for a while. I close my eyes for a moment, breathing in the summer air, just enjoying having her in my arms at last.

"You okay?" she asks eventually. "Saxon told me about your meeting. Damon said someone walked out. Was it Craig?"

"Yeah. It didn't go well."

"I'm so sorry."

"Don't worry about it." I lower my arms. My stomach is still churning from the unpleasant atmosphere in the room, but I refuse to let him spoil my time with Alice. I look into her baby-blue eyes. "I should have organized it so we were going home first. I don't know if I can wait until after dinner to make love to you."

She gives me a dazzling smile. "We've waited this long. And we need to keep our strength up."

"That is true." I sigh and release her, and pick my briefcase up as the Uber arrives. "Okay. Come on then."

We get in the car, sitting close in the back, holding hands.

"How's your mum?" I ask as the driver navigates the busy roads.

She tucks a stray strand of hair behind her ear. "She's good, thank you. She and Charlie are having a girlie few days while I'm away. I think they're going to watch back-to-back episodes of *The Bachelorette*."

"You don't like the series?"

She wrinkles her nose. "There aren't any elves or robots in it."

That makes me laugh. "You don't like romance?"

"Of course I do! I found the scene where Luke Skywalker snogged his sister very romantic."

"What about where Leia tells Han Solo she loves him?"

"And he replies, 'I know'? Did you know that was improvised?"

"Seriously?"

"He was supposed to say 'I love you too,' but he didn't think it fit with his character."

I glance across at her. She's looking away, at the shops and cafés as we pass. "It's such a great line," she says, clearly still thinking about *Star Wars*. "So Han."

I smile and look back at the road, conscious that I haven't felt as happy as this for a long time.

The Uber takes us through the city to Lambton Quay and drops us outside the Parliament buildings. Bringing my briefcase with me, I take Alice's hand and head toward the executive wing, which is called the Beehive because its shape resembles a traditional woven form of beehive called a skep. Alice's eyes widen as we approach the building.

"Wait," she says, "where are we going?"

"Le Soleil is on the third floor," I tell her.

"Of the Beehive?"

"Yep. You have to book a day in advance, and give your first and last names so security can check you out." Grinning at the look on her face, I lead her into the building. "Hey, Ian," I say to the guy on security.

"Good evening, Mr. Chevalier." He smiles at Alice. "Good evening, Ms. Liddell."

"Hello," she says, blushing.

She places her handbag and I put my briefcase on the tray, and then Ian gestures for her to walk through the security scanner. I follow her. "All good," he says, passing us our items, "have a great evening."

"Thanks, Ian." I pick up my briefcase, take her hand again, lead her across to the elevators, and press the button to call the car.

"You're trying to wow me, aren't you?" Her eyes are suspicious, although she's smiling.

"I like good food," I reply. "And it's no fun eating out on your own. So I'm making the most of you being here."

"Fair enough." She curls her fingers around mine, and we go into the car as the doors open.

I press the button for the restaurant on floor three, and the doors close. As the elevator rises, I move her so her back is against the wall and slide my free hand to the back of her neck.

"Kip!" She glances around, blushing. "There are probably security cameras in here."

"Don't care." I kiss her, marveling at the softness of her mouth. I sigh, which comes out as a low growl, and Alice moans in response, her tongue darting out to meet mine. Whoa, zero to sixty in, what, two seconds? Even faster than my Merc, which is saying something.

I release her as the doors part, and give her a warning look. "You're bad for my blood pressure."

"And you've wiped off all my lipstick."

I take her hand and lead her out toward the restaurant. "We definitely need to keep our strength up."

It's not a huge restaurant, but it's beautifully presented, with smaller round tables by the windows, and longer rectangular ones down the middle of the room for larger parties. The tables are covered with neat white tablecloths topped with small displays of fresh flowers, and the cutlery is all polished silver. The decor is dark, sophisticated, and intimate. A guy sitting at a grand piano is playing *The Nearness of You*.

It's relatively busy as it's a Friday night, with about two-thirds of the tables occupied, mostly by people wearing suits, with a few of the women in cocktail dresses. Alice stands out in her white summer dress, like a wild daisy in a world of concrete and glass.

"Oh God, I'm wearing totally the wrong thing," she says, pausing in the doorway.

"You look amazing," I tell her. "I can't wait for everyone to see you're with me."

She gives me a wry smile, but lets me lead her forward. We're met by the restaurant manager, who welcomes us in and shows us to our table. As I requested, it's the best one, in the corner by the window and therefore quiet and secluded, overlooking the flagpoles flying the New Zealand flag, and the neatly tended green. We sit at the round table in the comfortable suede-covered chairs, and the manager informs us that our waiter will be Wiremu, who'll take our drinks order in a few minutes.

I open the wine menu and run my gaze down it. "Shall we have some champagne, or would you prefer a cocktail?" I look up at her. She's looking around the room, her eyes like saucers.

"Are any of these MPs?" she whispers, gesturing at the other diners.

"Mmm... I recognize two or three. You get all kinds of people here. That guy's an All Black. The woman over there is an actor—she was in that James Cameron movie that came out last week. And that dude's the lead singer in Paua of One."

"Oh shit, you're right. Jesus, Kip, why did you bring me here?"

"Because it's the best place in Wellington, and I wanted to show you off."

Her gaze comes back to me, flattered but puzzled. "Why? I'm nothing special."

I look at her fine features, her bright-blue eyes, her wavy blonde hair, and her gorgeous figure, and feel a swell of smug pleasure that she doesn't know how beautiful she is, because she's not had any guy whispering sweet nothings to her in the darkness. I was the first man to taste her, to be inside her. I don't know why, but I find that an incredible turn on.

She blushes. "Don't look at me like that."

"Like what?"

"Like you want to eat me alive."

I let my lips curve up. "Now you're talking. I don't really need to see the menu."

She laughs and opens hers up.

"You haven't answered me," I say, "champagne, a cocktail, or something else?"

She nibbles her bottom lip. "I've never ordered champagne in a restaurant."

"Then champagne it is." I smile up at the waiter as he appears—a good looking Māori guy in a white shirt and black waistcoat and trousers.

"Kia ora," he says, "can I get you a drink while you look at the menu?"

"We'll have a bottle of the 2009 Louis Roederer Cristal, please," I tell him.

"Of course," he says without batting an eyelid, and goes off to fetch it.

Alice stares at me. "It's over five hundred dollars a bottle."

"Yeah. It's good stuff. It scored a hundred points in Wine & Spirits Magazine."

"Out of what?"

"A thousand." I give a short laugh at the look on her face. "Out of a hundred. Very rare."

"You like to tease me, don't you?"

"I do. It was created by Louis Roederer for Alexander II of Russia in 1876. He ordered that the champagne be bottled clear, with a flat bottom, so nobody could hide a bomb in the punt."

"The punt?"

"The dip in the bottom."

"I didn't know it was called that. Wow. That's a fascinating story."

"Plenty more where that came from." I open my menu. She doesn't reply, and after a few moments I look up to find her watching me with a smile. "What?"

"You," she says. "I was worried I wouldn't feel the same way about you."

My heart skips a beat. "And do you?"

She meets my eyes, and we lock gazes for a moment. "Oh yes," she whispers. Then she drops her gaze to her menu. "Ooh," she says, "risotto. I love a good risotto."

Smiling, I turn my attention to the food, and we spend a pleasant few minutes talking about options. Wiremu comes back with the bottle of champagne, pops the cork, and pours us both a glass. She takes a sip and gives a girlish giggle. "Mmm. Lovely."

I wink at Wiremu, who tries to hide a smile, and fails. "Have you made your decision?" he asks.

"Yes, thanks. We'll have the bread to start with, but we'll skip the starter." Alice said she didn't want to eat too much and was happy with just a main course. "I'm going for the Fiordland venison, and the young lady has decided on the smoked beetroot risotto. We'll also have a side of the thick cut truffle fries, please."

"Of course." He collects the menus and heads off.

"Please don't tell me you're vegetarian and I took you to a rib shack for our first date," I say.

She laughs. "No. I have a thing about risotto, that's all." She holds up her champagne glass.

I raise mine. "What shall we toast?"

"Great sex," she says.

"I'm more than happy to drink to that." Laughing, we tap them together carefully and take a sip.

She lowers her glass and leans forward, arms on the table. It pushes her breasts together and gives her an enticing cleavage.

"Have you got something in your eye?" she asks. "You're blinking a lot."

"It's taking every ounce of willpower I own not to eye-dip you."

That makes her laugh, and she glances down, then back up at me with mischief. "Eye-dip all you like."

I don't, but it makes me smile. "I missed you," I tell her again.

"I missed you, too. It's been nice chatting most evenings, though."

"Yeah. I look forward to it at the end of the day."

"Me, too." She sips her champagne again. "So… come on, tell me about Craig. He sprung that on you, didn't he?"

I inhale deeply and blow the breath out. "I don't want to sour the mood."

"Aw, come on. We're friends first, right? I like that you talk to me."

I sigh again. "He called yesterday and told Marion he wanted to see me this afternoon. She tried to put him off until next week, but he insisted, and in the end I thought it would be best to get it over with, rather than worry about it for a week."

"Makes sense."

"He turned up at four p.m. with Renée."

"Oh, shit."

"Yeah. She basically ran the meeting. Helen—she's our head of HR—kept trying to shut her up, but she wouldn't take a back seat. He hardly said anything. I asked if I could talk to him alone, but Renée said no, and he refused to look at me. Helen was amazing—she kept slapping Renée down and telling her to let him speak for himself, but he just wouldn't engage. I think Renée had forced him to go in."

"So I guess you raised the issue of his employment at Kingpinz," she says. "What happened there?"

"I asked why he hadn't given me his resignation. Renée said it was because he hadn't done anything wrong. Helen then made it clear that his behavior in the previous meeting was out of order: the way he spoke to Marama, who's the other member of our team, as well as the fact that he accused us of ganging up against him, and also that he told a reporter we'd made a deal with Sunrise when we hadn't. I tried to talk to him, and said we needed to find a way to work together, even though it galled me. He said things would be fine if we agreed to sell MOTHER to Renée. She then offered us fifteen million dollars."

"Jesus. I thought Craig had agreed to ten million."

"He had. She knows what potential the software has."

"What did you say?"

I turn the glass in my fingers. "I said no."

"I bet that felt good."

I give a small smile. "Yeah."

Alice studies me for a moment. "Do you regret it now?"

I tip my head from side to side. "It would have been good to feed that money back into the company. It would have benefited all of our employees. Just because Saxon, Damon, and I have money, it doesn't mean that everyone has. I wonder whether I was being selfish in making that decision."

"Selfish in selling a revolutionary piece of software for a decent price? Only you could think that."

"It sounds altruistic, but deep down, if I'm honest, can I say I'm not looking for admiration and approval? I don't know."

"Admiration and approval from whom?"

I shrug.

"From society? From your parents? Or from Saxon?"

I frown.

"There's a whole *Friends* episode where Joey tells Phoebe there's no such thing as a selfless act," she says. "She spends the whole time trying to prove to him he's wrong, but she can't do it. You're refusing to be guided by money because you know it's going to make a huge impact and advance lots of different areas of technology, and you want to work with the best company you can because it's going to be amazing. You'd be inhuman if you didn't get a kick out of that."

I study my glass, thinking about it.

"What happened after you turned them down?" she asks.

"Renée screamed at me, told me I was being an idiot, and she was offering me a fortune. I could see she hadn't expected me to turn her down. I... lost my temper a bit."

"You yelled at her?"

"No. I didn't raise my voice. Sunrise has been having trouble with working conditions and pay cuts in its factories. Plus I was with her at a meeting at the hospital once and she made fun of someone with a speech impediment. That didn't sit right with me. So I told her I'd never sell my software to a company run by Attila the Hun."

She laughs. "What did she say to that?"

"She called me a fucking cunt. It was almost funny watching Helen type that up. Renée said, 'Don't type that,' and Helen said, 'Everything's going in the minutes.' I thought Renée was going to tear her laptop out of her hands."

"What did Craig say while all this was going on?"

"He just put his head in his hands." I look through the window at the view. It's a few hours until sunset. The sun's rays have bathed the grass in a warm gold, and they're reflecting off the windows of the high-rise buildings, almost blinding me. I think about Craig—one of my oldest friends—and how he seemed almost broken, a completely different man from the witty, smart guy I thought I knew so well.

"How did it end?" Alice asks softly.

Wiremu arrives at the table with a plate of sourdough bread and house-churned cultured butter. Alice doesn't touch it, though, still looking at me. I take off my glasses, fold them up, and leave them on the table. "I told him I wasn't going to sell MOTHER to Sunrise, and if he were to continue working at Kingpinz, he would need to accept that. He said I was making him look foolish by going back on his promise. I told him he didn't need my help for that. Then I fired him."

"Ah."

"Renée said they were going to sue me for wrongful dismissal. Then they both walked out."

"What did Helen say?"

"I thought she was going to bollock me. I apologized, and she said, 'I'm glad you fired him. He's a knob.' She did add that it was going to be an unpleasant court case, but I think after he started seeing Renée, it was always going to end like that."

"How sad. I can't see that relationship having a happy ending."

"No, me neither."

"I'm so sorry," she says, holding out her hand.

I slide mine into hers. "Ah, it's okay." I lift her hand and kiss her fingers. "Let's not talk about it anymore. I don't want him to spoil our time together." I release her hand. "Come on, this bread looks amazing. Tell me about your day. What have you been up to?"

# Chapter Seventeen

## *Alice*

I can see how much the altercation with Craig has upset Kip, but he obviously wants to move on, so I start telling him about tomorrow's podcast which is already set up for release, and which looks at a TV series that's just come out based on a well-known fantasy novel.

He spreads some butter on a piece of sourdough, then holds it out to me. Smiling, I take it from him and nibble it while he butters himself another.

He talks about some of the other podcasts I've done, and it's obvious from what he says that he's really listened to them. I'm incredibly touched. It's one thing to be aware of Wonderland; it's another to have listened from beginning to end to more than one episode.

"Oh shit," he says suddenly. "I forgot! I got you a birthday present." He lifts his briefcase onto his lap, opens it, takes out a gift bag, and hands it to me, replacing his briefcase on the floor.

"Hmm," I say, shaking it and recognizing the shape of a book, "I wonder what this is? A watch?" I place it on my wrist. "A hat?" I put it on my head.

He just grins and munches on his bread.

Smiling, I unwrap it carefully. It's actually two books, housed in a red slipcase. The books are bound in what I think is red Morocco leather. The spines have raised bands and are lettered in gilt. One is *Alice's Adventures in Wonderland*, the other is *Through the Looking-Glass, and What Alice Found There*. Both the copies bear a dedication: 'Margaret Evelyn Hardy from the Author, Christmas 1871.' One of them contains a piece of paper that explains their origin.

Without lifting my head, I look up at Kip. He gives me an impish smile.

I look back at the paper. It explains that Margaret Evelyn Hardy is the daughter of the first Earl of Cranbrook, and Lewis Carroll sent copies of his books to Margaret at the earl's request.

"These are first editions?"

He nods.

"Signed by Lewis Carroll himself?"

He nods again.

"But…" I go to brush my fingers across one of the books and stop, afraid to touch it. "These must have cost you a fortune."

He shrugs. "You're worth it." He smiles.

It's a lovely thing to say, but it doesn't come anywhere near to explaining why he would have spent what has to be serious money on these. I don't know a huge amount about first editions, but I'm pretty sure that these signed copies would have cost him upwards of a hundred thousand dollars.

"I don't know what to say," I whisper.

"Thank you is customary."

I look up at him. "Why would you buy me something like this?"

He butters himself another chunk of sourdough. "Because you were named after Carroll's Alice. Because you've done so amazingly well with Wonderland." He puts down his knife. "And because I want to get in your knickers." He takes a bite of the bread, his eyes gleaming.

"You didn't need to spend money on me to do that," I point out. "I'm a sure thing, in case you haven't realized."

He grins and takes a sip of champagne. Then, as I continue to stare at him, he leans on the table and looks into my eyes. "It's your birthday," he says simply. "I wanted to buy you something nice."

"You're the king of understatements, aren't you?"

"The knight, not the king." He laughs and leans back as Wiremu arrives to clear our plates.

Carefully, I slot the books back into the slipcase, then into the bag to protect them. "Thank you very much," I say as graciously as I can. "It's a wonderful present, and I'm very touched."

"You can thank me properly later," he says.

Wiremu picks up the last plate, and I'm sure he's hiding a smile.

As he walks away, I scold, "Kip!"

"What?"

I shake my head. "You're incorrigible." I honestly don't know what to say. I guess he has so much money that he's used to spending a hundred thousand on books for a girl he's only spent one night with. "What do you buy a girl on a third date?" I ask. "A yacht?"

"Drink your champagne and stop worrying."

I take a sip, sniffing as the bubbles go up my nose. I'm worried. I agreed to come and see him because I assumed that even though I'm staying a few nights, we'd both accept that would be the end of it. But a gift like this doesn't suggest he's thinking the relationship is going to end after I go back to Gisborne. I think about the fact that Saxon took me to Kingpinz, and that Damon said, *I heard a lot about you.*

"Kip," I say gently, "I thought you understood. I came here today because I thought you were just after some fun. I haven't changed my mind. I can't have a relationship."

"Right," he says. "Just really, really fantastic sex. Got it."

I try not to laugh. "I'm serious."

"Me too."

"Kip…"

He sighs. "I know you have obligations, and I don't expect anything. I just want to spend time with you. I like you a lot. You make me laugh, and I haven't done a lot of that lately. You make me happy." He shrugs.

What can I say to that? How can I criticize him after he said something so incredibly sweet?

"All right," I say softly. "So what have you got planned for the next few days?"

"I was thinking you on top, then from behind, to start with," he says.

I giggle, and that makes him laugh, and we're both chuckling away by the time Wiremu returns with our mains.

"Seriously, though," I scold as we heap chunky fries onto our plates.

"I am serious. I want to spend as much time as I can with you in bed."

"I won't be able to walk."

"That's the plan." He grins.

"Saxon said he wants us to go around for dinner."

"He'll understand. He's permanently knackered. I think Catie's wearing him out."

I smile. "What about Damon? Is he seeing anyone at the moment?"

"No one serious." He cuts up his venison. "This time last year, his then girlfriend threw a Christmas party for all their friends and family.

Halfway through, she stopped the music and proposed to him in the middle of the room."

"Oh wow. That was brave."

"Some might say idiotic. If she'd assumed he'd be too embarrassed to say no in front of everyone, she didn't know him as well as she thought."

"He turned her down?"

"He was annoyed that she tried to force his hand."

"Well, you know all about that."

His lips twist. "Yeah. He just turned around and walked out. The following day, he went home to discover that she'd cut up all his suits and tossed all his belongings onto the front lawn, and changed the locks."

"Oh shit, really?"

"Neither Saxon nor I were surprised. She was mad as a box of frogs."

I laugh. "So has he dated since?"

"Dating is a strong word…"

"Ah, he's been on Tinder?"

He chuckles. "Yeah, he's been out with a few girls. He's also been working hard. Like me this year, he's thrown himself into the business instead. It seems like a sensible option until you go home to a dark house."

I have a mouthful of the risotto, which is marvelous. "Are you lonely?"

He studies his plate, then eats a piece of venison. "Sometimes I miss sharing things with someone."

"And sex, obviously."

His eyes meet mine. "Obviously."

"So… me on top?"

"That's the plan."

"You've been giving this some serious thought."

"You have no idea."

I giggle. The champagne is starting to have an effect. "How have you coped without sex this year? I'm guessing you have a close relationship with your right hand."

"I'm left-handed, but yeah."

"I didn't think about that. So which hand you use for… you know… depends on which hand you write with?"

"On your dominant hand, I guess, yeah."

"Ooh, dominant. I like that word."

He stops eating for a moment, studies his plate, and blows out a long breath before taking another mouthful.

"Sorry," I say. "Am I putting you off your food?"

"Nothing puts me off my food. You're just sending my thermostat shooting up, that's all."

I eat another forkful of risotto while I watch him. "Do you mind me talking about sex?"

"Not at all. In fact I encourage it." He glances around. "First time for me in Le Soleil, though."

"Glad I can be your first in something," I tell him.

"Oh, you've been my first for many things," he replies, somewhat mysteriously. I don't know what he means by that, but it gives me warm fuzzies in my belly.

"I joke about it," I say in a low voice, studying his warm brown eyes as they watch me with some amusement, "but I don't get it. You're rich, handsome, and smart. You could have any woman you want. Why do you want me?"

"Because I like the way your eyes light up when I do or say something unexpected. I like shocking you."

"Corrupting me, you mean."

"Po-tay-to, po-tah-to."

"That's it, isn't it? You like seeing the innocence fade from my eyes."

"Yeah. It turns me on." He gives a lazy, sexy smile as he reaches for his glass and takes a sip.

I have another forkful of risotto. "So how many times are you going to fuck me this weekend?"

He coughs into his champagne, then dabs his serviette to his mouth, giving me a reprimanding look. "Jesus. Don't say things like that."

I eat a chunky chip, chuckling. "And your answer?"

"As many times as I can manage?"

"Ballpark?"

"Dunno. Three or four?"

"Okay, I'd be happy with that." I think about what he said and frown. "Wait, you mean three or four times over the next few days, right?"

"Three or four times a night," he corrects. His brows draw together. "Although we'll probably be radioactive by the end."

"What?"

He finishes off his champagne, his eyes sparkling as much as the wine. "I finally have you within arm's reach. You really think I'm going to have you once and then roll over and go to sleep?"

I narrow my eyes, then say, "You're messing with me."

"No. Ordinarily, maybe once a night might be satisfactory, but our time's limited, and I want to make the most of you." His eyes gleam with amusement. "I don't know what you expected, but you're going to get seriously screwed this weekend."

I catch my breath. This competition to try to shock each other is pointless. He's always going to win.

He flicks open the buttons on his jacket, slides it off, and places it over the back of his chair. The front of his waistcoat is made from the same material as his jacket and trousers, but the back is satin, and a lighter blue with a gorgeous swirling pattern in the fabric. The contrast with the crisp whiteness of his shirt is startling.

"I'm guessing your suit is bespoke," I say, somewhat faintly. It fits snugly to his frame. "Where's it from?"

"A very nice Italian tailor."

"In Wellington?"

"In Italy."

My eyebrows rise. "You actually go to Italy to get your suits?"

"I do. My business suits are British, from Savile Row. My evening suits are Neapolitan."

I lean a chin on my hand, fascinated. "What's the difference?"

"The cut, as well as some of the features. Both styles have high armholes compared to the American suit. But Italian suits have less shoulder padding. They're snug fitting, with piped pockets." He lifts the jacket to show me. "British suits have flapped pockets and usually a ticket pocket. They developed from military uniforms, so they're stiffer and more structured. Great for the office. Italian suits are more flamboyant; they have brio. Perfect for the evening."

"Brio?" I've not heard that word.

"Panache. Style." He lifts an eyebrow and smiles.

"You fascinate me," I tell him, a tad breathless.

"It's not unusual to wear an Italian suit. Saxon and Damon are the same."

"Yeah, but they don't give me the feels."

He meets my eyes, and we study each other for a while.

"I like the way you look at me," he says eventually.

I smile, then lean back as Wiremu approaches to collect our plates. "Would you like to see the dessert menu?" he asks.

"Yes, please," Kip says. Wiremu takes the plates away, then returns with a menu for each of us.

I'm full of bread, risotto, and chunky fries, but the desserts look scrumptious.

"How about we share something?" Kip says when I tell him I don't want to eat too much if I'm going to get screwed senseless. "You choose."

"Tonka Chocolate Crémeux," I read out. "From Willy Tonka's chocolate factory?"

He laughs. "Tonka beans are the seeds from the kumaru tree from South America. They look like raisins."

"What do they taste like?"

"Vanilla with a touch of spice and tobacco. They're illegal in the U.S."

"Why?"

"They contain a chemical compound that's toxic when consumed in high quantities. You'd have to eat a shit-ton of dessert to get into trouble, though."

"We've got to try that, then. As well as the chocolate crémeux, it has banana bread, whipped milk jam, and salted caramel ice cream. I don't even know what whipped milk jam is, but it sounds amazing."

We give our order to Wiremu, and he tops up our glasses, then retreats.

The sun is low over the horizon now, and the room is flooded with a rich golden light. Every now and again, I can detect Kip's cologne. It smells expensive and sophisticated. Of course it does. No five-dollar supermarket spray for this guy.

"Thank you so much for this," I say. "I'm having a wonderful time."

"And it's not over yet," he teases.

The pianist starts playing *I Got it Bad and That Ain't Good*. Kip gives me a mischievous smile. "Dance with me," he says.

My eyebrows rise. "What?"

He gets to his feet and holds out a hand. "Come on."

My jaw drops as I glance around. "It's not the kind of place where you dance."

"There's music playing, isn't there?"

"Yeah, but there's no dance floor."

"There's room all around the piano." He picks up my hand and tugs it.

"I can't leave the books."

"I think they'll be safe," he says drily.

"Oh my God, no…" Protesting all the way, I let him pull me up and follow him the short distance across to the piano. Conscious of people looking over at us, my face heats as he turns me into his arms, takes my right hand in his left, and we start to move.

He tries not to laugh as he looks at my face. "Why are you blushing?"

"Everyone's looking."

"That's because they're all wishing they had the guts to do what we're doing." He bends his head and lightly kisses me. "You look amazing. I want everyone to see that, tonight, you're my girl."

I look up at him, trying hard to hold onto the reins of my racing heart. This guy… I want to keep this casual. To have fun but make sure I don't fall for him. But it's nigh-on impossible.

We move slowly, from foot to foot. It's nice just being close, and feeling his hand holding mine. His skin is warm, and he strokes his thumb with mine. At one point he lifts his hand and turns me in a circle before pulling me back into his arms. Someone nearby claps, and he chuckles and sends them a smile.

"Shame there's not more room," he says. "It would be nice to take a spin about the floor."

"You like dancing?"

"Yeah. Mum and Dad taught all three of us. They used to win competitions when they were younger."

"I'm afraid I've never danced."

"You mean ballroom dancing?"

"Any type. I've never been to a club."

He tips his head to the side, clearly puzzled. "Seriously?"

"Only danced to songs in my bedroom."

"But you must have had times when your aunt looked after your mum. Didn't you go out then?"

"I was supposed to stay at school until I was sixteen, but as Mum's health deteriorated, I took more and more time off. Friends drifted away, went to university, got jobs and boyfriends."

"There must have been help and support available through the system?"

I give a sad smile, because it's not his fault that he has no idea of the reality. "There are at least forty thousand young carers below the age of twenty-five in New Zealand and that figure is probably vastly underestimated. I've seen a global table that ranks a country based on its awareness and response to young carers, and we're well behind the UK and Australia. There's not enough funding or staff, and those who do exist are overworked and underpaid. There are Facebook groups and so-called support networks, but to be honest I never found them much help."

He studies my face, then pulls me closer to him, sliding his arm around me. I rest my cheek on his shoulder, enjoying his scent, and being close to him. The thought of unbuttoning his waistcoat and shirt later, and sliding my hands beneath the cotton onto his warm skin, sends a tingle down my spine. I don't care that this is undoubtedly going to end in heartache. Right now, I wouldn't rather be anywhere else but in his arms.

The pianist slides smoothly into another song, and we dance for a few more minutes before I say, somewhat reluctantly, "Our dessert has arrived."

"Come on, then." He leads me back to our table, the two of us smiling as a ripple of polite applause sounds around the room.

"Another first," I say, taking my seat.

"For me, too." He picks up his spoon and scoops up a little of the dessert.

"You haven't danced with another girl here?"

He laughs, shakes his head, and closes his lips around the spoon. "Mmm."

I have a spoonful. It's rich, smoky, and creamy. Oh my God, it's amazing. I close my eyes in ecstasy, savoring every second until I swallow, then brush the tip of my tongue across my lip so I don't waste any.

"Jesus," he says. "You're killing me here."

I laugh and open my eyes. "We should order a portion in a doggy bag. I could smear it all over you and lick it off."

He turns his spoon over and sucks it. "I've already got that sorted."

"You've ordered a portion?"

"No. But I bought some edible massage oil." He grins as my eyes nearly fall out of my head.

"What's it made from?"

"Coconut oil. With vanilla. I'm going to make you smell like custard, then lick it all off."

I give him a helpless look. "Oh my God."

He laughs and has another spoonful of the dessert, his eyes dancing as he watches me. He points at the dish with his spoon. "Eat up. You need to keep your strength up."

"I do. I feel a bit faint. Whereabouts is your house, is it far?"

"About ten minutes away. But we're going somewhere else first."

"Oh?" I'm disappointed.

He smiles. "I thought it might be best to give ourselves a little time for our dinner to go down before we indulge in bedroom gymnastics. And it's still your birthday. So we're going to Te Papa."

I haven't been to our national museum for a long time. "Oh, that'll be fun. Is there a special exhibition on?"

"There is." He doesn't elaborate. Gesturing for me to finish the dessert, he puts down his spoon and leans back in his chair. "Would you like a coffee?"

"No, thank you. I'm stuffed."

We chat for a bit while we finish off the champagne. I find him so easy to talk to. I like that he's interested in lots of subjects. He likes science and history and sport and music, and he always has something interesting to say.

When the bottle is empty, we go over to the desk and Kip pays, and then we head out, going back down in the elevator. I hold my birthday present tightly as we walk out to the Uber.

It's a short journey to Te Papa. Once there, we get out of the car, and Kip comes around to take my hand.

We cross the waterfront, holding hands. The sun has nearly set now, the late rays painting the harbor in plums, scarlets, and oranges. Ahead of us, Te Papa glows like a lighthouse. Out the front is a large banner advertising the current exhibition.

My jaw drops, and I laugh as I see the blonde girl in her blue dress with the white pinafore. It's an Alice's Adventures in Wonderland Exhibition.

Kip's eyes are alight with pleasure. "Come on," he says eagerly, "I'm looking forward to this."

# Chapter Eighteen

## *Kip*

I'm pretty sure ninety percent of my thoughts over the past couple hours have been about having sex with Alice. Okay, ninety-five. Possibly ninety-six.

It's impossible not to think about taking her to bed. Despite her lack of experience, the girl was made for loving. I can tell it's on her mind, and I think that's why I'm obsessing about it. Whenever I talk, she stares at me with a look in her eyes that suggests she's thinking about stripping me naked and getting down on her knees, and boy does that make my motor race.

Despite this, I thoroughly enjoy the next hour. We leave her books and my briefcase in one of the lockers near the entrance and head up to the exhibition. It explores the journey of Alice's Adventures in Wonderland from book to screen and includes films and TV programs, but the most fun part is the interactive exhibit, which takes place in a large maze. We meet all the characters from the stories: the White Rabbit with his waistcoat and pocket watch, the grinning Cheshire Cat, and the Queen of Hearts, as well as the Mad Hatter and the March Hare at the tea party. We eat sweets and then have to squeeze through a small door into a tiny house, then have another sweet and climb up a huge chair to look into Alice's room. It's full of bright colors and the crazy creatures from the stories, and by the time we finish, my Alice is smiling, and her eyes are sparkling.

We leave the exhibit and end up in the shop, and I treat her to a pair of flamingo earrings.

"What did you think?" I ask as we retrieve the books and briefcase from the locker.

"It was absolutely wonderful." She chats away about it as I call for an Uber, and before long we're in the car and heading for home.

"It's been a fantastic evening." She holds out her hand, and I close my fingers around hers.

"Has your dinner gone down?" I tease.

She gives a little nod, and her eyes meet mine as she shivers.

"Don't be nervous," I murmur, lifting her fingers to mine.

"I'm not. Well, only a little. It's like Christmas Eve all over again." Her gaze drops to my mouth. "Before you kissed me earlier, you said you were enjoying the anticipation. I know what you meant. I'm so excited. I can't wait… and yet I want this bit to last forever because it feels so good."

Her eyes have taken on a sultry look, the lids lowering to half-mast. She's thinking about kissing me, and maybe about doing more. The thought makes my heart race. She's right; it is like how I felt about Christmas Eve as a child: those glittering presents under the tree; the excitement of waiting for Santa; all that promise.

"I'm excited to have sex with you and not be a virgin," she murmurs so the driver can't hear. "I know you held back last time." She looks up into my eyes. "This time, you don't have to hold back."

My heart bangs on my ribs. "You're sure? You might regret that."

Her eyes flare. "Ooh. Am I letting the tiger out of his cage?"

"Just remember to be careful what you wish for."

She laughs, clearly intrigued.

The car pulls up outside my house, I thank the driver, and we get out.

Like many houses in Wellington, mine sits on the side of one of its hills and is on several levels. Normally I enter through the garage at the top, but today we go in the door to the side and down some steps to the open plan living and dining area. Alice's case sits there, which Saxon dropped off earlier.

She places the gift bag with her books on top, then says, "Wow…" She walks over to the window and looks out at the view of Brooklyn and beyond it the lights of the CBD. Then she turns around, wide-eyed. I look at it through her eyes. I suppose it is impressive. The cream carpet and light-gray suite make the room feel light and airy. The furniture is minimal, with clean lines.

She stops and looks up at a large oil painting of a woman dressed in white. It was inspired by the artist John Singer Sargent, not unlike his 'Portrait of Madame X.' It's beautiful, and still takes my breath away whenever I look at it.

Alice looks at me. "Is this Lesley?"

That makes me laugh out loud. "No. It's the Greek goddess Astraea. She's the virgin goddess of justice, innocence, and purity."

"Figures," Alice says, throwing me a wry look before turning her gaze back to it. "Who's the artist?"

I smile. "Damon."

She looks back at me, her mouth an O. "Seriously?"

"Yeah. He says it's just a hobby. Cocky bastard."

She looks back at the painting. "He's seriously talented. Wow."

I watch her for a moment, jealous of her admiration for my brother. She's not unlike the goddess, the remains of her innocence draped around her like the soft white material of her dress. I want to strip it from her, slowly. Watch her naivety fade from her eyes as I do things to her that she could never have imagined. Does that make me a bad person?

Mumbling beneath my breath, I toss my keys onto the dining table and place my briefcase down, toe off my shoes, tug off my socks, and then slip off my jacket and hang it over a chair. "I'm going to have a whisky," I tell her. "Would you like anything? Champagne? Wine? Whisky, brandy, gin?"

"I'll have a whisky, if you're offering." She walks slowly around the room, running her fingers across the back of the sofa, taking in the furnishings.

Leaving her to explore, I go through to the kitchen, retrieve two tumblers from the cupboard, and throw in a few ice cubes. After studying the bottles of whisky, I choose a Rare Collection Glenfiddich and pour a splash in each glass.

She comes out into the kitchen and stops. I glance over at her, raising an eyebrow at the look on her face. "What?"

Her gaze skims down me, making the hairs rise all over my body. "Look at you," she whispers, "barefoot and gorgeous in the kitchen." She walks up and places her hands on my chest. "You look amazing." Fixing her gaze on me, she pushes me back up to the worktop and moves up close, until her mouth is only an inch from mine. "Will you keep it on?"

Her eyes glitter—she's hoping to shock me. Amused, I reply, "Sure. As long as you understand that you'll be naked." I turn to pick up the whisky glasses and pass her one.

"Don't I get a say in it?" she asks.

"Nope." I sip my whisky.

"Just because you have a Y chromosome," she grumbles and takes a sip of hers. Then her eyebrows rise. "Ooh. That's smooth."

"It should be, the price I paid for it."

She looks at the bottle. "1937? Jesus. How much did that set you back?"

It was over a hundred thousand dollars, but I'm not about to tell her that. "A decent amount. I've been saving it for a special occasion." I smile.

She wrinkles her nose. "That's a nice thing to say."

"What can you taste?"

"Mmm. Toffee. It's lovely."

I have another sip. "There's also a touch of pear."

"I can't taste that."

"I've drunk a lot of whisky. You get to be able to pick out the aromas."

She gives me an amused look. "Why doesn't it surprise me that you're an expert?"

"That's better," I tell her.

"What is?"

"That you're admiring me and not my brother."

Her lips curve up. "It made you jealous that I liked his painting?"

"Of course it made me jealous. You're my girl."

She sighs. "Kip…"

I put down my whisky, take off my glasses, then turn her so she's up against the worktop. "Tonight," I say. I slide my knuckles beneath her chin and lift it so I can look into her eyes. "Tonight, you're my girl."

Her lips part, and she gives a small nod.

"Mine," I murmur, lowering my head so my lips are close to hers. We barely touch, but a tingle runs down my spine.

"Yours," she whispers. "Tonight. One hundred percent."

The thought makes my head spin.

We stand there like that for a moment, lips almost—but not quite—touching. Our breaths mingle. Our chests are rising and falling fast, and I know her pulse is racing, the same as mine. But I hold back for a few seconds longer. Jesus, I want her so much it's making me ache.

I lift both hands to cup her face, brushing my thumbs across her cheeks.

Then, finally, I lower my head and kiss her.

She releases a little sigh as a puff of air against my lips, then opens her mouth to allow me access. I slide my tongue against hers, and she gives a little thrust of her own, entwining them together.

Resting her hands on my chest, she gradually slides them up around my neck. I wrap my arms around her, and we indulge in a long, sensual kiss that sends sparks shooting through me.

Slowly, I slide my hands down over her hips to her thighs, then begin to gather her dress in my fingers. Feeling her lips curve up against mine, I chuckle, but don't stop, drawing the material up over her body as she lifts her arms. Pulling it over her head, I draped it over one of the barstools, then admire the beauty it has revealed.

She's wearing a champagne-colored bra and matching underwear, lacy and pretty, but I want her naked. I move my arms around her back, undo the clasp, draw the straps down her arms, and toss the bra over the dress. Then I hook my fingers in the elastic of her underwear, draw it down her legs, let her step out of it, and put it to one side.

I stand back up and move close to her again. She's blushing a little, unused to being completely naked in a man's kitchen. Self-consciously, she brings her hands up to cover her breasts. I put my arms around her, holding her, shielding her, for a moment at least, until she's too aroused to think about it, and she snuggles up against me.

"I've got something to tell you," she murmurs.

I kiss the top of her head. "Okay."

"I'm on the pill, so… if you don't want to use a condom, you don't have to. It's up to you."

I lift her chin so she's looking up at me. "When did you start taking it?"

"A while ago, to regulate my cycle. I didn't mention it last time because, well, we didn't know each other, and I know you're supposed to use condoms for protection against diseases, but we know each other better now. I've read it's supposed to make it more sensitive for you."

"That's very thoughtful," I murmur, my voice husky with desire.

She nudges me. "I'm just saying. It's up to you."

"I'm clean," I tell her. "I've never had sex without a condom."

Her eyebrows rise. "Not even…"

"Not even. Another first with you." I brush my thumb across her bottom lip. She takes it into her mouth and sucks, looking up at me with her big, innocent, blue eyes.

Oh Jesus, this girl…

My erection springs to life as she sucks. I remove my thumb and kiss her again, this time allowing the full heat of my passion to sear through us both.

She's so soft—her skin, her breasts, her mouth. I cup her left breast in my hand, feeling its weight like a ripe fruit. I've never seen such pale nipples on a woman, the lightest pink, barely darker than the rest of her skin, and they also feel soft, like velvet petals. I tease one with my thumb, then tug it gently until it stiffens. She gives a little moan against my mouth, so I do it again, harder this time, and she sighs, then leans her forehead on my shoulder.

"What's the matter, Alice?" I kiss her ear, then the skin beneath it. "We've only just started."

"I know, but I've been…" she tips her head back, "aaahhh… thinking about this for weeks, and… aaahhh… you make me ache…"

I tease her earlobe with my tongue while I continue to tug her nipple. "Where?"

"Aw, don't make me say it."

I laugh and tug her earlobe between my teeth. "Why not?"

"Don't forget I'm new to all this."

"Oh, I haven't forgotten. You're still gleaming with it."

"With what?"

"Virginity."

"I'm not a virgin," she states as I run my tongue around her ear. "You made sure of that last time, if you remember."

"All right, then. Innocence. It radiates from you. But not for long."

"No," she says sarcastically, "you're going to make sure of that."

I kiss back down her jaw to her mouth. "Yes, I am. I'm going to fuck it right out of you."

She pushes me. "You're so wicked."

"And you love it."

"I do not. I'm horrified. I'm clutching my pearls at your disgusting language."

"I'll give you a pearl necklace if you really want one." I kiss down her neck and draw my tongue across her throat.

"Oh Jesus." She shudders.

Laughing, I lift her and rest her bottom on the edge of the worktop. Then I part her knees and move between them. "Tell me where you ache," I ask, as I cup her breasts and kiss her.

She loops her arms around my neck and arches her spine, pushing her breasts into my hands. "Mmm… everywhere…"

I brush down to her knees, push them wider apart, then slide my hands up her thighs. She shivers and holds her breath as I stroke my thumb across her mound.

"Here?" I murmur, sliding my thumb down into her folds. "Oh, Alice. Already wet and swollen?"

She moans as I draw some of her moisture up over her clit, then circle the pad of my thumb over it.

"Poor girl," I say softly, "aching for me. You won't last five minutes at this rate."

"Ah, don't embarrass me."

"But I like embarrassing you. Watching your cheeks flush. Your lips part." I kiss her, dipping my tongue into her mouth before lifting my head again. "I'm going to keep doing it until your halo slips and that pure light fades into something much dirtier."

"You want me dirty?"

"I do, my innocent little girl. I want to watch the naivety vanish from your eyes and know it's all my fault that you've been corrupted." Slowly, I kiss down her body, pausing by her breasts to suck each nipple, before I drop to my knees in front of her. I run my tongue up her thigh, then press my nose to her and inhale.

"Jesus," she says, and she lowers back onto her elbows.

I place a hand on either side of her and part her folds, groaning at the sight of her all swollen and glistening. My trousers tighten as my erection strains at them, eager for action, but I ignore it. This time is for her. I intend to spend as much of the next few days as I can in bed with her, and I need to make sure she's well lubricated if she's not going to get sore.

Dipping my thumb down inside her, I collect more moisture and spread it through her folds, then lower my head and brush my tongue all the way up to her clit. She moans and clenches, sinking a hand into my hair as I circle the tip of my tongue over the swollen bud. Making her come isn't going to be hard, but I'm not going to draw it out this first time. Once I've released that initial tension, we can start properly, and that's when I get to torture her for as long as I can bear it.

I suck, and lick, and stroke, and tease her entrance with a gentle finger, and it's only a couple of minutes before her breaths turn to gasps, her fingers tighten in my hair, and she cries out loud as her orgasm hits. I feel that deep satisfaction a man feels when his girl comes, and stroke her thigh until she falls back, quivering and gasping.

Getting to my feet, I unzip my trousers, push down the elastic of my boxers, guide the tip of my erection into her folds, and slide inside her with one smooth thrust.

"Oh!" She shudders, looking up at me with her mouth open in surprise.

I close my eyes at the sensation of being inside her without barriers, skin on skin. She's hot, wet, and tight, and it feels exquisite.

"I can't believe we didn't even make it to the bed," she whispers as I lean forward to kiss her.

"Oh, we'll get to bed in a minute," I assure her. "I intend to take you in as many positions as I can manage over the next hour or so."

Her eyes widen. "Hour?"

"Well, don't hold me to it. I'm only human, and you feel amazing without a condom, so I might only make a few minutes." I pull almost out of her, then sink into her soft flesh again with a groan.

"Mmm..." She wraps her legs around me, leaning back on her elbows again, tipping her head back so her hair spools across the worktop like coils of silken rope. "That feels so good."

I sigh and thrust slowly. It's wonderful just to be inside her again.

Leaning over her, I lift her head so I can kiss her, sliding my tongue into her mouth to mirror the movement of me inside her. We stay there for a while, moving together, kissing leisurely, and I think there's never been a moment as perfect as this, with Alice's skin lit by the glow from the stars and the lights of the city.

Eventually I slow and withdraw gently, and she sighs.

"Come on," I say, tucking myself back in. I help her down from the worktop, pass her whisky glass to her, pick up mine, then take her hand and lead her down the stairs to the lower level, where the bedrooms are located.

I take her through to my room, leaving the curtains open because I like seeing the light on her skin, and I lead her over to the bed.

"It's very minimalist," she says, leaving her glass on the bedside table and looking around. It's a large room, and it contains only a bed and two bedside tables, with all my clothes in the walk-in wardrobe.

"I like space. It gives me room to breathe."

"It's very you." She brings her gaze back to me and brushes her hands down my chest, over my waistcoat. "You look like James Bond."

I lift her, wrapping her legs around my waist. "And now I'm taking you to double-oh heaven."

"Jesus, that's a terrible joke," she says, and we both laugh.

"Yeah, sorry about that." I tug the duvet back, then climb on the mattress and fall back onto the pillows so she's on top of me. I push her up, and she sits astride me, her moist folds pressing against the base of my erection through my boxers. She rocks her hips, biting her bottom lip as I press against her. "Go on," I tell her. "You do it, slow as you like."

Her eyes light up. She pushes the elastic of my boxers down, then guides the tip of my erection beneath her until it parts her folds. Pushing down so I enter her a fraction, she leans on my chest, closes her eyes, and then slowly impales herself on me.

"Ah…" I close my eyes too, lifting my arms above my head as she begins to ride me. The sensation of her slick walls grasping and massaging me is exquisite, and I breathe deeply, knowing this is going to take every ounce of self-control I possess.

My eyelids flicker open, because seeing a woman on top of you is half the beauty of this position, and discover her watching me, a sultry smile on her face.

"I'm fucking you," she says.

I lower my hands so I can cup her breasts. "Yes, you are."

She arches her back, sucking her bottom lip as I play with her nipples, still moving slowly, then takes my hands in hers, interlacing our fingers. "I like being in control," she says. "I think I might be a dominatrix."

"Yeah, I don't think so." I pull her hands over my head, bringing her breasts in line with my face, and fasten a mouth onto her nipple.

"Oh!" She squeals, then groans as I suck hard. I don't stop, teasing with my teeth and tongue, then swap to the other one, and continue to do that for a while, until she's squirming against me, moving faster, grinding against me.

"Time for a change." I hold her around the waist, then lift up and turn her onto her back.

"Ooh! It's warm in here," she says. "Can you put the aircon on?"

"Nope. I want you hot and sweaty."

She laughs as I bend and kiss her neck. "Your lovely suit!"

"I can always get it dry cleaned." There's something sensual about being dressed and having her naked beneath me. I loosen my tie, then lift up onto my hands and start to thrust with purpose.

Ah, as much as I love girl on top, being in control turns me on more. I look down and watch myself sliding into her, and fuck me, that's hot. I sit back on my heels so I can get a better look, resting a hand on her belly, then slipping my thumb down to tease her clit.

"You're so gorgeous," she says, breathless, looking up at me the way she does, with wonder in her eyes, making me weak at the knees.

"And you're divine." I stroke up her pale body and caress her breasts. She lifts her arms above her head, purring, and I bend and take one of her nipples in my mouth. She shudders, arching her back. She's like a statue of Astraea, her curves captured in white marble, all purity and innocence—at least she was, until I got hold of her.

The thought sends fireworks shooting through me, and I lift up, holding her hands above her head, and change the angle of my hips so I'm thrusting down into her.

"Oh shit," she says, teeth tugging at her bottom lip. "Ah… Kip… please…"

"Please what?"

"You're making me ache again."

I know how she's feeling, because I'm feeling the same, heat pooling in my groin, an ache growing deep inside me. I'm not going to make an hour. I'm not even going to make five minutes at this rate. I relieved myself in the shower this morning before I went to work, thinking it would help me last longer this evening, but it's not made a blind bit of difference. She's too hot, too gorgeous, and as much as I'd like to make it last hours, this first time is going to have to be hard and fast.

Her skin has started to flush and take on a slight sheen. I bend and kiss her, claiming her lips with long, deep kisses, delving my tongue inside her mouth, and she moans and tightens her legs around my waist, trying to push up and make me grind against her.

"No," I state. "Not yet." I withdraw, move off her, then rotate my finger in the air. She blinks, then rolls onto her stomach. I pull a pillow down and tuck it beneath her hips.

"What's that for?" she asks.

"It changes the angle and makes it easier for me." I move between her legs, push up one of her knees, and slide the tip of my erection down through her folds. Then I stop and lean over her, a hand either side of her shoulders.

Bending, I murmur in her ear, "I'm going to fuck you hard now until you come, okay?"

"Oh God," she whispers. "Yes, please."

Despite my words, I enter her gently, wanting to make sure I've got the angle right. I know it's going to feel deeper for her, and this is the first time any man has taken her this way.

Jesus, that's so hot.

She groans and buries her face in the pillow as I fill her up, until my hips meet her bottom. She's so wet that there's no friction at all.

When I'm all the way inside her, I wait, letting her adjust, and kiss her ear. "All right, Alice?"

"Ohhh… mmm… it feels so good…"

I begin to move. "You like being fucked from behind?"

She gives a little helpless sigh.

"Tell me." I scoop her hair over her shoulder so I have access to the soft skin of her neck and kiss down it.

"Mmm… yes, I like it. Ah, God, I love it…"

I trail my tongue across her skin, heat building inside me. "I want to mark you," I say with a growl. "Make you mine. Will you let me?"

She looks over her shoulder at me, her blue eyes huge, a tad puzzled. She moistens her lips. "Okay," she says in a small voice.

I kiss down, fasten my mouth on the place where her neck meets her shoulder, and suck. She groans, so I suck harder, letting my teeth graze her tender flesh, and she shudders, then squeals and says, "Oh shit. I'm going to come."

At any other time I might have changed position again to draw it out for her, but I'm too turned on now to hold back. I lift my head and push up onto my hands again, and thrust hard and fast, plunging down into her.

"Aaahhh… Oh God, oh God, oh God…" She exclaims every time I thrust, her hands tightening on the pillow, and then I feel her clamp around me as she comes. She cries out, long, deep moans, which turn me on so much that I know I'm not going to last long. I ride her through her orgasm, feeling heat burning inside me, waiting for my own climax to hit.

Despite how turned on I am, it takes a while to build, and I lose myself in her, in the sensation of being surrounded by her, of being inside her. I place a hand between her shoulder blades and press her into the pillow as I thrust myself senseless, and still my orgasm remains elusive. Ah... it's going to hit me like a train when it happens... almost there... everything's tensing... and then my muscles tighten and I shudder as I come inside her, several long, hard pulses that leave me groaning and gasping and almost dizzy as she drains me dry.

Whoa.

I blink and try to focus as I come back down to earth. Alice lies sprawled beneath me, breathing hard. I kiss her neck—soft, gentle kisses now the intensity of emotion has passed. She inhales and then exhales in a huff, and I laugh, withdraw, and fall back onto the pillows. Man, that was intense.

Reaching across to the bedside table, I pick up my whisky, have a big mouthful, and let the cold liquid slide down inside me. Shit, it's hot in here.

I look across at Alice. She hasn't moved. Her face is still buried in the pillow; I don't know how she's breathing, but her chest heaves with exhausted gasps. Her body is shining with sweat. The mark I made on her neck is turning into a light bruise.

"You okay?" I ask, amused.

Slowly, she lifts her head and turns it on the pillow so she's looking at me. Her eyes are wide with something—shock? Bewilderment?

"You've literally fucked me senseless," she admits.

I smirk. "My work here is done."

"Jesus," she says. "Is it always like that?"

Turning onto my side, propping my head on a hand, I hold out my glass and rest it on her back, cooling her skin. "No, Alice. It's very rarely like that."

She meets my eyes, and we study each other for a while.

"I'm so hot," she says eventually. "I'm melting into the mattress."

"You're hot? I'm the one still fully dressed." Her cheeks are flushed, though, and her skin is still shining.

Lifting up, I have another mouthful of whisky, and then take one of the ice cubes into my mouth. I put the glass back on the bedside table, then move over her. Lowering down, holding the ice cube between my teeth, I rest it at the top of her spine.

"Ooh," she says, and shudders. "Oh, actually, that's nice."

I draw it across her neck from one side to the other, watching as water runs over her, then slowly move down her body, dragging the ice cube across her skin. She grunts and wriggles.

"Lie still," I demand.

"Bossy Y chromosome," she says, but she stops squirming.

I continue down her spine, and shift between her legs. The cube is now small and smooth in my mouth. Mischief surges through me, and I part the cheeks of her bottom.

She pushes up onto her elbows and looks over her shoulder. "Kip," she says in a warning voice.

I slide the ice cube into the dip at the base of her spine, and then move it down between her cheeks. She gasps, but I don't stop; I press the ice against the tight muscle there, then push it inside with my tongue.

She squeals, and I lift up and lie on top of her, holding her there with my weight as the ice melts. She moans, shuddering with little rhythmic jerks.

"Did you just come again?" I ask, amused, nibbling her ear.

"Oh…" She buries her face back in the pillow. "What are you doing to me?"

I press the root of my growing erection against her butt. "Did you really think I'd finally get you into my bed for a decent amount of time and not explore every inch of your beautiful body?" I kiss her back. "Not take you every way I can think of?" I kiss her neck, over where I bit her. "Not fuck you until you can't breathe, until we're both exhausted?" I kiss her cheek. "Silly, silly girl."

# Chapter Nineteen

## *Alice*

Kip lifts off me, rolls over, and gets up. He takes off his waistcoat, then his shirt while I watch, unmoving, and goes over to turn on the aircon. The cool breeze wafts over my hot skin.

"I'm going to lock up for the night," he says. "I'll bring your case down." He pauses and asks, with some amusement, "You okay?"

Without moving, I give him a thumbs up.

He chuckles. "I'll be back in a minute." He goes out of the room.

I watch him go, then turn my face and groan into the pillow. Finally, I roll over and get up, moving as if I'm a hundred years old.

Crossing the room, I go into the en suite bathroom, turn on the light, and close the door.

It's large and spacious, decorated with simple, clean lines. I pee, then wash my hands, looking at myself in the mirror. Unsurprisingly, I look as if I've had wild monkey sex. Talk about a mess. I'm sweaty and disheveled. My hair is all over the place. My makeup is smudged. The edges of my lips are blurred from his demanding kisses.

My eyes widen as I look at the growing bruise on my neck. When he said he wanted to mark me, I didn't know what he meant, and agreed because I didn't want to show my ignorance. I've heard about hickeys, of course, but obviously never had one. It was an erotic mix of pain and pleasure, and I didn't expect that, or the possessive growl he gave when he did it.

But then I didn't expect any of it. It's only now that I realize how gentle he was before. But this time... I guess it's my own fault. I did tell him not to hold back. *Just remember to be careful what you wish for.* He wasn't kidding. I had no idea what I was asking. I thought he might be a bit more enthusiastic. I didn't expect him to be quite so... intense. So passionate. To completely consume me like that.

I think about what he did with the ice cube, and my face flames. I didn't think I was a prude. I've watched porn, and I can see why the taboo nature of anything involving slot D is both forbidden and exciting. But for some reason I didn't expect him to go anywhere near there only the second time we slept together! That tiny thrust of his tongue, the insertion of the ice, so insignificant, and yet so kinky to my uninitiated mind, shocked me. As did the way he lay on top of me, holding me down while the ice melted... I shudder as I remember the aftershocks of pleasure that rippled through me.

I thought lovemaking would be a tender expression of our growing affection. I thought he'd be gentle, respectful, and considerate, the way he was the first time.

Instead, I feel completely and totally fucked. I'd say used, except that implies he gave no thought for my pleasure, and that's not true. But it was abandoned, raw, and feral. He held me down and completely took what he wanted from me. And the most surprising thing is that I loved every minute of it.

I feel a little ashamed of that. As a modern woman, shouldn't I be indignant and disgusted at his caveman-like behavior? But I'm not. It turned me on. He completely possessed me. I was totally unprepared to feel like that, and for the first time I hear warning bells, way off in the distance. I feel as if I've fallen into the rabbit hole, and I'm tumbling farther and farther into a fantastical world that's making my head spin.

Is every time going to be like this? Have I signed up for three whole days of being screwed witless? I already know I'm never going to be the same again. And I know I've made it twice as hard—no, a hundred times as hard—to walk away from him.

I glance somewhat shyly at the masculine items on the shelves and around the sink. I've existed in a woman's world since my father died, our cupboards at home filled with perfume, contraceptive pills, makeup, tampons. It's strange to see his razor and beard trimmer, a men's deodorant, his comb and hair products, the bottles of cologne in elegant, expensive bottles. I pick one up and sniff it, comforted by the familiar smell.

Replacing the bottle, I take the hairband from around my wrist, scoop my hair up, and fasten it in a loose, scruffy bun. I take one last look at my flushed cheeks, the mark on my neck, sigh, and look away.

I go out into the bedroom. I can hear him moving around upstairs. It's a little cooler in the room now. I'd like to put some clothing on, but my dress and underwear are in the kitchen, and he still hasn't brought down my case. I cross to the walk-in wardrobe and go inside. I've never seen anything like it—it's a whole other room. Three walls are filled with both hanging space and shelves. The fourth side has a dressing table and chair. The table bears a box filled with cufflinks, tie pins, and wristwatches too big for a woman's small wrist. The whole place smells faintly of his cologne. It has a very masculine vibe. Very Kingsman.

I go over to the shelves and run my fingers across the shirts on the hangers. Over half the shirts are white. Some have thin red, blue, or green stripes. Others are pastel colors—light blue, pale pink. On quite a few, the placket and underside of the collar are contrasting colors, clearly a style he favors. Another rack contains more casual dress shirts—mostly dark colors: purple, black, and navy-blue, some of them patterned: paisley, checked, or with flowers.

He has numerous suits—navy, pinstripe, gray, black, and a couple of summer linen ones. They have different lapels, pockets, and vents at the back. Now I know the design is connected to where they're from, and I can tell the difference between the smart, formal British suits, the elegant, flamboyant Italian ones.

A rack contains a huge number of ties—most of them plain or with elegant stripes or patterns, a few fun ones, including one with red hearts. Bought by a previous girlfriend? There are no signs of a woman anywhere in this house, though. No girly items in the bathroom, no leftover clothing in here. For that I'm thankful. I know he's had girlfriends. I don't particularly like to think about him with other women, though.

Hmm, are we jealous, Alice? That's a new emotion for me.

Another wardrobe holds more casual wear: polo shirts and slacks on hangers, and the rest folded on shelves: jeans, sweaters, rugby shirts, and tees. I take out a plain white tee and pull it on. It's too big, of course, and hangs over my bottom, the sleeves coming almost to my elbow, but I like wearing something of his.

I go out into the bedroom just as he comes into the room, carrying my case and my purse. He glances over and smiles as he sees me in his tee.

"I hope you don't mind," I say.

He shakes his head. "Suits you better than me." His eyes dip down. "Are you cold?"

I follow his gaze and realize my nipples are protruding through the thin cotton like pencil erasers. Embarrassed, I glare at him, and he smirks.

He puts my purse beside the bed and takes my case into the walk-in wardrobe, and I return with him, watching him place it to one side. "Did you bring a toothbrush?" he asks as he takes off his trousers and hangs them over the chair. Now he's only wearing his black boxer-briefs.

I nod, unzip the case, and take out my washbag. I follow him into the bathroom, place it beside the sink, and take my toothbrush out. He puts some toothpaste on his toothbrush, then offers the toothpaste to me. I put a little on mine, and then we brush our teeth standing side by side, glancing at each other in the mirror.

I've never done this with a partner, and I watch my face flush at the thought of sharing the oddly intimate routine with someone else. He notices, and his lips curve up.

"You okay?" he asks, rinsing his toothbrush. "I don't think your eyes could get any bigger."

I nod, spit, and rinse, conscious of my hot cheeks.

"You're trembling," he says. "Are you sure you're not cold?"

I shake my head and wipe my mouth with the towel. I'm suddenly intensely aware of him, of how gorgeous he is, how relaxed and confident.

He studies my face, frowning, then turns and cups my cheeks in his hands. "Did I hurt you?"

"No. I'm okay. Just… overwhelmed. I haven't done any of this before. I've never shared myself with a man. It's all new to me." I give a self-conscious laugh. "I know I'm twenty-six now, but I feel like how I imagine a fourteen-year-old medieval virgin must have felt when she was married to the lord of the manor."

"Aw," he murmurs, frowning, "I didn't think of that." His eyes search mine, and then he pulls me into his arms and hugs me tightly. "I'm so sorry."

I snuggle up against him, my arms close to my chest. "It's okay. It's just… I think maybe because I lost my dad a long time ago, I'm not used to being around a man."

He rubs my back, and I feel him kiss my hair. "I didn't even consider that," he says.

"Neither did I. And even if I had, I wouldn't have thought you would feel so... different from me."

"In what way?"

"In every way. Physically. The way you act. The clothes you wear. The way you speak. You're very much a man."

He kisses my hair again. "I hope that's a compliment."

"Oh, it is, very much so. I don't know if I'm explaining myself very well."

"I understand. I feel the same way about you."

I lift my head to look at him. "In what way?"

He smiles, cupping my face again. "In every way. Physically, of course. There's nothing angular about you. You're all soft, hairless curves. Smooth skin. Hair like silk. Delicate hands." He brushes a thumb across my bottom lip. "And you're also different in other ways men aren't supposed to comment on nowadays."

I'm intrigued. "Like what?"

"The way you're more thoughtful. Compassionate. Gentle. But so incredibly strong and resilient. When I'm cornered, I use my strength and height and weight to influence the other person, but you can't do that. You have to be smart. You're so in control of your emotions. You fascinate me."

His words warm me all the way through. He brushes my cheeks with his thumbs, and presses his lips to mine, his tender, gentle kiss telling me he's sorry, and my heart softens.

He takes my hand. "Come on." He leads me out, turns off the light, and closes the door. We climb on the bed, bringing up the duvet, and he turns off the bedside lamp. Now the room is lit only by the stars and the lights of the city.

Lying back, he pulls me into his arms. I curl up against him, and the two of us nestle down beneath the duvet.

He lifts my chin and gives me a gentle, lingering kiss. Then he strokes my face while he looks into my eyes. "I am sorry," he says. "I didn't consider how strange this must be for you."

"You know when you stare at a very bright light," I reply, "and everywhere you look, all you can see is the after image? That's how I feel."

He brushes my cheek with his thumb. "You're sure I didn't hurt you?"

"No. Well, my neck's a little tender..."

If I thought he'd look remorseful and apologize, I'm to be disappointed. He moves the neck of the tee aside to look at the mark, and his lips curve up.

"No need to look so smug," I say sulkily.

"You did tell me not to hold back."

"You were right. I should have been careful what I wished for."

"Disappointed?" he asks.

I give a short laugh. "No. Not disappointed."

"Then…"

"I'm shocked, Kip."

"At what?"

"Everything! And don't look surprised, I know that's what you wanted. Well, it worked. You shocked me." I'm being sarcastic, but a small part of me is annoyed that I performed exactly the way he wanted. "Are you happy now?"

"Yeah," he says, annoying me even more at his cockiness.

I punch his arm. "Ow," he says. I go to punch him again, and he catches my arm, rolls on top of me, and holds me down. Ooh, he's so strong. I wriggle, but I can't pull free.

My heart bangs against my ribs. "Get off me," I say, irritable that he has such an effect on me.

"No." His brown eyes are sultry, amused. "Stop squirming."

I huff a sigh, but stop moving. He kisses my nose. "Good girl."

"Don't 'good girl' me like I'm a schoolgirl."

"Are you trying to turn me on?"

I try not to laugh. "You're obnoxious."

"And you love it." He kisses me then, sliding his tongue into my mouth, and even though I've already come three times, and I'm exhausted, my body stirs, and I give a long sigh against his lips.

He grins, releases my hands, and tilts his head to kiss me deeply, and I wrap my arms around his neck and kiss him back, so happy right then that I think I could explode.

When he eventually lifts his head, his eyes are full of affection. "I am sorry I shocked you."

"No, you're not."

"I sort of am. I've been thinking about having you in my bed for weeks, and I kinda lost the plot."

I can't help but be flattered by that. "So you're sorry you marked me?" I ask, already knowing the answer.

"No. I'm not sorry about that."

"Why did you do it? It's not like I'm going to let anyone see it."

He shrugs. "I know it's there."

I can almost feel it, like a brand. "I'm glad you asked me, even if I didn't know what you were asking."

"Why did you agree, then?"

"I didn't want to look like an idiot. I note that you didn't ask before you did the vanishing ice trick, though. You knew I'd say no to that."

"Yeah, and yet it felt so good it still made you come," he says smugly. "Maybe you should trust me."

"Depends what else you're going to shove up there. Anything bigger than an ice cube and we might have a problem."

"I promise not to insert anything else unless you beg me to."

That makes me laugh. "Fair enough."

He kisses my lips, long and luscious, then lifts his head and kisses my nose. "Am I squashing you?"

"Yes, but I like it. All the things you said about me—I like how we're different, too. Women are encouraged to believe they can do anything men can do, and it implies we're the same, but we're not."

He moves his hips against mine. "Clearly."

"Mmm, but it's not just about that. You're taller, broader, stronger, and more muscular." I run my hands up his biceps, feeling the hard bulges there. "Your hands are larger. You have hair in places I don't— your face, chest, and belly. Your voice is deeper, and you have this." I brush a finger down his Adam's apple.

"But it's not just that," I continue thoughtfully. "Before she fell ill, my mum was spirited and independent, and she brought me and Charlie up to be the same. But she also thought it important that we be ladylike and feminine. She taught us to sit with our knees together, and to be conscious of our posture and our movement. You don't think about that, though."

"I manspread, you mean?"

I smile. "You're not too bad, but you do sit with your knees apart. You move confidently, as if you expect the world to be watching you. And you speak differently. You're more succinct, you use fewer adverbs, and you don't use flowery language." His eyebrows rise; he didn't know that. "You're also less apologetic than me," I add. Maybe some of that is due to him having money and influence. He's used to being a billionaire boss. I guess that might be one reason why he's so aggressive in bed. I wonder whether his brothers are the same? I won't ask him. It's obvious there's some measure of competition between all three brothers, and somehow I don't think he'd like me thinking about them and sex in the same sentence.

"You like these differences," he observes, and smiles.

"I do," I admit, "but the thing is that I hadn't considered any of it whenever I wondered what sex would be like. I don't know why—I've watched enough nature shows on TV. In the animal kingdom, although the female often chooses her mate, it's the male who mounts her, and she just has to wait for him to do his thing."

"Sounds about right," he says.

I stroke a finger along his jaw, scraping my nail against his bristles. "Hardly. I just didn't expect you to be so…"

"Bossy?"

"Yeah."

"I guess it's always beneath the surface, covered with a thin veneer of civilization." He kisses my nose. "It's different in the bedroom. It's a place to explore fantasies. I'm guessing you wouldn't want a man to tell you what to do in everyday life."

"No," I admit.

"But did you like me taking charge when we had sex?"

I suck my bottom lip.

"Be honest," he scolds.

I give a reluctant nod.

His lips curve up. "Good," he murmurs. "Because it's going to happen again, and the sooner you get used to it, the better."

He kisses me, and his words whirl around in my mind, while I brush my hands up his back to his strong shoulders.

Eventually he shifts off me, pulls me toward him, into his arms, and we settle down, pulling the duvet around us. He sighs and kisses my hair. "There's not enough time in the world to do all the things I want to do to you. With you. So many delights. So little time. But it's not just about sex. I'd love to watch *Game of Thrones* with you. See you record one of your podcasts. Eat at every restaurant in town. Take you places—Fiji, Singapore, Tokyo. We could have such fun."

I draw circles on his chest, fascinated by the brown curling hairs. "It's a nice fantasy."

He's quiet, and I guess he's thinking about the fact that it's just not a possible future for us.

After a while, his hand stops moving on my back, and I assume he's fallen asleep, but when I lift my head, I see the starlight glint in his eyes, and I know he's still awake.

"Turn over," he murmurs, and I roll and let him pull me back against his chest and wrap his arms around me.

I can just see the tattoo of the cross on his upper arm, and I brush a finger across it. "I'm so sorry about Christian," I murmur.

He sighs.

I follow the line of the cross. "Are you religious?"

"Not now."

"You were?"

"My mum is," he admits. "My dad isn't. When they got together, they made the decision not to have us christened so we could make our own decision when we were old enough. Mum spoke to us about it sometimes. She'd tell us stories from the Bible, especially at Easter and Christmas. She taught us the Lord's Prayer. We went to church with her a few times, just to see what it was all about. It may be because Damon's younger, but he was probably the one of us who succumbed to it the most. He even talked about becoming a priest."

"Seriously?"

"Yeah. And then Christian died. Mum tried to talk to us about it, but you can't tell three angry teenage boys who witnessed their cousin's awful death that it's all God's plan."

"No, I guess that didn't go down well."

"Saxon got very angry, not with Mum but sort of at her, and said religion was all a lie, and God didn't exist. I just felt powerless. When the rocks fell, I was the one who swam back to shore to fetch help, and I swam so hard, I could barely breathe, but it still wasn't enough to save him. Afterward, I had panic attacks every time I felt out of control."

I'm quiet for a moment, genuinely shocked at that. I wonder whether he chose this moment to tell me, in the darkness, so I can't see his face.

"I'm so sorry," I whisper, stroking his arm. "Do you still get them?"

"Not now."

I wonder whether he conquers it by staying in control. Whether that's why he's on the verge of being OCD. Maybe even why he's so bossy in bed. I decide not to ask him that. "Do you still believe in God?" I ask instead.

He's quiet for a moment. Then he says, "I suppose it's hard to un-believe something." He clears his throat. "I don't think about it much."

I think about his younger brother, and the beautiful painting on the wall. "Why do you think Damon paints pictures of gods and angels?"

"He says it's the only place that God exists for him now."

"That's incredibly sad."

"I guess. I hadn't thought about it before." He kisses my hair. "Are you religious?"

"Kind of. Mum and Dad were both brought up Anglican, although they didn't go to church regularly. They brought Charlie and me up in a similar way. We believe, but don't practice as such. Sometimes I pray, I suppose. Not in a get on my knees by the side of the bed type of way, but yeah, I do believe."

"And losing your dad didn't change your faith?"

"No. Everyone dies. I don't pretend to understand God's purpose. I don't get too theological about it. I keep my feet on the ground. I believe in faith, hope, and love, and try to apply that to the people around me."

He kisses my hair. "That's a nice way of putting it."

We're facing the window, and I watch the stars flickering in the night sky, thinking about the shooting star I saw on Christmas Eve. I didn't wish for a future for us, because I knew it wouldn't come true. What's the point in wishing for a man and marriage and babies when it can't happen? Instead, I just wished for happiness, deciding to leave the manner of it in the hands of God, or Fate.

My eyes drift close, and I'm almost asleep when he murmurs, "I'm not going to let you go."

I frown, knowing I should argue with him and tell him it's not up to him. But I'm too tired, and instead I let sleep carry me away.

# Chapter Twenty

## *Kip*

When I wake, the sun is just coming up, filling the room with a white-gold light. I stretch and yawn, and then, as the memories from last night come flooding back, roll onto my side to face the woman who's sharing my bed.

She's still asleep, lying on her tummy, cheek pressed against the pillow. The sun has cast her pale skin in a rosy flush, and her blonde hair, while messy in its untidy bun, shines like gold thread.

I don't know what it is about this girl that rings my bell. I'm sure there are more beautiful women out there, although it's hard to think how her features could be perfected. I love her baby blue eyes, now hidden behind her lids, her long, fair lashes, her straight nose, the scatter of faint freckles across her cheeks, the attractive curve of her Cupid's bow. And her body couldn't be improved—she's neither too thin nor too curvy, her waist dipping and her hips flaring in perfect proportions. And I love her breasts, and her pale pink nipples that point up, begging to be kissed.

But it's not just a physical thing. I like her. She's warm, funny, and genuine. Like I told her, she makes me smile, and that's no small thing in this world.

I think about last night, how she trembled, blown away by our lovemaking and the sheer experience of being with a man. I feel humbled by that. I'd enjoyed introducing her to the wonders of sex, and I have to admit I thought it was funny to shock her with the ice, but I didn't consider how my very masculinity might unsettle her.

I've never considered myself or my brothers as alpha males, but I can see how she might see us that way, with our confidence bordering on arrogance because of our money. I've never thought of myself as intimidating before, but her description of me, hot on the heels of

Lesley's comments, makes me wonder whether others—especially women—view me like that sometimes. That makes me uncomfortable. I don't want Alice to feel bullied or browbeaten. Did she understand what I tried to explain last night? I have no desire to control her in real life. The thought of controlling her pleasure during sex, though, of drawing out her orgasm, teasing her until she can't bear it any longer, definitely turns me on.

Best not to think about that if I want to go back to sleep.

I visit the bathroom, then come back to bed. She's lying on her side now, facing away from me, and I curl around her, enjoying her warm, soft skin, the feel of her nestled against me, the smell of her hair as I nuzzle the silky strands. I lower my arm around her, and I'm content to just hold her as I doze in the early morning sun.

*

A couple of hours later, I'm in the kitchen in a pair of track pants frying bacon when she comes in wearing my white tee and—I soon discover as I slide a hand up her thigh to her bottom—nothing else.

"Hey you," she says, hugging me. "I woke up and you'd gone."

"I thought you probably hadn't had breakfast in bed for a while, so I decided to cook for you."

"I've never had breakfast in bed," she admits, sniffing the bacon.

"Never?"

"We weren't allowed as kids, and I've cooked my and Charlie's breakfast since I was fourteen."

"In that case," I say firmly, "we're definitely having it in bed. I've decided—we're not getting up today." I flip the bacon with one hand, keeping the other on her soft butt.

Her lips curve up. "You're kidding."

"Nope."

"That's so decadent. I couldn't possibly spend all day in bed."

"Do I need to tie you to it?" I look down at her.

She meets my eyes, and hers are lit with amusement and a touch of excitement. "You're so wicked," she murmurs.

"It's you," I tell her, releasing her so I can crack a couple of eggs into the pan. "You bring out the animal in me."

She giggles. "Is there anything I can do?"

"Butter the rolls, if you like."

She does that while I start making the coffee. Within a few minutes, the egg-and-bacon rolls and two steaming mugs of coffee are ready on the tray. I carry them back to the bedroom, and we climb on and sit back against the pillows, me with my legs stretched out, her cross-legged, while we eat.

We talk about all kinds of things, her upcoming podcasts, her recording setup and studio, my work, AI, gaming... We talk, and we sip our coffee and watch the sun rising in the sky, filling the room with bright-gold summer sunshine.

I've never done this with a girl. Never shared the same tastes in books, movies, and music, and been able to lie there for hours talking, laughing, and enjoying just being together.

It's nearing midday when Alice finally says, "This is lovely, but I really should have a shower."

"No point," I tell her, reaching out to lace my fingers through hers.

"Why?"

I pull her hand toward me, and laugh as she falls onto my chest. "Because I've got some very dirty things planned," I murmur, sliding a hand to the back of her head and pulling it down to kiss her.

"Mmm." She kisses me back, then lifts her head to look at me with wide eyes. "But it's the middle of the day."

"So?"

She looks genuinely surprised. "I just thought..."

"We had to wait until it was dark and the lights were out? Come on, Alice, I thought you knew me better than that."

Her face flushes. "But we only had sex last night."

"Yes, and now you're in my bed, wearing only a T-shirt, with a bare arse and no bra, and you smell amazing, and I want to make the most of you while I have you, so stop complaining and take the T-shirt off."

"Make me," she says.

"Oh-ho, it's going to be like that, is it?" I grab her and roll her beneath me, then easily strip the T-shirt off her so she's lying naked on the sheet. It's pleasantly warm in the room, but her nipples have stiffened to hard points, and I chuckle as I kiss down to one and suck it.

She moans and writhes, and I sit back on my heels and reach over to my bedside table. "You're going to have to learn to stop wriggling unless you want to be tied down," I inform her. Finding the bottle of massage oil, I bring it back, then lean over her. "Unless that's what you're hoping for."

She looks up at me, and she has that look on her face again, as if I've turned into the star of her favorite movie. God, I hope she never stops looking at me like that.

Sitting back on my heels, I show her the bottle. "Edible," I point out.

"Oh dear," she says.

I smirk. "Turn over."

"Take your boxers off first."

"Are you giving orders now?"

"Please?" She pouts.

I laugh and take them off. My erection springs free, ready for action, and her eyes widen. "Ignore it," I tell her. "I don't have any control over it. It's going to have to wait."

She laughs and rolls over, resting her head on her arms. I straddle her legs, trying not to think of all the things I could do to her in this position, then pick up my phone. Pulling up the playlist I put together for this session, I set it playing, and Jack Johnson begins singing *Better Together*. I put the phone back on the bedside table, then pour some of the oil onto my hands. Rubbing them together, I warm the oil up, then place them on her shoulders.

Slowly, I begin to massage her. I'm no expert and this isn't a physio session—this is about connection, about being sensual and sexy, so I keep my touch light, and just enjoy the feel of her soft skin beneath my fingers.

I straighten each arm in turn and stroke them, following with my mouth, kissing her palms and sucking her fingers, before bending them back beneath her. I use a little more pressure on her shoulders, but I'm gentle as I caress around the love bite, placing tender kisses over it. Smoothing the oil down her back, I work either side of her spine, running my fingers up her ribs to the sensitive skin under her arms, and scolding her when she wriggles.

Shifting to the other end of the bed, I work on each foot, sliding my fingers and then my tongue between her toes, up the insteps, and around her ankles, then knead her calves and the backs of her thighs. By this point she's giving long sighs with each stroke, and when I finally reach the plump muscles of her bottom, she twitches and groans as I place my now-warm hands over them and massage. I stay here a while, stroking down her back, over her bottom, and down her thighs, then back up again, and by the time I ask her to turn over, I'm as hard as a rock, and finding it increasingly difficult to control myself.

She lies with her arms above her head, and her cheeks are flushed now, her lips parting as I sit astride her hips. With the root of my erection pressing against her mound, I turn the bottle of oil upside down. I drizzle it from the hollow at the base of her throat down between her breasts, and she gasps.

"You're supposed to warm it first," she scolds.

"I forgot." I watch her soft nipples tightening, desire coursing through me. This is backfiring big time.

Still, I continue, stroking over her arms and around her shoulders, then finally down over her breasts. Her nipples have softened again, and they're like velvet beneath my fingertips, as I stroke and squeeze them, tugging slightly until she's squirming beneath me.

"Lie still," I scold, and she moans.

"I can't."

Moving off her to the side, I pour more oil on my hands, lots and lots of it, so it runs over my palms and dribbles over both of us, and now she's wet and shiny and so am I as I stretch out beside her, our skin sticking together and peeling apart with a delicious sucking sound. I smear the oil across her bottom lip with my thumb and then kiss her hungrily, too fired up to go slow. She opens her mouth to me, though, and our tongues tangle, while I slide a hand over her breasts, then continue down to between her legs.

I drizzle some more oil there and begin to massage it in. My fingers slide easily through her swollen folds, and we both groan.

"You're so fucking wet," I murmur, plunging my tongue into her mouth.

"I wonder why?" she asks when I lift my head. "You're driving me crazy."

"That's the idea."

Her eyelids flutter shut as I slip two fingers inside her. I move them in and out of her gently for a while, then ease them out. This time, I slide my middle finger further down to the tight muscle beneath, bringing the oil with it and massaging it over her skin.

Her eyes open and she gives me a wry look. "You promised."

"I believe I said I wouldn't insert anything unless you begged me to." I keep stroking my finger there, and she blinks in slow motion, her lips parting.

"You're so bad," she whispers.

"All I want is to give you pleasure," I tell her, brushing my lips across hers as I continue to stroke the oil across her skin. "And aren't you here to try new things?"

"Yeah…" She sucks her bottom lip, her eyelids fluttering again as I press my finger against her very lightly.

"That's all I want," I murmur. "Like this." I tease her lips with the tip of my tongue. "Doesn't that feel good?"

She moans. "Yes…"

"So can I?"

"Ahhh… yes…"

Making sure my finger is well-coated with oil, I press it a fraction of an inch inside her. Remove it. Then do it again. I know the act of just teasing the tight muscle is going to be enough to drive her wild.

"Mmm…" She brushes her hand down my chest, coating her fingers with oil, then closes them around my erection and begins to stroke.

Whoa. I'm already hard, but her firm touch makes me swell, my erection straining toward her as if begging her for more. Oh man… I was totally unprepared for that.

I sit up and kneel between her legs, and the two of us continue stroking each other. She looks so sexy, her eyes sleepy with desire, her skin flushed, her lips parted as she gives deep, shuddering breaths. She's not far from coming, and neither am I.

My heart racing, I study her breasts thoughtfully.

"What are you thinking?" she whispers.

I lift my gaze back to hers. "Pondering on where to come."

Her lips curve up. "What are the options?" She looks down at my erection, her fingers slipping easily up and down its length, occasionally stroking over the head with her thumb.

"Right now?" I give her a helpless look. "Shooting my load across your stomach is looking pretty likely."

She giggles, her eyes lighting up. "Mmm. Do that."

"Seriously? You don't want me to come inside you?"

She tips her head to the side so she can get a better view. "Later, maybe. Now, I want to watch." She lifts her hand. "And I want you to do it."

I groan, missing her touch. "You're sure?"

"Oh yeah."

"Okay. I will, if you get yourself off, too."

Her eyes widen, and she laughs. "Seriously?"

"Yeah. Why should you have all the fun?" I sit back on my heels, sliding my knees under her thighs. I move her hand between her legs. Then I take myself in hand and start stroking.

She gives a short laugh, her cheeks flushing a rosy pink. But she begins to move her fingers, lifting her other arm above her head, making herself comfortable.

Once again, this is backfiring on me. The sight of her touching herself, her fingers slipping down through her folds, brings my climax racing toward me at a rate of knots. I watch her swirl her fingers over her clit—she has great hands, slender and yet strong, with short, neat nails painted a light pink, and it turns me on big time to watch those fingers teasing her swollen, glistening flesh.

Her gaze slides down to my erection, and she gives a helpless sigh as she watches my hand moving more quickly and surely, used to the movement, and her tongue flicks out across her lips. Ah, jeez. When she lowers her hand to her breast and begins to tease her nipple, I tip over the edge.

I lift up, bracing myself on a hand, and come over her shiny skin, sending thick, creamy jets shooting across her tummy and breasts. She watches, fascinated, her fingers pausing for a few seconds, and then her gaze lifts to mine and our eyes lock, and something passes between us, like an electric shock, something hot and fast and exquisite that makes me catch my breath. Her fingers continue to circle again, and then she closes her eyes and bites her lip, obviously feeling the approach of her orgasm.

I can't resist her—I'm still hard—and so I slide right into her in one smooth move, and thrust her through the climax, grinding my hips against hers so I'm touching her clit. I kiss her, plunging my tongue into her mouth, capturing her moans. She squeals and comes around me, clenching with such strong pulses that it makes me groan.

We stay like that for ages as she drifts down to earth, me thrusting gently, just enjoying being inside her, and her limp on the mattress, arms above her head, powerless to do anything but lie there and sigh.

Eventually, she opens her eyes to look into mine and starts laughing.

"I'm so incredibly sticky," she complains. "Oil and sweat and… you know."

"Half of it's on me," I remind her. "I think we need a shower."

Her eyes widen. "Together?"

I kiss her again, tenderly this time. "Of course. I don't want to spend a second more than I have to apart from you this weekend."

I lift up, my skin peeling from hers and making us both laugh, and then I help her up, and we go into the bathroom. I set the shower running, and when the water's hot, we go into the cubicle and stand beneath the spray.

I like showers and so the cubicle isn't small, but I stand close to her anyway as the water soaks us both. I dip my head beneath the spray, then say, "Can you grab the shampoo?"

She picks it up and squeezes some onto her hand, then begins to massage it into my hair. I sigh as she works her fingers across my scalp, then turns me to rinse it beneath the water.

"My turn." I wash her hair, too, and then it's time to wash our bodies. We pour a generous amount of shower gel onto the sponge, and then I give it to her and lean back against the glass and let her smooth the sponge across me.

"You're all brown and shiny," she murmurs. "Like polished wood." She cleans me almost reverently, moving the sponge across my shoulders and down my chest, exploring my muscles, and drawing a finger through the wet hairs.

She seems fascinated by my pecs and abs and nipples, and I let her take her time, enjoying the attention, and liking the fact that I'm the first guy she's done this with.

"You have a magnificent body," she says.

"Why, thank you."

"I mean it. You're so handsome, Kip. So gorgeous. How come you're not married with six kids right now?"

*Because I was waiting for you.*

I don't say it. But I think it.

Instead, I say, "I'm a free spirit."

She laughs, turning me around so she can soap my back. "That you are, my friend."

I lean on the glass and let her stroke the sponge over my shoulders and down my spine. Then she gets to my butt and spends an inordinate amount of time soaping it.

"I think it's clean," I say after approximately an hour.

"I'm enjoying myself," she protests.

I laugh, turn back, and take the sponge from her. "My turn."

"Oh dear." She looks down at my erection. "Already?"

"Just ignore it. It's like a dog chained up in the garden. It's gonna bark at everything that walks past the house."

She giggles, and I grin and start washing her. I cover her torso in soapy suds, cleaning her shoulders, her arms, her breasts, and down over her tummy. Then I drop to my haunches to wash her legs. Finally I pass the sponge between her thighs, wash the suds away, then lean forward and slide my tongue into her folds. She sighs, and I swirl my tongue over her clit a few times before kissing up over her belly and back up to her mouth.

She puts her arms around my neck, and we stand like that for a while, kissing while the water spray rinses us, just enjoying being together and touching one another.

Eventually I turn off the shower, and we get out and dry ourselves, pull on clean tees and underwear, change the bottom sheet, laughing at all the wet patches of oil and other fluids, then go upstairs to get ourselves some lunch. I make us a chicken salad sandwich, and we take it with a packet of chips and a coffee back to bed. We check our phones, reply to a few messages, then sit and talk while we eat.

She says she's had a text from Charlie saying her mum's well and they're enjoying their time together. I ask her about her father, and for the first time she tells me about the day he had a heart attack, and what a shock it was for her and Charlie. And she tells me how it was only weeks afterward that her mother started getting eye pain, blurred vision, and electric-shock sensations down the left side of her body.

We talk about her mother's disease and its progression. She explains how Penny has constant fatigue, and the pain means she only sleeps for a couple of hours at a time. Alice helps her visit the bathroom and bathe, pushes her in the wheelchair, and basically does most things for her. But it soon becomes clear that her main worry is Penny's mental health.

"Depression is common in people with M.S.," Alice says, "because of the pain and the fatigue and constant complications. We work hard to focus on the positive things in our lives, but she has days where it all gets too hard for her. And she hates that she's holding me back from living a normal life. When she's really bad, she cries and says it would be better if she wasn't here. I find that hard to handle."

"Of course you do. I'm so sorry."

"Her dark moods don't tend to last long because she knows they upset me. I try to keep little treats for days like those. We go out in the car to the waterfront and look at the statues of Captain Cook and Young Nick—he was Captain Cook's cabin boy, and he was the first person on the Endeavour to spot the New Zealand coastline."

"Oh, I didn't know that."

"Yeah, Mum's quite into Kiwi history. Sometimes we go to Dad's grave and sit there and chat about him. Or we go to the Eastwoodhill Arboretum and just immerse ourselves in nature. I'll make us something special for dinner, or get out a box of chocolates I've saved, and we'll eat the whole box while we watch an old movie. Things like that, to try and take her mind off it all."

We're both sitting back on the pillows, finishing off our coffees. I've opened the sliding doors onto the terrace outside, and I can hear traffic way off in the distance, but here it's quiet, with just the sound of birds in the nearby trees, and the rustle of the tulle nets as they blow in the breeze. Alice's hair is nearly dry, shining like a halo with the afternoon sun behind her. I know she's no angel, but she certainly has the heart of one.

"You don't think she would feel better to know that you had a normal life," I say gently. "A home of your own, a husband, children?"

She rests her head on the headboard, her blue eyes bright as the summer sky behind her. It's just another minute in our day, another moment together, but I realize my heart is racing as I wait for her answer.

"Maybe," she says slowly. "But I can't have those things and look after her."

"I understand. What about some sort of compromise? If we could find someone to look after her that she got on with?"

"She'd hate that. And it wouldn't change the fact that I live in Gisborne."

"Would you consider moving to Wellington?"

She looks into my eyes, and maybe she also realizes now what we're discussing.

"I can't ask her to move out of the home she shared with my father," she says gently. "And the place where his grave is. She would never leave. And anyway, this is only the second time you and I have slept together. We can't make such big changes in our lives for each other."

"Maybe not yet," I add. "But this won't be the last time we'll have this conversation. Just so you know."

She looks into my eyes, her brows drawing together. "Don't make me choose," she whispers.

"I'm not. I won't." I put my arm around her, and she snuggles up to me. I kiss the top of her head. "You're the sweetest girl I know," I tell her simply, "and I don't want to do anything to hurt you."

"Let's just concentrate on today," she says, looking up at me. "On what we have right here, right now."

"Okay." So I kiss her, moving my lips slowly across hers.

But I don't care that this is only the second time we've been together. I know I want her, and I'm used to getting what I want. And I'm not going to give up easily.

# Chapter Twenty-One

## *Alice*

"Red or white?" Saxon asks.

It's Sunday evening, and we're at Saxon and Catie's house, about to have dinner. She's baked some focaccia, and we're currently dipping chunks of it in olive oil, salt, and dukkah.

I look at where he and Catie are sitting opposite me and Kip at their dining table, noting that neither of them has a wine glass in front of them, and say, "I'm happy to stick to soft drinks."

"Aw," Catie says, "I don't mind if you have a glass of wine. I'm living vicariously at the moment. Saxon won't let me have mayo, soft cheese, alcohol, or too much coffee. He's like Hitler with food and drink at the moment."

"Harsh," he says. "But probably true."

Kip chuckles. "I'm happy with Sprite, too."

"All right," Saxon replies good-naturedly, and he pours us all a glass from the bottle he brought out for himself and his wife.

"So," Catie says, picking up her glass and sipping it, "what have you two been up to this weekend?"

"Playing Scrabble," Kip says without missing a beat. Saxon laughs, and Catie suddenly realizes what she's asked and giggles.

My face grows lava hot. We've hardly gotten out of bed the whole weekend. Kip has made love to me numerous times, in multiple positions, leaving me drifting up somewhere above the clouds, bathed in warm sunshine.

Catie glances at me, sees me blushing, and smiles. "Where do Viking warrior Scrabble champions go when they die?"

"Don't know," I say.

"Vowel-halla."

"Jesus." Saxon dips a piece of bread in the oil. "Your jokes don't improve with time."

"I'd like to see you do better," she scoffs.

"All right." His eyes gleam. "I cheated on my girlfriend. When we were playing Scrabble, I was supposed to take four letters and I took five instead and won the game. Then I went upstairs and fucked her sister." He grins and pops the bread in his mouth.

Kip coughs into his Sprite and wipes his mouth. "Now *that's* a joke," he says.

"Last week I picked up gonorrhea," I tell them. "Best Scrabble game ever."

That gives Catie a fit of the giggles. She points at Kip. "Your turn."

"Why is it impossible to keep Oedipus from cheating at Scrabble?" he asks. "Because he's always trying to look at his mother's rack."

It's my turn to laugh. Saxon grins and says to a puzzled Catie, "It's a Greek story. Oedipus killed his father and married his mother."

"Oh." She sends Kip a wry look. "Trust you to tell me a joke I don't understand."

"I was going to say one about wanting to play 'clitoris' but not being able to find it," he says, "but I didn't want to embarrass Alice."

That makes us all laugh, and Saxon gets up to clear the plates. "Wasn't the bread amazing?" he asks. "It was Catie's first attempt at making it."

"It was lovely," I say, surprised. "Wow, well done you."

"So tasty," Kip adds, "and loved the rosemary on top."

She flushes. "Thank you. I've never done much cooking, but Saxon's been teaching me."

"God help us all," Kip says.

His brother gives him the finger, and Catie laughs. "He's a lot better than me. But we've been watching cooking videos together and trying out some of the recipes." She also gets to her feet and collects the empty bread board. "Back in a sec." She follows him out.

I smile at Kip. "They seem happy."

"I've never seen him like this," he admits. "It's cool. He deserves it."

I study him, wanting to say that he deserves it too, but I can't say that when it's me who's holding back from letting this develop into something more.

He took off his glasses when he sat down, and his brown eyes are thoughtful, contemplative. I lean forward and kiss him, long and lingering, and he slides his arm around me and kisses me back, his fingers skating across my shoulders, making me tingle.

"Put him down," Saxon says, coming back in carrying a casserole dish, "you don't know where he's been."

We part with a laugh, and he puts the dish in the center of the table and removes the lid. "Chicken chasseur," he states, releasing a wonderful smell of onion, garlic, and red wine into the air.

"And mash," Catie adds, returning with a big bowl of mashed potatoes and putting that beside it.

"It smells fantastic," Kip tells her.

"It's just a one-pot recipe," she says modestly.

"Yeah, but it took quite a bit of prep," Saxon adds. "Credit where credit's due."

She smiles. "Shall I be mum?"

"Seems appropriate." He hugs her from behind, brushing his fingers over her bump, kisses her neck, then takes his seat.

Catie dishes up the dinner, and we eat while we chat. Their house is just across from the beach, and where the sliding doors are open, the sea breeze brings with it a salty tang and a welcome evening coolness, as it's been so warm today.

We talk about all sorts of things—their pregnancy and how the babies are doing, Kingpinz, Craig, and their younger brother.

"Kip told me about Damon's ex destroying all of his suits," I say. "I'm guessing he doesn't buy off the peg either. Cutting those up has to be a crime."

"He didn't care about that," Kip says. "He did care when he found scratches all down the side of his E-type Jag."

"That's what happens when you stick your dick in crazy," Saxon comments, helping himself to more mashed potato.

Catie and I exchange an amused glance. "Was she mad, then?" Catie asks.

"Certifiable," he says, adding a generous second helping of the casserole. "But she was young and blonde, so he didn't stand a chance."

"How old is he?"

"Twenty-seven in April," Kip says.

"And Rachel was only twenty, with big..." Saxon suddenly remembers whose company he's in. "Eyes," he finishes lamely, and Catie snorts.

I grin and get to my feet. "Can I use your bathroom?"

"Of course," Catie says, "just along there on your left."

I visit the bathroom, then come out and sit back at the table. "I was thinking that you could have asked Damon to join us," I say. "Or would he have felt like a third wheel?"

"Probably," Catie says. "Kip, can you pass me your plate, please?"

He hands it to her, putting his arm around me as he leans back, resting it on the back of his chair. Opposite me, Saxon laughs. I give him a curious look. His eyes are dancing. Catie presses her lips together, clearly trying not to laugh.

Puzzled, I glance at Kip. "What's going on?"

"Nothing," he says, "don't mind them. Give us a kiss."

I give him a strange look—it's not something he'd normally say. Then as I stare into his eyes, I feel a prickle of warning. It looks like Kip—same black shirt, same mouth, same brown eyes... but it doesn't feel like him, and it doesn't smell like him...

I look back at the other brother, who's watching me with amusement.

"Very funny," I say, and smile at Catie. "Did they do this to you, too?"

"Yep," she says as they both laugh and get up. "Luckily I spotted it, too."

Kip pulls off Saxon's tee, and Saxon unbuttons Kip's shirt, and they swap, going around the table to take each other's places. "We're identical," Saxon complains. "What gave it away?"

"Your cologne," I tell him, "partly. But not just that."

"It's the eyes, isn't it?" Catie says. "The other one just doesn't feel right."

"That's it," I reply, "exactly."

Kip leans forward and kisses my temple. "Good to know," he murmurs, and I inhale the subtle scent of his cologne, which never fails to send goose bumps rising all over my skin.

When we've finished the casserole, we clear the table, then they serve up a chocolate cheesecake they made together.

"Oh my God, I'm so full," I declare after I finish the last mouthful. "That was divine."

Saxon gathers up the plates, looks at his brother, and gestures to the kitchen with his head. "Come on, bro. Let's do the dishes and let the girls put their feet up."

Kip chuckles. "Yeah, all right." He gets to his feet and kisses the top of my head before following Saxon out to the kitchen, carrying a pile of dishes.

Catie looks at me and smiles. "Would you like to see the nursery?"

"Oh, I'd love to!"

"It's not finished yet," she says as we get to our feet, "but I've started getting a few bits for it." She leads the way along the corridor to the other end of the house. "That's our room," she says, "and here's the nursery."

We go into the room. It's empty apart from a table covered with magazines and swatches. The carpet is covered with newspaper. The wall is divided by a dado rail. She's painted it light blue above the rail and light green below it, so it looks like the sky and grass. I can see the faint pencil marks of animals sketched out on the paint—a tiger, a lion, and a giraffe.

"I'm doing a kind of mural," she says. "I've never done anything like it before! Do you think it'll work?"

"Oh, it's going to be amazing," I tell her. "You're so clever. I can't paint at all."

"I've never done much of it, except at school." She smiles as she looks at her project. "Saxon bought me a load of paints and canvases. He's such a sweetie. I really don't deserve him."

"I'm sure that's not true," I scold.

"I don't know," she murmurs. "The guys are very rich. I still worry his family is going to think I'm after his money. Does it bother you?"

"Not really, but then ours isn't a long-term thing. It's just a fling."

"Yeah, right. Mine was just a one-night stand." She laughs and strokes her bump as she looks around the room. "Saxon wants to get one big crib for the boys. I thought he'd want to encourage them to be independent, but he says they'll miss each other after spending nine months so close together, and I thought that was so sweet."

I smile as I wander over to the table and flick through some of the swatches. "It is. Do you find it weird that Saxon has a brother who looks identical to him?"

She joins me. "Not now. I did, but I've gotten used to it. I don't even think about them being twins, actually. Although they are very close, of course. They have a connection that goes a step beyond mere siblings."

"Does it bother you?"

"No, not at all. You?"

"No," I say, "I feel the same. I think it's nice they have support for each other. I know it bothered Kip's ex, though."

"Oh, really?"

"Yeah. I think she was jealous of Saxon. It seems a shame. I don't think they should have to give up that relationship to be with someone."

"Me neither. I asked Kip if he liked being a twin once. He said it was cool because you get a ready-made best friend. He said the boys will always have someone on their side, looking out for them." She strokes her bump.

I smile. "That's sweet."

"He's a sweet guy."

"Not a word I'd choose for him," I say, thinking about what he did with the ice cube.

Her lips curve up. "So… how's it going, then? Has he kept you busy?"

"Just a bit. Haven't you noticed me walking like a cowboy when he gets off his horse?"

She giggles. "I guess he's making the most of you being here."

I pause, glance over my shoulder to make sure the doorway is clear, then murmur, "Can I ask you something?"

"Of course."

"Is Saxon… bossy? You know, in bed?"

Her eyes light with amusement. "He'd say no, that he's just enthusiastic. Why do you ask? Is Kip bossy?"

"Just a bit."

"Ooh. Is he all Fifty Shades?"

"I haven't actually read that."

"Oh you should. I learned so much." She laughs. "Does he have a playroom?"

"He has a PlayStation."

"No, I mean that in the book, Christian has a room that he takes Ana to, where he ties her up and does naughty things to her. Whips and paddles and stuff."

My eyes nearly pop out. "Oh, jeez, no, nothing like that. Nothing I've seen, anyway. God, I'm so naïve." I think about the love bite he gave me on my neck and try not to blush as I flick through the swatches. I had to wear a shirt with a collar this evening to cover it up. "I don't know if Kip's told Saxon, and if he has, if Saxon's told you, but... um... he's the first guy I've been with."

"Oh..." Her eyebrows lift. "No, I didn't know. So that night we met at Red's Rib Shack..."

"Yeah, it was my first time with a guy that evening. So I don't have anything to compare him to. I just wondered if all men were... you know... bossy."

"Well, I only had a few partners before Saxon, so I'm not exactly an expert. I would say that guys have to do most of the movement, right? So it's instinctive for them to direct the action. After saying that, it wouldn't surprise me if the fact that the Chevaliers are rich and privileged makes them borderline arrogant and bossy. Money buys obedience. They're used to getting what they want, and to telling people what to do, and I guess that's going to stray over into their sex lives. We just get to be the lucky girls who benefit from it." She smirks.

"Kip said it's different in the bedroom," I reply. "That's it's a place to explore the differences between us. But I'm beginning to think he's bossy most of the time, not just in bed."

I stop talking as there's a sound from behind us. We freeze, glance at each other, then slowly turn. The guys are both standing in the doorway, watching us, lips curved up with amusement.

"How much of that did you hear?" I ask.

"Enough to make me want to put you over my knee," Kip says wryly, and Saxon gives a short laugh.

Both Catie and I blush scarlet, and the guys chuckle.

"Come on," Saxon scolds, holding out a hand. "We've made coffee."

Kip puts his arm around me as we walk back to the living room.

"How long were you standing there?" I whisper, embarrassed to think he heard me talking to Catie about what we'd done.

"A while," he says.

"Did you hear us talking about you having a playroom?"

His eyebrows rise almost comically. "No. But you're absolutely going to have to tell me about that."

There's no time to say anything because we're going into the living room. Kip and I sit on the sofa, and Catie curls up in one of the armchairs, while Saxon pulls up a beanbag and sits in front of her, with her feet in his lap. He massages her feet while we talk, and she rests her hand on her bump, her gaze drifting occasionally, so I'm sure she's thinking about her boys.

I remember what Kip told me about her—that she had a tough upbringing, and she lived on the streets for a while. How strange it must be for her now to be living in such a beautiful house, to be married to such a gorgeous guy, and to be pregnant with his twins.

I've never really thought much about marriage and babies. It's always felt like such a far-off dream, like visiting New York, or meeting the King of England, something I can't imagine ever doing in real life. Is it possible, though? Not yet, but maybe a few years down the line, when Charlie has come home to work, and I have more free time on my hands? I can't imagine ever meeting a man who would be interested in dating a girl who has responsibilities like I have. Kip is, but then he's one in a billion, and I can't imagine there are many men out there like him.

For a moment, while he and Saxon chat about the upcoming All Blacks game, I let myself fantasize about a possible future where I'm married to Kip, and pregnant with his child. The thought makes the hairs rise all over my body. How amazing would it be to have sex and know you could be making a baby? To have it grow into a person inside me, to give birth and hold a tiny person who was part of me, part of him? To have him put his ring on my finger and promise to love me until death parts us?

Oh jeez, I've never even let myself come close to imagining anything like that, and it takes my breath away.

He looks at me then, straight into my eyes, our gazes lock, and I can't look away.

Oh no. Surely not. I haven't been that stupid.

We haven't known each other that long. We've only slept together a handful of times. We're not even dating properly.

I can't have fallen in love with him.

I blink and realize he's looking at me because someone's asked me a question, and they're all waiting for me to answer. "Sorry, what?"

He grins. "Saxon asked you who you're interviewing next on your podcast."

"Oh shit, sorry." I try to bump-start my brain and steer it away from the thought of saying I do to Kip Chevalier. "I'm talking to the guy who wrote the Ruffpunk series on Wednesday."

"I haven't read that," Saxon says.

"I have," Kip tells him. "You'd love it. It's a historical fantasy set in a Tudor steampunk world, where Shakespeare invents a new form of magic using poetry and casts spells with his words. It's fantastic, and it's won loads of awards. It's quite a coup to get the author on."

"I'll definitely listen in," Saxon says. "I'd like to read that."

"She did an AMA on Reddit," Kip says. "She had so many questions."

"Most of them were from you," I say, and Saxon and Catie laugh.

"No they weren't," he scolds. "You were really popular."

"I'm so impressed," Catie says. "I'm tempted to ask for your autograph."

"Oh, stop it."

"I'm serious," she states. "I've never known anyone famous before."

"I'm not famous," I say, embarrassed, but I can see that to her, someone who interviews well-known authors, who publishes a popular podcast, and who does an AMA on Reddit, *is* famous.

"Did you go to the Wonderland exhibition?" Saxon asks, and I nod.

"Kip took me. It was so good, and really clever how it made you feel as if you were actually in the story."

"Especially for you," Catie says with a smile. "Alice!"

"So who are you, the Mad Hatter?" Saxon asks Kip.

"If I am then you're the Cheshire Cat," he replies, and Catie and I giggle, because that seems so appropriate.

Kip smiles. "Finished your coffee?" he asks me.

I have the last mouthful. "Yeah, done."

"Come on, then. Let's leave these good people and head home."

We exchange hugs and kisses, and Catie makes me promise to stay in touch so I can keep recommending books for her. Then Kip and I head out to his Merc.

"That was a fun evening," I say as he heads back toward Brooklyn, the Merc gliding quietly through the traffic.

"It was. So... what was this about a playroom?"

"Oh God, I can't believe I told you that..."

"Come on. Spill the beans."

I sigh. "I was talking about you being bossy in bed, and Catie asked whether I meant like in Fifty Shades. Apparently the hero had some kind of playroom with... um... whips and stuff."

"Did you put her straight?"

"I said I hadn't seen anything like it... You haven't, have you?"

He laughs. "No. But now you're giving me ideas."

"Really?"

He gives me a wry look. "Alice. I'm into pleasure, not pain."

"Hmm." I touch my neck and narrow my eyes at him. He just smirks.

I look out of the window, at the bright lights of the city flashing by. "When we were talking about Craig and the woman he's with, I said I didn't understand the whole power play thing, and you said it was about giving up control for a while, and about trust."

"Yeah, I guess."

"Why do you think he feels the need to give up control? Is it because he's just had a baby and he feels overwhelmed by that?"

"Maybe. But apparently his affair with Renée started last Christmas, just before Chloe became pregnant." He indicates at a roundabout, then pulls away, his expression thoughtful. "He does have a lot of responsibilities though. His mother died a couple of years ago after a long battle with breast cancer. His father's an arsehole—I think he used to knock him around when he was young. Craig's eldest sister is an alcoholic, and she's in and out of rehab. His youngest sister has three kids, and she's bringing them up alone because her husband walked out on her, so Craig helps out with her a lot."

"So maybe because he has all those pressures in his life, he feels he can escape with Renée? It could explain his actions."

"Perhaps. But it doesn't excuse cheating on his wife. I don't care what pressures a man is under. Nothing excuses that." His jaw knots, and I know he's gritting his teeth.

I put a hand on his thigh. "You're the sweetest guy, Kristopher Chevalier."

"If you're going to full name me, you have to know there's going to be punishment."

I bite my bottom lip and repeat, "Kristopher."

"Just don't say I haven't warned you."

My pulse speeds up a little. We had sex early this morning, slow and lazy, as the sun came up. He's been gentler since I mentioned how much he shocked me the first time at his house, but as I look across at him, I feel a flutter of dark desire, an urge for him to possess me the way he did before.

I can't get enough of this guy. He looks gorgeous in his black shirt, the sleeves rolled up a few times to reveal his muscular, tanned forearms. I want to unbutton the shirt, push the sides apart, and touch the defined muscles of his chest. I want to nuzzle his neck and smell his cologne, and brush my fingers against the short hair on the back of his head. And I want him to kiss me the way he does, as if he's hungry for me, and he can't get enough of me.

"Don't look at me like that," he says, glancing at me before signaling and turning the car.

"Like what?"

"Like you're thinking about wicked things."

"I am. You've corrupted me, *Kristopher*, turned me into a sex addict. All I can think about is fucking you." I say the word purposefully, wanting to fire him up.

"Jesus."

I nibble my bottom lip. "I like that you took into account what I said about not being used to this. I know you've held back a bit, and I think that's sweet. But… I want you to know… you don't have to anymore."

He glances in his rearview mirror, slows the car, and turns onto his road. "And I've told you before, you have to be careful what you wish for."

"I know what I'm wishing for this time. I want to let the tiger out of his cage."

He pulls up outside his house, opens the garage door, and slots the car in. Then he turns off the engine and looks across at me. "You're sure?"

I unbuckle my seatbelt, lean forward, and cup his face. My heart is racing now, and when I moisten my lips, I see his gaze drop to them. "Yes. It's our last night together, Kip. So don't hold back. I want all of you, one hundred percent. So give me everything you've got."

# Chapter Twenty-Two

## *Kip*

My heart is banging on my ribs, but I make myself sit still as I study Alice's face in the semi-darkness while she strokes my cheek.

I don't like her talking about this being our last night together, but I'm not yet sure what I can do about it, and the answer isn't going to come to me sitting in the car. I'm wasting valuable time that could be spent in bed. All I can do is show her how I feel about her, and hope that she misses me so much she can't bear to be apart from me.

I study her mouth and watch her lips part and the tip of her tongue emerge to moisten them. She's right that I've tried to be gentle after she told me how she was so unused to being with a man. I felt more than a tad guilty that I shocked her, and so I've spent the past couple of days taking my time to make love to her, and reining in the darker desires that threaten to rise when she's in my arms. But her words, *Give me everything you've got*, make me instantly hard.

Unbuckling myself, I shift in the seat to face her, resting an arm behind her. After lifting my glasses onto my hair, I cup her chin in the V between my thumb and forefinger and lift her face so she's looking at me, and lower my lips to just above hers.

Then I wait, letting my breath whisper across her skin.

"You're such a tease," she whispers.

"The anticipation is half the fun," I murmur, brushing my lips across her cheek, her eyebrow, and back down her nose.

"Are you going to fuck me when we get in?" she asks, eyes sparkling.

"Within an inch of your life," I promise, and then I lower my lips to hers and kiss her.

This time, I don't bother with gentle butterfly kisses to warm us both up. I'm already volcanic, and I crush my lips to hers and let my passion pour through. Alice gasps, and I take the opportunity of her open mouth to plunge my tongue inside and kiss her hard.

I slide my hand into her hair and hold her there, kissing her deeply until the blood is soaring through my veins, until I'm dizzy with love and lust and desire. Then I tear my mouth away from hers and tell her, "Inside, now."

"Ooh," she says as we get out of the car, "Mr. Bossy is back."

"Yes he is, so you'd better do as he says." I unlock the door and follow her into the house. Then, tossing my keys and glasses onto the table and not bothering with the lights, I push her up against the wall, take her face in my hands, and kiss her again.

She moans, finds the bottom of my shirt, and slides her hands beneath it, onto my skin. I groan as she moves her hands up my back, then scores her nails lightly down either side of my spine.

"I love your body," she whispers as I move back, helping me to push the buttons through the holes. "I never get tired of touching you."

"Likewise." Impatient with how long it's taking, I pull the shirt apart, sending the last few buttons flying, rip the garment off, and toss it away. She laughs, helping me out with the buttons of her shirt, and soon that joins mine on the floor. Next, it's our trousers and her bra, and then we're in our underwear, and we're still standing only a few feet from the front door.

But I can't wait to get her into the bedroom; I can't stop touching her long enough to walk down the stairs. My mouth claims hers again hungrily, and I slide my hands onto her butt and clutch the soft muscles there while I walk her backward to the dining table.

She glances over her shoulder at the large windows and says, "We should pull the curtains."

"Forget the curtains." The lights are out anyway, and it's not as if the house is overlooked, as it's on a hill. Anyone who can be bothered to get a pair of binoculars to spy on us is welcome to drink their fill.

"Kip," she says, laughing as I lift her onto the table, "don't you want to do it somewhere comfortable?"

"Can't wait." I hook my fingers in her underwear, slide it down her legs and over her feet, then press it to my nose and inhale before tossing it away.

"Jesus," she says.

"You smell amazing." I drop to my knees in front of her. "I have to taste you. Open your legs."

She parts her knees, and I push them wide, taking big bites up her soft thighs. When I get to the top, I slide a thumb down through her folds, not surprised to find her already moist. She's so easily aroused, which I love. But it's not enough; I want her swollen and soaked, so that when I slide inside her, there's no friction at all.

Parting her folds with my fingers, I brush my tongue right up her core and then swirl it over the bud at the top. She moans and drops back onto her elbows, and I murmur, "There's a good girl. Nice and wide, now. You can wrap your legs around me if you want. Yeah, just like that. Now, relax and enjoy."

I proceed to pleasure her, turning myself on in the process, because how could I remain immune when I'm surrounded by the smell and taste and feel of her velvet flesh? I slide my fingers inside her and fasten my mouth on her clit, and tease her orgasm out of her inch by inch, second by second. Gradually my hand grows wet and her moans grow louder as I suck and stroke. I slow down and then, as she starts giving deep, ragged breaths, I lift my head to look at her glistening folds, remove my fingers, and blow softly across her sensitive skin.

"Oh my God," she says, and groans.

Just lightly, I stroke a forefinger down through her swollen folds, then turn my hand and slide my fingers inside her, caressing her lovingly, because I want to make it good for her, and to make it last.

"Kip…" she whispers, and it's as if she's stroked a feather down my spine.

"Slowly, baby," I murmur, removing my finger, now coated with her moisture, and smoothing it up through her folds so she's shiny and slippery. I lean forward and taste her again, and it's like hot, sweet, salty, sticky, tangy candy, like addictive nectar, and I can't get enough of it. I lap at her, my tongue flat against her folds as I give her long licks all the way up.

She moans, full of heartfelt longing, and lifts her hands to her breasts, and oh Jesus, that's so hot. Still licking, I watch her pluck her nipples with her thumbs and forefingers, and eventually close my eyes as I fight to keep control. I can't draw it out any longer. Slipping two fingers inside her, I fasten my mouth over her clit and suck, and it's amazing how I feel her orgasm sweep over her, starting deep inside, like an earthquake beneath the ocean. It sends out ripples that make her clench around my fingers, all her muscles pulsing, and her back arches and her toes curl, and she cries out my name.

As her body gives up its tension, and she flops back onto the table, I place tender kisses on either side of her thighs, then get to my feet and lean over her, pressing my throbbing erection between her legs through my boxer-briefs.

Her arms are across her face, and she lifts them a little to peer up at me. "You have a magnificent tongue," she states.

I thrust my hips, driving my erection up through her swollen folds, and she groans and wraps her legs around me again. I continue to move my hips, and Jesus it's so tempting to stay there and thrust myself to a climax, but this is our last night together, and it's only been minutes since we walked in the door.

Gritting my teeth, I move back, take her hand, and pull her upright. "You drive me wild," I tell her, pressing my lips to hers.

"I drive *you* wild? I'm the one who just lost the plot." She lets me kiss her, grumbling, "I can taste myself."

I slip a hand beneath her, coat a finger with her moisture, then lift it and smear it across her bottom lip. She jerks and squeals as she pushes against my chest, but I hold her face in my hands and kiss her, licking it off her lips, and she groans.

"You're an animal," she whispers when I eventually move back.

I lift my hands to her hair. I watched her put her hair up into a bun before we went out, and I was fascinated by this device she used, which consisted of two strips of plastic joined at either end by two hooks. She pulled her hair through the gap in the middle, turned the device over and over until the long strands were wound around it, then hooked the two ends together to form a bun. Carefully, I unhook it, then unwind her hair, which twists in crazy curls, bouncing around her shoulders as I slide the device out. Leaving it on the table, I sink my hands into her soft hair, fascinated as it curls around my fingers as if it's grasping hold.

"Astraea's watching us," Alice says, looking across at the painting of the virginal goddess who stares down at us with her startling eyes, not unlike those of the girl in front of me. "Do you think she's disapproving?"

"Oh, I don't think she's as innocent as she makes out, the saucy minx."

Alice looks back at me, her lips curving up. "That's why you like the painting, isn't it? The thought of her losing her innocence. Of her being corrupted by earthly desires."

"Yep. Just like you."

I take her hand and lead her toward the stairs. "Like my virginal Alice, with her big blue eyes that widen in shock every time I show her something new."

"It's probably best that this is our last night," she states. "You'd only lose interest in me now I'm not squeaky clean anymore."

I stop walking, and after a couple of steps she has to stop too, because I'm still holding her hand. Her lips have quirked up, so I know she meant it to be funny. But I'm not amused. I'm obviously not doing this right if she's still thinking she can walk away from me.

"Uh-oh," she says.

"Yeah," I tell her softly, "you should be worried. Do you really think your virginity was the only reason I slept with you?"

Her eyes are cautious, wary. "Um…"

I lead her down the stairs toward the bedroom. "I hope you're ready for this. It's going to be a long night."

*

### *Alice*

I'm already regretting teasing him like that. As soon as the words left my mouth, I felt him stiffen. I can tell he doesn't want to talk about this ending tonight. And I suppose that's fair enough—why spoil the last hours we have together? Still, I'm not quite sure why he's glowering.

"Are you angry with me?" I ask as we get to his bedroom.

"No." He shucks his boxer-briefs, his erection jutting toward me, apparently eager for some action. "I'm just conscious we've got a lot to get through."

"What do you mean?"

He pulls the duvet off the bed and tosses it onto the floor. "You told me that if you ever dated someone for real, you didn't want to look like a fool."

"Yes… but—"

"I promised I'd show you everything I know so you're ready for when you meet that other man." His eyes gleam.

I give him a wry look. "Kip…"

"Get on the bed," he says.

My eyes widen. His lips curve up, just a tiny bit.

He points at the bed.

"All right," I mutter, and I climb on.

"Not like that," he says as I go to lie on the pillows. "I want your head at the edge."

Puzzled, I turn so I'm lying on my back, my head at the edge of the bed.

"Back an inch," he says, looking down at me. I shuffle back. "Bit more," he says.

I move back so my head is just hanging over the edge of the bed. He comes to stand over me, and I look up to see him stroking himself before he leans forward on the bed and moves the tip of his erection to my lips.

Oh my.

I open my mouth and take him inside, and he purrs and says, "Good girl. You're going to let me fuck your mouth now, nice and deep. And I want you to touch yourself while I do it." He moves my hand between my legs.

I slide my fingers into my folds, finding them swollen and wet after he went down on me. As I circle the pad of my forefinger over my clit, he pushes his hips forward, sinking into my mouth.

Oh jeez, this is hot, and I moan around him, my fingers moving through my folds as he slowly thrusts. The angle I'm at means he can go nice and deep, and soon my mouth is wet, and he's giving deep sighs every time I brush my tongue across him.

He gives a deep, guttural groan, then pulls out and leans on the bed, looking at me upside down.

"Yum," I say, and lick my lips.

He mutters something unintelligible, then says, "Up you get. On all fours, facing the pillows."

I do as he says, my heart hammering as he climbs onto the bed between my legs, and I feel him press the tip of his erection into my folds. Gently, he pushes forward, and I gasp as he sinks into me, so deep from this direction.

Oooh, that feels good. My hands tighten into fists, and I shudder as he begins to thrust, setting up a fast pace and driving into me, filling the air with the slap of his hips against my butt. Leaning over me, he fills his hands with my breasts, and I drop down onto my elbows and lower a hand between my legs, an ache growing inside me again, even though I only came a short while ago.

I circle my fingers over my clit, and he says, "Yeah, make yourself come for me," his husky instruction turning me on almost as much as the fact that he's sliding inside me. I suck my bottom lip and concentrate on the growing sensations inside me, then shudder and clench around him as my orgasm hits, squealing and crying out his name as he continues to pound into me, riding me all the way through it.

When I'm done, he waits a moment, stroking my back, then slowly withdraws, leaving me feeling empty and disappointed that he hasn't come.

It doesn't last long. He puts a hand flat on my back and pushes me forward so I fall onto my tummy. I bounce and go, "Oof," but I have no time to recover, because he's pushing up my knee, positioning himself against me again, and then he's inside me, right up to the hilt in one easy thrust.

"Oh…" I bury my face in the pillow, groaning as he lowers down on top of me, pressing me into the mattress.

"No rest for the wicked, Alice," he teases as he begins to thrust. "And you're very wicked."

"I wasn't," I mumble, clutching at the pillow, "until I met you."

He gives a throaty chuckle, then starts moving with purpose. One of his hands snakes under me and starts playing with my nipple, and I bite my bottom lip as my body begins to stir again. Not another orgasm. I can't stand it. I'll melt into a puddle, and he'll have to scoop me up into a bucket.

But he's obviously not going to stop, and all I can do is hold on for dear life as he lifts up onto his hands to give himself a better angle and plunges down into me.

Dear God, the guy's unstoppable. We've had sex enough times that I can tell how turned on he is, but he's clearly decided he's not going to come yet. He thrusts and thrusts, until the room grows warm and we're both covered in sweat, until I'm panting and groaning, and then

I come again, clenching around him, before collapsing into the pillows in a shivering, shaking mass.

"Come on, Alice," he teases, withdrawing and smacking my backside before rolling over and getting up. He tugs my hand, and I grumble but let him pull me up.

"Mercy," I mumble, but he just laughs and moves me over to the window. Picking me up easily, he wraps my legs around his waist, then presses me up against the glass as he sinks inside me again. It's cold on my skin and I gasp, but all he does is take advantage of my open mouth to dip his tongue inside.

Sinking my hands into his hair, I kiss him, sliding my tongue against his, determined now to drive him to the edge, and he groans and begins to thrust. Oh, I like this, up against the window, his big strong hands holding me up. I tell him, murmuring against his lips how much I like it.

"I knew you would," he says back, his voice now tinged with that huskiness that makes me shiver. "You were made for sex, baby. Made for me."

It's not at all an appropriate thing to say considering we both know it's our last time, but he likes making possessive statements, and I'm not about to berate him right now, when my body's throbbing with need, so wet and swollen from all my orgasms that it's practically humming.

And still, he doesn't come. He continues to take me in as many positions as he can think of—standing, sitting, lying, from behind, on our sides, sometimes slowing down as if he wants to make every second last, sometimes speeding up, as if his body is taking over and urging him to get to the finish line.

But it's only after I've come so many times I've lost count, and when we're finally in missionary, my favorite, because I can see his face, and my legs are wrapped around his waist, that he lifts up onto his hands, and I feel him tremble.

"You're shaking," I whisper, running my fingers up his arms and across his muscular shoulders.

"I can't hold on much longer," he says hoarsely.

I swallow hard. "Come for me, honey."

His eyelids drift shut for a moment before he opens them again. His gaze skims down me, noting, I'm sure, the way my breasts move with each of his thrusts. "Jesus, you're so beautiful."

My eyes prick with sudden, unwanted tears. "Kip…"

I don't think he notices. He's too busy taking my hands in his and pinning them above my head, and his gaze rakes down me, his fierce hunger taking my breath away. He shifts, moving his hips up an inch, and this time when he thrusts, he's grinding against my clit, and oh I'm going to come *again*. I'm so exhausted that all I can do is shudder and let it wash over me as if I'm driftwood lying on the beach. I moan loudly, and that's obviously enough to push him over the edge. He gives a couple more thrusts, then groans and shudders, and I force my eyes open so I can watch his climax claim him. I've seen the satisfied look on his face when I come, so I know that's how I must look as his hips jerk and he spills inside me. I've done this for him—even if he directs the action, it's my body that's driven him over the edge. Oh, he's so gorgeous, with his fierce frown, his deep groans, his muscles turning to rock as he thrusts again and again, until he's finally spent.

"Jesus Christ," he says, opening his eyes to look at me, dazed. "Holy shit."

"You all right?" I ask. "Still in one piece?"

"No."

I cup his face. "My Kristopher," I whisper. And then I wrap my arms around him and hold him, wishing I never had to let him go.

# Chapter Twenty-Three

## *Kip*

I'm not sure what happened at the end there. I'd held my climax in for so long that I was shaking with the sheer effort of not coming. And when I did, I think I actually shifted into an alternate dimension. Or maybe I died for a few seconds before being hauled back into this world blinking like a new babe. Whatever happened, it felt as if it went on forever, and now I feel faint and exhausted and dizzy and elated all rolled into one.

"You sucked me dry," I tell Alice. "I must look all desiccated and withered like an Egyptian mummy."

She giggles and strokes my face. "You're a god in the bedroom. I'm the luckiest girl in the world."

I lower onto my elbows—carefully, shakily, afraid of collapsing on top of her and then suffocating her because I'm unable to move—and kiss her. A slow, luxurious, heart-achingly tender kiss now all my passion and energy is spent.

Then I lift my head and look at her. "Don't go," I say.

Her expression softens as if she's been expecting this. "Kip…"

"Stay another couple of days."

"I can't."

"We'll go away somewhere. Mum and Dad have a bach up in Paraparaumu, right on the beach. It's huge and quiet, and all you can hear is the sound of the waves and the seagulls. We'll make love on the beach with the waves washing over us."

"And get sand in all our crevices."

"I'll help you wash it out."

She laughs, then kisses me again. "Come and lie beside me."

I move my hips, still inside her, and her eyelids flutter shut for a moment. "Seriously?" she demands, "How are you still hard?"

"It's you and your magnificent body. Want to go again?"

"You're kidding me."

"Actually, I am. I might give myself a coronary." Carefully, I withdraw, then move off her and collapse back onto the pillows with a groan. She curls up beside me, and I wrap my arms around her.

I kiss her hair. "So what do you think?"

"I can't. But I'm flattered that you want me to stay."

"Why can't you?"

"Because Charlie's heading off in a couple of days to meet some friends in the South Island, and I want to spend some time with her before she goes."

That's tough to argue against. It's not fair of me to demand more of her time when she has so little to go around.

I brush my fingers down her back, then back up her sides. "Uni doesn't start until the end of February though, right? Is she going back to Gisborne after her trip south?"

"No. She's there for a couple of weeks, camping, and then she'll be working in Wellington right up to the beginning of the term."

"When is her next break? When is she home again? Easter?"

"Yeah."

"What about your aunt? When do you think she'll be able to look after your mum again?"

"Not for a while. Her oldest daughter, Gina, is getting married, so she'll be saving her holiday for that. You can see my predicament, Kip. I'm not being obstructive on purpose. It's just too hard."

"Every problem has a solution. Finding answers to difficult questions is what I do for a living."

"Maybe." She props her chin on my chest and studies me. "But I'm not a project you need to analyze. I'm not a puzzle to solve."

I play with her hair. "I know. But I don't know any other way to be."

"I understand why you're frustrated. I am, too. But this is how it is. I'm sorry, but you just need to accept it."

It comes to me then that Alice is arguing with me—in the most gentle, civil, grown-up way possible. She doesn't want to shout or accuse or ruin the blissful moment we've had. But she's not going to drop to her knees and beg for me to help her find the answer either. She's already decided this is it, and she's come to terms with that.

I haven't, though. "I can't just accept it," I tell her. "Because I want you."

"And you're used to getting what you want."

I shrug.

She sits up. "You need to let me go, Kip," she says gently. Then her lips curve up a little. "Don't glare at me."

My brain is furiously trying to come up with an answer. She's already told me she can't move to Wellington because her mother can't bear to leave the house Alice's father lived in, and I understand that. Unfortunately, even though some of the work I do can be done remotely, a lot of it can't. I need to meet with my clients, so I can't move to Gisborne.

"I've got my own plane," I tell her, full of frustration. "I'll fly up after work and fly back in the morning."

"It's still an hour, and we're fifteen minutes' drive from the airport. And you work such long hours."

"Lots of people have long commutes."

"That's true, but it's not a practical solution, honey."

"It doesn't have to be every day. I could come up on Friday night and fly back Monday morning."

"You usually work at the weekends," she reminds me. "All it would do is make it harder when we eventually realize there isn't a long-term solution. I'm so sorry, but there just isn't. And the thing is, this," and she gestures between us, "what we have here, it's been so wonderful, but it's just sex. It's not like it's the love of a lifetime."

Silence settles before us as our eyes meet. Her hand drifts down and rests on the duvet like an autumn leaf.

"Right," I say.

She bites her lip. "Kip…"

I shake my head. My chest is hurting so much that for a moment I wonder whether the coronary I foretold earlier has actually come to pass. But it's just my throat muscles clenching, locked in a spasm of grief that I fight to hold in.

I don't know whether she truly meant that, or if she said it to make both of us feel better. It must be the latter? Surely I'm not the only one here who's fallen in love?

I look into her eyes. They plead with me not to say it. And they shine with all the emotion she's trying to hold in.

Clearly, I'm not the only one.

There is no obvious solution. The path ahead is blocked by brambles, and I can't see my way clear. I can't control this situation, any more than I could control what happened with Christian. For the first time in years, panic rises inside me at my impotence, a word no man ever wants to encounter.

I take a deep, shaky breath, and blow it out slowly. Alice has feelings for me, and I need to take consolation from that, and hope that the way ahead will become clear. For once, I'm going to have to have faith.

Faith, hope, and love. I guess I do still believe in something.

"Come here," I say.

I tug the duvet around us as our skin begins to cool, and just hold her as the stars wheel across the sky. Eventually she falls asleep, but I lie awake a lot longer, my brain like a computer that's been charged with a problem, unable to shut down until it's solved.

*

I don't get a lot of sleep, and I'm not much closer to solving the issue by morning. I make her tea and toast and take it to her in bed, and then we shower together, which inevitably ends in gentle lovemaking, as it's impossible to be that close to her with her skin all hot and slippery and not get turned on.

But even though I would be prepared to form my own debating society and argue the point, I have to accept that all good things come to an end, and by eight a.m. I'm driving her to the airport in my Merc. She offered to catch an Uber, but I want to make the most of the last few minutes she's here.

It's raining, which seems appropriate, considering my mood. When we get to the airport, I park across from the domestic terminal, and we sit there for a moment, watching the rain running down the windscreen.

"Don't come in," she says. "I couldn't bear it." Her bottom lip trembles.

I raise her hand to my lips and kiss her fingers.

She lifts her chin. "I've had a fantastic time. Thank you so much. You're a wonderful guy, and it's been such fun."

I look out of the window, at the rain clouds overhead. I want to take her back home and chain her to my bed. Lock the front door so she can't leave. Force her to promise to see me again. But I remind myself that I need to have faith, and that I need to let her go, and hope that, like a homing pigeon, she'll find her way back to me.

I turn my gaze back to her and unclip my seatbelt. Take off my glasses and slide my hand to the back of her head. Then I lean forward and kiss her.

She returns it, and I can feel her relief that I'm not going to argue with her. I won't get my way by sheer force of will. I'm going to have to find another route.

Eventually, I lift my head and brush my thumb across her bottom lip. "Let me know when you get home safe."

She swallows. "I shouldn't. We should just make the break now."

My throat tightens. "Sorry, sweetheart, but I'm not going to stop talking to you just because it's hard for you. I love being with you, and making love to you, but we're friends first and lovers second. I have to accept that you're leaving. Don't take your friendship away from me as well."

*

### *Alice*

Kip's voice breaks, right at the end. Rain dances on the windscreen, and the light that comes through it casts a reflection of the rivulets over his face. It makes it look as if he's crying. He's not, but I can see he's very emotional.

We sit silently for a moment, just listening to the rain. Although I know it would still be incredibly hard, in the long run it would be easier for me if we parted now, and we agreed not to talk again.

But looking at him, it's impossible not to think back to last night, and that moment when he trembled with passion because he wanted me so badly. I don't want to lose him either. And I can't bring myself to insist.

"All right," I say softly. "I'll message you later."

The relief on his face almost makes me cry. "Thank you," he says, and he kisses me again.

"I'd better go now." I give him a quick hug, then get out of the car, pulling the hood of my jacket up over my hair.

Despite the rain, he gets out too and takes my case out of the boot for me. Then he hugs me tightly.

"You'll get soaked," I scold, not wanting his beautiful British suit to be spoiled.

"Don't care," he says, hanging on for a few more seconds before releasing me.

I give him a quick, hard kiss, then take my case, run across the road, and go into the airport without looking back.

*

The pain of saying goodbye is alleviated a tiny amount by the piping hot latte and the cinnamon roll that Immi brings me on the plane. I eat the sweet, warmed pastry while I fly through the clouds, feeling the distance growing between us deep inside my heart. God, how can I miss him so much already, and we've only just parted? Leaving the roll half-eaten on my plate, I lean back in my plush leather chair and look out of the window, trying not to cry. I knew it was going to be hard to leave him, but I chose to do this anyway, so I only have myself to blame. He hasn't purposefully made it harder for me. This is all self-inflicted, and if I'm going to flay myself, I have to deal with the pain after the event.

Was it worth it? I suppose only time will tell me that. At the moment it hurts so much. Part of me wishes I hadn't gone to Wellington, had told him after that first time that I didn't want to keep in touch. But then I wouldn't have had the last few marvelous days. I can feel every second of the moment he spent worshiping me in my body—my muscles ache, my mouth feels bruised, and I'm tender down below, which isn't a shock considering how many times we managed to make love. At least he tried to make sure I was well-lubricated each time. My lips twitch. He worked very hard at that.

I put my elbows on the table and cover my face with my hands. How long is it going to take me to stop thinking about him kissing down my body, burying his mouth in me, sliding his tongue inside me? Oh Jesus, how can I give that up now I've tasted it? Now that I've tasted *him*? He's going to haunt me, I know it already. All I can do is deal with the visions when they come, and hope they gradually fade as the days go by.

*

When we land, there's already a text message waiting for me. My heart sinks a little as I open it, convinced he's going to tell me he's missing me, which is only going to make me feel worse.

It's a picture of an Egyptian mummy lying desiccated and withered in its sarcophagus, and underneath the message, *Love from King Tut x*

It makes me laugh out loud, and for days to come, every time I think about it, I smile.

\*

The next week is busy, as Mum and I cram in as much time as we can with Charlie before she heads off to the South Island.

Kip messages me all the time, but I can't bring myself to tell him to stop. If the messages were heavy, declarations of undying love, constant assurances that he missed me, or all about sex, I might have resented them, but they're not. He sends me small, funny messages and memes, links to songs on Spotify or books on Amazon, and sometimes selfies if he goes somewhere interesting or sees something he wants to share with me. I tell him about a book I'm reading and enjoying, and he starts reading it too, and we begin messaging each other when we've finished a few chapters to discuss them. It's such fun that we continue with the next book, and it's lovely receiving his messages, especially late at night, when we're reading at the same time. I like imagining him stretched out on his sofa, soulful music playing in the background, the sliding doors open and the curtains blowing in the breeze, and a whisky glass resting on the table as he flicks through the pages.

He doesn't mention calling, though, so I don't have to turn him down, and for that I'm thankful.

On Thursday 26th, we take Charlie to the airport. She's sad to be leaving, but I can see she's also super-excited to be going to Christchurch. She and her friends are going to be hiring a car and driving down to Queenstown and then Dunedin before flying back to Wellington for her last year at university, and she's really looking forward to it.

We go with her as far as we can, me pushing Mum in her wheelchair, then stop just before the entrance to the gates. She gives Mum a big hug, promising to call and text regularly. Then it's my turn to say goodbye.

"You're sure you don't mind me going?" she asks for the umpteenth time.

"Of course not." I make a shooing gesture.

Still, she hesitates, glancing at Mum, who's ferreting in her purse for a tissue, before saying to me, "If you'd rather me stay so you can go back…"

"Charlie," I say firmly, not wanting Mum to hear, "it's done, and I'm fine. Go on. Have a great time."

Reluctantly, she gives a final wave and heads off.

We wait until she disappears around the corner, then make our way slowly back to the car. It takes a few minutes to get Mum and the chair in, and then I drive home. We don't say much on the way. It's almost unbearably hot. It's the height of summer now, and it makes me think about Kip's bedroom—the way the tulle curtains fluttered in the breeze when he had the sliding doors open, and the sunlight that fell across the bed like gold bars.

My memories of those days don't seem to be fading like I'd hoped. If anything, they seem to be intensifying. I find myself thinking about him at odd times—while I'm doing the dishes, weeding the flower beds, and in the shower—especially in the shower. It's impossible not to remember his hands sliding over my wet skin, his hot mouth on mine as the water poured over us. I've given up trying not to think about him, though. Actually, I find the memories comforting, like having a box of treasures I can open, take out, and examine whenever I feel low. And I'll always have them, I realize as I drive. No matter what happens now, they're something that nobody can take away from me.

When we get home, I retrieve the wheelchair from the back, help Mum into it, and push her inside. I take her into the living room, help her out and into her armchair, and make sure she has a drink. Then I say, "I think I might have a lie down, if that's all right."

"Actually," she says, "I wondered whether we could have a chat."

Surprised, I nod and take a seat on the sofa. I've opened the doors to the garden, and I can smell the lavender and roses I planted beneath the window for her. "What's up?" I ask. My heart gives an unexpected knock in my chest. The last time she did this, it was to tell me the results of a test that revealed a deterioration in her eyesight. "Are you feeling okay?"

"I'm fine." She folds her hands in her lap, takes a deep breath, and fixes me with a determined gaze. "Do you love Kip, Alice?"

# Chapter Twenty-Four

## *Alice*

I stare at my mother. "We haven't said that to each other. I haven't known him that long, Mum."

"Okay, let me rephrase it. Are you *in* love with him?"

Totally. Crazily. Head-over-heels.

"I'm trying not to think about it," I reply.

"Why?"

"Mum…"

"I know you don't want to have this conversation," she says, "but we're going to have it."

Something twists inside me. "Please, don't."

"Alice, you're a sweet, sweet girl. I know how much you've given up to look after me. You've missed out on the end of your schooling, on university life, on having a normal job, and on dating."

"I don't want—"

"Alice," she says firmly, and I close my mouth. "Please, let me speak. I haven't argued with you because, well, I haven't really had an option. I can't live on my own, and we haven't had the money to pay for someone to look after me."

"And you'd hate that anyway."

"I can't deny that. And of course, maybe most importantly, I love having you home. You're the light of my life, sweetheart. You have a beautiful heart, and no matter how bad I'm feeling, you only have to smile at me, and you fill me with joy."

My eyes sting with unshed tears. "Mum…"

"Of course I love you and Charlie both the same—she's wonderful, too, such a ray of sunshine. But Alice, there's something special about you. You're so giving, so generous. So unselfish. I'd miss you so much if you weren't here. But…"

"Don't," I say, dashing away a tear as it spills over my lashes.

"I knew it would happen one day," she says, ignoring my plea. "You're far too beautiful not to have some man fall in love with you. And now it's happened, and sweetheart, I don't want to be the reason you don't find happiness with the man you love."

"I know. But there are lots of reasons why it wouldn't work. We come from very different backgrounds. He's not just wealthy, Mum, he's a billionaire." Her eyes widen. "We get on very well, but I know that long term it would never work. He travels a lot, and even though he says he doesn't enjoy them, he has to go to functions and parties and conferences all over the world. And I'm... me. I like my life, Mum. Even if I didn't live here with you, I wouldn't be going to parties and living the high life. I love Wonderland, and the house, and our garden, and just being with you. I don't want anything more than that."

"That's a lie, Alice. At least be honest with me."

"I'm not lying. I'd hate that kind of lifestyle."

"How do you know unless you've tried it? And anyway, even if that's true, you can't tell me that deep down you don't want a partner, and maybe marriage, and children. That you don't want to hold your own babies in your arms."

That makes me falter, because saying no, I don't want that would be a lie, and we both know it.

"I don't want to talk about it." Close to bawling my eyes out, I get up from the sofa. "Can I get you anything before I go?" I turn on the baby monitor and slip the small receiver with its band over my hand onto my wrist. We bought it a couple of years ago, and it means I can move around the house and hear as soon as she needs anything.

"Don't go, sweetheart," she whispers. "Stay and talk to me."

"There's nothing to talk about, Mum."

"Alice..."

I walk out of the room, something I've never done, even when I was a teenager. I barely make it to my bedroom before the tears start falling, and by the time I shut the door and lie on my bed, I'm crying for real, trying to muffle my sobs so she can't hear them in the living room.

I can hear her snuffling a little through the baby monitor, trying to hide the fact that she's crying, and that breaks my heart. We're lucky in that we get on so well and hardly ever argue. And despite both of us being kind of housebound most of the time, she's always ensured that

I get out regularly on my own, encouraging me to go out for a walk or to the local shops when she has an afternoon nap, or to have a few days away whenever June comes to stay.

But it doesn't change the fact that we both know there's an invisible tie between us, and it's always going to be there. I know Mum wants our relationship to be like any other mother and daughter—close, but not so close that we have to live together for the rest of our lives. She wants me to be independent and to have my own life. But, as Mick Jagger pointed out, we don't always get what we want.

My phone buzzes in the pocket of my jeans. I roll onto my back and, wiping my eyes, take it out.

Kip: *Has Charlie gone? How are you doing?*

I sigh.

Me: *Yes, she's gone. I'm okay.*

I hesitate before I send it. It would be best if I didn't tell him about our conversation, but it's at that moment that I realize he's the closest thing to a best friend that I have, and I miss him, and I want to talk to him.

Me: I just had an argument with Mum. Well, a disagreement, anyway.

Kip: Aw, sweetheart. What about?

Me: I'm sure you can guess.

Kip: Ah. I'm so sorry.

Me: She feels bad, and I don't know what to say to her. She wants me to have a normal life, and we both know that's impossible.

Kip: Maybe. Maybe not.

My shoulders sag.

Me: I don't want to argue with you as well.

Kip: We're not arguing, we're discussing. It's what couples do.

That makes my breath catch in my throat.

Me: We're not a couple.

Kip: You can deny it all you like. The fact is that I want to be with you and you want to be with me. We just haven't figured out the logistics yet.

I put my face in my hands. Why is everyone torturing me like this? I'm trying to do the right thing, and everyone seems determined to make it harder.

I struggle to control my tears for a while, ignoring my phone, and therefore it's not a huge shock when it starts ringing. I wait for a moment, wondering whether to keep ignoring it, then decide that's childish and answer it.

"Hello?" I whisper, wiping my face.

"Hey, sweetheart." Just the sound of his husky voice makes me cry even more. "Hey," he says, obviously realizing as I sniffle and snuffle, "come on. I didn't mean to upset you."

"I'm okay," I squeak.

"You're obviously not. Blow your nose and listen to me for a moment. I'm not going to patronize you and say this isn't a tricky situation. But there are ways around it, ways that are a lot easier when you have money. The fact is that things are going to get a lot easier for you when Charlie comes home permanently. You'll be able to share your mum's care, and that will give you a lot more free time. I don't know how you plan to work it, but maybe you can consider looking after her for half the week each rather than splitting your days? And that means you could fly down to be with me for half of each week?"

I wipe beneath my eyes. "But Charlie's not moving home until the end of the year."

"I know. You'll be surprised how fast the time will go. In the meantime, you can come down whenever Charlie's home or when your aunt is available. And otherwise maybe I'll come up to see you."

My head is spinning. "You'd wait a whole year for me?"

"Well, it's nearly February now, and university semesters normally end in November, so it's not a complete year. But yes, baby, I'll wait a year for you, I'll wait as long as you need me to so we can be together."

His declaration, and the accompanying endearment, make me melt. What girl could turn that down?

"I'm crazy about you," he continues. "I haven't told you yet because I didn't want to freak you out, and I'm aware that we haven't known each other long, but I'm in love with you. I think it was love at first sight, if I'm honest, the moment I looked up outside the restaurant and saw you standing there. Maybe even from the moment I saw your bio where you described yourself as a shield maiden."

That makes me laugh. "Yeah, Mr. Twenty-Seven-Percent Rogue."

"Was I accurate?"

"A vast underestimation, I'd say." I listen to him chuckle, warmed all the way through by his wonderful words.

"Look," he says, "I know it's not the easiest situation, but like I said, we can work around it."

I lie back on my bed, too afraid to hope. "But surely there's no point in starting something when we don't know where we're going?"

"I don't agree with that. You never know what life is going to throw at you."

I wonder whether he's thinking about Christian. "You mean something might happen to Mum," I whisper.

"Ah, no, that's not what I meant at all. I meant more that you really don't know what might happen. At the moment it'd be difficult for me to move away from the office, but it doesn't mean it'll always be like that. Perhaps I'll open another office up there! Or you'll all decide to move to Wellington. You never know."

I do know that it would break Mum's heart to leave this house, but I don't say anything.

"I can't expect you to wait," I tell him. "It's not fair."

"Well, I'm afraid you don't actually have a say in it."

"Are you being bossy again?"

"Yep."

I smile. "You're a naughty boy."

"And you're a super-hot, gorgeous, beautiful, sexy girl, and I'm not letting you escape my clutches, so you'd better get used to me being around. Talking of which, I was thinking… your cousin's called Gina, isn't she?"

"Yes."

"When's her wedding?"

"Actually, it's on Valentine's Day."

"Do you have a date for it?"

My lips curve up. "No…"

"Would you like one?"

"Seriously?"

"Yeah."

I hesitate. "I have to look after Mum at the wedding."

"Jesus, Alice, I know that. I'm not saying I expect your undivided attention. I'm saying I want to be a part of your family, if you'll let me. I'd love to meet your mum and your aunt. And I'm sure your mum wouldn't mind if we had a dance or two."

"Would you… um… just fly up for the day?"

"I'll stop over, if you have the room and if your mum didn't mind. Otherwise, I'm sure there'll be good hotels nearby."

"I'd like you to stay with me," I murmur. "As long as you realize the house isn't quite what you're used to."

"It doesn't have a bathroom?"

"Yes, Kip, it has a bathroom."

"What about a kitchen?"

"Stop it. You know what I mean."

"What kind of a snob do you think I am? I know not everyone's house is like mine."

"Catie told me you grew up in a mansion."

"Well, yeah, okay, that is true."

"She said it has a pool and a billiard room and a theater room, and you all had your own separate apartments there."

"Yes, that's true…"

"She said you get to it via a cable car."

"Look, I'm not saying my family isn't wealthy. I know not everyone is the same, that's all, and I don't judge other people by what they do and don't have. Give me some credit."

My face warms. "I'm sorry."

"It's okay."

"You want to put me over your knee?"

He gives a short laugh. "You keep teasing me and one day I'm going to do just that."

It's the first time he's mentioned sex in our conversations since I came home, and it sends heat all the way through me. "Ooh. I've just had a hot flush."

"Oh… that idea turned you on, did it?"

"Everything about you turns me on."

He sighs. "I miss you."

"I miss you too."

"Not long until Valentine's Day, though."

"No, that's true. Well, I'd better go and tell Mum you're coming up. I think she was crying when I left her."

"Aw, you two. Yeah, go on, go and tell her. What day is Valentine's Day this year?"

"Tuesday."

"And they're getting married that day?"

"Yes."

"How about I come up on Friday night? Stay five nights and go back on the Wednesday?"

"Really?"

"Yeah. I can hire a car and we can take your mum out to a few places, or we can just stay in and watch TV, I really don't care. I just want to be with you."

It feels too good to be true, but he's offering, and I can't turn him down. "Okay," I reply, my voice squeaky. "That would be lovely."

"All right. Let me know what she says. Speak soon."

"Yeah, speak soon."

"Love you," he says.

I hesitate. Then I smile. "Love you, too."

"Good girl," he replies, and then he ends the call.

I roll my eyes and pocket the phone. I check my reflection quickly—my eyes are a bit red, but I'm sure hers will be too—then go back out to the living room.

She's still in her chair, resting her head on a hand, looking sad, but she lifts her head as I come out.

I go straight up to her, sit on the arm of the chair, and give her a hug. "I'm sorry," I tell her.

"I'm sorry too." She squeezes me back. "I didn't mean to upset you."

"I know." I kiss her cheek and then pull up the stool she rests her feet on and sit beside her. "Look, I've just spoken to Kip."

She brightens. "Oh?" Then she looks wary. "What did you say?"

"I told him what we'd been talking about." I take a deep breath. "And he said we're going to find a way around it. He said he wants to be with me, and he's willing to wait until Charlie's graduated and moved up here."

She inhales, her eyes widening. "Oh, Alice."

"Yeah, I know. He said until then, we'll see each other whenever we can, and to start with he's going to come here for Gina's wedding."

"Oh my God!"

"He wants to meet you. And... I hope it's okay, but I said he could stay here, if you didn't mind."

"As long as he sleeps in the spare room," she says. Then, when I bite my lip as I think how I'm going to tell him that, she adds, "I'm joking, Alice. You're twenty-six. Do you really think that I believed you went down to Wellington to play Scrabble with him?"

I grin. "He told me a joke about that. Why is it impossible to keep Oedipus from cheating at Scrabble?"

"No idea."

"Because he's always trying to look at his mother's rack."

"I like him already," she says. "Oh wow, I can't wait to meet him."

"He said he'll fly up the Friday before and stay until Wednesday, so we'll get to spend some time with him. He said he'll hire a car and take us out if we want, or just stay in and watch TV." For some reason, that makes my eyes prickle again.

"He sounds very sweet," Mum says, also emotional.

"He is." I try not to think about his statement regarding putting me over his knee. "I hope you like him."

"I like him already, Alice, because you like him."

"He told me we're a couple, and he said he loves me."

"Aw." She pulls me toward her, and I give her another hug. "I'm so pleased for you," she whispers. "If you can have even a fraction of the love I shared with your father, it will be amazing."

"I'm sorry he's not here, Mum. I'm sorry you've had to spend all these years without him."

"I know."

"I miss him, too."

"I know, darling. I know." And we sit there like that for a while, mother and daughter, holding each other in the warm summer sunshine, thinking about the men that we love.

# Chapter Twenty-Five

## *Kip*

The next couple of weeks pass quickly. I visit Genica on a daily basis, working closely with Jack Evans and his team in the beginning stages of the integration of MOTHER with the new voice synthesizer. There are always going to be hiccups in the evolution of new software, and although I made sure the project was in good shape when I delivered it, there are still flaws to iron out that have only just come to light.

Running alongside this is the Craig situation, which continues to be like a nagging toothache. I've tried several times to see him alone so we can talk without Renée constantly interrupting, but he still refuses to answer his mobile when I call him, and I'm determined not to go to the house again as if I'm begging him to forgive me. Instead, we're conducting all our communication through lawyers. He's suing for wrongful dismissal, as well as a host of other complaints. Helen is convinced he doesn't have a leg to stand on, but lawyers are smart, and although I wouldn't admit it to anyone, I'm nervous.

Saxon knows what's going on, of course, it would be impossible to hide it completely, but I'm doing my best to keep it off his desk. Catie is now seven months pregnant, and although she's feeling well and looking great, he's preoccupied a lot of the time. He's still flying back to Auckland every other week to oversee Titus's company, so he's under a lot of stress, and I want to alleviate that as much as I can.

Despite everything that's going on, the guys insist it's fine for me to take some time off in February. "It's not as if I'm doing anything," Damon mutters when I ask if he minds covering for me for a few days over Valentine's Day.

So on the evening of Friday the tenth, after I finish work, I go home, shower and change, pack a bag, and take it and my suit bag with me to the airport, where I board the Knight Sky.

Immi brings me a coffee, because I'm hiring a car in Gisborne, and as the plane soars above the clouds, I finally let my brain turn to what it wants to think about: the gorgeous Alice Liddell.

Since I told her I loved her and that I was willing to wait for her, something has shifted between us. She's still wary, unsure how it could work, and nervous about thinking too hard about the future. But I believe she's accepted that I'm serious about her, at least.

I'm excited to see her. I speak to her most days, and we message each other all the time, but obviously it's not the same as being together. When the plane lands, I almost run to the hire car desk like a schoolboy, and I shift from foot to foot impatiently while the guy behind the desk completes the paperwork.

The keys finally in my hand, I find the car—a rather nice Range Rover—throw my bags in the back, program Alice's address into Google Maps, and head off.

It takes about fifteen minutes to get there. She's out at Wainui Beach, in a medium-sized house with a small front garden and what appears to be a largish back garden. It's a nice neighborhood, and I can imagine the house would fetch a decent price on today's market. I know her father was the manager of a computer store in the town center, and her mother worked as a secretary before she fell ill, and it makes me wonder if the family was more affluent when her father was alive. I'm surprised they haven't sold the house and downsized, but then I remember Alice saying that her mother refused to move because she couldn't let go of the memories she had of her father. I understand that, but it seems a little unfair when it would release some of the equity tied up in the house. But it's none of my business, and I remind myself that I mustn't judge when I don't know all the facts.

I slide the Range Rover onto the house's drive in front of the garage, turn off the engine, and get out. I'm in the process of retrieving my bags from the back when the front door opens. It's Alice, dressed in a long green summer skirt and a white vest, her hair scooped off her neck, and she looks young and fresh-faced and so goddamn beautiful that I just drop everything, stride up to her, and sweep her up into my arms.

"Kip," she whispers in my ear, throwing her arms around my neck, and then she's kissing me, and I let her slide down me until her feet touch the ground, and kiss her in the early evening sun until she's breathless and laughing. "Oh my God," she says, "I've missed you." She hugs me again, and I bury my face in her neck and inhale her sweet scent as I hold her tightly.

"I've missed you, too."

"I'm so glad you came."

"I'm not going to pass up on the chance to see my girl, am I?"

She giggles at that, girlish and joyful, then moves back to look into my eyes. "I'm not imagining this, am I? You're really here?"

"You can poke me, if you like."

Mischief lights her eyes, and she reaches out a finger and prods me in the stomach. "Hard as," she says.

"Not yet, but if you keep kissing me like that, it won't take long."

She laughs. "Come on. Get your bags and come inside."

I collect them, lock the car, and follow her in. The front door leads into a hallway where I leave my shoes, and I follow her down and into the open plan living and dining room.

The room is clearly laid out to allow for wheelchair access, with an absence of clutter, which appeals to me, and floorboards instead of carpet. Alice's mother sits in one of the armchairs with a view of both the TV and the garden beyond. She looks very like her daughter, with the same blonde hair, although hers is braided into a long plait that hangs over her shoulder. She's very slender and looks quite frail, but her face is bright, and she beams at me as I walk in.

"You must be Mrs. Liddell," I say, leaving my bags by the door and going over to hold out a hand. "I'm so pleased to meet you at last."

"Oh goodness, call me Penny," she says, shaking my hand. Hers feels like a tiny bird in my massive paw, all fragile bones. "And it's lovely to meet you too, Kip."

"I'll just check on dinner," Alice says, flushing, and she walks through the dining room and disappears through a doorway. I smile at Penny and sink onto the sofa.

"How has your day been?" she asks.

"Real busy, actually. I wanted to clear the decks before I came away."

"Alice has been telling me about MOTHER. How is the production coming along?"

"Two steps forward, one step back. But I expected that. We're looking at August as a date to roll out the first units. I'm hoping we'll meet that."

Penny glances over at the doorway, then looks back at me and smiles. "She's been so excited to see you. Thank you so much for coming up."

"It's my pleasure. I've been looking forward to it. Haven't been to a wedding for ages."

Alice comes back out and stands before us. I can tell she's nervous. "You two getting acquainted?"

"You should relax before you strain something," I tell her.

She gives me a wry look. "Come on, I'll show you around."

Chuckling, I get to my feet, take the hand she offers me, and follow her through the dining room. "That's where I sit when I call you," she says, showing me the outdoor table and chairs. The deck overlooks the garden, which consists of a paved pathway that winds around pretty flower beds and trees, and a patch of lawn at the bottom on which I can see a couple of rabbits. I can picture Alice pushing her mother along the pathway, and this is also where the picture of her was taken that she used on Tinder.

She takes me through the kitchen, which is small but neat, past the laundry room, and then through to the bedrooms. "Mum's room," she says, "my room, Charlie's room, and this is my studio." She opens the door and takes me inside. I recognize it from the Tinder photo, her desk with the computer against one wall, the microphone set in a stand, and the shelves of fantasy and sci-fi books. The first editions I bought her have pride of place in the center of her shelf.

"I'll be able to picture you here now," I tell her, but there's no time to say anything more because she presses me up against the wall, slides a hand into my hair, and pulls my head down to kiss me.

It takes me two seconds to get over my surprise, and then I wrap my arms around her and kiss her back. Her soft lips part beneath mine, allowing me to sweep my tongue into her mouth, and she gives a quiet moan as I pour out all the weeks of heartfelt longing into a long, deep, slow kiss.

When I lift my head, she looks up at me dreamily. "I'll be able to think about this every time I do a podcast in here," she murmurs.

I cup her face and kiss her eyebrows, her eyelids, her nose, and back to her mouth. "I'm happy to provide as many memories as I can."

She sighs, slides her arms around my waist, and rests her cheek on my shoulder. "Mum likes you. I can tell. I'm not surprised. What's not to like?"

I kiss her forehead. "I'm glad. It's always important that the people you love get on. Next time you're in Wellington, I'll have to take you to meet my folks."

"It's going to be a slightly different experience from this one. Do they wear tiaras when they're at home?"

"Dad has a scepter. Mum wears the crown." I grin. "They're very normal. They weren't born rich."

"Catie said last time she went for lunch there, they had caviar, lobster, and oysters."

"So what? They like seafood."

"Seafood to most people in our position means prawn cocktail that's more sauce than prawn."

"Yeah, I can see how it might be a tad intimidating. But they're lovely people, and they're both going to adore you. Now come on. We should get back to your mum or she'll wonder where we've got to."

In the living room, I watch while pretending not to as Alice helps her mum into the wheelchair, then takes her over to the dining table. Clearly they've got everything off to a fine art. There's plenty of space to maneuver the wheelchair, and Alice parks it away from the table after she lifts Penny into the chair at the head where there's the most room.

"Can I help bring something in?" I ask, following her into the kitchen.

"Sure." She hands me the salad, and then she carries in the lasagna she's made, placing it in the center. I bring in the bottle of white wine and the glasses, open it, and pour us all a small glass before taking my seat across from Alice. She dishes the lasagna up, giving her mother a small serving of the pasta with just a spoonful of the salad beside it. She's told me that fatigue is a major issue for her mother, and it's clear by the way Penny cuts her food and lifts the cutlery to her mouth that it's taking an effort just to eat.

But she chats brightly enough and eats everything on her plate, and after we've eaten, we continue to chat for another hour in the living room, while the sun sinks toward the horizon, flooding the garden with a warm orange light.

At about eight thirty, Penny says, "Okay, I think it's time I went to bed."

"Are you sure?" Alice asks, surprised, so I'm guessing it's earlier than she usually retires.

"All our chat has worn me out," Penny says, although she glances at me and smiles. She wants to give us some time alone, I think, which is sweet of her.

"I'll do the dishes," I tell Alice.

"You don't have to do that," she scolds.

"I don't mind." I get up, go over to Penny, pick up her hand, and kiss her fingers. "It's been so nice to meet you at last. I hope you sleep well."

"It's been lovely to meet you, too."

I leave Alice to take her mother to bed, clear the table, and run the hot water into the sink. She has a dishwasher, and I rinse the plates and glasses and put them in while the lasagna dish soaks, then start cleaning it, looking out at the garden from time to time and watching the rabbits.

If only Saxon could see me now. I give a wry laugh. I know he'd be amused, but pleased. He likes Alice, and he's frustrated that I'm taking my time with her. It's difficult to explain how I feel I need to move slowly.

"Now that's what I like to see." Alice comes up behind me and slides her arms around my waist. "A man being all domestic. What a beautiful scene."

I grin, put the dish on the draining board, then turn and cup her face with my wet hands.

"Argh," she complains, but she stops when I kiss her, and lifts her arms around my neck. Tilting my head a little, changing the angle, I turn her so her butt is resting against the sink and delve my tongue into her mouth.

She sighs, and we kiss for a long while, taking our time, just enjoying being together, being close.

"Is your mum okay?" I ask when I eventually lift my head.

"Tired, but fine. She thinks you're wonderful."

"She doesn't think I'm leading her daughter astray?"

"She knows you are—that's why she likes you."

Laughing, I take her hand and lead her through the dining room and into the living room. I sit on the sofa, but before she can sit beside me, I pull her toward me so she falls forward, catching her by the hips. She laughs and climbs on top of me, sinking down with a knee either side of my hips, resting on my thighs.

Looping her arms around my neck, she bends her head and kisses me, and I'm hard instantly, aroused after weeks of daydreaming about her, playing through the memories I have of her in my bed, in my arms.

"You want me inside you now, baby?" I ask, pushing her skirt up so I can rest my hands on her silky thighs.

Her eyes flare, and she says, "Here?"

"Unless you have any objections." It's clear that Penny can't lift herself in and out of her wheelchair without help. It's sad, but it does mean we're not going to be interrupted.

"No," she whispers. "No objections."

I tap the monitor on her wrist. "That's one way, right?"

She laughs, slips it off, and places it on the arm of the sofa. "Yeah. It's just so I can hear her if she needs me." She hesitates. "Do you want me to turn it off?"

"Of course not. Makes no difference to me."

She takes my face in her hands and studies me for a moment. Brushing a thumb over my bottom lip, she murmurs, "I'm glad you're here." Then she lowers her lips to mine.

We kiss for a long while, as our bodies stir and awaken, responding to each other while our hands begin to rediscover the delights beneath our clothes. She strips my tee off, and her vest follows after that, and then I spend a pleasant few minutes admiring her breasts in the gorgeous lacy bra she's wearing before I finally unclip it at the back and draw the straps down her arms. I fill my palms with her breasts while we continue to kiss, and she sighs against my lips when I take her soft nipples between my fingers and thumbs and tease them gently to tight peaks.

"Mmm," she murmurs, moving up close to me and rocking her hips, arousing herself on the erection that juts through my jeans. I have no issues with that, and encourage her to move, giving small thrusts of my hips so we're moving together in a slow, graceful dance.

It's not long before she lifts off me and removes her skirt and her underwear, and she lets me undo my jeans and release my erection from my boxer-briefs before she climbs back on me, guiding the tip of my erection beneath her. Then, slowly and carefully, she sinks down, impaling herself on me.

I groan at the sensation of sliding into her warm, wet, velvet flesh. "That feels amazing."

"Ah, Jesus, yes." She rocks her hips a few times, coating me with her moisture, enabling me to sink right into her. "You feel so good."

"Ride me," I say gruffly, cupping her breasts. "Take your pleasure from me." I cover one of her nipples with my mouth. It's softened again, but it soon hardens as I tease it with my teeth and tongue, and then I suck, massaging it with the flat of my tongue, which makes her tip her head back and give a soft moan.

We move together, my hands skating over her skin—down her silky back, around her ribs, and up to play with her breasts—while she strokes my shoulders and the back of my neck, making me shudder.

I'm not touching her clit, but I'm not surprised that it only takes a few minutes before her hips begin to move more urgently. I think both of us have been dreaming of this for weeks, and imagining it all day. I stroke down her back to her butt and squeeze the firm muscles there, encouraging her to rock harder, and she moans and crushes her lips to mine.

"I'm going to come," she whispers against my mouth, and I growl and thrust up hard into her. Her lips part and she screws her eyes shut, and then her teeth tug on her bottom lip, and I watch as her orgasm sweeps over her, and she clamps around me, six or seven fierce pulses that are almost too much to bear. I hold on, though, waiting for her to finish because I know she likes to watch me, too.

Eventually, she opens her eyes and blinks at me, and her lips curve up. "I love you," she whispers shyly, brushing her lips over mine.

"I love you, too."

"Come for me." She begins to move on top of me again, and I close my eyes as pleasure spirals through me. "Come on, baby," she murmurs, teasing my lips with hers as the rock of her hips drives me in and out of her. "Let me hear those wonderful deep groans. Let me feel your muscles tighten as you come inside me."

There's no stopping it now—her body is slim and soft and warm in my hands, all sensual curves and dips, and she's so warm and wet, and I don't have to claw my way to a climax, I just have to lean back and relax against the sofa cushions and let it wash over me in wonderful waves. It feels amazing, my muscles tightening deep inside, and her mouth is on mine, drinking in my gasps of pleasure, my body jerking and pulsing what feels like a dozen times, before it finally calms.

I open my eyes and look straight into hers
"Hello," she says, and kisses my nose.
"Hey." I sigh.
"Missed you," she says, and then she nestles against me, with me still inside her, and we sit like that for a long time, making the most of just being as one.

# Chapter Twenty-Six

## *Alice*

The next day passes in a kind of dream. It feels surreal having Kip here in Gisborne, in my house. Whenever he walks into the room, my eye is drawn to him, as if he's too big for the room, like he's taken a bite from the 'Eat Me' cake and grown to twice his normal size.

At first I was anxious about what he was going to think of the house in particular, and my life in general. I was nervous he was going to be bored and restless. Although we spent three days together at his place, when we weren't in bed, we were busy. Here, of course, much of my day is devoted to looking after Mum. On the first morning, we all have breakfast together out on the deck, but then it's time to help Mum get washed and dressed, and I come back into the living room expecting to find him on his phone or laptop. Instead, I discover him lying on the sofa, listening to one of our Pink Floyd albums on the record player, reading.

"Having a nice rest?" I ask, dropping to my knees by his side.

"Mm. This is good." He shows me the cover of a sci-fi novel I recommended.

"I thought you'd like it."

He puts the book on his chest and looks at me, lips curving up. "Oh, you think you know me, do you?"

I lean over him and kiss him. "I'm getting there."

He slides a hand to the back of my neck and holds me there, and we have a long, leisurely kiss. When he eventually lets me go, I study his face while he strokes my cheek, and I sigh. "I wish we could spend all day in bed."

"Me too. But anticipation is half the delight, remember." He kisses my nose. "What are we up to today?"

"As the weather's nice, I thought we might go for a walk along the waterfront."

"Sounds great. Come on, then."

Mum's all ready, and we make our way out to the car. I don't want him to feel as if he has to help me look after her at all, which I'm sure she'd hate anyway, but without asking he folds up the wheelchair and lifts it into the back of the car while I help her in. When we get to the waterfront, we stop to buy an ice cream, and when I take our rubbish to the bin, I come back to find that he's pushing Mum, and they're chatting away. I walk beside him, touched by his attentiveness and care for her. For some reason I hadn't expected that.

After a couple of hours and a stop in a café for lunch, the fresh air has worn Mum out, and when we return home I take her into her room for an afternoon nap. I come out, half expecting him to drag me into my bedroom, and I wouldn't complain if he did. But instead I discover he's making us both a cup of tea. We take it into the living room and sit on the sofa, he pulls me into his arms, and we drink our tea while we chat about the morning. Then he puts our cups on the table, and he turns me and lies back so we're squidged together on the sofa. He kisses me for a while, and then he hugs me, and we snooze together, wrapped around each other, his breath warming my forehead, and my lips an inch from the hollow at the base of his throat.

The weather turns in the afternoon, rain pooling on the deck and making the flowers wilt, so when Mum gets up, we sit up at the table, put some music on, and play cards for a couple of hours. We start with Rummy and Blackjack, and we teach Kip Solo Whist, and he teaches us Poker, which we're terrible at, meaning he wins all the coins from our spare change pot. Then we go into the kitchen, and Mum sits at the table and crochets while Kip helps me make dinner—crispy chili chicken, with chicken strips marinated in dark soy sauce, garlic, ginger paste, and sesame oil, dipped in egg and corn-starch and fried in a wok with spring onions, and stirred into a sauce made from honey, lemon juice, dark soy sauce, and sriracha.

After we've eaten, we watch a movie together. It feels strange to sit on the sofa with Kip instead of in my armchair. And it's odd to cuddle up to him in front of Mum. I feel anxious about showing my true feelings for him in front of her, worried it's only going to increase her fear that she's holding me back. But Kip is relaxed, happy to include her in the conversation, and she seems to enjoy his presence, so in the end I try to stop the gnawing fear inside me and just enjoy the moment of being with two of my favorite people in the world.

When she gets tired and says it's time for her to go to bed, Kip gets up to give her a hug and a kiss on the cheek. I take her into her room, and as I help her into her nightie, she says, "He's wonderful, Alice. You make sure you hold onto him. Whatever it takes."

"I'll try," I say, not quite sure 'whatever it takes' means.

I told Kip earlier that I need to spend half an hour answering a few emails and posting on social media about my upcoming interviews on Wonderland, and he said that he should catch up on his emails too. So when I go back out into the living room, he collects his laptop, and we pour ourselves a glass of wine and go into the studio. He sits on my spare chair, props up his feet, and works quietly while I record a video for TikTok and post on Insta and Facebook. I tell him about what I'm planning to read next, and he tells me about the latest email he's had from Helen from Craig's lawyers, and we talk for a while, just chatting the same way we do when we're messaging, asking each other's advice and sounding off.

It strikes me that actually we're very good friends first and foremost, almost before we're lovers. Maybe that's because although we looked at each other's photos, our first connection was via messages, talking about things we had in common. Or perhaps it's just that I feel comfortable in his company, able to open up about the things I feel passionate about or I'm worried about, and I know he's going to have good advice, or at least be able to make me feel better in some way.

But that doesn't mean our connection is purely cerebral. He's put down his laptop and we've been talking for a while when I lean forward to pick up my pen after dropping it, and his voice trails off mid-sentence. I sit back up and raise an eyebrow at him, and he says, "Sorry. You gave me a view right down your cleavage and it distracted me."

I inhale, and something shifts between us, as if the temperature in the room has risen sharply by a few degrees. Our gazes meet, and his lips slowly curve up as he tucks a foot beneath my office chair, which is on wheels, and pulls it toward him.

I laugh and let him pull me up, and I sit astride him on the chair, settling onto his lap and looping my arms around his neck. "You don't know how many times I've dreamed of you while I was in this room," I murmur, rubbing my nose against his.

He kisses my bottom lip and nibbles it. "And did you touch yourself while you were in here? Make yourself come?"

"Might have."

He finds the bottom of my tee and slides his hands up it onto my back. "My sexy Alice," he whispers, "there's no stopping you now we've set you free, is there?"

"Not while you're around."

I meant that I feel sexy whenever I think about him, but he says, "I'm not going anywhere," and I realize that he thought I was saying our time together is finite. "I'm not letting you go now I've found you," he tells me fiercely, and then he pulls my head down to his, turning the dial up to eleven for a searing kiss.

He kisses me until I'm breathless with longing, and strokes me until my body's throbbing with need. And then I remove my jeans, climb back astride him, and make love with him, our bodies moving together in perfect unison. I know we could come together, but I also know that he enjoys watching me as much as I enjoy watching him, and so I let him take me all the way, clenching around him with powerful pulses that make us both gasp, and then I get to watch his face as his climax takes him, feel his body tighten, and his deep groan rumble through him as he spills inside me.

I lean against him while we calm and quieten, his words echoing through me as if my whole body is a bell. *I'm not letting you go now I've found you.* For the first time I feel a glimmer of hope. Is it possible there could be a future for us? I'm still not sure how it could work long-term. But maybe he's right, and I should put my fears to one side, and just concentrate on the here and now, on him still hot and hard inside me, on the smell of his cologne, and the warmth of his neck against my lips.

\*

Sunday and Monday pass in much the same way. The weather is changeable, but rather than rant and rail against it, we organize ourselves around it, going out when it's fine, and staying in when it's wet. Tuesday—Valentine's Day—dawns gray and overcast, but the forecast suggests the clouds will clear before midday, so we're hopeful it's going to be nice for Gina's wedding.

SERENITY WOODS

Kip is asleep when I wake up, so I go out to the kitchen and start making us all a cup of coffee. Mum's awake, but she'll sit in bed while she drinks hers before I help her into the bath and we start getting ready for the big day.

I'm just steaming the milk when he comes out, looking sleepy and gorgeous, dressed in a tee and track pants, his feet bare, and his hair all ruffled.

"Hey, gorgeous," I say as he walks up behind me and slides his arms around my waist.

"Hey you." He nuzzles my neck. "You smell divine."

"Mmm. So do you."

He kisses my neck. Then he places something on the counter in front of me. "Happy Valentine's Day."

I stare at it. It's a long, rectangular, black velvet box. The kind that contains jewelry.

"Oh Kip." Suddenly, my hands are shaking.

"Go on, open it."

Gently, I lift the lid. It contains what I think is called a tennis bracelet—a line of gemstones connected by a precious metal chain.

"Are they…" I gulp. "Are they diamonds?"

"Ten carats total," he says, "in white gold."

I've never even seen such an expensive piece of jewelry, let alone touched it, let alone *worn* it.

"I thought you might like to wear it to the wedding." He pries it from the box, loops it around my wrist, and fastens it.

I turn my wrist, watching the gemstones sparkle in the early morning sunlight. "Kip… it's beautiful."

"You like it?"

"Of course I like it. You shouldn't have, of course."

"I can't buy nice jewelry for my girlfriend?"

It's the first time he's called me that, and I give him a shy smile. "I'm embarrassed to show you my gift now."

"Ah, you didn't have to get me anything."

I reach over for the box containing his present and pass it to him. His arms still around me, he takes off the paper and opens it. It's a guitar capo, engraved with the phrase 'Love from Alice' and a heart.

"Aw," he says, "I love it."

"It's not much…"

He turns me in his arms and kisses me. "I love it," he repeats. "Nobody else could have bought that for me. Thank you." He kisses me again, but for once I don't close my eyes—instead I look at the bracelet over his shoulder, feeling a similar spangle and sparkle deep inside my heart.

*

Charlie wanted to come up for the wedding, and Kip kindly offered to fly her up on his plane, so we all go and pick her up mid-morning. She's super excited to be here, and she loved the plane flight, and took full advantage of Immi's offer of a glass of champagne and chocolate cake on the way. She's thrilled to see Kip, and when I show her my bracelet, she gives me a big hug and whispers, "I love it. You're so lucky."

The weather does indeed clear up by midday, and we all arrive for the wedding just before one-thirty. Gina has chosen to get married at a church in the small village where her Māori fiancé is from, about ten minutes north of Gisborne. Kip parks the car and retrieves the wheelchair, and I help Mum into it. He locks the car, and I push Mum up the slope toward the church.

She was too excited to nap at lunchtime, and as a result I can see she's a little tired, but she pins a bright smile on her face that lasts until we get to the church entrance. My uncle, Don, is there to greet us. He gives us an apologetic smile. "I'm really sorry," he says, "there's no room for the wheelchair in the aisles because of all the flowers. We'll have to put you at the back."

Mum reddens, but says, "That's fine, Don, don't worry about it."

I introduce him to Kip, and then we go into the cool interior. Don indicates a space right at the back of the pews. "I'm so sorry," he says again. "June's really cross because the wedding organizer let the florist set up without her, and she didn't remind her about the access." Sure enough, there are elaborate displays on stands at the end of each pew. It looks beautiful, but there's no way we could get the wheelchair down there, even if we were to remove it after Mum was seated.

"I'll be fine here," Mum says, embarrassed by all the fuss.

Kip looks at the front of the church. Then he looks back at Mum. "Come on, Penny. You're not sitting at the back."

She looks up at him, her blush deepening. "I'm fine here."

"Nah," he says, "you're not hiding in the corner." He bends and rests his hands on the arms of the wheelchair. "Put your arms around my neck."

My eyes widen, and I bite my lip. Mum is incredibly shy and self-conscious, and she hates it when people try to help her by moving chairs and tables for her wheelchair, or making any kind of fuss that draws attention to her.

To my surprise though, her lips curve up and, with a delightful, girlish laugh, she puts her arms around his neck. He lifts her easily, slides a hand beneath her to catch her skirt so it doesn't drape and reveal her legs, adjusts her in his arms so she's comfortable, then, murmuring something to her that makes her laugh again, he carries her down the aisle to one of the empty pews close to the front.

I look at Charlie, who's as startled as I am, and at Don, who knows what she's like about accepting help. He glances at me, and he grins. "That's some fella you've got there."

I sigh. "Tell me about it." Leaving the wheelchair tucked in the corner, I go down the aisle and sit between Kip and my mum.

"Thank you," I murmur, kissing his shoulder. He's wearing a smart navy suit, Italian cut, I know now, with a white shirt and a light-blue paisley tie, and he looks good enough to eat. In fact, I might do that later, I think mischievously, as a reward for being the best boyfriend in the world.

\*

We watch the service, and while we sing the hymns, I imagine the music spiraling up and dancing like dust motes in the light streaming through the stained-glass windows. And then I watch Gina and her fiancé exchange their vows, promising to love each other before God and their family. Kip's hand tightens on mine, and I wonder whether he's thinking about Christian, but when I glance up at him, I discover him smiling at me, and it strikes me that he might be thinking about saying his own vows to someone one day. To me? I blink, watching him look back as the groom places the ring on Gina's finger, wondering if I'll ever be the one in the white dress, promising to love and honor the man by my side. It's not a future I ever thought I'd have. Is it a possibility now?

\*

After the service, Kip carries Mum back to her chair, and then we make our way to the hall for the reception. They're holding it in his parents' paddock, in a large marquee, with a wonderful self-serve banquet with lots of fresh fish and seafood, salads, sliced meats, and freshly baked bread.

Kip comes with me to meet June, Gina, and the rest of my family. It's the first time, of course, that I've ever done this, and we're greeted with smiles and teasing comments that make me blush and him grin. I introduce him as my friend, because he seems too old to be called a boyfriend, and I'm not comfortable yet referring to him as my partner. But he holds my hand the entire time, so I think it's quite obvious what our relationship is.

After we've done the rounds, he fetches Mum a plate of food and a drink before we help ourselves, and then he sits beside me with his arm around the back of my chair, and makes me try bits and pieces from his plate while we talk to June and Don and various guests who come up to chat.

After the dinner and the speeches, the tables are cleared and the band begins playing. The bride and groom start the dancing to *You To Me Are Everything* by the Real Thing, and then when the singer encourages everyone else to take to the floor, Kip gets to his feet and holds out his hand to me.

I glance at Mum, but she winks at me and says, "Go for it."

Unable to resist, and anyway Charlie is with her, I take his hand and let him pull me up and take me onto the dance floor. He turns me into his arms, and we begin to move to the music.

"I asked your mum if she minded us dancing, and she said not at all," he says.

"She wouldn't have said no to you," I point out, "not after the way you carried her in the church."

"Ah, I know that embarrassed her a little, but it seemed wrong for her to be seated at the back."

"It was a lovely thing to do," I reassure him. I straighten his tie with my free hand. "You're a wonderful man."

"How many glasses of bubbly have you had?"

I giggle. "Only two. I'm serious." I look up into his eyes. "You're the best thing that ever happened to me, Kip."

His smile fades, and his eyes take on a serious, intense look. "What brought that on? You're normally very reticent to say things like that."

"I'm afraid," I admit as we turn slowly to the music. "Of losing you."

"You're not going to lose me."

I study the stitching on his lapel.

He tucks a finger under my chin and lifts it so I'm looking into his eyes. "Alice... Why don't you believe me?"

"I don't know." I think of all the hurdles I've had to jump and all the walls I've run into in my life. My father dying. Discovering my mother has M.S. The various pits we've fallen into along the way with her health. Realizing I wasn't able to finish school, or go to university. Knowing that choosing to send Charlie meant I was restricting my ability to live a normal life. So many little disappointments. And having to do it all while trying to be supportive for Mum, and not make her feel as if she's letting me down. "Experience, I guess."

He slides his hand to the base of my spine and pulls me even closer, then lowers his head and brushes his lips across mine. "Nothing's set in stone," he murmurs. "Your future hasn't been written. And no problem is insurmountable with time, effort, and money. We'll find a way to be together. All you need is a little faith."

"Faith, hope, and love," I mumble, letting him kiss me again. And it's impossible not to let the seed of excitement that's been growing in my belly flourish and begin to sprout. Because maybe, just maybe, there's a chance it'll all work out.

# Chapter Twenty-Seven

## *Alice*

I drive Kip to the airport the next morning while Charlie stays with Mum. While we wait for the plane, he pulls me into his arms, and we stand like that for a long time, enjoying the warmth of each other, and just being close.

"You take care of yourself," he says, his voice husky. "I should be able to come back up in a couple of weeks."

I nod, trying not to look disappointed. I know he's flat out at work with MOTHER right now. I just have to be grateful that he has his own plane and can fly so frequently.

He gives me a last kiss and walks away, and I watch him until he disappears around the corner, feeling tears prick my eyes. It's not forever, but it feels like it. It was lovely having him here, waking up next to him, being with him all day, every day. But nothing like that lasts forever.

Charlie stays another couple of nights, and then she packs up her bags ready for university. June is working so I can't drive her down. Kip offers to send the plane for her, but she announces she has a friend who's driving down from somewhere up north who's willing to come and pick her up.

When her friend's car pulls up, Charlie gives Mum a long, long hug and promises to call her tonight. I pick up one of her cases, and we go out to the car. Her friend turns out to be a guy, who she introduces as Jake. He's young, gorgeous, and friendly, and I give her a suspicious look as she puts her bags in the back, but she just smiles and comes over to hug me.

"This is my last year," she promises, "then I'll be up to share the load with you, and hopefully you can work something out with Kip."

"Don't worry about that now," I tell her, kissing her cheek. "Go and enjoy yourself."

"Oh, I will," she says mischievously, getting in the car as Jake goes around and gets in the driver's side.

They wave and pull away, and I watch them until they turn the corner.

Then I send her a text. *Jake's nice.*

She comes back immediately with: *Relax! We're just friends!*

I text back: *Are you mad? He's gorgeous.*

She replies: *LOL. Yes he is, but honestly, we're just friends. I don't need any complications :-)*

I realize then that she's aware she's leaving Wellington at the end of the year, so she's probably right; she doesn't want to start something and then discover it's something she doesn't want to end.

I feel a tad ashamed. It's the first time I've really thought about how all this has affected Charlie. I've assumed because she's been able to live the life I never have that she's lucky and has everything, but of course it must have affected her, knowing she has all this freedom and is then going to have to leave it behind to come back home. It must have affected her relationships, male and female, and obviously it's limited her job opportunities.

The thought puts a damper on my day, and my mood hasn't been great anyway since Kip left. I miss him so much, more than I thought I would. That's the main problem with only spending a few days together every now and then. When we're apart, I long for him, and the yearning is almost unbearable.

We get a surprise the week after he leaves though that reminds me what a wonderful guy he is. There's a knock on the door mid-morning, and I answer it to discover a guy standing there with a clipboard, his van parked out the front. He tells me he has a delivery from a mobility center in the town, and asks me to sign. Puzzled, I scribble my name, then stare with a slack jaw as he lowers the tailgate and brings out something we'd never have been able to afford—an electric wheelchair.

Oh my God. I know who's organized this.

The guy runs through how to charge and operate it, and how to fold it down, and I listen as best as I can while my head spins. When he's done, I bring the chair inside and take it into the living room. Mum looks up from her crochet and stares at it.

"It's from Kip," I say, my voice squeaky with emotion. We both know it'll mean increased freedom for her around the house, and maybe even when we go out, if I can figure a way to get it in and out of the car.

"Oh my God," she whispers. "Seriously?"

I feel such a surge of love for him that it makes my throat tighten. "Are you going to try it?"

She takes one look at my face and bursts into tears.

After we've both wiped our faces, I help her up and into it, and we spend the next hour going around the house and garden, reorganizing the furniture so she has space to reverse and turn. Eventually she returns to her armchair, worn out from the excitement, and settles down for a doze, and I go out into the garden and message Kip, asking him to call me when he's free. He comes back within five minutes.

"Hey you," I say, still feeling emotional. "Mum's spent the previous hour zooming about the house in her chair."

He chuckles. "Oh, it came? Is it okay? It's not too big? I went for one of the slimmer ones."

"It's amazing, Kip. I don't know what to say."

"Next time I'm up, we'll take a look at your car," he says. "Luckily you've got an SUV. They told me you can get a bumper-mounted rack on the back and then you just hook the wheelchair onto it. Or we can get you a ramp. I don't want you putting your back out trying to transport it, but I thought it would be nice for you both if she could use it while you go along the waterfront or around the gardens."

Tears run down my face. "You shouldn't have," I whisper. "But I really appreciate that you did."

"I'd do anything for you," he says simply. "Silly girl."

*

Mum and I soon slip back into our normal routine. Kip messages me all the time and calls me most evenings, and we spend hours on the phone, talking about our day, and what we're going to do the next time we meet. He's super busy, spending most of his days with Genica, working on MOTHER, as well as covering for Saxon, who's working his socks off trying to get a lot of his work done before the babies come.

My work is busier than ever, which is good, because that takes my mind off him for a while. After my AMA on Reddit, I received an influx of requests from authors and publishers for interviews and reviews. Whereas I normally only do an interview once a week, I start doing them more frequently, and I up my social presence, too. My Kickstarter is going well, which means I should be able to refit the studio with a soundproof booth and buy some new quality equipment.

Kip comes up every other weekend in February and March and stays until Monday morning. Our feelings for each other show no signs of waning. He's loving and affectionate, and we make love with the same ferocious intensity as always, enough to make me joke that I'm glad he only comes up every two weeks, because I need a fortnight to recover.

As April nears, I start getting excited, because Charlie's coming home for Easter, and I'm going down to stay with Kip for a whole five days. Saxon and Catie's twins are due any moment, so I'm hoping I'll be able to see the babies, too.

I schedule a couple of interviews on YouTube for while I'm away, and do the same with TikTok, Instagram, and Facebook, so I don't have to worry about it while I'm with Kip. I also order a bunch of clothes online and do a little fashion show for Mum, choosing our favorites for my holiday.

On the evening of the Friday before Easter, Kip finally calls and says the big moment has arrived, and Catie has gone into labor. I'm relieved when he finally messages the next day to say she's had the babies, two healthy boys they've called Aidan and Liam. I'm super excited at the thought of being able to hold them when I go to Wellington! Well, it's not often you get a chance to get your hands on newborns.

Kip spends the day at the hospital with them, helping out where he can, and then I get an amusing drunk text from him in the evening— apparently Catie sent Saxon home with him to 'wet the baby's head', which basically means knocking back a few whiskies and then passing out in front of the TV.

On the Thursday before Good Friday, Mum and I finally go to pick Charlie up from the airport, as she agreed to Kip's offer of a flight this time. I'm spending the weekend with her and Mum, and then I'm flying to Wellington on Easter Monday to be with Kip.

I smile as she appears through the gate and walks toward me. Then my eyebrows lift in surprise. She's lost weight since the last time I saw her, and normally at this time of year we're both nut-brown after spending weeks in the sun, but she's a pasty white, with dark shadows under her eyes.

"She doesn't look well," Mum says, concerned.

I don't reply, frowning as she runs up and gives Mum a big hug. "Hey!" she says. "I've missed you both so much!"

Mum hugs her back, and then Charlie comes and hugs me.

"Hey, sweetie." I step back and hold her arms as I look at her. "How are you doing?"

"I'm okay!" She pins a smile on her face.

"Did you enjoy the flight?" I ask as we make our way out of the airport, Mum driving herself in her new wheelchair, while I pull Charlie's case for her.

"It was a-mazing," she says. "I had a glass of champagne and a piece of a fantastic chocolate torte. So good."

I grin as we cross to the car. "There's something to be said for having a rich boyfriend." I open the car and start helping Mum into the passenger seat.

"Absolutely." Charlie concentrates on getting her suitcase into the boot, helps me attach the wheelchair to the rack at the back that Kip had fitted for me, then gets into the back seat.

I glance at her in the rear-view mirror before starting the engine and pulling away. "Everything okay, sweetie? You've lost weight, and you're very pale."

"Oh, just been working super-hard. I've got a dissertation this year, and the assessments are coming thick and fast, too."

"Are you eating well?" Mum asks. Charlie has a student allowance and a loan, and she works in a bar in the evenings and at the weekends, but Mum and I both know money is tight for her. We suspect that, like with a lot of students, her diet suffers occasionally so she can pay her rent and other bills.

"I'm fine," she insists and changes the subject, asking what we've been up to. She seems chirpy enough, so I wonder whether maybe she has just been working hard, and I'm imagining it.

We have dinner together, and in the evening we chat for a while, then watch a movie, and she seems fine, although I notice her gaze drift off occasionally while the movie plays, as if she's not really watching it. Something else that's odd is that normally her phone is glued to her hand, and she spends a lot of time texting, but tonight it sits up on the kitchen counter, face down, and she doesn't touch it all evening. When I query her about it, she says she's trying to cut down her screen time as she's been having trouble sleeping, which seems like a fair enough explanation.

At nine, Mum declares she's going to bed, and I think that maybe now I'll get a chance to talk to Charlie alone. But she says, "Yeah, I'm really tired, too," and before I can argue she gives us both a hug, then heads off to her room and closes the door.

I help Mum to bed, making sure she's propped on the pillows as she likes to read before she goes to sleep.

"Do you think there's something wrong with Charlie?" she murmurs.

I hesitate. "I'm sure she's just tired after studying so hard." I know she wants to get a good job when she moves up here, and she's always been the type to get her homework and studying done before she goes partying.

"I hope so," she says. "I thought when I had kids that I'd stop worrying when you grew up, but I don't think I'm ever going to stop!"

I kiss her cheek. "Whatever's bothering her, I'm sure it'll sort itself out."

\*

The next day, Good Friday, Charlie looks a little brighter, and by Saturday she's almost back to her normal self. Despite this, her phone remains on the kitchen counter, and she looks a little lost without it. The explanation that she's trying to cut down her screen time doesn't quite work for me, and I try to talk to her a couple of times, but she insists she's fine and just exhausted from studying, and in the end I drop it, sure she'd talk to me if there was anything actually bothering her.

I'm distracted anyway by my upcoming trip to Wellington. I spend the morning having Charlie trim my hair and then waxing myself so I'm smooth all over, and take my time on Sunday morning deciding what clothes to take.

And then I walk out of my room intending to start lunch around one p.m., and I go into the kitchen to find Mum and Charlie sitting at the table. Charlie's face is in her hands and she's sobbing, and Mum looks up at me, clearly upset.

"What's going on?" I ask, pulling out the seat next to them and rubbing Charlie's back. "What's up, sweetie?"

She just shakes her head and sobs louder. I look at Mum, whose eyebrows draw together.

"I've been trying to get her to tell me what's wrong," Mum says. "I know something's bothering her."

"I can't," Charlie says, hiccupping between the words.

I kiss her shoulder. "Hey, come on. You can talk to us about anything, you know that. We're here for you."

She lowers her hands a little so she can look at me. They're red and shining, filled with pain. "I fucked up," she says.

"Why?" I continue to rub her back. "Is it something to do with your studies?"

She shakes her head.

And then it hits me. The phone left on the kitchen counter. The fact that she's lost weight, and looks completely lost. And the guy who came to pick her up in February.

"Is this about Jake?" I ask.

Tears leak from her eyes, and she covers her face with her hands again and sobs.

"Aw." I squeeze her shoulders. "I knew you weren't just friends. What happened? Did he break up with you?"

To my surprise, she shakes her head.

"Come on," I prod, "tell us what happened."

Still, she refuses to speak. Baffled, I continue to talk to her, trying to get her to tell us why she's crying, but she refuses to tell me.

Now I'm frustrated and getting upset too, and so's Mum. I've been as gentle as I can up to this point, but that approach isn't working, and eventually I sit back, my tone turning sharper. "This isn't going to work," I tell her firmly. "You can't just sit there, bawling your eyes out. What are we supposed to think? I can't leave you like this. I'm going to call Kip and tell him I'm not going tomorrow."

"No!" She drops her hands then, clearly distraught. "You can't. You *have* to go."

"Why?" Her insistence has sent fear fluttering in my stomach. "Charlie, what's going on? Just tell me, and we'll deal with it together."

"I can't," she whispers. "I don't want to ruin everything."

"Jesus, Charlie! You're upsetting Mum, and me. Please, just tell me. I know this about Jake. If he didn't break up with you, what happened?"

She presses her lips together and wipes her face. Then she says, "I broke up with him."

"Why?" I ask softly. "I thought you liked him."

"I did. I do. I fell in love with him."

My lips curve up. "But that's a good thing, right?"

Tears continue to trickle down her face. She shakes her head. "He's a couple of years older than me. He's just finished his Master's in Engineering. And... he's got a job in Auckland."

My mouth opens as I go to reply, but nothing comes out. And then it all slots into place. Her boyfriend's moving to Auckland. And she can't go with him. Not just because she hasn't finished her degree yet. But because at the end of the year, she's coming home to look after Mum with me.

I meet Mum's eyes, and the depth of sadness she's feeling is obvious. The absolute last thing she wants is to be a burden to her daughters, but it's out of her control. She just can't look after herself.

Charlie tears off a sheet of kitchen towel and wipes her face. "I'm sorry," she whispers. "It's okay. Really. I miss him a bit, that's all. But it's not like I've known him for years. We only started dating in January."

My eyebrows rise. "Oh... he's the one you went to the South Island with?"

She nods and smiles through her tears. "He's the brother of one of my friends. I'd met him before, and he asked me out, but I told him I wasn't on the market. Then when Ria came up with the idea of a camping holiday, he said he wanted to come. And while we were away, we just..."

"Hooked up?" I ask.

She gives a shy smile. "Yeah. I couldn't resist him. Since then, we've seen quite a lot of each other, even though I've kept telling him I can't be with him long term..."

"What brought it to a head?" I ask. "When he got the job?"

"Sort of." She presses a hand to her mouth.

"Come on," I say gently. "You've told us the rest."

She puts her face in her hands again for a while. Then finally, she says, "He asked me to marry him."

My jaw drops. It's impossible to untangle my feelings at that moment. Joy for her, and a huge wave of pity because she obviously loves him so much. And hot on the heels of that, a deep ache in the pit of my stomach, because I know what it means.

I inhale deeply, and slowly exhale. Didn't I know this was going to happen all along? *Life isn't a fairy tale, Alice. You knew it would never work out.* I know what I have to do, but ohhh… it stings. Oh Kip. We came so close.

"Aw," I murmur. "Charlie…" I lean forward and cover her hand with mine. "It's okay. I want you to call him and say you'll move to Auckland with him when your course is done. And you are going to marry him."

She blinks and stares at me. "What?"

"Alice," Mum whispers, "no."

"Yes," I say. "You have to do this, sweetheart. Love like this doesn't come around often, and you have to grab it when it does."

"B-but…" she stutters, "what about you and Kip?"

"We'll work something out."

Her eyes grow hard. "You mean you're going to tell him it's over between you?"

I look at the table. "He'll understand."

"What the fuck!" Her eyes blaze. "No, he won't. He loves you, and you love him. You absolutely are not going to tell him that."

"Yes, I am. You deserve to have this," I tell her desperately. "I want you to have it all—love, marriage, and children."

"Because you don't deserve it? Come on, you've given everything up for me. School, university, and dating."

"She gave it up for me, not you," Mum adds quietly, but we both ignore her.

"I'm the oldest," I reply, "and I wanted to do it for you."

"And I appreciate every single thing you've done with all my heart, but you've done enough. I can't let you continue to sacrifice your life for me, Alice. It's my turn to give something back to you."

"No." Unable to continue sitting for some reason, I push my chair back and get to my feet. "I can't go and have a wonderful life with Kip knowing that you've given up being with Jake for me!"

"And you think I can do it the other way around?" She looks at me incredulously. "How can I go to Auckland with Jake, knowing you're not seeing the love of your life because of me?"

"Stop it, stop it!" Mum's yell cuts through our argument, and we both stare at her, shocked. "I can't bear it," she screams. "I can't bear the two of you arguing over who's going to give up their future because of me. I don't want it to be like this! How can I live with myself if either of you miss out on the chance of what I had with your father because of my fucking illness?"

It's the first time either of us have ever heard her swear, and we stare at her in shock.

And then she puts her face in her hands and burst into tears, and at that point I'm sure I can actually hear my heart fracture in two.

All three of us are crying now, because life is shit. Mum is never going to be well again. No fairy godmother is going to swoop in, wave her wand, and make all our problems disappear.

Charlie isn't going to just let me make this sacrifice, and I don't want her to make it for me, either. I couldn't live with myself if she lost Jake over this. And now we've upset Mum, which is the last thing either of us wanted. I hate that she feels like a burden.

Oh God. How can I make everything all right?

# Chapter Twenty-Eight

## *Kip*

Even though it's Sunday, I've been at work this morning, trying to clear the decks ready for Alice's visit tomorrow.

I'm in a strange mood—a mixture of excitement at the thought of spending some serious time with her, and frustration from issues at work. The integration of the software with Genica's hardware isn't going as well as I'd hoped. The software is sound, but they're having trouble getting the voice synthesizer to sync with it, and it's giving us all a major headache. Jack Evans wants me to change a part of the software to fit his hardware, but so far I've balked at the significant amount of work that'll involve. I've taken a long time to get MOTHER to a state where I feel she's ready for integration, and I'm reluctant to change it now.

Add to that the fact that Craig's lawyers have started legal proceedings for his claim of wrongful termination, and my irritability levels are higher than usual. I definitely need some Alice time, and the ability to work off my frustration with some serious sex. I hope she's prepared, because I'm considering handcuffing her to the bed for five days.

Tired and a little cranky, I leave the office and head home. I've got a few hours to myself, and then I'm heading over to my parents' house because they're having a small party to celebrate the birth of Saxon and Catie's twins.

I throw on a tee and some track pants, and text Alice. *You around for a chat?*

Usually, she comes back within five minutes at the most. Today, though, the phone is still silent fifteen minutes later.

Thinking that maybe she's in the middle of an interview, although she'd told me her last one before she comes down was yesterday, I fix myself a sandwich, crack open a beer, open a book, then end up dozing for half an hour. When I wake, the only message is from my cousin, Kennedy, asking what time I'm getting there tonight.

I text back, telling her that Damon's picking me up at five, then bring up the text I sent Alice to check it went. It did, and I purse my lips.

I'm not the kind of guy who expects the girl to be at his beck and call, and who gets annoyed if she doesn't respond immediately. It's not that. I have a strange niggling feeling in my stomach that something's awry. I don't know why, though, and, cross with myself, I go into the room I've set up as a gym and work out, lifting weights, rowing, and then running for a solid half an hour.

After that I text her again, then have a shower, neaten my beard, trim my nails, and get dressed for the evening in a casual shirt and jeans.

Still nothing from Alice.

I check my watch. It's nearly four o'clock. Too early for a drink, really, but hey, the sun's over the yardarm somewhere in the world, right? And I feel anxious, and need something to help me chill out. I pour myself a whisky over ice, add a splash of mineral water from the fridge, and take it into the living room.

Then I text her again. *Hey! Just checking, is everything okay? No worries at all if you're busy, but just want to make sure all is well :-) x*

I sip the whisky while I browse the 'Today I Fucked Up' subreddit, pulling a face as I read a post by a guy who mistakenly used some kind of facewash for lube while he masturbated and ended up losing the top layer of skin on his family jewels. Jesus. Now I need to go bleach my eyeballs. I'm engrossed in the comments and physically jump when the phone buzzes in my hands. I feel a swell of relief—it's Alice calling.

"Hey," I say. "Good to hear you. How are you doing?"

"I'm okay." Except she doesn't sound okay. Her voice is low, and not filled with the breathless, bubbly excitement it normally holds when we speak.

I sit up and put my whisky on the table. "What's going on? Is there something wrong?"

She's quiet for a moment. I can hear birdsong in the background— she's sitting outside on the deck. "I'm sorry," she says.

I frown. "What for?"

"Kip... I really am sorry. I appreciate everything you've done for me. All the presents you've bought me. All the time we've had together."

Alarm bells ring in my head. "Wait, what's the—"

"But I can't see you anymore," she finishes.

My heart seems to shudder to a stop, clattering against my ribs like a rack of saucepans. "Hold on," I say, surprised at how calm I sound. "What's happened?"

"It doesn't matter. I really don't want to argue with you about it."

"I don't want to argue with you either, but you do need to tell me what's going on. I deserve an explanation if you're abandoning me, don't I?" It comes out half-amused—she can't be serious, surely?

"That's fair," she murmurs. She takes a deep breath. "Charlie's home. And she told me today that she's fallen in love. He's an engineer, and he's got a job in Auckland, and he's asked her to marry him and go with him. She's broken it off because she promised me she'll come home and share Mum's care. But she's absolutely devastated. And... I can't have that, Kip."

I get to my feet and walk over to the window. I'm not seeing the beauty of the view, though. It feels as if the hills and harbor have been turned into a wasteland by a nuclear bomb.

"So you're breaking up with me?" I whisper.

"I can't have her give up the chance to be with him for me," she says. "I just can't."

My spine is rigid, and I'm surprised the phone isn't buckling under the strength of my grip. "And how does she feel about you doing exactly that? Giving up the chance of happiness for her?"

"She's not happy about it. We've been arguing all afternoon. She didn't want me to call you. But maybe now I've done it, she'll have to accept it." She sounds calm, resigned. And I know why.

"You expected this," I reply, stunned. "You didn't ever think we'd end up together."

"Life's not a fairy tale," she says.

"So you're not going to fight for me?"

"Don't make this about you, Kip. It's got nothing to do with my feelings for you."

"I didn't mean it like that. I meant you're not going to fight for *us?*"

"Don't." Her voice is a hoarse whisper. "This is incredibly hard. You're the best thing that's ever happened to me, and I miss you so much it hurts. But I've made all these sacrifices over the years, and if Charlie doesn't get her happy ending, it'll all have been for nothing."

"Honey, I'm sorry for sounding so harsh, but that's bullshit. You've dedicated your life to caring for your mother, and that's extremely admirable, and I'm so proud of you I want to burst, but there's a point where it becomes a martyr complex. Neither of you have to give up everything. I told you that there's a solution to every problem, and I still believe that."

"It's easy for you to say when you have unlimited funds and a wealthy family to support you. I have an aunt who's a full-time nurse with four children who generously gives up a few days of her precious holiday to look after Mum. We have my carer's allowance and Mum's benefit and whatever I can make through Wonderland. And that's it. That's not me being dramatic. And I wasn't being a martyr when I made the decision several years ago to give Charlie the things that I couldn't have. I didn't want both of us to lead empty lives."

"That's very honorable, but it's not your fault you're the eldest, and I'm sure that Charlie feels uncomfortable with your decision."

"I know it's not my fault, but I am the eldest, and because of that I get to make this decision."

"Alice, you're not listening. I'm saying that neither of you have to give up everything for your mum. There are ways around it. I can help."

"Kip—"

"I can try to find her boyfriend a job down here."

"He doesn't want to stay in Wellington—he's working at the family firm in Auckland and quite happy about it, I believe."

"But if he wants Charlie, he might be willing to change that for her."

"She doesn't want that."

Jesus. These women.

"That still doesn't mean you have to stop seeing me," I tell her. "What we're doing right now is working, isn't it?"

"Not really, Kip. When you go, it kills me. I miss you so much. It's so hard."

"Then I'll come up every weekend."

"That's not an answer. You're tired anyway when I see you. Every weekend is going to kill you."

"People commute all the time."

"We've had this conversation. And anyway, even if you did do that, it's not a permanent answer."

"I thought we decided not to worry about the future."

"All we're doing is sticking our heads in the sand. At some point we're going to have to come to the conclusion that it's just not going to work. Your life is in Wellington, and mine is here."

"It doesn't have to be. I know Penny loves the house, but I'm sure she doesn't love it so much that she wants to make her girls miserable over it. Move down here, and come and live with me. With your mum, I mean."

"I… look…" She's getting flustered. "Your house is on three floors. Practically half of it is stairs."

"I'll get stairlifts put in."

"Christ, Kip…"

"I'll fucking move! I'm not losing the best thing I've ever had when I know there's a solution. I just haven't found it yet."

"Stop it!" she yells. It's the first time I've ever heard her raise her voice. "You can't just throw money at this and make it go away. I'm not a problem to be solved, and you've got to stop trying to dazzle me with dollar signs. This is my decision, and I'm not making it lightly, or being browbeaten into it. Don't bully me."

That makes me stop in my tracks. "I'm not bullying you. We're a couple, and we're having a disagreement, so we're discussing it, that's all."

"No, you're trying to force me to see things your way. And I need you to see it my way."

This is pointless. She's not listening to me. She's made her decision, and she's going to see anything I say as me trying to convince her out of it. And maybe it is. But what's the answer? I just roll over and accept we're done?

"I love you," I say simply. "And I don't want to lose you."

She doesn't reply. I think she's crying.

Just then, in the distance, I hear someone say, "What are you doing? Are you talking to Kip?" It's Charlie.

"I've told him it's over," Alice says.

"No!" Charlie sounds distraught. "I'm not letting you do this!"

"It's not up to you."

"So I don't get a say in my own life?"

"That's not fair. Why can't anyone just let me make this decision for myself?" She doesn't swear much, unless we're having sex, so I know how upset she is. I think she's forgotten I'm on the phone.

"I didn't want to talk about this," Charlie snaps, "but you both made me do it."

"You were sobbing like a baby. I didn't really have a choice."

"Both you and Mum want me to talk about everything. It never seems to occur to either of you that sometimes a person doesn't want to talk."

"Charlie, grow up, for God's sake. You can't come home and be so obviously unhappy and expect us to ignore you."

"I didn't want to talk about it, but Mum pushed me until I was in tears, and then you started. And now she's upset, and talking about ending it all because she's such a burden on the two of us—"

"Oh my God, don't say that…"

"And I know how much you love Kip, and you're breaking up with him, and it's all my fault…" She starts sobbing.

"Honey… Ah shit."

The phone goes dead.

I look at it, blinking, unable to understand how my whole life has crashed within the space of a few minutes.

I stare out at the view for a whole minute, my hand clenching and unclenching, fighting the urge to throw my phone at the wall and smash it into a billion pieces.

What will that achieve, though? Angrily, I turn from the window, go back to the sofa, pick up the glass, and have a big mouthful of whisky. It sears down inside me, but I welcome the burn.

I can't believe she's broken up with me. What the hell is the point in having all this money and not being able to help the woman I love? There are a hundred ways we could solve this problem, but she won't consider any of them because of some foolish sense of pride that makes her feel as if she has to figure it all out for herself.

*Don't bully me.* Jeez, that stings. Was I bullying her? Where's the line between being organized and dominant? Being confident and bullying? One of my favorite movies is *Master and Commander*, and in it Russell Crowe states that men have to be governed, to which the doctor replies that it's the excuse of every tyrant in history. I've always believed that most people prefer to be led than to lead—that's been my experience in business, anyway. But maybe in putting myself in a position of power, I take away a person's ability to think for themself.

It makes me think of Craig's comment: *You put yourself on the fucking pedestal and then wonder why we try and knock you off it.* Jesus, was he right? Is that what I do?

Is that what I've done with Alice? *You've got to stop trying to dazzle me with dollar signs.* I've bought her expensive presents, flown her on our private plane, brought her to my house, and taken her to the best restaurant in the city. I've tried to wow her with money, it's true.

For the first time I understand what Saxon's been through with Catie, who had even less money than Alice. She was homeless for a while and was malnourished because she couldn't afford a decent diet. I've watched Saxon tease her with food, coaxing her as if she's a child, and been puzzled by it. I was baffled by her reticence and her refusal to accept his help even though he'd gotten her pregnant, and I still am. Why are poor people so proud? Poverty isn't a character flaw any more than having wealth is proof of a powerful personality, unless you're in a mafia movie. I don't get it, and it makes me angry that I'm sitting here in this huge house with a bank balance containing nine zeroes and I can't do a single thing to get Alice back. There's no point in flying up there and banging on her door. Or transferring a million dollars into her account. She'll see everything I do now as trying to bully her into doing things my way. If she wants to act like a martyr, like fucking Joan of Arc, then there's nothing I can do about it.

I knock back the rest of the whisky in my glass, get up and fetch the bottle, and pour myself another splash, trying desperately not to think about what I did with the ice last time Alice was in this house.

Having a big mouthful, I turn toward the living room and stop as I see Damon's painting of Astraea on the wall. For the first time, it strikes me how much it looks like Alice, from the blonde hair to the pale, curvy figure beneath the flowing robes. I think of how shy she was that first time, how eager for my touch, how perfect. It would have been so much easier if I hadn't gone on Tinder that night, not sent her a Super Like, not immediately messaged her. And yet I can't bring myself to regret it. *You're the best thing that's ever happened to me, and I miss you so much it hurts*, she said, and I feel the same way. So why are we not together? None of this makes any sense.

Grabbing the bottle of whisky, and fighting the urge to slice a knife through the painting, I take the bottle into the living room, stretch out on the sofa, and decide that the Lagavulin is going to be the answer to all my problems.

# Chapter Twenty-Nine

## *Kip*

Which is all well and dandy until I hear the door open and Damon call out, "Kip?"

Fuck. I forgot all about the party tonight.

"Down here," I yell, pushing myself upright on the sofa. It's a struggle, and my eyes take a moment to focus on him as he comes down the stairs.

He takes one look at me and frowns. "We said five, right?"

"Uh, yeah."

He picks up the bottle of Lagavulin, which is a quarter empty, and his gaze slides to me. "Are you drunk?"

"No." I do my best to sound indignant, which isn't easy when I'm seeing double.

"Did you forget about the party?"

I run a hand over my face and through my hair. "Kind of. Sorry, I should have texted. I'm not going."

He slides his hand into his pockets. "What's going on?"

"Nothing. Tell them I'm sorry, but I couldn't make it."

He studies me calmly for a moment. Then he says, "Go and get dressed. I'll make you a cup of coffee."

"I'm not going."

"Yes, you are. I've also got better things to do than play happy families, but Mum wants us to be there, and we're doing it for Saxon, who's had a tough time and deserves some support. So go on, get a pair of jeans on."

Irritation flares inside me. "I just said, I'm not going. Saxon doesn't need me there."

"He's your twin, dude. Obviously something's going on with you, and I'm sorry about that, but you need to show some solidarity. I'll get the coffee going." He walks off into the kitchen.

Grumbling, I heave myself off the sofa and go downstairs to the bedroom. Normally I wouldn't let him tell me what to do, but deep down I know he's right.

I tug on a pair of jeans and a shirt, run a comb through my hair, glare at my bleary eyes in the mirror, then go back upstairs, slotting on my glasses. Damon pushes a cup of espresso across the kitchen counter to me. I have a mouthful and wince at its bitterness, but finish it off while he watches.

He nods. "Come on. We're going to be late anyway."

I shove my feet in my Converses, grab my keys and phone, and follow him out to his car.

"So what's going on?" he asks as he heads toward our parents' place, which is only a short drive away.

"I don't want to talk about it."

"I'm guessing Alice has broken up with you?"

"Jesus, which part of 'I don't want to talk about it' is so fucking difficult for you to understand?"

"Knock it off," he snaps. "You're being a dick, and if you ruin this evening, I'm going to break both your legs."

I glare moodily out of the window, and we don't talk again.

When we get there, Damon parks on the top level, and we make our way into the house. It's a mansion really, built on several levels on the side of one of Wellington's hills, with a billiard room, a theater room, a huge pool, and three separate apartments that Saxon, Damon, and I used to live in while we were at university.

I've always loved it here, but today it brings me no pleasure to see the fine furnishings and numerous rooms. It feels wrong to be surrounded by such opulence when Alice has left me because she feels it's the only option when she doesn't have the money to solve her problems.

We go into the main living room and discover that everyone else is already here—Saxon, Catie, my dad's twin brother, Brandon, his wife Jenny, their daughter, Kennedy, her husband, Jackson, and baby Eddie. Their family dog, Pongo, sits patiently by Catie's side, fascinated by both the baby in her arms and the other one in the car seat at her feet.

Everyone cheers as we walk in, and we go around and exchange hugs and kisses. I feel oddly out of it all, as if I'm on the outside looking in, and at the first chance I can, I go over to the drinks cabinet and pour myself another whisky. I turn to see Saxon and Damon exchanging glances, but I ignore them. I'm not interested in discussing my problems, and I have no interest in listening to their opinions on my love life. As soon as I can, I'm going to get out of here, head home, and collapse into an alcohol-induced stupor.

"Hello, honey," Mum says, sidling up and slipping her arm around my waist. "Are you okay?"

"I'm fine." I give her a tight smile and squeeze her shoulders.

"Hungry?" she asks. "We've got some great food tonight."

"Not really."

She studies my face and tips her head to the side with a frown. "Are you sure you're all right?"

"Mum, I'm fine." Irritably, I drop my arm, walk over to one of the armchairs, and drop into it. I know I'm being mulish, but it's taking all my willpower just to stop myself walking out. I'm too miserable to make an effort.

I've never been the sort of person to want to talk through my problems, and to be fair my family knows this and they all ignore me for the next hour or so, while Pamela, our housekeeper, brings in the food that Pierre, the chef, has made. I pass on all of it, sickened at the thought of swallowing anything except the whisky. Why have I never thought about the fact that we have our own chef? How decadent is that?

About every five seconds, I check my phone to see if Alice has texted me, but the screen remains dark, and my Apple watch refuses to buzz against my wrist to announce an incoming call. Slowly knocking back the whiskies, and taking off my glasses, I grow more morose as the evening goes on, having to sit there and listen to everyone cooing over the babies and telling Saxon and Catie how wonderfully they're coping with their newborns.

He looks obnoxiously happy, and it's with some surprise that I realize I'm jealous. Despite all the odds, he got his girl, and he didn't even really have to try. She fell pregnant after their one-night stand, and she came and found him. All he had to do was persuade her to be with him, and although it took him a little time, it was always going to happen. Saxon has always found it easier to turn on the charm. Maybe

I should send him up to Gisborne for me. The thought that he'd probably be able to talk her around doesn't help my feelings of inadequacy.

He chooses that moment to look over at me, and sees me glaring at him. He studies me for a moment, then says, "All right. What's up?"

"Nothing."

"You've had a face like a bulldog chewing a wasp since you got here. What's going on?"

The others fall quiet and look over at me. I squirm under their concerned gazes, my empty stomach rumbling. "Just leave it," I mumble, finishing off my whisky.

"No, come on," he persists. "It's not like you to be such bad company. You're normally the life and soul of the party."

"Are you drunk?" Dad asks me, more out of surprised concern than because he's angry.

"He was drunk when I turned up," Damon states.

"What's happened?" Saxon asks. "Is it something to do with Alice?"

"I really don't want to talk about it."

"Oh shit," Kennedy says, "she hasn't broken up with you?"

I turn my gaze on her, but I lost the ability to subdue my cousin with a glare long ago. "Aw," she says, "Kip. Why?"

"Jesus." I put my glass down on the table with a little more force than I mean to, sending a clang throughout the room. "Just leave it."

"Dude," Saxon says with a frown as the baby in the car seat stirs and wails.

"Sorry," I say, knowing I don't sound sorry at all.

Saxon stands and picks his son up, then straightens, rocking the baby as he frowns at me. "Come on, what's happened?"

"I knew I shouldn't have come." I get to my feet as well. "I'm going home."

He hands the baby to Mum, then turns back to me and slides his hands into his pockets. "No you're not. You're going to stay here and talk to us."

I give a short laugh. "No I'm not, *boy*." A reference to the fact that he's fifteen minutes younger than me. "I'll call an Uber," I tell Damon, and take a few steps toward the door.

Unfortunately, Saxon moves with me, blocking my way. He looks more amused than annoyed, even though I know me referring to being the eldest always annoys him.

"Don't be an ass," he says. "Talk to us like an adult."

Irritation flares inside me. "Don't talk to me as if you're the grown up."

"Kip!" Mum scolds, but I ignore her.

"You're not superior because you're married with kids," I snap. "You knocked your girlfriend up by mistake."

He glances at Catie, then looks back at me. "That's a bit below the belt," he says calmly, although his eyes flare.

I look at her and see her face has reddened. "I'm sorry," I apologize, feeling a wave of tiredness. I've never been a rude person, and I feel ashamed to think I've embarrassed her. "Just leave it," I tell him, desperate to go home.

"No, you don't get to ruin our celebration without at least a semblance of an excuse."

"Yes, Alice broke up with me, okay? Her sister's boyfriend is moving to Auckland and has proposed to her, and Alice wants her to go with him, which means she has to stay in Gisborne. So she's told me it's over."

"What the fuck?" He looks bemused. "And you're just going along with that? Didn't you suggest she move down here?"

"Of course I suggested it, and a hundred other things, but she's made up her mind, and anything I say now is going to look as if I'm bullying her."

"Suggesting isn't bullying."

"Well you know that and I know that..."

"Want me to talk to her?" he asks. "I'm better at it." His lips curve up. He's probably referring to the moment I told Catie I'd teach her the guitar because I'd do it better than him, but for some reason I feel a flare of jealousy, maybe because I had the same thought a few minutes ago. All I can think is that he got his girl, and I didn't get mine.

"You're really starting to piss me off," I say irritably.

"Am I? I'd never have guessed."

"Boys," Dad says. "Act your age and not your shoe size."

Saxon raises an eyebrow at me. "Yeah, bro. Grow up."

I know what he's doing—he's goading me, trying to make me get it all out in the open. He's always done this—whenever I've had issues in the past, when I've said I didn't want to talk, he's always provoked me until I've lost my temper and we've had it out. To be fair, it does normally resolve the issue. But Dad's right, we're not twelve anymore.

I step around him. He steps as well, blocking my exit.

Irritation flares through me. "Get out of my way." I place both hands on his shoulders and push him hard, so he stumbles back.

Normally that would have made him lash out, but this time his lips curve up and he holds both arms out to the side, palms up, like he's Jesus. "Whatever you need, bro." Because he's so grown up, and I'm so immature.

Looking at him has always been like looking into a mirror, and I recognize his smug superiority, his insistence that he knows best, because it's such a big part of me. Both of us are used to getting our own way, but although his determination to go after Catie meant he got the girl, it's not going to work for me. I'm so envious that fury blazes inside me, and all the anger that's been building up explodes behind my eyes.

I draw back my arm and, being left-handed, give him a left hook, feeling my fist connect with his nose with a satisfying crunch. Blood sprays over us both. Catie squeals, Pongo barks, and both babies begin to wail.

"Fuck!" Saxon holds his nose and his eyes blaze.

"Not so grown up now, are you?" I ask him. I try to be smug, but I'm talking to myself, and I wish I was the one feeling the pain.

He comes for me, and, numerous whiskies down, I'm slow and unsteady, and I lose my footing. Amidst squeals from the girls and yells from the guys, I fall back onto the carpet with him on top of me, and for a moment we grapple, as furious with each other as we were the day after our sixteenth birthday, when he told me he was going to ask Sarah Cunningham out, and I asked her first just to annoy him, and she said yes.

He punches me, catching my cheekbone. That's going to give me a black eye. His blood drips onto my face, making us both slippery. We roll and, welcoming the pain at last, I lift up to hit him again, but I'm stopped as Damon grabs me by the back of my collar. An inch taller and twenty pounds heavier, he hauls me off Saxon, half-choking me. I cough and scramble to my feet, but my father puts a hand on my shoulder and bellows, "Kristopher Chevalier! Stop this nonsense right now!"

I shake myself loose from his grip, chest heaving, but stay put, watching as Saxon sits up, putting a hand to his nose. Blood is pouring down his face, covering his clothes, with droplets scattered all across the carpet and table. "Feel better now?" he asks sarcastically, taking the towel that Kennedy has rushed to get him and pressing it to his nose.

Jackson, who's a GP, bends to take a look at him. "We need some ice, Kennedy," he says, and she runs off to get some.

I glance at Catie, who has tears rolling down her face as she tries to comfort the baby in her arms, and at Mum, who's rocking the other twin, also looking upset. She's always hated us fighting. It wasn't a frequent occurrence when we were kids, but it did happen. It's been years since we've scrapped like this, though. I look at my hand—it's covered in his blood.

Damon looks at Dad, then picks up my glasses and slots them in the front of my shirt. "I'm going to take him home."

"Good idea," Dad says grimly. He points to me and then to Saxon. "But I want you both back here tomorrow morning, and we're going to talk about this."

I hesitate, feeling guilty at the sight of Catie sobbing and Kennedy trying to stop the bleeding of Saxon's nose, but Damon slides a hand under my arm and propels me toward the door. "Come on, bro," he murmurs, "I think you've done enough damage here tonight."

"I should say sorry to Catie," I say hoarsely as we go out. "We made the babies cry."

"She'll be all right," he says, closing the door behind us. "She was upset to see you both fighting, that's all. She hasn't grown up with you like Kennedy and I have." He takes me to the passenger side of his Bentley, opens the door, and pushes me into the seat, putting a hand up to make sure I don't hit my head. It's only as he does it that I realize how drunk I am. My head's spinning, and I feel sick.

"Are you going to throw up?" he asks as he gets in.

"Dunno. Maybe." I swallow. "Yes."

"Jesus." He pauses, then gets out, comes around to my side, and lifts me out again. I stand by the flowerbeds, bent over with my hands on my knees, then vomit over the lobelia.

He sighs, goes back to the car to get a water bottle, and hands it to me. I take a mouthful, rinse, and spit, then let him lead me back to the passenger seat.

He drives me home, not saying anything, and takes my keys from me to open the door.

"I don't want coffee," I mumble.

"You're going to drink a bottle of water, and then you're going to sleep," he informs me. He grabs a bottle of water from the fridge, takes me down the stairs to my bedroom, and guides me to the bed. He stands over me until I've drunk the whole bottle, then makes me lie back and pulls off my shoes.

"Lock the door on your way out," I mumble as he heads for the door.

"I'm not going anywhere," he says. "You'll only choke on your vomit, and if you have a rock-star death I'll never hear the end of it from Mum. I'll be back in a minute." He disappears up the stairs.

I look out of the window. The sun has set, and the stars are popping out on the night sky. I remember Christmas Eve, when Alice told me the theory about the Star of Bethlehem being a conjunction of… something. I'm too tired and drunk to remember, but I remember her soft voice, and the way she whispered, *I miss you too*. I miss her so much it's a physical pain in my stomach, my head, my chest, in my heart.

Footsteps sound on the stairs, and Damon comes back into the room carrying an ice pack wrapped in a cloth. He toes off his shoes, goes around the other side of the bed, climbs on, and sits up against the pillows, pressing the pack to my bruised face.

"I'm lonely," I tell him, "but I'm not that desperate."

"Ha ha. You're an idiot."

"Tell me something I don't know. I didn't mean to hit him."

"Yes you did. And he deserved it. Honestly, I feel about five years older than both of you."

I sigh.

"I'm sorry about Alice," he says, moving the pack to my cheekbone. "Maybe she'll feel differently when she calms down."

"I don't think she will."

"You never know. It's funny what love makes people do. Apparently. Not had much experience with it myself."

"Yeah, yeah," I mumble. "Don't tell me you've been going down to Christchurch just to see Alexander." The guy was his best mate at school and university. Damon's been helping him out with a project, but he's been going down more than I would have thought was necessary, and Saxon and I have privately wondered whether he's seeing someone down there.

"I'm working for him," he says, amused.

"Nothing to do with his two young, beautiful sisters?"

"Alex would kill me if I went near either of them."

"True. So why are you smiling?"

"Fuck off," he says mildly, covering my eye again.

"Ouch." I sigh.

We don't talk for a while. Holding the pack to my eye, Damon flicks through his phone. I'm dog tired, but thoughts keep racing around.

Eventually I say, "Do you ever feel guilty for having money?"

"I thought you were asleep."

"Brain won't stop. So, do you?"

"No. Dad worked hard for what he has, and so do we."

"Why do those without money refuse to accept help?"

"Not all of them do. Rachel was more than happy to accept any contributions I was willing to give." His tone is icy.

I lift the ice pack and look up at him. "She was after your money?"

"I overheard her telling a mate on the phone that she was close to landing me."

"Shit. I never knew that."

"So actually, I'd rather be with someone who was reluctant to accept help. It means she loves you for you, bro. Not for your bank account."

"I guess. It's just so hard when I think I could solve her problem for her."

"Maybe the issue is more that she wants to work it out for herself, rather than that she's upset about the money? She must feel powerless, with her mother's illness and her father's death. Perhaps helping her sister, and making decisions about her own life—good or bad—makes her feel as if she has control over something."

"That's profound."

"If I'm sounding deep, you're really drunk." He takes the ice pack off. "Go to sleep."

I close my eyes. Then I think about my twin, and feel a stab of guilt. "I shouldn't have hit Saxon."

"No, you shouldn't."

"I spoiled the celebration."

Damon sighs. "He'll get over it."

"He was only trying to help, and I broke his nose and made his wife and babies cry."

"Kennedy texted me—Jackson's stopped the bleeding, and he says Saxon will be fine. Stop worrying and go to sleep." He picks up his phone.

"Do you think I'm arrogant?"

"Jesus." He puts the phone down again. "Where's this come from?"

"Craig said I put myself on a pedestal and then wonder why people try and knock me off it."

"Craig's a cunt. Go to sleep."

"Do you think he had a point?"

"You're one of the good guys, Kip. You work hard, you're good to women, dogs, and children, you're generous and kind. Bossy? Yeah, sometimes. You're a Chevalier, for Christ's sake. We're all bossy. But no, I wouldn't say you were arrogant. You're one of the humblest people I know. More than Saxon or me. You're softer inside than we are. You care more what people think, and you try harder to please. Craig's just pissed because you don't return his feelings for you."

"You think he's gay?"

"No. I think he has a man crush on you, that's all. He's envious of your relationship with Saxon, and me, I guess, because he doesn't have any brothers, and he has a shit father. He admires you. He wants to be like you when he grows up."

I give a short laugh, and he picks up his phone. "Go to sleep, for fuck's sake," he says.

And, warmed by his words, I take his advice.

# Chapter Thirty

## *Kip*

I vomit twice more in the night, but luckily Damon's there to help me stumble to the bathroom, and to encourage me to drink more water. So when I eventually wake up for real, I feel a tad fragile, but not half as bad as I might have done if he hadn't been there.

I check the time—07:14. The sun is up, flooding the room with pale yellow light. The sky is such a light blue that it's almost white.

The bed next to me is empty, and I can't hear Damon upstairs.

Still no message or calls from Alice, but there are a few others waiting for me. The first is from Damon. *Hey bro, I left around two a.m. once you stopped throwing up. Take the Panadol and drink the orange juice, then go apologize to Saxon and Catie and I'm sure you'll feel better. D*

The second is from my father. *I'd like to see you here at eleven a.m., kiddo. Make sure you're not over the limit. Dad x*

He hasn't called me kiddo for years. It's obviously a reflection of my behavior last night.

The third and fourth are from Saxon. The third, sent early this morning, just says: *You're a twat,* with the middle finger emoji. I give a short laugh. The fourth says: *Hope you're feeling better today.*

I look at the bedside table—Damon's left a glass of orange juice and a pack of Panadol. I pop two out of it and drink the whole glass of juice. Then I get up and take a shower.

I stand under the water for a long time, thinking. Not so much about Alice—that wound is too raw and painful—but about my brother's insightful comments regarding Craig. That he's envious of my relationship with my brothers because his father is an arsehole, and he doesn't have any brothers. That he admires me, and obviously thought we were close, and is disappointed that my relationship with my brothers will always be special.

It doesn't excuse his affair, or his behavior toward me and the others in the office. But maybe it does explain it. And after last night, I'm the last person who can get on their high horse where good behavior is concerned.

After turning off the water, I get out and dry myself. Then I stand in front of the mirror and examine my face. My right cheekbone has swollen, and the skin under my right eye is already bruising up. It'll be black in a day or two.

I wonder what Saxon looks like. In the past, I'd have smiled at the thought, but today I feel sick to my stomach. We're grown men, and I hit him in front of our parents and, more importantly, in front of his wife and children. All right, they're only babies and they won't remember it, but that's not the point. It obviously upset Catie, and I feel terrible about that. Saxon has spent months trying to give her a stable, secure lifestyle after the horrifying things she's been through. I think of that God-awful day when I waited outside her apartment until Saxon could come and rescue her, and how fragile she looked. The thought that I've distressed her, even in a small way, makes me feel about an inch high.

I go into the walk-in wardrobe, pull on my jeans, and take out a plain white T-shirt. It reminds me of Alice wearing it, and I hesitate, then pull it on. It's only then that my gaze falls on the dressing table, and I see the gifts I meant to give Saxon and Catie last night. Guilt floods me once again. I completely forgot about them. I'll take them with me today as a peace offering. I'm not sure if Catie will be there, but Saxon can take them home for her.

Bringing them with me upstairs, I leave them on the kitchen counter and decide I should have some breakfast. Technically I should make myself a fry-up to combat the alcohol, but my stomach's still a little uneasy, so instead I have a bowl of cereal with fresh fruit and a large, strong coffee, and take them out on the deck to eat.

I've just sat down when my phone rings. My heart leaps for a second, and then I see the number and realize it's Marion, my PA. Surprised, as it's Easter Monday and I know she's gone away with her husband, I answer it, "Hello!"

"Good morning," she says. "I'm so sorry to bother you at home."

"Hey, it's fine. Everything okay?"

"Oh yes, it's just that I check the general office voicemail a couple times a day, and there was a call on there from late last night that I thought you should know about."

"Oh?"

"It was from Penelope Liddell."

For a second I don't recall the name, and then it comes to me. "It's Alice's mother. What did she say?"

"I can give you the voicemail number so you can listen to the message yourself, if you like, but I wrote it down in shorthand exactly as she said it so I could save you some time and read it to you."

"Please."

"She said, 'Good evening, my name is Penelope Liddell. I would like to leave a message for Mr. Chevalier please, sorry I mean Mr. Kristopher Chevalier. I know it's Easter Monday tomorrow, and so I don't know if he'll get this in time, but would he please be able to call me on my mobile between one and two p.m.? If he doesn't get this, then maybe he could do the same on Tuesday instead.'" Marion reads out Penny's number, and I program it into my phone.

"Thank you," I say. "I really appreciate you taking the time to do that."

"Of course, no worries. Is... everything all right?"

I've known Marion for five years, and, like any good PA, she's more than a secretary. She practically runs my life for me, and she's been a good friend, nursing me through my breakup with Lesley by bringing me healthy food and bullying me to go to the gym and not just sit around moping and eating donuts.

"Alice broke up with me," I say softly. "She wants her sister to go with her boyfriend to Auckland, which means she won't be around to share the care of her mother, and she thinks that means we don't have a future together."

"Aw, Kip. You're not going to give up on her, though, are you?"

I smile. "I'm guessing her mother's going to ask me the same thing. I'll let you know tomorrow."

"All right. Good luck."

"Are you having a nice weekend away?"

"Lovely, thank you. The Coromandel is so gorgeous at this time of year. See you tomorrow."

"Yeah, 'bye." I end the call.

I know why Penny has asked me to call after one p.m.—that's when she normally goes into her room for her afternoon nap. She obviously doesn't want Alice to listen to our conversation, and she also wants to speak to me without Alice knowing. I wonder what she's going to say?

I feel a flicker of fear at the thought that she might tell me I'm upsetting Alice too much and I need to leave her alone. Obviously Alice and Charlie were arguing yesterday, and Charlie mentioned that Penny was talking about ending it all because she felt as if she was a burden on her daughters. Somehow, though, I can't imagine Penny's warning me off. I don't think she'd want Alice to stop seeing me. She wants her daughters to be happy, and ending their relationships isn't going to achieve that for either of them.

Well, I won't know until one p.m. I text her and tell her I've got her message and I'll ring her just after one, and she comes back almost immediately and says *Thank you x.* The kiss is a positive sign, I think, and that gives me hope.

After I've eaten my breakfast, I get my laptop and compose an email to Craig. I take my time, thinking carefully about each sentence. We're not supposed to talk directly, and I don't want to make things worse, but equally Damon's comments last night made me think. In the end, I come up with:

*Craig,*

*I know we're supposed to be communicating through lawyers, but there are a few things I'd like to talk to you about, face to face, and alone. I might be mistaken, but I don't think either of us really wants to drag this through the courts. We've known each other a long time, and I like to think that, egos and hurt feelings aside (yours and mine), we should be able to solve this with a decent, honest conversation, man to man.*

*Let me know if you're up for it. If not, well, I guess I'll see you in court.*

*Kip*

I read it several times, then send it.

It's time to head over to my parents' house. Dad bought each of us a breathalyzer when we were younger so we could make sure we weren't over the limit after a few drinks. I haven't used it for a while as I don't tend to drink at all when I'm driving, but I take it out of the cupboard and blow into it, relieved to find I'm well under.

Taking the presents with me, I get into the Merc and head out into the sunny morning.

When I pull up at the house, Saxon's Aston is already there, gleaming in the sunshine. I pick up the parcels and make my way inside, my stomach fluttering. It's been a long time since I've had the need to apologize for bad behavior.

As I pass the kitchen I see Mum there, talking to Pamela as they load a tray with cups of coffee. They both look over as I stop and walk in. Pamela gives a wry smile, and Mum gives me a look that says, 'What am I going to do with you?'

"Morning," I say, going up to Mum, leaving the parcels on the counter, and putting my arms around her. "I'm so, so sorry."

"Aw." She slides her arms around my waist, and we have a big hug. "It's not me you have to apologize to."

"Well, I do, because it's your house, and you're my mother, and you brought me up better than that."

She lifts up and kisses my cheek. "I know you wouldn't have done it unless you were very upset. I'm sorry to hear about Alice."

"Thank you. Her mum has asked me to call her at one o'clock, so I'm hoping that's a good sign."

"Oh, me too."

"How's Saxon?"

"Sore. Grumpy."

"And Catie, is she here?"

"Yes. She's been very quiet. You really upset her, you know."

"I know." I release her and pick up the parcels. "I'm going to go and try to put things right."

"Want a coffee?" Pamela asks.

"Please, that would be great."

"Come on," Mum says, and she picks up the tray and leads the way out, through the living room, and out onto the terrace.

Saxon and Catie are sitting out there with Dad, the babies in the twin carrycot they use when they're out and about. Dad straightens as we come out, and Saxon and Catie look over.

"Hey." I cross to them and put the parcels on the table. "Morning, Dad," I say.

"Hey, boy," he says as Mum puts the tray on the table.

I turn to Saxon and Catie. He meets my gaze, unsmiling, challenging. He has a big mark across the bridge of his nose, and both of his eyes are already blackening.

Catie gives me a small, wary smile.

I hold my hand out to her. She looks at it, and then her lips curve up as she slides hers into it. I pull her to her feet and into my arms, and she hugs me and rests her cheek on my shoulder.

"I'm so, so sorry," I murmur, rubbing her back. "I ruined your celebration, and I upset you and the babies, and that was unforgivable. I really regret it, and I apologize with all of my heart."

"It's okay," she says, her voice husky. "It was just so horrible to see you angry with each other. I love that you're best friends. Bros for life, right?"

"Bros for life," I repeat, looking over her shoulder at my brother. He meets my gaze, still glaring, but a little mollified now I've apologized to his girl.

She steps back, and I go over to him as he stands up.

"Double trouble," I say to him, which is what Dad has always said about us in the past.

He huffs. "You're an arsehole."

"Takes one to know one."

He gives a short laugh.

"How's the nose?" I ask.

"It fucking hurts."

"I really am sorry."

He sighs. "Yeah I know." He opens his arms, and we have a bearhug.

My throat tightens as he refuses to release me for a moment. We've been together since we were in the womb. I guess it's no surprise that we've experienced the best of times and the worst of times together.

When he releases me, I can see he's choked up, too. I don't comment on it, instead saying, "I've brought you the presents I should have given you last night. You first." I give Saxon his.

We all sit, and Mum hands out the coffees as Saxon tears off the paper. She winks at me and ruffles my hair as she passes, so I know she's forgiven me.

He screws the paper up with one hand as he examines the box and laughs. It features eight LEGO superheroes in a frame, and it says, "Daddy you are…" then, "Stronger than, cooler than, quicker than, mightier than," and so on above each corresponding hero. At the bottom, it states, "You are our favorite superhero!"

"I love it," he says, smiling. "Thank you."

I grin and hand Catie two presents. "For the babies," I say, tapping one, "and that one's for you."

Cheeks flushing, she opens the babies' one first. It's a pair of white baby onesies. Both have line drawings of computer keys, and one says 'Ctrl + C' while the other says 'Ctrl + V', meaning 'copy and paste', a nod to the fact that they're identical twins, as well as that she's about to start a degree in computer engineering.

She laughs. "Aw, they're fantastic. Thank you." She picks up the second present, giving a shy smile, and opens that too. It contains a square velvet box, and she lifts the lid and studies the contents.

It's an oval pendant, made from white gold, engraved with a picture of a mother holding two babies. Twin diamonds decorate either side.

"It's a locket," I explain. I show her how to open it to reveal the hollow in each side. "You can put a photo of each twin. Or one of the twins together, and one of Saxon, whatever you want."

She looks up at me, eyes wide.

"I had it made especially," I say awkwardly. "You don't have to wear it if you don't like it, but—"

She presses her fingers to her mouth. "I love it," she squeaks. Then she bursts into tears.

"Shit," I say to Saxon, "sorry."

He puts his arm around her. "It's amazing," he says softly. "Thank you." The last ounce of resentment has vanished from his eyes.

"They're lovely gifts," Mum tells me. "Well done."

One of the babies—Liam, I think, because he's wearing red—stirs in the cot, waving his tiny fists in the air.

"Can I pick him up?" I ask, and Catie wipes her eyes and nods. "Of course."

I lift the baby out and walk beneath the umbrella so he doesn't have the sun in his eyes.

"Hey, little fella," I murmur, and he looks up at me with his big blue eyes. He smells sweet, of milk and talcum powder, and when I stroke his cheek with a finger, he grabs it and tries to suck it. I chuckle and look at Saxon, who's watching me with a smile.

I feel a huge swell of relief. It's the first step to putting things right with the people I love, and it feels damn good.

I just hope I can do something similar with Craig and Alice.

*

I stay for another hour, drinking my coffee and chatting to my family. Then, just before midday, I get a text from Craig. It says *Got your email. Are you at home today? Say, three p.m.?*

Heart racing, I text back, *Yep, I'll be there.*

*I'll see you then*, he replies.

I blow out a long breath. "I'd better get going," I say. I don't tell them about Craig for now, wanting to keep that to myself in case it ends badly.

I've told them I'm ringing Penny at one, and they all wish me good luck. We exchange hugs and kisses, and then I head off, feeling a lot better about myself than I did a few hours ago.

I go home, make myself a sandwich, and try to answer a few work emails, although it's difficult to concentrate. Then, just after one, I take my mobile out onto the deck and make myself comfortable in a chair in the shade.

My mouth's gone dry, and I have to take a few deep breaths before I can pluck up the courage to call, hoping I've given Penny enough time to get settled in her room.

She answers after five rings. "Hello?"

"Hey, Penny," I say, smiling and hoping she can hear it in my voice. "It's Kip."

"Hello, Kip. I'm so glad you got my message. Thank you for calling."

"No worries—I'm really pleased you rang. How are you?"

"I'm not too bad, all things considered. Thank you for asking. How are you?"

I sigh. "I got drunk last night, then punched my brother and nearly broke his nose. He gave me a black eye."

"Oh, goodness!"

"Yeah, not too proud of myself at the moment. But anyway, enough about me. How are Alice and Charlie?"

It's her turn to sigh. "Things aren't great here. No punching, but a lot of crying. They've always been very supportive of each other, and they argue so rarely, so it's upsetting to see them at loggerheads. I'm guessing Alice has told you what's going on?"

"She said that Jake proposed to Charlie, and he's asked her to move to Auckland with him. And Charlie broke up with him."

"Yes."

"Alice then broke up with me so Charlie could go to Auckland. But I'm guessing that didn't go down very well."

"No. Alice knew Charlie would protest, but she thought she'd eventually cave and agree to the arrangement. Charlie's very upset though. Both of them feel too guilty about the other one having to sacrifice their relationship. So at the moment, neither of them have what they want."

"It's a very tricky situation."

"It is, and it's not easy knowing I'm the cause of it."

I lean forward, elbows on my knees, and run a hand through my hair. "Aw, Penny."

"I'm not saying that looking for sympathy, Kip. I'm just stating a fact. It's not my fault, and there's nothing I can do about my illness or the fact that I need looking after. It is what it is, and we have to make the best of it. I upset both my girls yesterday because I said it would be better if I wasn't here, and I need to do something… to at least try to put it right."

"What do *you* want?" I ask. "Because that's important, too."

"I think the first thing is that I need to ask you a question. I know Alice has broken up with you. And I know it's a messy situation. You're a very sweet guy, but I'm sure that having a girl's mother permanently around is not what a guy looks for when he starts dating. Whatever you say now, whatever the outcome of this conversation, I want you to know that I'm not going to go and do something silly—I said what I said because I was upset and frustrated, but I'd never harm myself because I couldn't make my girls' lives even harder. We'll work it out between us, whatever happens. But I wanted to talk to you before I start thinking about solutions. So I guess my question is, are you still interested in Alice? Do you still want to be with her?"

"A hundred percent, yes," I say without hesitation, my heart swelling.

"Really?" Her voice is almost squeaky with hope.

"Of course. I love her. With all my heart. I want to be with her. And the thing is, I'm a family guy. I love my parents and brothers and aunts and uncles and cousins. And I want to be a part of your family, too. You're very important to me, Penny. Not just because you're Alice's mum, and I want to make sure you're happy and safe because I want *her* to be happy. But because I like you! You're fun and you're a lovely person, and I like being with you."

"Jesus, Kip, are you trying to make me cry?"

"I'm sorry. I'm just telling it like it is."

"Okay." She clears her throat. "Well, in that case, maybe we should talk about where we go from here. I think we should both be brutally honest, yes? There's no point in tiptoeing around this situation."

"I agree," I say, pleased.

"I won't be offended if I suggest something and you say no or that you'd prefer to do it a different way, okay?"

"Okay."

"Right," she says. "Here goes."

okay

## Chapter Thirty-One

### *Kip*

After my long phone call with Penny, I send a text to Sam, the pilot of the Knight Sky, then take my laptop out onto the deck and spend half an hour browsing and jotting down some notes until the doorbell goes. I answer it to find Craig standing there. To my relief, there's no sign of Renée. I'm tempted to say, 'So she let you out on your own, then?' but I manage to restrain myself.

"Jesus," he says, staring at my eye, "what happened to you?"

"Don't ask," I reply wryly. "Come in." I stand back and let him pass, close the door, and follow him down the steps. "You want a coffee?"

He shrugs. "Okay."

I take it as a sign that he's planning to stay at least long enough to have a drink, and turn on the machine. "Thanks for coming," I say as I start the espresso pouring. "I wasn't sure you'd agree to it." I glance at him. "Was Renée okay with you coming?" I'm genuinely curious, as I was convinced she'd arrive with him.

He sits on one of the barstools and scratches at a mark on the counter. "Renée and I broke up."

I stop in the process of retrieving the milk from the fridge and stare at him. "Oh, shit. When?"

"A week ago."

I study his face, and for the first time I spot the exhaustion and unhappiness on his features. Slowly, I lift out the plastic milk bottle, bring it over to the counter, and pour some milk into the jug. "I'm very sorry," I tell him, taking the bottle back to the fridge.

"Are you?"

"Yes," I reply sincerely. "Of course. Breakups make you feel like shit. Despite what you think of me, I don't wish you ill."

He doesn't reply. I pour another espresso, steam the milk, pour it into the mugs, and turn off the machine. "Come on."

I lead the way out to the deck, and we sit in the afternoon sunshine.

He has a mouthful of coffee, slides down in the chair a bit, and rests his head on the back. Then he exhales in a long sigh.

"Where are you staying?" I ask.

"In the Richmond Hotel for now."

"Have you seen Chloe?"

He nods. "I looked after Sammy for the afternoon a couple of days ago, so she could have a break."

"How is she doing?"

He shrugs.

I inhale and blow out a long breath. We've been through a lot together. Maybe not as much as I have with Saxon and Damon, but I took Craig out for a drink after his mother died, I talked to him a lot about his sister when she was in rehab, I've gotten drunk with him when he's been miserable about his father, and he bullied me into going out with him when Lesley went to Australia. It hurts to think of how he turned on me and the firm we built up together. Walking out on Kingpinz can't have been an easy decision, and it makes me wonder how much of a part Renée played in that. I'm not saying I understand, exactly, but we've all done crazy things for love.

"I want to apologize," I say.

His eyebrows rise—he didn't expect that. "What for?"

I think about my reply. "For if I made you feel shut out of the decision making at the company at any stage."

The truth is that Saxon, Damon, and I are directors and thus the only ones who deal with the board and make the major decisions. But Craig and Marama are part of the senior leadership team, and we all tend to discuss issues about the company, whether it's the staff or the projects.

His reasons for choosing Sunrise were unethical, but it doesn't change the fact that he felt I made the decision without him.

"I made the decision to go with Genica," I continue, "because I thought their hardware would more easily integrate with MOTHER and we'd be able to get the product out more quickly. In actual fact, we've run into some problems, and I'm not sure it's necessarily going to be quicker or easier to produce than it would have been with Sunrise or any of the other companies we looked into. But it wasn't the only reason I chose them. I also thought Jack Evans' work ethic fitted better with the way we work. I still do."

I lean forward, elbows on my knees. "At our meeting in November, when we discussed the various companies, I was aware that you and Marama favored Sunrise. But Saxon and I thought Genica was the best option, and Damon eventually agreed, and the fact that it was three to two was the reason why I didn't bring it up again, or ask for an official vote. But maybe I should have done. Whatever the reasons behind your choice, you should have had the chance to discuss it in more detail rather than be blindsided, and I'm sorry for that, if nothing else."

He blinks. Looks away, out at the view. And then his chin trembles and, to my shock, his eyes gleam and he presses a fist to his mouth, fighting his obvious emotion.

"Craig," I say gently, puzzled and worried, "what the hell's going on? I thought we were friends. Why didn't you tell me you were having trouble with Chloe?"

"It's not easy admitting your faults to Mr. Perfect," he says, attempting humor as he wipes beneath his eyes.

"Dude, I'm so far from perfect it's not even funny. My girlfriend's just broken up with me. And last night I punched Saxon and almost broke his nose."

"Seriously? He gave you that black eye?"

"Yeah. I was a dick to him and deserved worse. So, like I said, nowhere near perfect."

He sighs and runs a hand through his hair. "Things hadn't been great with Chloe for a while, but I know you adore her, and I didn't think you'd see things from my point of view."

"I like her, yeah, she's a great girl. But nobody knows what goes on behind closed doors. I wouldn't have judged." I have strong opinions about things like cheating, but I do my best not to be judgmental most of the time.

He sighs again, and then the words just start flowing. "I guess I was ashamed of myself for not making the break with her earlier. I stayed with her because, well, it's what good guys do, and I thought I was a good guy. But I wasn't happy, mainly in the bedroom. When we were first together, we had sex a lot, but she's always been very vanilla. I hadn't been with many girls before I met her, though, and guys don't talk about this kind of thing, so you don't know what other people's relationships are like, right? Over the last few years, I've tried to suggest we give a few things a go, but she wasn't willing to try anything. She called me dirty and disgusting, and I thought I must be, you know? So I stopped asking and tried to be happy with what I had. And then she wanted a baby, and I wasn't against having kids, and I thought maybe it might put things right between us and stop me feeling so restless. So we started trying. We'd been trying for a few months, and then I met Renée at the conference in Auckland. Dude, I can't explain that moment when our eyes met, it was electric. And I know it makes me weak, and I'm ashamed of myself, but when she asked me back to her room, I just couldn't say no. And it was amazing. She was far more experienced than me, and willing to try everything I suggested. I was completely mesmerized. I'd have done anything for her at that point. Anything."

He speaks simply, and gives me a resigned, sad smile. I don't say anything, because I have no idea what to say. I don't condone the way he's treated Chloe. I don't like people who cheat, or who aren't willing to work through their problems. But I'm not a saint. Relationships do break down, and when you're in the middle of things, sometimes it's impossible to see the sky, because you're too busy looking at all the obstacles on the ground.

And sex is such a tricky issue. I would think it's very unusual to meet someone whose sex drive and likes and dislikes completely match your own. I would imagine it's common to have one person want it more, or to want to be more adventurous. And I've read enough threads on the Marriage subreddit to know how many settle, only to have to fight dissatisfaction later in life.

It makes me think of Alice, and how she'd only just dipped her toe in sexy waters before she was ripped away from me. I don't know how compatible we would be if we were to stay together, but I suspect we have a lot more in common than most couples.

There'll be time to think about Alice later. For now, Craig is talking again, seemingly unable to stop now he's started.

"When I went home from that conference," he continues, "I didn't plan to continue seeing her. I thought it was just a fling. But then I found out she lived in Wellington, and she contacted me and said she wanted to see me again. And I just couldn't keep away from her. I went to her place, and it was amazing again, and I went home that day determined to end things with Chloe. I walked in with the words 'it's over' ready on my lips, and before I could say anything, she told me she was pregnant."

I sigh. "Shit."

"Yeah. She was so happy, and I just couldn't bring myself to say it. I kept thinking about the baby, and I knew I had to try and make a go of my marriage for the baby's sake. So I stayed. I told Renée I couldn't see her again. She texted me occasionally, but we didn't meet up. I tried, I really did. But Chloe had morning sickness for the first few months, and after that she just didn't want sex—she said it felt weird while she was pregnant. And then the baby was born, and even a few months after, she still wasn't interested. I tried to be understanding, and accept she was tired and probably sore, but... I know it makes me a terrible person, but I just kept thinking about how Renée wanted me, and how good she made me feel... And then one day she contacted me again and asked to see me. And I'm only human, Kip. I was lonely, and I know it sounds pathetic and childish and makes me an arsehole, but I was angry with Chloe for not wanting me, and for not taking my needs into account. It had been a whole year since we had sex, and she wasn't showing any sign of wanting it. And so I went to Renée's house. And after that, I couldn't stop."

"How long before she brought up MOTHER?"

"Not long," he admits. "Deep down, I knew what she was asking me to do was unethical, and I knew she was using me. But at the time, I told myself I didn't care. I told myself we had something special, and it was just a coincidence that I worked at Kingpinz. But of course, it wasn't. When she didn't get the software, she was very angry. We've argued a lot, and it turns out it's not only your wife who withholds sex when they're pissed off with you." His lips twist. "I've had a lot of time to think since I left Kingpinz. And last week I finally told her it was over."

"What did she say?"

"She was shocked. She actually begged me to stay. Physically got down on her knees, which was a first. Once that would have turned me on, but it just sickened me. I walked out there and then, and went straight to a hotel." He swallows hard. "I've acted abysmally, to Chloe, and to you and the others at Kingpinz. I know that."

I blow out a long breath. "You know we can't take you back."

He gives me a long look, disappointment in his eyes. Then he says, "Yeah, I know."

"Even if I wanted to," I say, although I don't—as much as I feel sorry for him, I couldn't work with the guy again after what he's done—"Saxon and Damon wouldn't agree to it."

"Fair enough."

"Are you going to try to make it up with Chloe?"

He shakes his head. "She wouldn't have me back anyway. And I don't want to go back. Life's too short to spend it with someone who makes you feel bad for who you are, you know? I need to find someone who loves me for me."

"Yeah," I say, thinking about Alice again, and sighing.

"You said your girlfriend had broken up with you," Craig says. "Who's that?"

"Her name's Alice. I met her on Tinder. We've been seeing each other for a while, but she lives in Gisborne. She looks after her mum, who's got M.S."

"Ah, shit."

"Yeah. She doesn't think there's a way we can be together, but I'm hoping to convince her otherwise."

A couple of dry leaves drift down from the oak tree to one side of the house. Autumn's here, and the mornings are growing cooler, although it can still be fairly warm in the afternoons, like it is today. I think of Alice sitting in her garden, watching the rabbits playing on the lawn, and my heart aches for her. I miss her so much.

"Do you love her?" Craig asks.

I nod, and my lips twist.

"Fuck Cupid," he says.

I give a short laugh. "Yeah. Fuck Cupid."

"I'll call the dogs off," he says. "The lawyers. I'll cancel the case. I never wanted to do it anyway. It was all Renée's idea."

I feel a wave of relief, and give a big sigh. "Thank you. What are you going to do?"

He shrugs. "Probably freelance for a bit."

"You're an excellent engineer. You shouldn't have any trouble finding a job."

"Yeah." He hesitates. "I'm sorry it ended the way it did. We've been friends for a long time, and I know what I did was wrong."

"Water under the bridge, dude. Time to move on."

"I can't imagine Saxon and Damon saying that."

I smile. "No, maybe not."

We can't really talk about the underlying problem. It's rare for guys to talk about their feelings at all, and he'd never admit to my face that he's jealous of my relationship with Saxon. I think he expected the closeness I have with my twin brother to fade as I got older, but I don't think that will ever happen, even though I broke his nose last night. Alice told me: *You're twins. You're going to have a special connection. Anyone who doesn't accept that is going to have a problem*, and I think she's right.

He gets to his feet, I stand as well, and we walk into the house and up to the front door. When we get there, he turns and holds out his hand, and I shake it.

"Thank you for apologizing," he says. "I know it sounds childish, and that I'm the one who did everything wrong, but it meant a lot to me. People don't say they're sorry enough."

"You take care," I tell him. "Good luck."

He nods and goes out, and I close the door behind him.

I exhale in a long breath, go down into the living room, and collapse in one of the armchairs. I feel wrung out, but my day isn't over yet. I check my watch—it's not quite four p.m.

I text Mum: *Hey you. Are you in?*

She comes back: *Yes! Going out to dinner at six. How are you doing?*

Me: *Good—can I call in quickly? I want to ask you something.*

Mum: *Of course! See you in a bit.*

Me: *I'll be about fifteen minutes.*

I go into the bedroom and through to the walk-in wardrobe, take out a case, and throw in a pair of jeans, a couple of tees, and some underwear. I wash my face and change into a clean pair of jeans and a fresh tee, comb my hair, and glare at my bruised eye. Then I collect my car keys, take the bag to the car, lock the house, and set off for my parents' house.

When I'm done there, I get back in the car and head off to the airport.

Sam and Immi are ready and waiting, and soon I'm in the air, heading for Gisborne.

Excitement bubbles in my stomach at the thought of seeing Alice, and of our upcoming conversation. Nothing is certain, that much I know. It doesn't matter what conclusions her mother and I come to—she's the one we need to convince.

I think about Craig, feeling a sweep of sadness that his marriage is irreparable. He cheated on Chloe, so I understand why she doesn't want him back, and I can imagine that living in a sexless marriage is tough. Should he have tried harder to make it work before leaving her for someone else? Almost certainly. But relationships are two-way streets, and while obviously a man needs to be understanding when his wife is pregnant and has given birth, and I can imagine some people thinking a guy should learn to deal with a lack of attention and sex in that situation, as Craig said, we're only human. We all need to feel loved, admired, and wanted. Can I blame Craig because he felt the need to look elsewhere for love and sex?

I look out of the plane's window at the late afternoon sun that's turned the clouds the color of coral. If I get a second chance with Alice, I intend to make sure she always feels wanted and loved.

*I don't pretend to understand God's purpose*, she told me. *I believe in faith, hope, and love, and try to apply that to the people around me.* And that's what I need to do now. I need to have faith that her feelings for me are strong enough to get us through this. I have to hope that our future is a lot brighter than she obviously thinks it is at the moment.

And I intend to prove that I love her, and that I want to be with her for the rest of our lives.

The plane begins its descent through the clouds, and I buckle myself in for the ride.

# Chapter Thirty-Two

## *Alice*

I'm absolutely shattered.

Charlie's revelation yesterday threw all three of us into a whirlwind of heightened emotions, and it's been very difficult to stop them spinning us around.

Mum went to bed early last night, exhausted from the whole thing, and the two of us stayed up until very late, checking on her from time to time, both frightened of leaving her alone.

"We have to sort this," Charlie told me at one point, long after the sun had set. "We can't keep doing this to her."

"I know that," I snapped. But I couldn't see a way clear through the thick forest of our problems.

In the end, both of us were so tired and irritable and upset that we decided to sleep on it and talk again the next day.

I lay awake for about an hour, thinking about Kip, missing him, and feeling miserable, and fighting with myself because he's my best friend, and I wanted to call him and talk it over with him, and I couldn't. Eventually I crashed out, slept too long, and I've woken with a headache, grouchy and frustrated that the solution hasn't miraculously come to me in my sleep.

But I get up and have a shower, and feel a bit better when I'm clean and dressed and my hair is pinned up. I come out and make us all some breakfast, and then Charlie suggests that the three of us go out for a walk along the waterfront. I drive us down there, and we purposefully don't talk much about the men in our life, letting the sea breeze blow the cobwebs from our troubled minds.

When we get back, Charlie cooks us a bacon sandwich, and then Mum goes in for her afternoon nap while Charlie and I sit out in the garden.

We try to talk again, but it soon becomes clear that we're at an impasse. Charlie feels I've made too many sacrifices for her already, and she says she'll feel terrible if she agrees to go with Jake, which means that I'll have to give up Kip to look after Mum. Equally, I don't feel able to continue my relationship with him if it means she has to break up with Jake. She accuses me of being a martyr, and I accuse her of being a drama queen, and we both cry again, and then hug because we love each other, and we only want the other to be happy.

There's no easy answer, and by the time Mum wakes up, we're no closer to a solution, and we're both exhausted again, wrung out by all the emotion.

We try to talk to Mum again, but she just says, "Let's think on it," and refuses to discuss it again. She seems cheerful enough, though, so we leave her to her crocheting, and I go off to my studio, while Charlie does some uni work up at the dining table.

It's getting close to six when I decide I should really start getting dinner ready. I check my phone before I leave the studio, annoyed that I'm disappointed. I can't tell Kip not to message me, then get angry that he's done what I asked. I shove the phone into the back pocket of my jeans, go into the kitchen, and start chopping an onion, hoping that the spicy chili I have planned perks all three of us up a bit.

I'm in the middle of frying the mince when I hear the doorbell.

"I'll get it," Charlie calls, and she disappears down the hallway. I suspect it's a parcel, maybe with some books I've ordered, although it's late for the delivery guy. I add some tomato paste and the chili I've already chopped, hearing voices at the door. Then it closes, and I look up, expecting to see Charlie standing there holding a heavy cardboard box.

Instead, I see Kip, standing there hesitantly, hands in the pockets of his jeans. He's wearing a gray sweater over a white tee, and he looks tired, but he gives me a small smile.

"Hey you," he says.

He's come here despite the fact that I told him to stay away. I should be angry with him, and tell him to turn around and go back to Wellington.

I don't, though. Instead I say, "Kip!" in a breathless voice, drop the wooden spoon with a clatter, run up to him, and throw my arms around his neck.

He laughs and spins me around, holding me so tightly he's close to breaking a couple of ribs, but I don't care.

Charlie slips by us and goes into the kitchen to stir the chili. In the living room, Mum puts down her crocheting and smiles.

Kip lowers me to the floor, and I move back and look at him, lowering my arms. I thought he looked tired, but now I'm closer to him, I can see he has a big bruise darkening under his eye.

"What happened?" I ask, surprised.

He lifts his glasses onto his hair so I can inspect it. "You should see the other guy," he says, and gives a boyish laugh.

"Who did it?"

"Saxon."

My jaw drops. "What? Why?"

"Long story." He looks over his shoulder. "Hey, Penny."

"Hello, Kip."

Something about her lack of surprise has my spider senses tingling. "You knew he was coming?"

"Might have," she says.

Charlie comes out, and we both look at them curiously.

"What's going on?" I ask, heart racing. Now my initial shock has worn off, I'm worried about him being there. I don't need him adding his two cents to an already tricky situation.

"Come and sit down," Mum says.

Charlie sits in the other armchair, and Kip and I sit on the sofa. I look at him. He's resting an elbow on the arm of the sofa, and his fingers are covering his lips.

"I spoke to Kip today while you thought I was having a nap," Mum says. She's sitting very upright, her hands in her lap, and she looks calm and determined. "We talked for a long time, and I think we've come up with a solution that might work for all of us."

I frown at him. He just lifts his eyebrows.

"I want to start by saying that I really appreciate how both of you girls want to do right by each other," she begins. "You're good girls, and I know you both love me, and you love each other. I'm so grateful for everything you've done for me, and I'm touched at how much you're willing to sacrifice to look after me. However." She glares at us. "You've both frustrated me so much over the last couple of days that I want to bang your heads together."

I glance at Charlie, a little ashamed. She looks back at me, her lips twisting.

"I don't think it occurred to either of you to ask me what I want," Mum says. "And every time I tried to talk about it, you shut me down."

I stare at her, horrified. Is that true? I suppose it is. She did try to say she wanted to find a solution that would mean neither of us would have to give up the men in our lives, but we both steamrollered over her, insisting we weren't going to cave.

"When I talked to Kip, though," Mum continues, "he said, 'What do *you* want?' I was so touched I nearly cried."

I glance at him, but he's looking at her, his lips curving up behind his fingers.

Mum looks at me. "As I said, I appreciate everything you've done for me. But I'm not going to let either of you pass up on the chance of happiness with the man of your dreams for me. Alice!" She snaps as I open my mouth. "Please!"

I close my mouth again, shocked at her sharp tone.

"I know that over the years you've had to step up and make the decisions for this family," she says. "And I have so little energy that I tend to take a back seat. I find it too exhausting to argue. But for now, I need you to let me speak."

"I'm sorry," I whisper.

"It's all right. I didn't mean to sound so sharp. But I need to say this, and I need you both to listen. Charlie, you're going to get right back on the phone with your young man, and you're going to tell him you'll marry him, and that you're moving to Auckland."

Charlie stares at her. "But—"

"Goodness, please, just listen. You'll go to Auckland, and Kip has kindly offered the use of his plane for you to fly back as often as you like to visit us. Now, Alice. I know in the past I've said that I can't bear to leave this house because of your father. But he's been gone eleven years now. I still miss him as much today as I did the day he died. But he's not here."

"His grave is, though," I remind her, finding it difficult to speak.

Her expression softens. "He's not there either, sweetie. I don't need a gravestone to remind me to think about him. It's time I moved on. Time *we* moved on. You're twenty-six now. You've found a wonderful man who loves you, and you deserve to have a home of your own, and a family. You want babies, don't you?"

Tears rush into my eyes, and I cover my mouth with a hand. I look at Kip. He's watching me, his eyes crinkling at the edges as he smiles.

"So," Mum says. "We're going to be moving to Wellington."

My eyes widen, and I dash the tears away. "What?"

"I'll still be living with you, but Kip says his current house is on several levels and isn't suitable for someone in a wheelchair. We talked about getting stairlifts put in, but in the end we decided it'll just be easier to get somewhere new."

"I had a browse this afternoon," Kip says, "and I've been thinking maybe somewhere near where Saxon lives in Island Bay. A property on one level, with plenty of space. I'll get onto the real estate agents tomorrow and start asking around to see what's available."

"We'll put this house up for sale," Mum says. "Kip has suggested Charlie take most of the proceeds to put toward a place for her and Jake as he can pay for our house. And then we're going to look around for a private nurse to come in and take care of me from time to time."

"Mum!" I say, jaw dropping. "You'd hate that!"

"Sweetie, no person in their right mind dreams of being disabled or needing to be taken care of, and it's true that in the past I've felt embarrassed and worried about losing my dignity by having a stranger look after me. But Kip has connections through the hospital, and he's going to help me find someone I like, maybe a woman of my own age, who can be more like a friend. It's what I want, Alice. You've been so good to me, and I want you to be able to go out, to travel, to live a normal life, as much as possible."

I can no longer hold the tears in, and they run down my face. "Oh Mum…" I look at Charlie—she's crying, too.

I turn my gaze to Kip. "I can't expect you to do all this for me," I whisper.

"Alice," he says firmly, "it's what I want, too. I'm a big family guy, you know that. I adore you, and I want to be with you… but it's not all about you. I want Charlie to be able to marry Jake. And I want to help your mum. I want to be a part of your family, and for you to be a part of mine." He glances at Mum. "I forgot to say on the phone, but actually I think you'll get on really well with my mum, Mae. Her best friend is a nurse, and I think she might be able to help find you someone to help with your care."

"What about June?" I ask. "It'll make it more difficult for her to see you."

"We can fly her and her family down whenever you want," Kip says.

"It's not great for the environment," I grumble.

He gives a short laugh. "Maybe not, but we'll have to save the world in other ways." He clears his throat and looks at Mum. "Would it be okay if I have a few minutes alone with Alice?"

"Of course," she says.

He holds out a hand to me. "Let's go outside."

Meekly, my head whirling, I let him pull me up and lead me out into the garden. It's dark now, and a couple of moths are fluttering around the kitchen window, but there's enough light for us to see each other clearly, and it's not cold.

Still standing, he turns me to face him. "What do you think?" he asks.

"I don't know what to say. I… I'm ashamed Mum feels that Charlie and I didn't listen to her. She's right of course. I was determined to make the sacrifice because I thought it was what I should do. But she is still my mother, and she deserves to have a say in it."

I look down at where he's holding my hands. "But it's not easy. It would be a huge change for her to move, and I know that change is one thing she really struggles with. When anything big happens, it always makes her unwell."

"That's fair enough, but we'd make sure we did it in small steps so it didn't become too overwhelming." He lifts my hands and kisses my fingers. "Whatever you need, we'll do it."

I look up, into his eyes. "I really don't know what to say. It's so incredibly generous of you. I don't understand why you're willing to go to so much trouble."

He gives me a puzzled look. "Because I love you."

I frown. "Why?"

That makes him laugh. "All right," he says, "maybe this will convince you." He slides a hand into the pocket of his jeans and extracts a small, black velvet box. My eyes widen. He gives me an amused look, then cracks it open. It contains an unusual ring—a large sapphire, surrounded by small diamonds.

"It's Easter Monday," Kip says, "and all the shops are shut, and I didn't have long because I wanted to see you today, so I couldn't buy you a ring. This was my grandmother's. I asked Mum for it today. You don't have to wear it if you don't want to, and I'll happily buy you one of your own tomorrow, but I thought I could use it today."

He takes it out of the box and leaves the box on the table. Then he lowers down onto one knee. "Alice," he murmurs, "will you marry me?"

I stare at him. "Huh?"

"Will you be my wife, and come and live with me in Wellington? We'll choose a lovely home by the sea where your mum can be comfortable, and you can build a brand-new studio there with everything you need. And we'll have an amazing bedroom with the biggest bed where I can make love to you all night every night." My jaw drops, and he stifles a laugh. "Say something."

"I… are you serious?"

He sighs, gets up, and pulls me into his arms. "Of course I'm serious," he says warmly. "I love you. You're my best friend. I talk to you every day. I miss you when we're not together. And when we are… I can't keep my hands off you. Your body drives me crazy, and I spend hours daydreaming about things I can do with you and to you that will make those lovely innocent eyes widen in shock."

My lips curve up. "You're such a naughty boy," I whisper.

"So will you? Marry me?"

I study his face, looking at the bruise on his cheekbone, his gorgeous brown eyes. I want to say yes…

Panic fills me. He's doing this wonderful thing, and I should be squealing and throwing my arms around him and saying *Yes, yes, yes!* But the word won't come.

I wait for frustration to cross his face, or even anger—I'd understand if it did. But instead, he lowers his head and touches his lips to mine briefly.

"You've been through so much," he says quietly. "You've had to cope with your father's death, and with taking care of your mum, for such a long time. You had to grow up quickly, and make some big decisions, pretty much on your own. And because of all that, I think being in control has become a big part of your life, because it's the only way you've been able to cope. But I'm trying to say that you don't have to do it on your own anymore."

I swallow hard. Give up control? I don't know if I can do that.

"I'm sure during those first few years after your dad died, when your mum was diagnosed," he says, "she leaned very heavily on you. But she understands that her disease isn't going away. She's learned to live with it. And I think she needs to take back a little of that control.

It's not a criticism of you at all—she totally needed you to take charge. But she's ready to claw a little of her life back. I know she doesn't make friends easily, and she's chosen to isolate herself here, but she talked to me about getting out a little more, meeting women of her own age, maybe even taking a few classes or something."

I stare at him, shocked that the two of them have discussed this in detail. There's obviously something about Kip that encourages people to talk. Maybe it's because he's not judgmental, or just that he's willing to listen.

"I wouldn't dream of telling you how to live your life," he tells me. "You've done such an amazing job with your mum, and with practically bringing up Charlie single-handedly. But now you have me, maybe you can think about having a life of your own. Of *our* own? Think about what you'd like to do with your life, Alice, if you could do anything you wanted? Would you like to go to university? You haven't had the chance before. Or you could throw yourself into Wonderland and take it to the next level—take it out on the road, travel around New Zealand, go to the States! Meet your fans. Interview authors face to face. On your own, or with me if you like. I'd love to be a part of it."

Tears pour down my face again. "Oh, Kip…"

"Whatever you want, sweetheart," he says. "It's up to you. Do you want to share my bed? To make love to me whenever you want? Do you want to have my baby growing inside you?"

I cover my mouth and nod. "I do."

"Do you want to wear a beautiful white dress in church, and promise our friends and family, before God, to love me and cherish me for the rest of our lives?"

I nod again, my chest heaving.

"Then will you marry me?"

Marry him?

Spend the rest of my life with this guy, worshiping his body, having him worship me? Knowing he's mine, and that he's never going to kiss anyone but me? Having his baby growing inside me?

"Yes," I say with a sob. "Yes, yes, yes!" And this time I do throw my arms around him and hug him tightly.

He nuzzles my neck and kisses me there. "I'm so glad," he whispers fiercely. "Ah, thank you."

Thank me? As if I'm not the one who got the best deal in this relationship!

Is this real? Does he honestly want to be with me forever? I can't believe it. He wants to marry me. I didn't believe in fairy tales, but this really is a dream come true. I fell down the rabbit hole, and I really did end up in Wonderland.

"Here." He moves me back and slides the ring onto my finger. "I'll get you a new one tomorrow," he says.

But I shake my head, watching the diamonds glitter in the light from the kitchen window. "This one is absolutely beautiful. I'd love to wear it, if you're sure your mum doesn't mind."

"She bawled her eyes out when I told her I was going to propose with it. So no, she doesn't mind."

He holds my face and looks into my eyes. "I love you, Alice Liddell. I have since the first moment I saw you, and I just know I'm going to love you until my dying day."

"I love you too."

He kisses the tears from my cheeks. Then my nose. Then finally my lips, wrapping me in his arms as if he's afraid to let me go.

# Epilogue

## *June 21st (two months later)*

## *Kip*

It's the winter solstice, exactly six months after I met Alice, and Mum and Dad's house is full of people who've come to celebrate the renewal of Saxon and Catie's vows and their baby-naming ceremony. Saxon sprung a wedding on her after Christmas while they were on holiday, because he wanted to marry her but knew she'd be overwhelmed by having to say her vows in front of lots of people. However, six months have gone by now, and she's settled down a lot, to the extent that when he suggested they combine a naming ceremony with a vow renewal ceremony, she jumped at the idea.

Dad's twin brother, Brandon, and my aunt, Jenny, are chatting to Mum and Alice's mum. Penny has been spending a lot of time with Mum, and I'm so pleased that they genuinely seem to get on well. Penny's holding one of Catie's twins and Mum's holding the other, and the two of them are clearly enjoying themselves.

Kennedy's helping Catie get ready. Her husband, Jackson, with baby Eddie, is over talking to my cousin, Titus, and his wife, Heidi, who are visiting from the U.K, and Charlie and her partner, Jake, who's visiting from Auckland. Titus's parents are here, and I'm also pleased to see that he seems to be getting on better with his hard-nosed father, Julian.

There are a few other family and friends present, and a couple of people from work, all gathered on the terrace, as it's a clear day, and Saxon wanted an outdoor ceremony providing it wasn't raining.

Damon, Alice, and I are chatting to Mack and Sidnie, Elizabeth and Huxley, Victoria and Evie, and Hal and Izzy, all close friends of ours who've come down for the ceremony.

"How are the house alterations going?" Mack asks me.

"Good," I reply. Alice and I found a place in Island Bay only days after we started looking, and within five weeks the place was ours. It's a beautiful, one-level house just a few minutes from where Saxon lives, with only a short walk to the beach, and magnificent views across to Taputeranga Island. "We've had builders in, putting in a few ramps and improving access for Penny's wheelchair," I tell the others. "They've almost finished, then they're going to make a start on Alice's studio. We're planning on moving in by the end of July."

"We've found a buyer for our house in Gisborne," Alice explains.

"That must be hard," Sidnie says. "It's tough to say goodbye to your childhood home."

"It'll be difficult to leave it," Alice agrees. Then she slides her hand into mine and smiles at me. "But I'm moving on to better things, and that makes it easier."

"Aw," Elizabeth says, rocking from side to side with her baby boy in her arms. "Young love."

Huxley snorts. "Kip's thirty this year. He's hardly young."

"Thanks for that," I say wryly.

Alice giggles. "That's okay. I don't mind being with an old man." Her eyes sparkle.

She's referring to earlier this morning, in bed, when she said Charlie had told her about a romance novel she'd been reading that had a Daddy Dom/Little Girl theme. Alice teased me that the book was about me, and I then told her I'd happily take care of my little princess providing she stopped being a brat, which led to a fun half hour's lovemaking.

I raise an eyebrow at her and she blushes, and the others laugh.

"So, Damon," Victoria says, probably trying to turn the attention away from Alice's red face, because she's nice like that, "who are you seeing at the moment?"

"Yeah, totally not having this conversation," he says, swigging from his beer bottle.

"I think there's someone special in Christchurch," Alice says. "Right?"

He looks at her, startled, then narrows his eyes as everyone goes, "Ohhh..."

"No," he says.

"I saw your new painting," she states. I remember then that he's just hung a new oil painting in his house. I hadn't thought anything of it, because he's always painting Greek goddesses. It's a good one, though, a tad too revealing for his office, with the woman's slender figure encased in a diaphanous gown that doesn't hide much. "It's called Limerence, right?"

"Yeah..." His lips curve up.

"What does Limerence mean?" Hal asks.

"It means obsession, or all-consuming passion," Alice replies. "I looked it up."

"Artistic license," Damon states.

"Yeah, right," she says.

He just gives her a wry look.

"Come on," Elizabeth says, "spill the beans."

He mumbles something and walks off, and we all laugh.

Over by the door, I see Kennedy come out, and she looks me, then gives me a nod. "Okay," I call out, "guys, we're ready, if everyone could take their seats."

Gradually everyone sits down, and Saxon walks through the two groups of chairs to the celebrant, who's standing by the makeshift altar. I make sure Penny is settled in the special place they made for her chair next to Alice, and then I nod to Charlie, and she disappears.

I walk to the front, next to Saxon. We're both wearing dark-navy three-piece suits, and I know we look more alike than ever today. Our black eyes have faded, and it's only my glasses that tell us apart.

He glances at me, and can see then that, oddly, he's nervous.

"Shall I take my glasses off and switch places with you?" I murmur to him. "See how long it takes her to notice?"

He gives a short laugh. "Shut up."

"I'm just saying."

"Yeah, bro, not long and our roles will be reversed, and it'll be me teasing you. Just remember that."

Alice and I have set the date for December. She wants to get married in church, and I'm more than happy to do whatever she wants, so we're going to have the big white wedding, which I think everyone will enjoy.

"Whatever," I say. "I'm just glad you'll be there."

That makes him smile. "I'm glad you're here today. It was odd doing it without you." Our friend Hal stepped in as his best man when he married in the Northland. It was my suggestion, but Saxon's told me more than once that he should have flown me up for the day.

"All that matters is that you got the girl," I whisper. "And the babies."

"Yeah," he says, chuckling. "You're right."

He stops then as she appears in the doorway on the arm of our father. Saxon visibly inhales, which makes me smile. She's wearing a simple white dress and, with her figure on the way to returning to normal after the birth, she looks graceful and gorgeous, blushing lightly as she walks down the aisle toward him with Kennedy behind her.

I glance at Alice, who's pressing her fingers against her lips, obviously surprised by her sudden emotion. She meets my eyes, and her eyebrows draw together, and I wink at her. She and Catie have become great friends, and both Saxon and I are pleased that the two of them are so supportive of each other.

"Wow," Saxon says as Catie draws levels with him.

She's trembling a little, and I know she's going to be feeling nervous to be the center of attention like this, but her face when she looks up at him makes even my cynical heart melt.

Someone turns down the music, and the celebrant begins the ceremony.

"Good afternoon," he says, "and welcome to all of you attending this joyful vow-renewal and baby-naming ceremony."

He talks for a while about marriage, of it being a union founded on mutual respect and affection. He explains how this is a symbolic, sentimental ceremony that Saxon and Catie are holding because they want to declare their love for each other in front of their friends and family. And then he asks them to read out the vows they've prepared.

Saxon clears his throat and holds Catie's hands. "With my whole heart," he says clearly, his voice ringing out across the terrace, "I promise to remain devoted to you, to continue to grow with you in mind and spirit, and to practice patience, kindness, and understanding. Once more, I vow to cherish you for as long as we both shall live."

"Oh dear," I hear Mum say behind me, as tears start rolling down her cheeks, and Penny pats her hand.

Catie takes a deep breath and repeats the words. As she speaks, I look across at Alice again, and I'm not surprised to find her watching me. We both know that we'll be doing something similar very soon, and I'm sure the thought fills her with as much joy as it fills me.

Once they're done, the celebrant goes on to do the naming ceremony, saying that Saxon and Catie want to share with everyone they know and love their hopes and dreams for their children's futures, and that the babies represent a new chapter in their lives, as well as strengthening the bond between them.

He formally names the babies—Aidan and Liam—and then asks the Guide Parents to come forward. Damon, Kennedy, and I approach, and he invites us to pledge our commitment to playing a supportive and caring role in the babies' upbringing.

We give our promises, and I can tell from the way Kennedy's voice is little more than a squeak and Damon's has turned husky that they're feeling as emotional as I am.

The celebrant wraps things up, and everyone claps and cheers, then gets up to come forward and toss confetti over Saxon and Catie. The two of them look elated, touched to be able to declare their love in front of everyone.

"That was wonderful," Alice whispers to me, coming up and sliding her arm around my waist.

"Wasn't it?" I wrap my arms around her and bury my nose in her hair. She smells of lemon and mint. "You make my mouth water."

"Likewise. But then you always do." She lifts up and kisses me. "You look so gorgeous in your suit. I truly am the luckiest girl in the world."

For some reason, her words make my throat tighten. I realize then that love—true love—is wanting to be with that person more than you want to be with anyone else. And it's about finding someone who feels the same way about you. I've never been with anyone who makes me feel like Alice does—that I'm her favorite person on the planet, and that she'd rather spend time with me than any other man. She'd rather kiss me, make love to me, than any other guy. It's humbling and thrilling in equal measure, and it makes me want to take her home, strip off her clothes, and make love to her for the rest of the day to say thank you for choosing me.

I settle for kissing her lips, and that turns into a long smooch that starts people whistling, until we eventually break apart with a laugh.

"Trying to hog the limelight as usual," Saxon jokes, clapping me on the back. "I'm glad you got the girl."

"You too."

Unusually soppy, we have a bearhug, our two girls watching us with a smile.

"I'm so glad you made up," Catie says. "Watching you fight was the worst thing in the world."

"I dunno," Alice states. "If you stripped them off and threw some custard over them, I can see it being quite a turn on."

Catie giggles, and Saxon and I exchange a wry look, then laugh.

"Come on," I say to Alice, throwing an arm around her shoulders. "Time for the photos."

We take our place next to Saxon and Catie, and smile at the camera, letting him capture us in a shot that I decide I'll have enlarged and hung on the wall in our new house. The women in our lives have made us both into better men, and I hope the four of us have many happy years together ahead of us.

# Newsletter

If you'd like to be informed when my next book is available,
you can sign up for my mailing list on my website,
http://www.serenitywoodsromance.com

## About the Author

USA Today bestselling author Serenity Woods writes sexy contemporary romances, most of which are set in the sub-tropical Northland of New Zealand, where she lives with her wonderful husband.

Website: http://www.serenitywoodsromance.com
Facebook: http://www.facebook.com/serenitywoodsromance

Printed in Great Britain
by Amazon

38522007R00195